The Cruise Club

Caroline James is a celebrated author of later-in-life fiction and her vibrant storytelling stems from her colourful career. Before becoming a full-time writer, she carved out a fascinating path in the hospitality industry, owning a lively pub and then a charming country house hotel. As a media agent, she worked closely with celebrity chefs, giving her an insider's perspective on the glitz, glamour and grit of the culinary world. When she finally turned her focus to writing, she discovered her true calling, penning bestselling novels that have garnered her legions of fans.

Also by Caroline James

The Cruise
The French Cookery School
The Spa Break

The Cruise Club

CAROLINE JAMES

avon.

Published by AVON
A division of HarperCollins*Publishers* Ltd
1 London Bridge Street
London SE1 9GF

www.harpercollins.co.uk

HarperCollins*Publishers*
Macken House, 39/40 Mayor Street Upper
Dublin 1, D01 C9W8, Ireland

A Paperback Original 2025
1

Copyright © Caroline James 2025

Caroline James asserts the moral right to be identified as the author of this work.

A catalogue record for this book is available from the British Library.

ISBN: 978-0-00-876935-2

This novel is entirely a work of fiction. The names, characters and incidents portrayed in it are the work of the author's imagination. Any resemblance to actual persons, living or dead, events or localities is entirely coincidental.

Set in Sabon LT Std by HarperCollins*Publishers* India

Printed and bound in the UK using 100% Renewable Electricity at CPI Group (UK) Ltd

All rights reserved. No part of this publication may be reproduced, stored in a retrieval system, or transmitted, in any form or by any means, electronic, mechanical, photocopying, recording or otherwise, without the prior written permission of the publishers.

Without limiting the author's and publisher's exclusive rights, any unauthorised use of this publication to train generative artificial intelligence (AI) technologies is expressly prohibited. HarperCollins also exercise their rights under Article 4(3) of the Digital Single Market Directive 2019/790 and expressly reserve this publication from the text and data mining exception.

This book contains FSC™ certified paper and other controlled sources to ensure responsible forest management.

For more information visit: www.harpercollins.co.uk/green

For Mika Mei, the magic in all our days.

Chapter One

"A cruise is more than the start of a journey, it is the beginning of a love affair with the sea, where every port brings a new adventure."

Carmen Cunningham fought the impulse to murder her mother. If Carmen's life was a novel, Betty Cunningham would have been edited out long ago, for no matter how hard she tried to please, Carmen could never satisfy the old lady's relentless demands.

At eighty, Betty was a force to be reckoned with. Despite pleading infirmity, she moved with surprising agility, and whenever Carmen felt the old lady's silver-topped cane prod into her arm, she found it hard not to snatch it from her mother's hand. It would be easy to pick up a cushion, hold it to Betty's face and muzzle the endless nagging, for whatever Carmen did to make life easier it was never to her mother's liking, and at times, Carmen despaired.

'For heaven's sake, Carmen, can't you do anything right?' Betty watched her daughter struggle with a laden tray. 'You know I like my tea at five o'clock, and you're ten minutes late.' Betty's permed grey hair bounced like a cloud of silvery spaghetti, as she snapped out each word.

Carmen, named after her father's favourite opera, bit back a retort. Long ago, she'd learned that arguing with her mother was like trying to hold back the tide. Instead, she offered a placating smile. 'Sorry, Mum, I was busy.'

'Busy? How can you be busy?' Betty muttered. 'Look at this room. When was the last time you cleaned? My asthma wouldn't be half as bad if I didn't have to live in a dust bowl.'

Carmen placed the tray down and sighed. Betty's asthma had a schedule of its own and only flared up if there was a job to be done. It was no use reminding her mother that Agnes, their delightful home help, was on a much-needed break in Cornwall, and Carmen made a mental note to try and remember to run a duster around the room as soon as she cleared the tea things.

Her latest manuscript would have to wait.

Cosy crime writer Carmen Cunningham was behind on a deadline, and, like Agnes, her ideas had gone on holiday too. Carmen's current writer's block meant staring at a blank page while her imaginary friends stayed silent.

'I'm sorry, Mum, but I'm trying to finish my new novel, and the hours seem to slip away,' Carmen said.

'No wonder your skin is ageing, slouched over that TV all day.' Betty's tone was cruel. She sat stiffly in her armchair and lifted a salmon paste sandwich to her lips. 'Do you want to end up like Mrs Mitchell down the road?'

Carmen removed her heavy-rimmed glasses and touched

her face to smooth her skin. She'd be delighted to end up like Mrs Mitchell, who, despite chronic osteoarthritis, was on her fourth husband. Her life was one long, happy holiday, and the woman always had a cheery word and a beaming smile, telling Carmen that she was a saint for putting up with her mother.

'It's not a TV,' Carmen said. 'I work on a laptop. It's how I write,' she patiently explained and handed Betty a folded napkin.

'What's wrong with a pen and paper?' Betty chewed with exaggerated slowness, dabbing at her mouth with the napkin balled between her fingers. 'No wonder you need glasses if you use those new-fangled machines.'

Moving to the window, Carmen tucked her glasses in a pocket and tweaked a curtain to shade the late afternoon sun from blinding Betty while she ate. As Betty moaned that her tea was lukewarm, Carmen stared at the lawn where sparrows pecked the grass. *At least someone is enjoying their meal*, she thought. Even in the simple act of eating, Betty found something to complain about, her dissatisfaction with the world as unyielding as her tongue.

If Betty was a character in Carmen's current novel, she would have been killed off by now. But as Des and Betty Cunningham's only daughter, Carmen was bound by a promise to her dad. On his deathbed, Des, short for Desmond, weakly gripped Carmen's hand. 'Look after your mother,' he'd said, 'I know she's a dragon but there used to be a good heart in there. It just got a bit lost over the years.'

Resigned to seeing out her mother's days as chief carer,

cook and bottle washer, Carmen tried to ignore Betty's daily threats of leaving her estate to a cat's conservation charity. Carmen appreciated the house she lived in and knowing that she would inherit it if she bowed to Betty's demands, her unwavering sense of duty kept her going. But Carmen secretly hoped that the grim reaper would come knocking on Betty's door before Carmen called it a day and couldn't take any more.

'This needed salt,' Betty declared as she pushed the last round into her mouth and tapped her cane on the floor. 'Honestly, Carmen, why can't you make a decent sandwich?' she said. 'I don't see why you should inherit this house if you can't do a better job of looking after me; your father would be turning in his grave.' Betty sat forward to place her plate on the tray, her painful expression exaggerated for maximum effect. 'My arthritis is playing up something fierce today,' she continued and attempted to rub her side.

Carmen thought that if Betty's arthritis were an actor, it would win an Oscar. Like clockwork, Betty's pain appeared on the dot of washing-up time after every meal. Her arthritis knew precisely when there were jobs to be done.

Leaning back in her chair, Betty crossed her arms, tossed her newspaper on the tray, and pointed to her radio. 'Let me know when *The Archers* is on,' she ordered and closed her eyes.

Moments later, the elderly lady was sound asleep, and Carmen picked up the tray and tip-toed out of the room.

* * *

Carmen turned a tap and swished bubbles in the sink. Her thoughts about silencing Betty were only in her head and, gently washing the crockery, Carmen knew she lacked the courage of her fictional characters. She resigned herself to the fact that she would remain a diligent daughter until Betty popped her clogs. Her frustration towards her mother, meanwhile, was released through her writing with the continuation of her cosy mysteries.

But as Carmen dried her hands, she sighed.

At that moment, her frustrations were rampant. Her current novel, which needed rewriting following a nondescript first draft, had come to a grinding halt, and no matter how long she stared at the screen, words refused to form. Her first book had been moderately successful, gaining an Amazon bestseller badge, and her publisher insisted that to continue momentum for her readers, Carmen must keep to the deadline in the proposed series.

But time was running out and the deadline was looming. Carmen had three months to hand the novel to her publisher.

As she folded the towel and placed it on a rail, she remembered her joy when she'd been accepted by a major publisher. After many rejections, her writing dream had come true and, for the first time in her life, Carmen had achieved something she was proud of. At fifty-three, her debut, entitled *The Rainbow Sleuth*, stormed to the top of the cosy crime charts, and readers were eager for the next in the series. Her three-book publishing deal had made the trade press, and Carmen's cosmopolitan hero was due to solve a series of mysteries.

'Writing muse, where are you?' Carmen called out.

As though searching for inspiration, she looked around the kitchen at Desbett House and studied the 1970s retro designs. Bold burned orange was predominant on wooden cabinets, and woodgrain finishes patterned shelving and countertops. She stepped across the vinyl flooring, which was dented by decades of pounding heels, then flicked a pendant light to illuminate her laptop, which lay on a Formica table.

Carmen found her glasses and placed them on her nose. She sat down, and as she turned the pages of a notebook, she wondered if she could place her lead character in a time capsule like this kitchen. Would the Rainbow Sleuth discover a victim slain by a Pyrex dish smashed into their skull or strangled by the macramé plant hanger? Might the casualty slip on the contents of a fondue pot or be chopped into pieces by the whir of an electric carving knife? If only she could find inspiration, glue her fingers to the keyboard and set the story alight.

Carmen knew that she had to push her imagination. She'd led an ordinary life with little experience to draw on. Working in her father's hardware shop was hardly the environment to plot and plan a cosy mystery. Yet, somehow, she'd managed to write a novel that had sold well.

The problem was in writing the next.

Carmen dreamed of penning stories all her life. As a child, she spent hours cutting out images from magazines and adding text to make her own fantasy books, and at school, she bravely held up her hand when a career teacher asked the class what they wanted to do.

'I want to be a writer,' the teenage Carmen announced.

But her teacher was dismissive and told Carmen that she didn't have the talent for novels and must apply herself to work in her father's shop.

Carmen picked up a pen and began to doodle in her notebook. An image of her teacher, hanging from scaffolding, began to appear on the page. 'I proved you wrong,' Carmen said, as she drew a noose, 'I wrote a novel, and readers liked it.'

On her fiftieth birthday, Carmen had experienced an epiphany when, following the sudden death of her husband, Betty suddenly sold their business, and Carmen found herself out of work. Devastated not only by the loss of her dad, but by discovering herself at home with Betty all day, Carmen vowed that she would write her first novel.

Her dad's words kept Carmen going through her grief. *'You've got to have a dream to make a dream come true . . .'* Des had repeatedly told his daughter.

Now, as Carmen drummed her fingers on the tabletop, she thought of Des's own dream of owning a business. Cunningham's Hardware had been a successful shop in the Cumbrian market town of Butterly, and he'd hoped that one day, Carmen would fulfil her childhood dream too.

'You've made up stories all your life,' he'd told her. 'Don't die wondering what it might have been like to be an author. *Make it happen.* Let your writing dream come true.'

Carmen stood and began to tidy Betty's tray.

As she prepared her mother's supper of a mug of cocoa

and a plate of Bourbon biscuits, her eyes drifted to Betty's discarded newspaper where the pages were folded to reveal the daily crossword. She noted that all the clues had been solved. Betty zipped through a crossword faster than a knife through butter, and despite her insistence that her mind was failing, Carmen knew that the old lady was as sharp as a pin, her memory a minefield of clues and answers. Des and Betty Cunningham, in their day, had appeared in pub quiz teams and won many prizes.

As Carmen picked up the paper, a supplement fell out. Stooping to retrieve it, she saw that it advertised cruise ship holidays. The glossy brochure was colourful, and, sitting down again, she idly flicked through the pages, imagining what it would be like to pack her bag and escape to a far-flung location.

A holiday without Betty, imagine!

There were enticing cruises to the Caribbean, Asia, Antarctica and the South Pacific on giant passenger liners. At the same time, closer to home, one could enjoy a five-city break in Europe. Cruising on the Danube, the Rhine or even the Norwegian Fjords sounded fascinating. Carmen couldn't remember the last time she'd enjoyed a holiday. The annual pilgrimage to Bournemouth, pushing Betty's wheelchair along the promenade during two weeks in the summer, hardly made magical memories of sun, sea and shenanigans.

'How I long for some shenanigans . . .' Carmen said as she stared at the adverts and exotic locations.

But the words of an advert for a lesser-known cruise line suddenly caught Carmen's eye.

> **Discover the magic of**
> **The Mysteries of the Mediterranean**
> *Embark on an unforgettable journey as you join*
> *The Cruise Club on the* Diamond Star.
> This small luxury liner prides itself on memorable
> cruises for the more mature. Set sail on
> an adventure through crystal-clear waters and visit
> sun-drenched beaches and ancient cities.
> Enjoy a comfortable cabin with sea views, plush
> surroundings and gourmet dining.
> The *Diamond Star*'s talented team will entertain
> throughout with song, dance, comedy and
> knowledgeable enrichment speakers.
>
> **EXCLUSIVE:**
> Number One Bestselling Author of the award-winning
> TV Series *Detective Inspector Blake Investigates*
>
> **RUSKIN REEVE**
> will be on board to host a talk and workshops
> *For a cruise you will cherish forever –*
> *book your dream holiday today!*

Carmen felt her pulse quicken as she re-read the advertisement. Her hero, the crime writer Ruskin Reeve, was a guest speaker on this Mediterranean cruise. It must be a sign!

The famed Ruskin Reeve was her inspiration, and she

had all his books, in series order, placed prominently on a shelf in her bedroom. She adored the crime writer who wrote tales of intrigue and deception and whose works had captivated readers and critics worldwide, gaining many prestigious awards. Carmen loved Ruskin's keen eye for detail and understanding of human psychology, creating complex mysteries and believable characters. The writing gods had guided Carmen, and now, all she had to do was summon the courage to pick up the phone and book her place on the cruise.

'If only I could write like you . . .' Carmen breathed as she gazed at Ruskin's photograph, her fingers tracing the outline of the letters of his name.

A voice in her ear whispered, and tilting her head to one side, Carmen felt sure that her dad was speaking. *'Follow your writing dream!'* he urged.

Carmen desperately wanted to follow Ruskin onto the *Diamond Star* cruise, to draw inspiration from his crime writing. Her heart fluttered at the thought of attending his writing workshops. Time with the talented author would surely end her writer's block and get the words flowing again.

She *had* to go on the cruise!

Carmen's hazel eyes sparkled with anticipation, and she pushed her heavy-rimmed glasses along her nose before running her fingers through her shoulder-length brown hair. She could almost feel the warm Mediterranean breeze on her skin and hear the gentle lapping of waves against the ship. Indeed, such a setting would inspire her to write, and it might be the remedy she so desperately needed. After all, it wasn't as though she couldn't afford the holiday; Carmen had a tidy sum in a savings account.

She checked the sailing date and was pleased that the cruise began in just over a week. There was no time to cancel, if she decided to go. Carmen knew that Agnes would be back from her holiday in a couple of days, and with a little gentle persuasion and extra money in her wages, she felt sure that the kindly woman would step up and help with Betty.

Betty. The roadblock in her plan.

The pitfall to the holiday would be Betty's hysteria when she learned that her daughter was planning an exciting trip without her mother. Memories of dozens of disappointments, caused by Betty's interference, flooded Carmen's mind.

She mustn't let Betty spoil her plans!

Despite the building guilt, Carmen picked up her pen and circled the cruise agent's number. For years Carmen had allowed her mother to dictate, often sacrificing her hopes and dreams for peace. But now she felt an unfamiliar, steely resolve.

Straightening her shoulders, Carmen set her jaw with purpose and gripped the pen. This wasn't just a trip – learning from Ruskin Reeve was a necessity, and she knew that she must seize the opportunity.

Carmen dreaded breaking the news to Betty but decided that she would deal with that disaster later. She reached for her phone and began to dial, her heart pounding with anxiety and excitement. With a hesitant voice, Carmen began the booking process. Each word she uttered felt like a brick in the foundation of her ongoing writing dream.

The friendly voice from the *Diamond Star* team made the booking process seamless and told Carmen that as a member of The Cruise Club, she was entitled to discounts on future cruises, complimentary excursions and special occasion onboard cocktails. Moments later, the booking was complete.

'I'm going on a cruise . . .' Carmen whispered in amazement as she ended the call. 'Carmen Cunningham is about to set sail!'

Chapter Two

Ruskin Reeve studied his reflection in his bathroom mirror and decided he looked exhausted. At sixty, he had the rugged handsomeness that only deepened with age, but at that moment, his chiselled features were prominent, and his piercing blue eyes lacked vitality.

Running his fingers through tousled hair, Ruskin frowned. The thick wavy locks were now more salt than pepper, but the silvery gleam was attractive. Ruskin thought he looked the part of a world-weary wordsmith and given that he'd just completed a twenty-stop book signing tour of Great Britain, he felt justified in his tiredness.

'Any self-respecting author would now settle down, stay home and put their feet up, enjoying a break before embarking on the next novel,' he told himself as he reached for a razor and began to shave.

Having been away for several weeks, he knew that as soon as he stretched out on his sofa, the door would pound, and Venetia would insist on making her presence felt. Only a restraining order would keep his ex-wife from barging her way in, throwing herself at his mercy and begging for a second chance. Venetia was a force to be dealt with and still clung to the hope of rekindling their long-gone marriage. During his recent tour, a dishevelled Venetia appeared in a book signing queue and, to his embarrassment, publicly pleaded for another chance when she reached Ruskin. It had taken security to stand by the door and bar Venetia from entry as the tour progressed.

As Ruskin held the razor to his skin and stroked gently over two-day-old stubble, he felt a glimmer of regret. Venetia's tears stirred a sense of responsibility, but he couldn't shake the relief he'd felt when the constant arguments and misunderstandings had ended.

'After thirty years of marriage I simply fell out of love,' Ruskin told his reflection.

The devotion they'd once shared had faded as their two boys grew up and had families of their own and was replaced by a yearning for freedom. Ruskin wanted to be alone, live as a single man and do what he enjoyed most. Writing was his life.

Yet, despite his longing for solitude, he adored his grandchildren – two precious girls – and cherished the moments they spent together. He would often smile as he recalled their curious questions, their little eyes wide, as they listened in awe to the stories he told. Even as he embraced his new independence, he held a soft spot for his sons and those little people who called him Grandpa, and Ruskin saw them as often as he could.

The creation of a character called Detective Inspector Blake had propelled Ruskin into the limelight, and his books were a huge success. Adapted for television, the fictional detective was a national treasure, a character so loved that mentioning his name elicited smiles and nods of recognition. With his dedication to justice, Detective Inspector Blake was the nation's favourite detective.

'You made me a ton of money,' Ruskin said and thought about his character as he rinsed the razor under the tap. 'Now, if I could extract myself completely from Venetia, I might be able to focus on the next book.'

Ruskin stepped into the shower. Sharp needles of piping hot water pummelled his skin as he soaped his still-lithe body. His early morning runs and regular swims had paid off, and Ruskin was in good shape. He remembered that his agent was pressing for an outline, something to hand to his publisher to stay within the terms of his current contract. Unlike many high-profile authors, Ruskin didn't give the research to a team or ask for plot ideas; he prided himself on being in control, every word his own. But he knew he needed a break, a place where Venetia couldn't find him, where the internet was sketchy and his agent would leave him alone.

Wrapping a towel around his waist, Ruskin walked into his bedroom, where a suitcase lay on the bed. He'd exchanged his usual tweeds as he'd packed and now chose lighter linens. When he'd been contacted by the marketing team at Diamond Star Cruise Lines and offered an opportunity of a luxurious Mediterranean cruise in return for a talk and a couple of workshops, Ruskin had jumped at the chance. How good it would be to trade stories of his writing life in exchange for the soothing embrace of the sea, and for days, he'd been dreaming of tranquil, sunlit decks. A space to relax, recoup and unwind.

As he dressed, Ruskin told himself that he could well afford a luxury cruise and had no need for a complimentary passage. But Ruskin was conceited and despite yearning for a break from the whirlwind of his literary life, he fed off public attention wherever he went. The promise of an eager audience, excited to listen to his tales, was almost as good as sex, and he revelled in the thrill of captivating a crowd.

Suited in pale cream linen and booted in soft leather brogues, Ruskin reached for his satchel and checked his lecture notes. Glancing at his watch, he saw that he was on time for the cruise line's driver, who would arrive at any moment. Draining a half-empty cup of coffee, Ruskin closed his case and carried it to the hallway, where his luggage was neatly lined up by the door.

Mustering the energy to charm a new audience, Ruskin gave a last-minute glance in a mirror. His eyes sparkled with the excitement of the upcoming trip and vainly, he stared at his reflection. Perhaps Ruskin would take Detective Inspector Blake with him, he thought when the doorbell rang. As he reached out to answer it, a book title popped into his head, and with a smile, Ruskin set off.

* * *

Two days later and the early morning easyJet flight from Manchester to Kefalonia was delayed by an hour. Passengers, already tired and cranky after rising in the middle of the night, had been told to move through the terminal to a new departure gate. Loaded with hand luggage, they wearily displayed their boarding passes. To everyone's dismay, a coach waited at the base of the jetway steps, and despite torrential rain, passengers were instructed that in order to board the plane, they were to be ferried across the tarmac to the aircraft's boarding steps.

Comedian and cruise ship entertainer, Dicky Delaney, dismounted from the coach and stood in a queue as the rain bucketed down. His spirits were as dampened as his clothes, as heavy drops fell with a furious intensity. The air was thick with the smell of jet fuel and passengers voiced discontent as they waited for their ordeal to end and to be allowed into the comfort of a dry aircraft cabin.

'This is no way to start a holiday,' a man with a thick Yorkshire accent called out.

Dicky nodded his head in agreement. It was no way to begin the start of his working stint on the *Diamond Star*, and he silently cursed Clive, his London agent, who'd organised his travel to the ship. Years ago, Clive would have insisted that Dicky travel first-class with a chauffeur to hand on both sides of the journey, but Clive had still not forgiven Dicky for an incident with a theatre manager's wife in a seaside town where Dicky had a summer residency. It had resulted in Dicky's contract being abruptly cut short and Clive losing his agent's commission. Dicky had also done a runner on a recent Benidorm gig, and the memory of Clive's furious, red-faced tirade, punctuated with veins throbbing at his temples, was still fresh in his mind.

'You'll travel with the masses and no arguments,' Clive growled down the phone from his Soho office. 'You may have redeemed yourself on the Caribbean cruise at Christmas, but you've still got a long way to go.'

The aircraft door suddenly opened, and smiling cabin attendants greeted the bedraggled passengers. 'Welcome to easyJet,' they said to the crowd climbing the steps and cramming into the doorway.

'It's good of you to arrange a complimentary shower before the flight,' a woman commented as she was directed to her seat. Her perfectly styled holiday hair, which hours ago had been set in curls and waves, now clung to her head in soggy strands.

'Is this a new water ride feature?' the Yorkshire man asked. 'I didn't know we were off to Splash Mountain.'

As Dicky entered the cabin, he was tempted to ask if standing in the rain for fifteen minutes was an innovative easyJet spa treatment. Instead, he flashed a toothy grin at the prettiest attendant and made his way down the aisle. Listening to the disgruntled northern holidaymakers, Dicky whipped out his notebook. Their remarks were comedy gold, and he wrote down a comment from a man in the seat behind, who asked his wife if he should be looking for a seat in a lifeboat, not a plane. Overheard gems of wit often made their way into Dicky's stage act.

The cabin crew checked seatbelts, and the flight took off. As it soared over the sodden sight of Manchester and arced gracefully into a turn to leave behind the rolling Cheshire plain, Dicky stared out of the window. They rose into marshmallow mountains of cloud, and he watched the play of light as the flight glided through a soft, ethereal world suspended between heaven and earth.

Dicky thought about the last few months which he'd spent in Spain. With a gig at a well-known club in Benidorm, arranged by Clive, he'd enjoyed a relationship with a pretty woman named Anne, whom he'd met on the Caribbean cruise. Their plans of starting a new life together had soon come to an end when Anne caught Dicky backstage with one of the dancers. As she packed, Anne's rage knew no limit, and Dicky, knowing when it was time to bow out, to Clive's fury, had also left town in a hurry to head back to his ex-wife in Doncaster.

'Women . . .' Dicky sighed as he watched giant cotton wool balls of cloud. He couldn't live without them, but he sure as hell couldn't live with them for very long.

Dicky had hoped that Anne was The One. But it turned out she was just another plot twist in his own romantic comedy. Back in familiar territory, his ex-wife's reception had been as chilly as an arctic blizzard, making it quite clear that he was no more than a passing shadow in her now well-ordered life. Dicky had stayed for one night only before heading to London to beg an angry Clive to find him work.

The drinks trolley was rattling in the aisle, and Dicky unclipped his seatbelt. When your luck ran out and your toast landed butter-side down, there was only one thing to do. He'd get back on stage, and during the cruise, push his autobiography. Dicky's book, *My Life in Showbusiness*, sold well on a cruise, and, if he kept under the purser's radar, there was always an opportunity to make an extra income on the side with the wealthy female passengers. Dicky had self-published his book after failing to reach the lofty heights of success he'd envisioned on the professional circuit with the big names in comedy. Unable to attract interest from a publishing house and take the traditional route, he forged his own path. Still, the book was engaging, and if he had embellished a few chapters here and there, no one seemed to notice.

'Coffee and a Scotch,' Dicky said to the attendant serving drinks.

Sipping slowly, he reflected on his career and remembered the highlights of performing on the comedy circuits at some of the largest clubs in the country. The thrill of the perfect punchline, when his timing was impeccable, and Dicky felt like he'd had the world at his feet.

But Dicky knew that those days were gone. Overshadowed by today's successful comedians, who were international stars performing to vast audiences for unheard-of amounts of money, Dicky had a sense of frustration mixed with a sad acceptance. Now, the best gigs Clive could find for him were on cruise ships or clubs on the Costas, where only the mature guests understood Dicky's age-old jokes. But despite the setbacks, Dicky clung to the belief that although he might be on the decline, he could still muster moments of brilliance that reminded him why he fell in love with comedy. He might not be the headliner he was in the past, but Dicky felt sure his journey wasn't over and that he could capitalise on the right situation.

'Maybe The Cruise Club on the *Diamond Star* will be a new start,' Dicky mused as he drained his drink.

Lowering the window blind, he closed his eyes. With the soft vibration of the aircraft engines his lullaby, in moments, Dicky was sound asleep.

Chapter Three

Carmen's bag was bunched on her lap as she sat on the back seat of a coach taking her to board the *Diamond Star*, berthed on the island of Kefalonia. As they drove away from the airport, she adjusted her glasses and stared at low hills and a landscape dotted with olive groves. The driver negotiated the winding twists and turns of the road, and Carmen caught her first sight of clear blue waters. Taking a deep breath, she counted to ten and, exhaling slowly, began to curse her mother.

On the front seat, Betty was chatting happily with a middle-aged man. Despite Carmen's insistence that she take a holiday alone, Betty had inveigled her way in.

'I don't understand why you would *want* to go on holiday alone,' Betty said when Carmen broke the news. 'You know how much I enjoy spending time with you, and as you've been so busy with that silly little novel, it will be good for us both to get away together.'

Within moments, Betty had seized the brochure on the kitchen table, dialled the number and booked herself a place.

'Yes, that's right,' she told the cruise agent, 'my daughter has already reserved her cabin, and I'd like one next door. I'm an invalid, you see.'

Betty's cane had been flung to one side, and with the agility of an athlete, she'd crossed the kitchen to dig into her bag, produce a payment card and read out the number. With the reservation secure, Betty grinned, then flopped into a rocking chair and picked up the cruise brochure. 'Just think, how nice it will be to have some mother and daughter bonding time,' she said, slowly turning the pages. 'You can take me on a shopping trip tomorrow, I could do with some new summer clothes.'

They entered the town of Argostoli, and Carmen gazed out of the window, wide-eyed with curiosity. She'd read about the devastating earthquake that had struck the town in the 1950s and knew the buildings she saw had been reconstructed in a neoclassical style, following the island's traditions. As they drove, she took in the houses and monuments, noticing how Argostoli was nestled around a deep lagoon, with a narrow bridge spanning the bay to create a convenient shortcut.

The vehicle jostled along a cobbled road, and a cruise ship came into view. A representative from the cruise line stood up, turned to face the group, and picked up a microphone.

'Hello,' he began, his voice warm and welcoming, 'and may I extend a heartfelt *Diamond Star* welcome to you all. My name is Peter Hammond, and I am your purser and entertainment director.'

Carmen joined the polite ripple of applause that followed, smiling faintly.

Peter continued. 'We are a small company, and personal service is something that the company prides itself on. You are now officially members of The Cruise Club on the *Diamond Star*, so feel free to come and discuss any queries you have with myself or my team.'

Carmen couldn't help but think that Peter might regret his warm welcome as she admired the charming Greek-style buildings and local shops. Betty would undoubtedly monopolise the purser's time, to ensure that she got her money's worth throughout the cruise. But Carmen was determined that nothing would dampen her own enthusiasm. This was her opportunity to meet Ruskin Reeve, and she intended to enjoy the amazing holiday. As the port came into view, she gazed at the bustling harbourfront and vowed to make the most of everything.

The coach stopped, and excited passengers pointed to the ship that rose majestically from the Ionian Sea, its bow painted navy with a regal gold stripe.

'Because of its size, the *Diamond Star* can dock port side,' Peter explained, 'unlike larger cruise ships berthed some distance away.'

Carmen could see that a walkway was carpeted in red, and a band was playing. Nervously, she wondered if Ruskin Reeve was already on the ship.

It's finally happening!

Soon, she would meet her idol. The thought of meeting the author she'd admired for years, filled Carmen with an indescribable excitement. Memories of standing in the rain early morning as they waited to board their flight, and Betty's constant complaints and rudeness to the airline staff, were forgotten. In the golden Greek sunlight, the *Diamond Star* looked like a floating palace, and Carmen would soon be stepping on board.

'CARMEN!' Betty's voice drew the attention of everyone around. 'Stop daydreaming at the back and give your poor old mother a helping hand.'

But Carmen's poor old mother had already made her way down the steps of the coach and was poking towards Peter with her cane.

Peter held a clipboard and checked his list of names. 'Ah, you must be Mrs Elizabeth Cunningham, accompanied by your daughter, Carmen?' He smiled at Betty.

'I'm glad you know who I am,' Betty snapped. 'Now find my wheelchair, young man; my daughter will be assisting me.'

Fully aware that crew members were waiting to help any passengers who needed assistance, Carmen wondered if she should hide. But Betty was making a fuss, and the only way to quieten her down and avoid a scene, would be to do what she was told.

'I'm sorry but Mother insisted on sitting at the front,' Carmen began as Peter, head and shoulders above the crowd, came forward to greet her. 'I'm afraid I got stuck at the back.'

Flustered, she slung her bag onto her shoulder, then attempted to straighten the creases from her cotton trousers. Her T-shirt felt damp in the heat and clung, and Carmen wished she'd worn something cool, gorgeous and flowing, like many of the glamorous passengers who were making their way to the ship.

'Don't worry, Ms Cunningham, or may I call you Carmen,' he said, 'such a beautiful name. I love the opera, don't you?'

Before Carmen had time to reply, Peter instructed a co-worker to help Betty into her chair and deaf to her protest, wheeled her to a linen-covered table where smiling uniformed servers were handing out drinks.

'Why don't you help yourself to refreshments,' Peter instructed as a server handed Carmen a cleansing hand towel while another offered champagne.

Carmen held the chilled flute and sipped.

The first taste was cold and delicious, and she felt a temporary release of the stress that lay on her shoulders. *This stuff should be on prescription!* Carmen asked for a refill.

For a moment, she forgot about her mother and let her mind drift to the turquoise water, sun-drenched coastline, and all the charming places she was about to explore. She visualised sitting close to Ruskin Reeve to listen to carefully chosen words of wisdom that would inspire and enable infinite possibilities in her writing. Reflecting on the adventure ahead, Carmen smiled. She was on the verge of an unforgettable journey!

'CARMEN!' Betty's voice screeched and Carmen's happy spell was broken. 'Don't stand daydreaming all day. Come and help your mother!'

Carmen turned to see the co-worker in charge of Betty shake their head and, with a shrug, walk away from the wheelchair. She wondered what Betty had said to cause upset. Finishing her drink, Carmen knew that she must get Betty settled in her room. If only she had the courage to throw away the key!

'Make sure you handle me with care!' Betty bossed.

Carmen contemplated breaking into a run and releasing Betty into the sea. But the thought of her mother's indignant shrieks echoing across the lagoon made Carmen grip the handles tighter. 'Relax, Mum, we're nearly there,' she said as they entered the ship, 'you'll soon be safe and sound onboard.'

'About time and not a moment too soon,' Betty grumbled impatiently. 'My arthritis is playing up and my cabin had better be to my liking.'

'I'm sure it will be perfect,' Carmen soothed.

With a wistful smile to Peter, who was helping check passengers in, Carmen made a mental note to order champagne from room service as soon as she'd unpacked.

Peter gave an understanding look. 'Don't worry,' he whispered, 'there are plenty of group activities for your mother. We call them the Golden Oldies Gang. You'll have lots of time to yourself.'

Carmen wanted to hug Peter. Perhaps the purser might ensure that the Mysteries of the Mediterranean cruise would be magical for Carmen after all.

Chapter Four

On the balcony of a suite on the *Diamond Star*, Fran Cartwright smiled as she held the rail and watched weary travellers disembarking from airport coaches. Greeted by cruise line staff, they stood in the warm sunshine, sipping complimentary drinks as they awaited to board the ship.

Tipping her broad-brimmed hat, Fran gazed over rainbow-rimmed sunglasses to see Peter, the purser, move amongst the new arrivals, dispensing *Diamond Star* hospitality as he mingled. He welcomed a middle-aged man and grinning, vigorously shook hands as they greeted each other.

Turning to her husband, who lay on a lounger alongside her, Fran commented, 'Sid, have a look at this. The ship is about to fill with new passengers.'

Straightening his shorts, Sid reached for his T-shirt, then tugged it over his shoulders before joining his wife. 'That looks like the comedian Dicky Delaney,' Sid said as they watched the two men below. 'His photo is in *Diamond Star Daily News*. It said he'd be joining the cruise in Kefalonia.'

Sid recalled the printed newspaper placed beneath their

cabin door each morning, informing passengers of the day's events.

'That's quite a tan he's got.' Fran said.

'Do you think he dyes his hair?' Sid asked.

'I think he's clinging on to the fountain of youth,' Fran replied as she gazed in wonder at Dicky's hair. 'He reminds me of Elvis.'

'That lass pushing the wheelchair looks exhausted.' Sid's eyes followed Carmen as she struggled to manoeuvre a cane-waving Betty along the walkway.

'The lady must have mobility issues,' Fran said. 'Perhaps it's her daughter who's taking charge, let's hope the cruise will do them good.' Fran's sculpted eyebrows knotted together as she watched the younger woman battle with the wheelchair as though it were a stubborn shopping trolley. 'The poor love looks frazzled,' Fran added, noting Carmen's rumpled outfit and bulging bag, weighing her down.

'The more passengers, the merrier,' Sid said and turned away to resume his position on the lounger.

The band was playing a selection of Greek tunes, and as Fran listened to the lively strumming of bouzoukis, she wriggled her ample hips beneath her colourful sarong and tapped her fingers to the infectious rhythm of drums and cymbals.

'Eh, it makes me feel like dancing,' she said and turned to Sid as a band member called out, 'Opa!' Fran held her arms aloft and swayed from side to side. 'Aren't we lucky?' she cooed. 'I still can't believe we're here.'

Had it been a year since they'd opened their fine-dining restaurant in Blackpool and watched food lovers flock to the Fylde Coast? After years of success with their fish and chip business, they'd finally fulfilled Sid's dream of putting Blackpool on the culinary map, and Fran's exquisite cooking and celebration of Northern cuisine had earned them many awards. This cruise was their well-deserved reward for countless gruelling days and the effort of training their staff to be competent in their absence. It marked the culmination of years of hard work and offered a chance to unwind and enjoy the fruits of their labour. Now, in their mid-sixties, Fran and Sid Cartwright reckoned they deserved a memorable break.

'I never thought we'd be living the high life like this,' Fran continued.

She grabbed Sid's hands and tugged him to his feet. Tossing her hat aside, Fran's brassy blonde hair spilled loose from her animal print scrunchie, and she urged him to dance. As the head chef and co-owner of their restaurant, Fran was accustomed to being in charge, but on this cruise, she was determined to let loose and enjoy herself.

'Opa!' Sid exclaimed, shuffling around Fran with his arms outstretched in a Zorba dance-like fashion. Narrowly avoiding the table, they spun in a circle, then collapsed in an embrace to lean over the railings as the music ended.

'It's like *Mamma Mia!*' Fran waved to the band, who held up their instruments and bowed before the applauding crowd. 'I can't wait for tonight. Do you think the musicians will come on board?'

'Aye, the *Diamond Star Daily News* says we're having a Greek night to welcome those joining today,' Sid informed. He touched his smooth bald head, which felt hot, and wondered if he should apply sunscreen.

'It will be a cracking event, and everyone will get to know

each other.' Fran reached for her factor fifty and began to slather it on Sid's head. 'Now, you'd better stay in the shade for the rest of the day, or we'll be frying calamari on that sunburned noggin of yours, Sid Cartwright.'

'Yes, boss,' Sid mumbled. Stretching out on his sunbed, he picked up the *Diamond Star Daily News* and placed it over his face.

As the ship gently swayed in the Argostoli lagoon, Fran sat down and found herself mesmerised by the sapphire blue water and the lush green hillsides. The whitewashed houses with their terracotta roofs stood out vividly against the Mediterranean sun, where distant mountains had an almost ethereal quality, and a gentle breeze carried a holiday scent.

'It's like a picture postcard,' Fran said, 'who'd think we were on a ship and not in a dream.'

Sid snored and, smiling, Fran turned to her husband of many decades. 'You deserve this holiday,' she whispered, 'sleep soundly, my lovely man.'

Fran inhaled the soothing scent of pine and salt water mixed with a hint of grilled seafood from the nearby cafés and bars. With a contented sigh and entirely at peace in this idyllic setting, Fran lay back and began to snore gently, too.

* * *

Propped up on a pile of fluffy pillows, Ruskin lay on his bed in his suite on the Bridge Deck of the *Diamond Star* and held a glass of whisky. He swirled the crystal tumbler and watched the amber-coloured liquid catch the light. Taking a sip, Ruskin tasted the smooth smoky flavour and stared out of patio windows which offered a perfect view of glittering sunlit mountains.

He'd boarded the ship two days ago and had so far enjoyed catching up on sleep and relaxing in the sunshine while the *Diamond Star* nestled in the bay of Argostoli. Today, as more passengers joined the ship, the ship would be at capacity with 900 passengers and 370 crew. Ruskin considered a small ship the perfect environment for Detective Inspector Blake to unravel a new mystery, and he would enjoy research and plotting during this trip.

Ruskin thought about the talk he would give during a sea day, and other than a quick rehearsal in his cabin, he was confident that it would go well. After all, he'd rolled it out at events a hundred times during his writing career. His workshops were well practised, too, and Ruskin knew that he gave the cruise line good value for money in return for his complimentary cruise.

Swinging his legs off the bed, he reached for a decanter and poured himself another whisky. His favourite tipple was helping him unwind. With his mobile switched off, it was a relief to be free of the barrage of messages and calls from Venetia, who stubbornly clung to the hope of reviving their defunct marriage.

Stepping onto the balcony, where the sun was fierce, Ruskin reached for his Ray-Bans and yawned as he scratched his naked chest. Coaches below were being unloaded, and he could see new passengers enjoying a welcoming drink as they waited to board.

A man greeted the purser, and Ruskin observed their easy manner as the two chatted. He wondered if they were mates catching up or had they worked together before? Ruskin noted the man's swarthy manner when a pretty crew member offered him a drink, his head turning to the sway of her hips as she moved away.

A couple dressed in matching baseball caps, T-shirts and shorts, stood arm in arm, occasionally stealing a kiss or nuzzling each other as they accepted their cocktails, and Ruskin wondered if the couple were later-in-life honeymooners, basking in newlywed bliss.

Good luck with that, he thought and looked away.

A frazzled-looking woman pushed a wheelchair along the walkway. Her arms were taut and a bag, wrapped around her shoulder, hung heavily, while the occupant of the chair waved a cane at any passengers in the way.

Ruskin grinned. The elderly lady wasn't going to make friends if she kept that up. He was tempted to shout down and tell the woman to stop, take a moment and enjoy the wonderful surroundings, but the elderly lady had reached the ship, and the pair disappeared.

Picking up his notebook, Ruskin sat down and thought about the diversity of passengers, knowing that each had the potential to become a character in his next novel. His mind wove details into his fictional world, turning observations into possible scenes as he jotted his thoughts. If his ideas for the next novel picked up during the cruise, his agent would be delighted.

Taking another slug of whisky, he settled into his seat and, resting his notebook on his knee, began to write.

Chapter Five

Onboard the *Diamond Star*, as new passengers settled into their cabins, crew members worked to decorate areas of the ship in preparation for the Greek evening. Blue and white banners lined the entrance to the Terrace Restaurant, where national flags had been hung over linen-covered tables decorated with Greek motifs. In the kitchens, the ship's chefs prepared a culinary menu that included traditional dishes, and in the Neptune Theatre, the entertainment team were rehearsing behind closed doors.

In a Terrace Cabin, on deck three, Carmen admired the layout of her room, marvelling at the clever design that maximised both space and comfort. Placing her bag down, she sat on the bed and studied the artwork, soft lighting and soothing décor. Having unpacked for Betty and settled her mother for a nap in the adjacent cabin, Carmen was grateful that there was no interlinking door, and Betty couldn't barge into Carmen's space whenever it suited her.

A knock echoed and Carmen called out, 'Come in!'

Carrying a tray with a half bottle of champagne in an ice

bucket, a cabin steward greeted her. 'Welcome aboard,' he said, 'my name is Fernando, and I am happy to assist you throughout your holiday.'

Carmen watched as the young man skilfully popped the cork. With her curious author's mind, she wondered about Fernando.

'Are you far from home?' she asked.

'Oh yes,' Fernando smiled, 'my home is in the Philippines.'

'Goodness, that's a distance away, how long are you at sea?'

'I work for six months then home to my family, then back on a ship,' he said as he carefully poured the champagne.

'Do you enjoy your work?'

Fernando's face lit up. 'I travel to different destinations and meet people from all over the world. I have the best job.'

Carmen thanked the steward and handed him five euros.

'Efharisto,' Fernando gave a slight bow, acknowledging her gratuity as he left the room.

Moving to the balcony, Carmen stepped out to enjoy the view. She felt a warm breeze and as she held her glass, stared at the bubbles rising slowly. The day's tension suddenly dissolved as the gentle sound of the sea and the distant call of birds blended into a welcoming blanket that wrapped around Carmen, creating a peaceful haven amidst the bustling ship.

Carmen drank the champagne and felt at peace. Her holiday had finally begun, and it filled her with excitement. The shimmering water and solitude felt like liberation. She closed her eyes and thought about the days ahead. Would she leave the ship and take part in any excursions? Would the cruise be the inspiration needed to kick-start her writing? Carmen imagined sun-kissed ports and, best of all, meeting Ruskin Reeve.

'CARMEN!'

The sharp screech of Betty's voice jolted Carmen and her hand jerked, spilling the remains of her drink on her trousers.

'I've been knocking on the wall and wondered where you'd got to.' Betty peered around the partition separating the terrace, her lips pressed into a thin line. 'Don't just stand there daydreaming. I'm ready for my afternoon tea.'

Betty's neck stretched out like a turtle appearing from its shell. Her new perm had a feather-like quality in the sunlight, and she reached out to pat and pull at the curls.

'This heat is ruining my hair,' Betty complained, 'don't be so selfish, leaving me alone and helpless when you could be in here with a can of lacquer and a comb.'

Carmen was tempted to tell Betty that her hair could wait and, if she picked up the phone and called room service, Fernando would soon appear with a tray of tea.

Dabbing at the stain on her trousers, Carmen realised she hadn't had time to change or unpack her own cases, but Betty would be unbearable in her demands until her daughter did as she was told. 'Coming, Mother,' Carmen replied.

She placed her empty glass on the table and stepped away from the terrace. Picking up her glasses and key, Carmen hastened to the adjacent room.

* * *

Dicky Delaney was not a happy man. After checking in, the entertainer was dismayed to see that his allocated cabin was in the interior and provided no natural light. To his further dismay, he realised that it was situated within a short distance of the ship's engines, which rumbled continuously. His accommodation was described as *'a compact space for travellers who require an economical, budget-friendly option.'* Dicky was furious that he would have to endure the limited living arrangement throughout the cruise and was tempted to call Clive and insist that his agent arrange an upgrade. But the comedian knew that Clive's response was likely to be abusive and end with the word 'off!'

Dicky's days of wrapping Clive around his little finger had ended. If he had any hope of continuing to work for a cruise line, the comedian would have to shut up and put up, as far as Clive was concerned.

'Let's hope my dressing room is an improvement,' Dicky mumbled to his reflection in the minuscule mirror as he stood in the tiny bathroom space.

Following a quick wash and liberal application of a new aftershave he'd purchased at the airport, Dicky straightened his hair and changed into a clean shirt. He hung his belongings on a rail and picked up a copy of his autobiography. Tucking his key in his pocket, Dicky slammed the door and made his way through the ship.

As Dicky ascended the floors to the duty-free shopping area, his mood brightened.

Wandering through lounges, he smiled at relaxing guests,

some taking afternoon tea while others strolled out to the sun decks to sit in the sunshine. Dicky felt at home amongst the *Diamond Star*'s mature, well-heeled clientele, noting with pleasure that one or two women were on their own. Mostly retired, widowed and wealthy, Dicky's familiar stomping ground looked fruitful.

He stopped to talk to a couple who recognised the comedian from the *Diamond Star Daily News*.

'Ey up!' the man said with a broad Yorkshire accent. 'You'll be making us laugh later, I hope?' He introduced himself and his wife as Don and Debbie from Halifax and told Dicky that they'd just joined the ship and were celebrating their wedding anniversary.

Pleased to make their acquaintance, Dicky congratulated the couple. 'I'm on stage for the ten o'clock show; make sure to be in the front row and I'll give you a shout out,' Dicky said. 'Thirty years married and still going strong?' he asked. 'They say patience is a virtue, so you two must be saints by now.'

As Don and Debbie moved away, Dicky heard Don mutter that he hoped Dicky's jokes improved for the show that night.

In the gift shop, Dicky paused at the entrance. Searching for copies of his book, he bit his lip as he realised there were none to be seen. An author by the name of Ruskin Reeve was showcased and stacks of his latest release dominated the bookshelves. The glossy covers faced outwards to catch passenger's eyes and a large poster featuring the author's smiling face announced:

Meet Bestselling Author Ruskin Reeve
Here on the *Diamond Star!*

Dicky marched over to an assistant, who was arranging a display of novelty items.

'Can I help?' the assistant asked and stroked the dorsal fin of Danny the Diamond Star Dolphin before placing the torpedo-shaped gift neatly on a shelf.

Noting the badge on the assistant's jacket, Dicky said, 'Hello, Jason.'

'Welcome aboard.' Jason touched his neatly styled hair as he looked Dicky up and down. 'How can I make your shopping experience sparkle today?' Without pausing for an answer, Jason continued. 'I can recommend the best cruise souvenirs and accessories, advise on the best spots for sunset views and know all of the ship's amenities.' He wrinkled his nose and sniffed at Dicky's aftershave. 'I can also recommend a decent fragrance.'

Dicky stood back.

Raising a well-groomed eyebrow, Jason pursed his lips. 'What's your pleasure?'

'My pleasure would be for you to find the stock of this book and make a decent display.' He held up his copy of *My Life in Showbusiness*.

'Ah, a comedian,' Jason sniffed and taking the book, flicked through the pages, 'but we already have a display for Ruskin Reeve.'

Dicky drew himself up. 'I'm the main act on this cruise and my book needs to be on those shelves.' He nodded and a quiff of hair fell forward. 'Where are they?'

'There's boxes of them in the back but I haven't put them out yet.' Jason folded his arms. 'Has anyone ever told you that you have a look of Elvis?' he asked, then added, 'In his later years.'

Dicky folded his arms and was tempted to return Jason's insult but knowing that he needed the assistant on his side, remained silent.

'Is this copy for me?' Jason asked with a cheeky smile.

'It might be,' Dicky said and wondered what he had to do to get Jason to promote his book. Lowering his voice and checking that no one else was in the shop, he said, 'How about I sign it for you, and you move Ruskin Reeve's books to one side and put mine out. Depending on my sales, I'll make sure it's worth your while?'

'You got it,' Jason handed the book back to Dicky.

Dicky reached for a pen and signed his name.

'Won't you buy a Danny the Dolphin?' Jason reached for the novelty gift.

'Maybe later.' Dicky shrugged and felt relieved when an elderly couple came into the shop and made a beeline for the dolphin display.

Ten minutes later, Dicky stepped on stage in the Neptune Theatre and made himself known to the choreographer of the *Diamond Star* Dance Troupe. Aware that he would work his act into the various song and dance routines and, having performed a zillion times with similar performances throughout his career, Dicky felt confident.

'Who's the headline singer?' he asked as he studied the show schedule.

'Melody Moon,' the choreographer replied, 'have you met her?'

'No, not had the pleasure.' Dicky studied the singer's songs for the evening show.

'She's just finished rehearsing and you'll find her in the dressing room you're both sharing.'

Dicky sighed. Gone were the days when he had his own dressing room. Regardless of gender, artists had to muck in, and he hoped the shared facilities would be more spacious than his box-like cabin.

Walking through the backstage area, Dicky wandered along an access corridor until he came to a door labelled *Melody Moon & Dicky Delaney*. Bristling that Melody's name came before his own, Dicky reached for the handle and stepped in.

To his surprise, the dressing room was generous. Newly carpeted and with a long counter against one wall, two comfortable swivel chairs sat before well-lit mirrors. A display of products was arranged on one side, and Dicky was delighted to see primers, concealers and bronzers of every shade and colour. His late-night shadows would soon fade with a dab or two of Melody's expensive cosmetics.

Dicky was about to reach out for Melody's professional stage makeup when he heard a toilet flush and a door in the corner of the room open. Turning to greet Melody, he was surprised to see a man in a silk dressing gown enter the room and walk past rails of glitzy outfits.

'Hello,' Dicky began, 'I'm Dicky Delaney.'

'Hello,' the man said and sat down.

Dicky noticed a faint trace of lipstick on his lips, and his eyes were lined with kohl.

'Er, I was hoping to meet Melody,' Dicky said, 'do you know where she is?'

'I'm Melody,' the man replied. 'But don't worry, my heels are higher than your expectations,' he added.

'*You're* Melody?' Dicky's jaw dropped.

'It's all. right, I don't often bite.' Melody shrugged.

Dicky quickly composed himself. He suddenly felt embarrassed. It wasn't as though he'd never met a drag artist before; the Spanish Costas were full of bars and clubs where he'd worked alongside numerous Zaras, Serenas, and Lolas. In fact, they'd been some of his most enjoyable gigs. But Dicky was taken aback that an old-fashioned company like the Diamond Star Line was moving forward with the times. He was delighted that they'd embraced inclusivity by introducing a drag act into its traditional stage show.

'I'm pleased to meet you, Melody,' Dicky said and held out his hand.

'I wouldn't be too pleased,' Melody said. Ignoring Dicky's hand, she took a cotton wool ball and slathered it with cream. 'I'm the headline act around here, so don't forget it.' Melody wiped at her skin and leaned into the mirror.

Dicky bristled. If that's how Melody wanted things to play out, she'd met her match!

'Well, that remains to be seen.' Dicky glanced at his watch. 'The show starts at nine, which means you've only five hours to bring your character to life.' He opened the door and as he stepped out, he retorted, 'It looks like you'll need every minute, good luck!'

Chapter Six

Fran was excited as she took Sid's hand, and they went from their cabin to the Terrace Restaurant. Throughout the day, Peter, the entertainment director, made announcements informing passengers about the Greek evening, encouraging them to dress in the theme, adding that the onboard fancy dress shop had plenty of available options.

As Fran and Sid waited for the lift to take them to the event, a couple wearing matching white togas joined them.

'I like your outfits,' Fran said as she noted the silky white gowns, worn off the shoulder and fastened with matching belts adorned with a small pineapple brooch.

'Good evening,' the man said. 'I'm Colin Scott, and this is my wife, Neeta.'

'I'm Fran and this is my hubby, Sid,' Fran said, 'did you join the ship today?'

Fran gazed at Neeta's cleavage and thought that it dwarfed the Grand Canyon. Studying the woman's wrinkle-free face and plumped-up lips, she wondered if Neeta's best friend was a cosmetic surgeon.

'Yes, we arrived on the Gatwick flight.' Neeta's glossy lips bounced like two balloons and as they stepped into the lift, she swirled the hem of her toga, showing a long expanse of tanned thigh. 'We're very excited about the cruise,' she added, flicking her blonde hair to one side. 'My husband is a retired airline pilot, and cruising is such a welcome change from flying now.'

'We're frequent cruisers,' Colin added proudly. 'Flying was great, but there's something about a ship that feels . . . well, grounded.' He smiled, clearly pleased with his wit. When he spoke, his teeth gleamed against the glow of his tan.

Sid, dressed in one of Fran's tunics over his shorts and belted at the waist, wore his faithful old leather sandals. Circling his head, he had a crown of plastic laurel leaves which Fran had found in the pound shop at the shopping centre in Blackpool. Fran, meanwhile, had fashioned a toga out of a sarong. She'd wound a length of braid that she used to identify their suitcases into an armlet and interspersed it with silver bracelets. As they waited for the lift to ascend, Fran glanced at Sid's feet. She wasn't sure the ancient Greeks wore white sports socks with their sandals but decided to let it pass.

'Here we are,' Fran said.

As the doors opened, her eyes sparkled with excitement as they stepped into the restaurant's reception area. The lively strains of bouzouki music, played by the band from the quayside, filled the air. Soft white lighting shifted to a serene blue, while servers in striped shirts and cotton trousers welcomed guests. As members of The Cruise Club, they were offered a selection of complimentary Greek wine, ouzo and cocktails.

'Don't mind if I do,' Fran said as she took a Santorini Sunset.

Colin and Neeta sipped on Athenian Mules, a drink combining ouzo, ginger and lime juice.

Fran's eyes popped at the potency of her own drink. 'This has got a kick,' she said, as fiery vodka, peach schnapps and grenadine hit the back of her throat.

They were shown into the restaurant, and when asked if they would like to join a larger table, the two couples happily agreed. Fran settled beside a woman who introduced herself as Carmen, with her mother, Betty, alongside.

'I saw you arriving today,' Fran said, 'have you settled in?'

'Yes, thank you, our rooms are lovely,' Carmen nervously replied.

Fran made more introductions to a couple from Yorkshire who told everyone their names were Don and Debbie. Don owned a successful construction company, specialising in building new homes. Debbie's makeup, in dark shades, covered most of her face, and in her hair she'd pinned numerous plastic snakes. Fran thought that Debbie's rather scary look was an interpretation of Medusa, while Don, wearing a cape and carrying a helmet and plastic sword, told everyone that he was a gladiator. Fran noted Don's cricket pads, improvised as gladiator shin guards above his Sketcher's walking sandals.

'And this is Colin and Neeta,' Fran said, 'we met them in the lift. Haven't they got gorgeous outfits,' she added.

'Toga-ther forever,' Don quipped as they studied Colin and Neeta's flowing white gowns.

'My daughter and I don't go in for all this dressing-up nonsense,' Betty announced.

Fran watched Carmen wince and grip her mother's arm in a gesture to prevent further comment. But Betty was in no mood to be silenced.

Staring at Debbie, Betty said, 'I didn't realise we've paid good money to watch folk make fools of themselves.'

Wearing a formal dress with a row of pearls at her throat, Betty picked up a napkin and shook it over her knees.

'I think you all look lovely,' Fran soothed and smiled at Carmen. 'That's a beautiful dress you're wearing.'

'Oh . . . thank you.' Carmen ran her fingers over the fabric of her plain navy dress. 'But it's quite frumpy in fairness. I only booked the cruise last week and didn't have time to shop for more appropriate clothes.'

'Nonsense, the colour is lovely with your gorgeous hazel eyes.'

Fran wondered what Carmen would look like if she removed her thick heavy glasses. She also wanted to ask if her mother was always so rude, but she could see that Sid had encouraged Betty to sample a Santorini Sunset. Fran hoped that a good slug of alcohol might soften the elderly lady into a warmer mood.

'Cheers, everyone!' Fran called out and held up her glass. 'Here's to a wonderful evening.'

Food was served, and the Greek-themed menu was a hit with the guests. Don was ecstatic over the moussaka and despite discovering that one of Debbie's snakes had come loose and fallen into his dinner, he told Debbie she must make the recipe when they got home. Colin and Neeta meanwhile, raved over plates of souvlaki, spanakopita, and tzatziki.

Betty picked at a Greek salad but brightened when she tasted a sweet baklava dessert. She ordered more then turned to Sid: 'And I want another of those orangey Santorini drinks.'

The head chef, Jaden Bird, appeared. Wearing neatly pressed whites, a colourful bandana and a starched apron tied at the waist, guests applauded his creative ice sculpture display of the Parthenon. Sid placed his fingers to his lips and whistled his praise.

'The chef is from Trinidad,' Sid explained to Fran, 'they say he's travelled the world.'

'Very nice.' Fran nodded as the chef stood beside his creation.

'Why did the ice sculpture refuse to come to the party?' Don asked everyone. 'Because it didn't want to melt under social pressure!'

As Don began to belly laugh, Debbie jabbed her elbow into his side.

At the end of the meal, Fran turned to Carmen. 'We're heading to the show in the Neptune Theatre,' she said. 'Would you like me to keep a seat for you and your mum?'

Carmen looked at Betty, and Fran noted a look of relief when they realised that Betty had fallen asleep. With arms folded, Betty's head rolled as she released a loud snore.

'As good as a knock-out drop,' Fran nodded to Betty's empty glass.

'If I'm quick, I'll soon get Mum in bed,' Carmen said, 'and I can meet you in the Neptune Theatre for the show.'

'In the bag with a bow on top.' Fran stood. 'Sid will give you a hand to get your mum to her room.'

Sid pushed back his chair and saluted. 'At your service,' he said.

He insisted on helping Carmen negotiate the route, and once inside Betty's room, Carmen removed Betty's shoes, and they carefully lifted the slumbering, slightly inebriated Betty onto her bed.

'It would be a shame to wake her; she's had a long day.' Sid said as he left Carmen to tuck a blanket around Betty and settle her for the night. 'I'll get off and see you in the Neptune Theatre.'

Carmen tidied Betty's room and a short while later, sighed with relief as she crept out. Closing the door she moved with an almost happy abandon. *That Santorini Sunset was a lifesaver!*

With any luck, Betty would be out for the count until breakfast time.

* * *

Fran had secured front-row seats in the Neptune Theatre. She was aware that the entertainment was about to begin and hoped that Carmen would be in time for the start of the show. Sid, sitting alongside, was chatting with Don.

Swivelling her head, Fran was delighted to see Carmen by the top of the stairs. 'Cooee!' Fran called out, and standing, she waved her hands. 'We're over here!'

Carmen dipped her head, conscious of onlooking guests. 'Thanks,' she whispered and sat down.

'This is exciting, isn't it?' Fran gave Carmen a nudge and, digging deep into her enormous bag, produced a bag of sweets. 'Grab a handful of these,' she said, thrusting a mound of jelly babies into Carmen's hand. 'They're my favourites.'

Carmen wondered how on earth Fran could continue to eat after the enormous dinner she'd put away. Tucking into each course, Fran had sampled all the dishes on offer, finishing off with two helpings of dessert. The jelly babies felt warm and with nowhere to subtly dispose of them, Carmen slowly began to chew.

The velvet-lined rows were packed and there was a buzz of anticipation as everyone waited for the start of the show. Background music began while latecomers searched for empty spaces, and people craned their necks as the house lights dimmed.

Fran gave Carmen a nudge. 'Are you looking forward to it?' she asked.

Carmen, her cheeks puffed out like a chipmunk, attempted to reply but only an unintelligible sound came out.

Taking to the stage, Peter stepped into a spotlight and the audience fell silent. 'Good evening,' Peter said, 'have you all enjoyed our Greek evening, so far?'

There was a murmur of approval.

'I want you to sit back and enjoy the *Mamma Mia!* themed show that our entertainers have lined up for you tonight,' Peter smiled. 'Please, put your hands together and let's give them a big *Diamond Star* welcome!' With an outstretched arm, which he swept dramatically, a band began to play.

The Neptune Theatre burst into a kaleidoscope of colour as dancers twirled onto the stage. In a dazzling array of costumes in fiery reds, vibrant blues and sunny yellows, they whirled into lively choreography as they moved to the pulsating rhythm. Wearing bell-bottomed jumpsuits with plunging necklines, the sleeves of the female costumes fluttered as they grooved in silver go-go boots. Metallic belts caught the lights as male dancers in flared pants and matching vests stomped their platformed boots.

Fran dug into her bag and produced a neon headband and a pair of funky sunglasses. Waving her hands, she bounced in her seat to the beat. The energy was infectious, and soon the audience was clapping along, engrossed in the performance, which moved skilfully through a medley of tunes.

'Eh, wasn't that lovely,' Fran said as the act finished.

The dancers gathered around Peter, who'd returned to the stage. 'Everyone, please,' he said, 'let's put our hands together for the one and only Melody Moon!'

Drums rolled, and a figure came into view at the centre of the stage. Fran gasped as she watched Melody Moon.

Wearing a jaw-dropping sequined gown that glittered when she moved and accentuated her traffic-stopping curves, Melody greeted her audience. The shimmering gold hugged her hips, while the plunging neckline and exaggerated shoulders added drama. At over six feet tall, a jewelled turban and heels of gravity-defying depth added height, and Melody's wig cascaded platinum-blonde curls to her shoulders.

'I wish I could do my face like that,' Fran murmured to

Carmen through a mouthful of sweets, nodding at Melody's bold paint and powders.

Carmen stared at Fran's makeup. Favouring bright shimmering blue eyeshadow, eyeliner and glossy peach lips, she'd done a cracking job of matching the artist on the stage. Carmen straightened her glasses and touched her own pale face, aware that her hint of tinted moisturiser was vastly overshadowed by Fran and Melody.

As Melody began to sing, disco lights captured the spirit of ABBA's heyday, and soon, the audience was swept up in the nostalgia and fun. She launched into 'Dancing Queen' and nailed every note, enhancing her performance by moving in step with the dancers. Between songs, Melody engaged with the crowd and her banter blended into a heartfelt tribute to the glory of ABBA. She moved effortlessly from 'Mamma Mia' to 'Take a Chance on Me', and each number had its own choreography, which Melody improved with flourish. Closing her act with a show-stopping rendition of 'Waterloo', Melody brought the audience to their feet.

'Let's hear it for Melody Moon!' Peter called out as Melody left the stage to rapturous applause. 'But don't worry folks, Melody will be back on stage throughout your cruise to entertain you.'

Still clapping her hands, Fran fell back in her seat. 'That was brilliant!' she muttered to anyone within earshot.

Carmen took a moment to look around the room at the grinning faces. Momentarily freed from Betty's clutches, Carmen realised that she was happy and turned to Fran, who returned her smile.

'Would you like a drink?' Fran asked, 'Sid's getting a round in.'

A server took their order, and as Peter announced the next act, Carmen sipped a creamy liqueur while Fran nestled beside her, cradling an Athenian Mule.

'Don says he met the comedian earlier,' Fran commented as the stage curtains opened. 'He and Debbie had a chat with him.'

'Did Don say that the comedian was funny?'

Fran slurped through a straw. 'I'm sure he'll be hilarious,' she replied. 'Hopefully, Don's observations will improve once Dicky Delaney's act gets started.'

'Why, what did Don say?' Carmen was intrigued.

Fran patted Carmen's arm reassuringly. 'Don is from Yorkshire,' she explained.

Carmen was puzzled.

'Don described Dicky as a joke book with the pages missing, a bit like watching paint dry.' Fran stared ahead. 'But I'm sure he'll be good . . .'

Chapter Seven

Dicky stood at the side of the stage as Melody took her curtain call and lapped up the thunderous applause. As he waited, aware that the stage manager stood alongside, Dicky's smile was strained, and he clapped too enthusiastically, masking the sinking feeling in the pit of his stomach.

Damn! Melody was good.

As Melody approached, Dicky took a deep breath, attempting to play it cool. He wondered how the hell he was going to follow her and hoped that the crowd hadn't peaked too early and some of the old-timers didn't drift off to bed.

When Melody saw Dicky, she stopped and gave him the once-over. 'Are you about to tell your jokes at a funeral?' she asked, taking in his black suit, crisp white shirt and patent leather shoes. 'From what I hear, when the audience gets wind of your act, they will be wishing they were dead.'

Dicky fumed. He had no idea what Melody had against him or why she was hostile, but there was no time to exchange insults. Peter was announcing his act.

'Please welcome to the stage,' Peter addressed the

audience, 'and give a big *Diamond Star* welcome to the one and only . . . DICKY DELANEY!'

'You did your best,' Dicky smiled at Melody, 'but now it's time for the real show to start. Thanks for warming up the audience and setting the bar low, now I'll go and raise it.'

Before Melody could snap out a retort, Dicky swept past and took the mic from Peter. Standing in the spotlight, he held up his hand and indicated to the band that they begin to play.

As the introductory bars of 'Staying Alive' by the Bee Gees began, Dicky launched into a lively, tongue-in-cheek rendition of the song. As he belted out the familiar chorus, the energy in the room returned, and by the time he finished, the audience was clapping along.

'You know you're getting on a bit when that song becomes less of a pop tune but more of a daily goal,' Dicky said, making eye contact and nodding to guests on the front row. 'On a cruise, staying alive means getting to the bar before the gin runs out!'

Laughter in the room was light, but Dicky continued.

'Welcome aboard to those of you who've just joined the ship. I hope you love cruising as much as I do, where you can eat and drink for twenty-four hours a day, and nobody judges you. At the seafood buffet, someone asked me what the catch of the day was?' Dicky looked puzzled. 'I replied – heart disease if you keep eating like this!'

'Is that the best you've got?' a man in the audience called out. 'Where's the real comedian?'

Dicky held his hand to his brow, shading the light as he searched for heckler. 'I'd like to thank this gentleman tonight for making me look good. It's a tough job, but someone had to do it!'

The audience laughed, but the heckler continued. 'I'm more entertained by the ship's emergency drill than you,' he said.

'I recognise that voice,' Dicky's eyes alighted on Don, who sat with folded arms in the third row. 'It's Don and Debbie from Yorkshire, everyone!' Dicky said as a spotlight highlighted the couple. 'Tell me, Don, what's a Yorkshire man's secret to a long life?'

Don, who'd been nudged into silence by Debbie's sharp elbow, merely shrugged.

'Come on, Don, you can do better than that,' Dicky encouraged, drawing more laughter from the audience. 'It's a strict policy of never spending more money than necessary,' Dicky quipped, then quickly continued, 'Why did the Yorkshire man bring a ladder to the pub?' He spread his arms to invite a reply. 'Because the drinks were on the house!'

Don sank low in his seat.

'And speaking of houses, did you hear about the two antennas that got married?' Dicky quipped, 'The ceremony wasn't much, but the reception was excellent!'

When the laughter died down, Dicky stood before Don and Debbie.

'But seriously, folks, this lovely couple are on the cruise for a very special occasion. It's their wedding anniversary, and I'd like you all to join me in acknowledging their special day.' Dicky turned to the band, who started to play, 'Congratulations'.

'Congratulations,' Dicky said and leaned forward to

shake Don's hand and, moving several snakes to one side, kissed Debbie on her cheek.

Confident that Don was unlikely to upstage his act again, Dicky continued.

Three songs and many jokes later, he had the audience in the palm of his hand. Many wiped away happy tears while others clutched their stomachs and shook their heads, almost exhausted from laughing.

'I'm going to close the show tonight with the result of our Greek-themed fancy dress competition,' Dicky said. 'Your entertainment director has been observing you all and has chosen a winner.'

Peter came forward and waved an envelope.

'Let me tell you that it has been a tough decision,' Dicky said, 'and those who participated are to be applauded.' He pursed his lips and frowned. 'However, one or two have confused the theme of the evening, and to the gentleman wearing a sack . . .' Dicky scanned the audience. 'Where are you, sir? Ah, over there, on the sofa in the corner,' Dicky spoke to an imaginary figure, 'you've got the wrong night, but thanks for being a couch potato.'

Peter, beside Dicky, clapped at the joke then handed over the envelope.

'For the lady standing in the corner looking lonely, don't worry,' Dicky smiled, 'we all know that you've dressed as a wi-fi signal, and I'm sure someone will connect with you soon.'

Dicky slowly undid the seal on the envelope and pulled out a card and a drum roll began. 'And the winners are . . . A toga-tastic twosome – Colin and Neeta!'

A round of applause rippled throughout the theatre as Colin and Neeta, hand in hand, hurried to the stage and Dicky exchanged words about their creative costumes.

'Congratulations!' Dicky beamed. 'You've won a soothing and relaxing couple's massage in our onboard spa.'

Colin and Neeta stood close together, their chemistry evident as Colin, with one arm around his wife, preened and tucked a thumb in his waistband, while Neeta, thrusting out her chest, flashed a length of thigh.

'I see you've both got a pineapple motif on your belts?' Dicky raised an eyebrow and, turning to the audience, winked. 'And if I'm not mistaken, you're wearing the pineapple upside down?'

Colin began to answer. 'It's part of our lifestyle,' he said, but before he could continue, Peter, whose complexion had paled, rushed forward and grabbed the mic from Dicky's hand.

'Let's congratulate them again,' Peter said, 'Colin and Neeta!' He hastily hurried the couple away.

'So that's it for tonight, folks,' Dicky said, 'why don't you all join in with me as I close the show.' He moved about the stage and began to sing the words of 'Sweet Caroline', and in no time, everyone was singing along. 'Goodnight, everyone!' he called out.

With a final bow, to a standing ovation, Dicky left the stage.

Chapter Eight

Dawn broke to a beautiful day in Argostoli, and Carmen was up early, having checked on Betty, who was mercifully still asleep. Dressed in shorts and a T-shirt, Carmen slipped her feet into comfy trainers and crept out of her room to take a stroll around the ship before everyone was awake for breakfast.

Early morning exercise enthusiasts jogged past Carmen, and she stared as they went by. It had been years since Carmen had jogged, and as she strolled on the exercise deck, she remembered running cross-country at school, where treks over the Cumbrian fells were as torturous as the rest of her lessons.

Whenever she felt the need to improve her health, Carmen attended aerobics sessions in the Butterly Community Centre, and she'd even tried yoga. Walks with Slipper, her dad's labrador, had been enjoyable but Slipper ascended to doggy heaven soon after her father died, and Betty had insisted they didn't have another dog in the house. Other exercise was in the form of swimming, and Carmen escaped to the local pool whenever she could.

That morning, as the sky lightened into soft shades of pink and gold, Carmen felt a sudden surge of determination and, removing her glasses, she broke into a slow and gentle jog.

A passing jogger scowled, while another raised an eyebrow and stared curiously. It wasn't until she reached halfway around the deck that Carmen paused and, replacing her glasses, noticed arrows pointing to the direction she'd come from, accompanied by the wording: *Joggers, please run anticlockwise around the deck.*

She'd been jogging in the wrong direction! There was a cruise ship etiquette that she'd been unaware of. Carmen felt foolish. Like the wi-fi signal the comedian had joked about – alone with no one to connect to. With her hands on her hips, feeling hot and sticky, she lowered her head to catch her breath.

Suddenly, a man came rushing by and, unaware of Carmen's presence, collided with her, knocking her off balance and sending her spinning to the floor.

'What on earth . . .' He towered over Carmen and removed earbuds from his ears.

Carmen was winded and didn't look up as she angrily replied, 'But what were *you* doing, careering along, not paying attention to where you were going?'

'I was listening to my audiobook,' the man said. 'I'm terribly sorry. Are you all right?' he asked and held out a hand.

Carmen felt firm steadying fingers circle her own as she wobbled to her feet. But her heart almost stopped when she looked up at the stranger. Panic surged as Carmen stood face-to-face with Ruskin Reeve. Her cheeks flushed as she struggled to find her voice in the shock of the encounter with her hero.

'It was m . . . my fault,' Carmen muttered as she pulled her clammy hands away. 'I wasn't looking where I was going.'

'No, it was *my* fault entirely. I realise I was accidentally running in the wrong direction, and will no doubt get a telling-off if I keep going.'

'Oh . . .' Carmen was tongue-tied, momentarily stumped that her hero had made the same mistake as her.

'Are you sure you're all right?' Ruskin asked.

'I'm fine, really.'

'Well, if you're sure?'

'Yes, quite sure, thank you.'

'I hope you enjoy the rest of your run.'

Ruskin's smile was like a burst of sunlight, and Carmen felt her heart flutter. It wasn't just the curve of his lips but the way his blue piercing eyes softly crinkled at the corners. She watched him replace his earbuds, and with a courteous nod, move swiftly away.

'Good grief,' Carmen muttered. Pinching herself to make sure that she wasn't dreaming, she set off again and soon got into her stride.

It was a most unexpected start to her day.

* * *

The Deck Café was busy as passengers gathered for breakfast, many eyes bleary thanks to a late night. Outside, under the shade of vast canopies, gentle conversation mingled with the distant call of seagulls swooping gracefully around the ship, their white and grey wings catching the morning light as they glided above.

'These birds are a bit different to the gulls we get at home,' Fran commented to Sid as she buttered a croissant and popped a chunk into her mouth. Dressed in a flowing kaftan in vivid shades of orange and yellow, she wore a wide-brimmed hat with a flower pinned to one side.

'Aye, the Blackpool birds would have whipped your breakfast right out of your hand,' Sid laughed as he tucked into bacon and eggs. 'Today's excursion looks like it's going to be good,' he added as he studied a copy of the *Diamond Star Daily News* and read out loud to Fran.

The Diamond Star Daily News
Today's Excursion: The ancient village of Maxos north of Argostoli, on a peninsula surrounded by the Ionian Sea, the charming village of Maxos, described as the jewel in the Ionian Crown, nestles at the end of a long and twisting road. Visitors are invited to relax on the beach, find Venetian buildings and dine in quaint tavernas. Your daytime excursion will leave you with many lasting memories.
Limited places available.

'It's a good job we booked early,' Fran said as she licked butter from her lips and dabbed her mouth with a napkin. 'Peter said the trip was full. Oh look, here's Carmen and her mum.' Fran held up her hand to wave and together with Sid, helped Carmen negotiate Betty's wheelchair to a place at the table.

'Did you sleep well?' Fran asked as Carmen sat down, 'You had a very long day yesterday.'

'Blissfully, thank you, my room is lovely,' Carmen replied.

'I was up all night and didn't get a wink,' Betty grumbled. She demanded attention from a passing server. Insisting that she couldn't go to the buffet table as her arthritis was playing up, Betty ordered lightly poached eggs, tea and two slices of toast.

Fran and Carmen exchanged glances.

'I'm going to grab another croissant.' Fran pushed back her chair. 'Carmen, why don't you come with me.'

As they moved through the room, Fran, a vibrant splash of colour, traded pleasantries with other passengers. At the same time, Carmen, feeling dull in khaki shorts and shirt, hovered behind.

'Fill your boots,' Fran said as Carmen stared at the sumptuous buffet table. With a blend of Mediterranean and traditional breakfast staples, fresh fruit and newly baked bread sat alongside pastries and Greek delicacies. 'Why not try a slice of spanakopita,' Fran suggested, sliding a slice of spinach and feta pie onto Carmen's plate. 'It's delicious,' she added, helping herself.

'Goodness, there's so much choice,' Carmen said. Her plate was full of mouth-watering concoctions as she stood beside Fran, who was ordering coffee. 'I'll need new clothes if my waistline expands during the cruise.'

Reaching for sugar, Fran studied Carmen and thought a few new outfits might brighten her appearance. So far, she'd only seen Carmen wearing the drabbest of colours in clothes that had seen better days.

'We can soon sort that out,' Fran said, gently patting Carmen's arm. 'There's a boutique on the ship, and I must confess that I treated myself as soon as we came onboard.' Fran smoothed her kaftan over her generous hips. 'You'd look lovely in something like this, and there will be shops and boutiques on the islands, I'm sure we can find something similar for you.'

Carmen stared at Fran. She was like a tropical sunset on legs and Carmen knew she'd never have the confidence to wear such an outfit.

'Don't look so worried, I know I'm a peacock, and you don't have to dress like me.' Fran added two sugars and stirred her coffee. 'Tell me something,' Fran lowered her voice, 'is your mum a bit difficult?'

Carmen sighed. 'Where do I begin?' she asked. 'Mum is very bossy. She used to rule the roost when Dad was alive and likes to dominate me.'

'I'm sorry.' Fran frowned. 'When did Dad die?'

'He passed away a few years ago. We had a hardware shop.' Carmen was thoughtful. 'I used to work alongside him, and a lady called Marion helped too, she was a bookkeeper, and I liked her. Marion was very kind to me.' She gave a shrug. 'I miss Dad terribly. He was the only person who gave me any confidence. Mum just knocks it out of me.'

'I imagine your mum misses him, too.' Fran gave an understanding nod.

'You'd hardly think so, she turns everything into a national emergency and has me running around after her.' Carmen paused. 'That's the only way I can keep in shape.' She smiled and thought of her feeble attempt at a jog earlier.

'You have a lovely figure and you're an attractive woman.' Fran resisted the urge to give Carmen a cuddle. She was like a tightly wound spring. Nervous and sad.

Carmen took a step back. No one had ever commented on her figure or described her as attractive, even on the rare occasion that she'd had a boyfriend.

'What's wrong?' Fran asked. 'You can confide in me, I'm good at keeping a secret.'

Carmen sighed. 'I thought that this cruise would be a lovely holiday all by myself, but Mum gate-crashed my booking.'

'Then why don't we find you a bit of "me-time".' Fran's tone was bright. 'The cruise offers lots of activities, and I noticed a group called the Golden Oldies Gang. We could see if we can involve Betty?'

'That would be as difficult as teaching a cat to swim.' Carmen shook her head. 'Mum never mixes these days and insists on tagging along with anything I do.'

Fran noticed that Carmen's shoulders had begun to relax and had an inkling that she was winning her over. 'Don't worry,' Fran reassured with a conspiratorial wink, 'we can sort it out. Are you going on the excursion to Maxos today?'

'Yes, I'm looking forward to it, though Mum is coming too.'

'We can chat more then, perhaps over a nice cool drink and a bite to eat.'

Carmen looked at Fran and for a moment, sensed that she had an ally. Fran's eyes were soft, and her expression warm. Beyond her garish makeup and flamboyant clothes, Fran appeared to genuinely care. Perhaps Carmen's holiday wouldn't be ruined after all.

'Thank you,' Carmen said, 'you're very kind.'

'Aw, don't go thanking me,' Fran chuckled, 'but we should get back. I have a feeling that Betty is chewing Sid's ear off.'

Carmen gripped her plate and hurried to keep up with Fran. 'Oh dear,' she muttered as she saw Betty lift her cane and prod Sid's foot, 'I think you might be right.'

Chapter Nine

Ready for their first excursion, Carmen and Betty made their way along the quay, where Peter assisted them into a minibus, one of three waiting vehicles.

'Be careful with my wheelchair!' Betty told their driver as she hoisted herself onto the steps and flopped on a seat at the front.

Carmen followed and reluctantly sat beside her. Next came Fran and Sid, followed by Don, Debbie and four more passengers.

After ensuring that everyone was comfortable, Peter joined them. 'Good morning,' he said as the minibus chugged into life, 'what a beautiful day you have for your visit to the magical village of Maxos.'

'It would be a better day if the air-conditioning worked,' Betty grumbled. She sat with her bag on her lap, arms folded, face grim.

'The air will cool as soon as we commence the journey.' Peter smiled sympathetically. 'Today, we're travelling north through the island of Kefalonia. Make sure you take in as much of the island's beauty as possible.'

'Everywhere is so dry,' Betty interrupted. 'Just look, it's all so parched, the ground is as cracked as my poor heels.'

Unperturbed, Peter continued, 'Please, sit back and enjoy the drive, which will take us through some of the island's most striking landscapes. Look out for olive groves and vineyards.'

'Oh, this heat, it's unbearable,' Betty continued to complain, 'I don't know how anyone gets used to it.' She took a fan out of her bag and waved it.

Peter reached into a cooler and began to distribute bottles of chilled water. Handing one to Carmen, he patted her shoulder when she mouthed an apology. When he reached Fran and Sid, Peter was greeted with beaming smiles.

'Lovely jubbly,' Fran said, 'and it's icy cold.' She thrust the bottle deep into her cleavage. 'Oh, that's cooled me down a treat.'

'If this is ouzo,' Sid said, 'I'll be dancing a Zorba in the aisle.' He grinned and took a swig.

'You can entertain us later, Sid,' Peter laughed, 'plenty of time for ouzo.'

As the road gradually climbed the hills, Peter pointed out a sweeping view of Argostoli surrounded by sparkling sea. Passengers noted the dry, rocky terrain, and a fragrant hint of wild thyme and pine which drifted through the now cool air of the minibus. Surrounded by hills on either side of the road, the view revealed deep blue bays and rocky cliffs plunging into the sea below.

'Look at these hills,' Betty moaned, 'steep as anything,

and they go on and on. You'd need to be a mountain goat to live around here.'

'Mum, will you *please* keep it down? You're spoiling everyone's journey.' Carmen nudged Betty.

'Excuse *me*,' Betty bristled with a pout, then turned away.

As their journey continued, whitewashed houses scattered along the coastline appeared. The road snaked higher, and a gaggle of goats wandered onto the hot tarmac, causing the driver to stop and hoot his horn.

Peter began to explain. 'As you see, the Kefalonian goat is quite unusual. With a black and brown coat which blends into the landscape, they are very independent and often wander the hills alone.' Peter paused as everyone stared at the creatures. 'The goats have a knack for popping up in the most unexpected places, on cliff edges, in the shade of an olive grove, or here in the middle of the road, and goat herders ensure that each goat has a bell around its neck to ward off predators and so they can be found.'

From the back of the minibus, Don called out, 'What do you call a goat that acts immature?' After a pause, he replied, 'A kid!'

The passengers laughed, and Peter told Don that if he wasn't careful, he'd make him a double act with Dicky Delaney.

'Double act with Dicky?' Don looked surprised. 'I'd sooner share a flat cap with a sheepdog, and the last time I was paired with anyone, it was with Debbie on a tandem, and we didn't speak for three days.'

More laughter rang out, but Debbie, grimacing, glared at Don.

Carmen studied the goats and envied their independence. She longed to wander the hills, as far away from Betty as she could. Gazing at the aquamarine sea, she thought it looked enticing and was entranced by the stunning views. The goats skipped off and ambled over the hillside, and as the minibus pulled away, Carmen felt Betty's head on her shoulder. Her eyes had closed, and to her relief, Carmen saw that her mother had fallen asleep.

Carmen watched the landscape pass by and thought of her lead character. She wondered if the Rainbow Sleuth might uncover a mystery in these mountains. Was there a murderer on the loose, and might Carmen create a story with a Greek setting in one of her future novels? Reaching for her notebook and careful not to wake Betty, she noted everything she saw. Who knew? One day, the notes might be helpful.

* * *

The drive to Maxos was almost complete, but before the driver negotiated the steep hill that led down to the village, he pulled over on the side of the road and Peter invited passengers to step out to see the view. The heat was intense, and a hot breeze blew as everyone stared at a cove below, glimmering like a jewel in the sunlight.

Peter explained that the beach they could see was called Myrtos. It was one of Kefalonia's most iconic places, having served as the location for the film *Captain Corelli's Mandolin.*

'Oh, we saw that film, didn't we, Sid?' Fran said excitedly.

She stood beside Sid, gripping his hand as the sun-soaked landscape before them dropped dramatically. With her other hand, Fran held her hat firmly as the breeze rustled her kaftan, the red floaty fabric flickering like flames in the heat.

They all gazed at the crescent of pure white sand and the vivid shades of turquoise and sapphire that shimmered in the sea.

'The waves can be quite lively,' Peter called out, 'I don't advise swimming at this beach, but for those of you who fancy a dip, the waters are calm in Maxos.'

'Eee, that sounds lovely,' Fran said, removing her giant sunglasses to mop her brow with a hankie. 'I'm roasted and glad I'm wearing my cossie under here.' She flipped up the skirt of her kaftan to reveal a baby pink tankini.

'Time to move on,' Peter called out.

Moments later, they began their descent to Maxos. The tight horseshoe bends required skilful driving, and passengers gasped as the vehicle neared the edge of the road where the drop was perilous. But soon, the reward was clear when a peninsular came in sight, and the small, picturesque village emerged, tucked into a bay with pastel-coloured houses spilling towards the sea. Framed by lush greenery of pine and cypress trees, a Venetian fortress loomed on the opposite side, high above a harbour.

'Oh, Sid, it's perfect,' Fran breathed as she stared at the bright blue shutters of the pretty buildings and terracotta pots overflowing with vibrant oleander.

The driver negotiated the narrow entry to a parking space, and as the engine died, Peter announced, 'Our transport will stay in this spot while you explore the village.

Despite past earthquakes in this part of the island, a few interesting remains of Venetian houses can be found. Please enjoy the beach, bars, and tavernas, and I shall be in the harbour area if anyone has any questions.'

'What's the fort like?' Don called out.

'It was built by the Venetian army in the fifteenth century and said to protect the villagers from pirate raids. As we aren't expecting any marauding pirates today, I recommend a visit, but it's a steep climb,' he warned, 'so if you intend to go, take plenty of water.'

The driver unfolded the wheelchair, and with Carmen's assistance, Betty was soon seated. Carmen gathered her bag and made sure that Betty had everything she needed. She placed a brimmed bonnet on Betty's head, and they set off.

'Why have we come here?' Betty grumbled. She reached for her fan and furiously waved it.

'Because it is a beautiful place,' Carmen replied, 'and I can't wait to look around.'

'Well, don't expect me to join you,' Betty was adamant. 'You can find a decent café in a shady spot, and I'll just have to sit on my own while you go off galivanting.'

Carmen breathed a sigh of relief. *Freedom!* The sooner she got Betty settled, the sooner she could escape and discover the mysteries of Maxos. She picked up her pace and navigated a winding path past an avenue of cottages and pastel-coloured houses. Wandering into the village square, Carmen gazed at pink and white blossoms bursting from woody stems of vines climbing along terracotta-tiled rooftops. She strolled by buildings hiding dark alleys that led to steep steps and noted properties further up the hillside.

'Isn't it lovely?' Carmen murmured as she looked around for a suitable taverna to park Betty.

A young man appeared. His glossy black hair gleamed in the sunshine, and as he grinned, Carmen saw his slightly crooked teeth.

'You need refreshment?' he asked.

'Well, er, yes, we are looking for somewhere shady and cool for Mum to relax for a little while,' Carmen said. 'Can you recommend a taverna?'

'Of course, come to Psara Taverna and meet my family. I am Spiros,' he added.

Before Carmen had time to consider the young man's offer, his olive-skinned arms reached out and strong hands grabbed the handles of Betty's chair.

'You will like,' he said as they set off and in moments, reached a bar shaded by colourful umbrellas on the side of the harbour. 'See, is good?' He grinned as he waited for Carmen's approval. 'My mána, she cooks.'

'It's perfect.'

Carmen picked up a napkin and as she removed her glasses to polish them, she looked around at the pretty harbourside setting, where tables were covered with gingham cloths and dotted with vases of wildflowers. Boats bobbed alongside in the calm water.

'I'm hungry,' Betty said as Spiros secured her chair by a table, shaded by a vast umbrella, where a cool breeze whispered across the bay.

Carmen reached for a menu and began to study the Greek specialities, hoping for something suitable for Betty.

'You try Mána's kolokythokeftedes and dolmades,' Spiros said.

Carmen read the translation and doubted that Betty would enjoy Spiros's mother's courgette balls and stuffed vine leaves. However, sensing her moment to escape, she nodded enthusiastically.

'Would it be all right if I left my mána here for a short while and looked around the village?' Carmen asked.

'But of course,' Spiros spread out his arms. 'Go, beautiful lady, enjoy, and when you come back, I have food waiting.'

Carmen patted Betty's arm and explained that she would be back soon. Not waiting for Betty to protest, she leaped like a gazelle, away from the taverna. 'Thank you!' she called out to Spiros.

The young man's smile was wide and touching two fingers to his lips, he blew her a kiss. 'Have fun!' he called out.

Flustered by Spiros's attention, Carmen's cheeks were hot as she left the taverna. Were all Greek men so friendly? But as she wandered around, Carmen embraced the hidden world. It was as though she'd stepped into a timeless, enchanted place, and the memory of Betty's continual protestations soon faded. No wonder Maxos was a highlight of the cruise's stopover in Kefalonia.

She came to a lane and noticed a small, three-storied, villa. With steps patterned in pretty mosaic tiles, terracotta pots stood either side of a blue front door. A sign announced, *Villa Galini*. Carmen noticed another sign in the window which read, *For Sale*. She considered the owner the luckiest person on earth to have such a gorgeous home, where shuttered windows on balconies overlooked a horseshoe-shaped beach. She couldn't imagine why anyone would want to sell it.

'How I'd love to live somewhere like this,' Carmen whispered as she stared at the villa, 'to write all day at that window, with a glorious view of the bay.'

Turning away, she was startled to see, draped over a rickety picnic table, the hunched figure of an old man in the shadow of overhanging fir trees. Moving closer, Carmen felt a stab of anxiety. *Is he breathing?*

Unsure of what to do, she reached out to shake his shoulder.

'Don't worry!' a voice called out. 'He's asleep.'

Carmen spun around and, to her surprise, realised that another man was sitting on a bench overlooking the beach. An open notebook lay on his lap, and he held a pen between his fingers. Wearing a Panama hat, linen trousers and shirt, he raised his Ray-Bans to stare.

It was Ruskin Reeve again.

Carmen felt her heart pound, and a flush spread across her perspiring face. Her breath caught in her throat as her eyes locked on Ruskin's authoritative figure. Beside her, the older man began to snore, and she noticed a dusty cap upturned on the table, beside several stacked jars.

'He sells honey, you should buy some,' Ruskin said. 'The old boy keeps bees, and they forage on herbs and thyme on the hillside.'

'I see.' Carmen felt starstruck. She'd unexpectedly come across her idol twice in one day, and now, in his presence, she hadn't a clue what to say. Unsure whether to speak or smile, she stood frozen, her eyes flicking from Ruskin to the older man.

'Are you all right?' Ruskin asked and leaned an arm along the length of the bench. 'You look awfully hot.' He tilted his sunglasses and stared. 'Don't I know you, have we met?'

'Y . . . yes,' Carmen stuttered, 'we bumped into each other on the jogging deck this morning.'

'Of course.' Ruskin patted the bench. 'Take a seat, this heat is terribly tiring.'

Obeying Ruskin's command, Carmen's feet felt like lead as she moved forward. She wished she'd worn something pretty and feminine, perhaps a cool kaftan like Fran's. Her khaki shorts and shirt hardly cut a dash in front of this handsome and educated man. Even her walking sandals were granny-like, and she knew that the floppy old hat she'd chosen to shade the sun had more of a boy-scout look than anything remotely fashionable, making her feel even more out of place on this picturesque beach.

'I mustn't disturb you,' Carmen said as she nervously sat on the edge of the bench.

'Don't worry, I was only jotting down a few thoughts.' Ruskin yawned.

Carmen knew that he was probably wishing that an attractive female had chosen to stop by. It was just his luck to be saddled with a dreary soul whose thickly framed glasses made her look like a 1950s librarian.

Staring beyond the beach where a fishing boat glided to the open sea, she heard Ruskin announce, 'I'm a writer.'

'Yes, I know.' Carmen wanted to tell him that he was the sole reason she'd come on the cruise but thought he'd believe her to be some sort of groupie and instead asked, 'What are you writing?'

'I'm not sure, but this place combines mystery and history, pirate legends and the ruins of an old fortress which gives it an inexplicable aura.'

'My thoughts exactly.' Carmen stared ahead, too, suddenly caught up in Ruskin's vivid imagination. 'It's easy to imagine how this atmospheric setting could inspire stories with all the legends that must be woven through the ages.'

'*You* should be a writer,' Ruskin added cynically and yawned again.

'But I am!' Carmen blurted out.

As soon as the words had left her lips, she wished that she could bite them back. What on earth would this world-famous man think of the mousey, drab woman dressed like a camp ranger about to go into the wilderness?

'Really?' Ruskin sighed.

He was losing interest, and Carmen could see that Ruskin was restless. He probably thought she'd self-published a cute little book of short stories that sold only to a handful of friends.

'Well, I mustn't keep you, and I'm going for a swim.' Ruskin closed his notebook and rose to his feet. 'Don't forget to buy some honey. It's terribly good for the mind.'

Placing the notebook alongside a jar nestling in his satchel, Ruskin wandered off without so much as a glance at Carmen or a wave goodbye.

'How discourteous,' Carmen mumbled as Ruskin's figure disappeared down the lane. She was annoyed that she'd been so quickly dismissed. 'But then,' she sighed, 'why on earth would a man like that want to stick around and talk to a woman like me?'

The old man had begun to stir, and Carmen saw him open one eye as he slowly raised his head from the table. Knobbly fingers reached for a jar, and he pointed to a sign that read, *Ten Euros*.

'Very well,' Carmen sighed and reached for her money. 'But, at that price, it had better be good.'

Chapter Ten

Fran and Sid enjoyed their walk around the village and now wandered along a path that bordered a horseshoe-shaped beach. Having stopped to buy souvenirs in a gift shop, Fran was pleased with her purchase of an embroidered tea towel, a glow-in-the-dark statue of Adonis, and a bar of olive soap. For Sid, she'd bought a T-shirt with the logo *Opa!* and insisted he wear it.

'You haven't needed your Greek phrasebook,' Sid said as he spotted a shady bench beneath a fir tree and guided Fran to the spot.

'You're right, and I think we're managing very nicely with my Greek greetings,' Fran agreed.

She placed the little book on the bench, then kicked off her sandals. Taking the bottle of water from her cleavage, she drank thirstily and offered it to Sid. Wriggling her toes, she looked up to see a couple approach. 'Kalimári!' Fran called out.

The couple, tall and tanned, wearing hiking boots and shorts, looked bemused. They stared curiously at the middle-aged woman, colourful in her vibrant kaftan. 'Kalimera,' they replied.

'Folk are very friendly,' Sid mused, 'those two look like serious walkers and must be heading up to the fort.'

'I expect they'll bump into Don and Debbie.'

'It's a very steep climb.' Sid stared up at the top of the hillside where the ruins of the Venetian fort peeked out.

Suddenly, an old man appeared from the shadows. An unlit cigarette hung from his lips, and a dusty cap dipped low over his weathered face. He held a jar of honey and a sign in his grubby hands.

Startled, Fran greeted him, 'Kalimári!' she said.

The old man looked bemused and thrust his hands out further.

'I think he wants us to buy his honey.' Sid reached into his pocket and peeled off a ten euro note.

'It's pricey, I hope it's good' Fran commented as she took the jar and smiled at the honey seller. 'Kalimári!' she called again and placed the purchase in her bag.

With a furrowed brow, the old man cocked his head and stared wide-eyed at Fran. Shaking his head, he turned and silently moved away.

'I'm hungry. Shall we find somewhere for a bite to eat?' Sid asked.

'Aye, that would be lovely.'

Taking Sid's steady arm, Fran slipped her feet into her sandals, picked up her phrasebook and they set off. Reaching a courtyard close to the harbour, Sid and Fran saw a man placing chairs around tables under a wooden gazebo. Tall and well-built, his stomach bulged from the waistband of his trousers, and as he prepared his taverna, he began to sing. His operatic voice carried across the courtyard to the gift shop, where a woman swept needle-shaped leaves, gathering them into piles.

'Ya, Jimmy!' the woman called out and nodded towards Sid and Fran. 'You'll frighten the tourists.'

But Jimmy continued to sing, his voice gaining momentum. 'Toreador! Love, love awaits you!'

Side-stepping cracks in the path, Fran and Sid stopped to listen, and when Jimmy ended his song, Fran clapped her hands. 'Kalimári!' she applauded. 'Your voice is wonderful, and I love that song from the opera *Carmen*.'

Jimmy began to laugh. 'But you just said, "squid",' he said. 'Next time, try "Kaliméra". Good morning is a more traditional greeting.'

'Oh, hell.' Fran felt her face flush, her fingers tightening on her phrasebook.

Jimmy grinned and placed beefy hands on his hips. 'Where are you going?' he asked.

'We're gasping for a drink and something to eat. Can you recommend anywhere?'

'My bar isn't open yet, but you could try the Psaro Taverna.' Jimmy pointed to tables beneath colourful umbrellas, a short distance away. 'Spiros will be happy to serve you,' he added.

'Aye, that sounds grand,' Fran thanked Jimmy.

'My pleasure,' Jimmy said and adjusted a chair. 'Squid!' he added with a wave of his hand and, with another belly laugh turned away.

Once they'd crossed the street to the Psaro Taverna, Spiros

greeted them warmly. 'Squid!' he called out to Fran with a grin and 'Opa!' to Sid when he saw Sid's T-shirt. Indicating that the couple joined others from the ship, Spiros guided them to a table overlooking the harbour.

Don, Debbie, Colin and Neeta sat alongside Carmen and Betty. Peter, who was pouring wine, stood at the head of the table.

'SQUID!' everyone chanted and began to laugh.

'Blimey, news travels fast.' Fran pulled at the collar on her kaftan and slid into a chair next to Don.

Don, his face flushed red and breathing laboured, looked like he'd just completed a marathon in ninety-degree heat, and drained a bottle of beer. 'We were at the top of the hill when a Dutch couple told us there was a strange lady by the beach calling everyone a squid,' he chuckled, 'Debbie and I knew that it had to be you.'

'That must have been the hiking couple,' Fran muttered. 'Whatever must they think of me?'

'How does a squid go into battle?' Don asked. 'Fully armed!' He guffawed.

'Did you get to the fort?' Fran asked, keen to change the subject.

'Oh yes, and it was worth the effort,' Don replied, wiping his brow with the back of his hand. 'You can see for miles up there, but the climb nearly killed me.' He held out his bottle for Spiros, who quickly refreshed the beer.

Peter handed Fran a glass of wine, and she noticed everyone had a jar of honey on the table. The old man had enjoyed a profitable day.

'I propose a toast to the honey seller,' Fran said.

'The best things in life are un-bee-lievably sweet,' Don added.

'What did you get up to?' Fran turned to Carmen.

'I went for a walk and found some ruins of Venetian buildings,' Carmen replied. 'A local man called Jimmy told me where to go and explained that an earthquake in 1953 caused a great deal of damage, but the ruins have been left as a reminder of the island's history.'

'How interesting,' Fran sipped her wine, 'and did this Jimmy sing to you?'

'Yes,' Carmen said, 'did you hear him too?'

'The whole village did, he has a wonderful voice,' Fran grinned.

Spiros appeared with an assistant, whom he introduced as his sister, and they loaded plates of delicious food onto the table. 'Eat, eat . . .' he instructed, and everyone began to tuck in.

To Fran's surprise, Betty was the first to reach out and dig deep into a bowl of moussaka, filling her plate and adding fluffy yellow potatoes bathed in olive oil.

'Your mum is hungry,' Fran commented as she helped herself to a stuffed vine leaf. 'Does she like Greek food?'

'Not to my knowledge, but she's been drinking ouzo for the last two hours and seems to have worked up an appetite.'

Fran looked at Betty, whose bonnet had slipped to one side. Several strands stuck out from her ordinarily neat hair and her cheeks were pink as she called out to Spiros to turn up the music. As ancient folk melodies sounded throughout the taverna, Betty closed her eyes and held up her arms to sway in a Zorba.

Fran turned her attention to Colin and Neeta.

'I like your headgear,' she said to Neeta, who wore a pink baseball cap with a pineapple motif. 'I wouldn't mind one of those for myself.'

Fran noticed that Colin's shirt had a pineapple print. 'Do you like pineapples?' she asked, remembering that the couple had a similar motif on their togas at the Greek night.

'Oh yes,' Neeta butted in. Wearing a tiny halter top, she leaned across the table and ran her pink-tipped nails softly along Sid's arm. 'Are you into pineapples, Sidney?'

Fran giggled as she watched Sid's eyes almost bulge out of his head. Neeta's pert breasts were threatening to spill into his souvlaki.

'Sid loves them, don't you dear?' Fran said.

'Really?' Neeta's eyes were wide, and she moved closer to Sid.

'Well, er . . . I like pineapple rings that come in a tin,' Sid spluttered and edged away from Neeta, 'and I'm quite partial to a pineapple chunk if Fran goes to the sweet shop.'

'Interesting . . .' Neeta smiled.

'Oh look,' Fran said, pointing to a figure coming out of the water. 'Isn't that man from our ship?'

Everyone turned to stare at the nearby figure on the beach.

'I think it's that writer fellow, Ruskin Reeve,' Sid said. 'What a good idea to have a cooling swim on such a hot day.'

'Have you heard of him?' Fran asked Carmen as she forked a cube of saganaki.

'Oh yes,' Carmen said, 'Ruskin Reeve is the reason I've come on this cruise.'

Fran noticed Carmen's eyes gleam. 'Really, dear, why's that?' She forked another cube of the crisp golden cheese.

'He writes novels and is a bestselling author. Have you heard of the TV series *Detective Inspector Blake Investigates?*'

'I certainly have. Sid and I love the series and save them for my night off.'

'Well, that's the author on the beach.'

'My goodness, I'm sure Sid will want his autograph, he loves reading detective novels.'

'Ruskin is going to host a talk and is running workshops.' Carmen grinned. 'I can't wait.'

'That's nice. Do you like detective novels?'

'Actually, I am an author, too.' Carmen lowered her head. She felt embarrassed to admit her career, fearing Fran would probe and want to learn more.

'Really?' Fran clapped her hands. 'But that's fantastic, what do you write?'

'I've only written one novel, and it's called *The Rainbow Sleuth*.'

Fran reached for her wine and called out, 'Oi, Sid! Have you heard of *The Rainbow Sleuth?*'

Sid turned, pleased to be diverted from Neeta, who'd edged her chair closer. 'Yes, it's a cosy crime mystery that came out a few months ago. I read it on my Kindle.'

'You'll be interested to know that our girl here,' Fran wrapped an arm around Carmen, 'is the author. Isn't she clever!'

'I'll say.' Sid grinned. 'I hope there's another book coming out soon. It's going to make a cracking series.' He raised his beer to Carmen. 'Well done, lass, now we can say that we've met someone famous.'

'I'm not famous,' Carmen insisted. Suddenly embarrassed, she removed her glasses. 'Ruskin Reeve is the celebrity you must meet.'

'So why are *you* so keen to meet him?' Fran asked as she lifted a dish of keftedes and spooned a meatball onto her plate.

'I'm hoping I'll gain some inspiration.' Carmen sighed. 'I've got writer's block and I can't seem to write a word, but my publisher has given me a deadline, and there's not a prayer that I'm going to make it.'

'Now, don't worry your pretty head about little things like deadlines,' Fran rattled on. 'A good holiday will soon sort all that out, with all the inspiration you're going to get during the cruise.'

'I hope you're right.' Carmen frowned.

'Of course I am, and Sid and I will help. You need a good plot for your rainbow sleuth and some interesting characters?'

'If only . . .'

But Fran patted Carmen's arm. 'Don't worry,' she said reassuringly and tore a slice of pita, dipping it into a bowl of tzatziki.

A writer, how interesting! Fran thought and turned her gaze to Betty, who'd heaved herself out of her chair and was now gripping Spiros's hands to shuffle across the cobbles.

Spiros, who'd been handing out complimentary shots of ouzo, supported Betty with care and guided her movements to the lively Greek music, causing Fran to smile as she watched the two strangers, generations apart, sharing a moment of connection.

'Your mum's a dark horse,' Fran whispered to Carmen, 'and not as infirm as she'd like us to believe. Will she be doing cartwheels next?'

'You never know . . .' Carmen set down her glass and sighed.

'A couple of drinks and a handsome Greek, and she's away.' Fran chuckled.

After another round of ouzo, Sid rose out of his chair. Sensing that Neeta, who was squiffy, was about to grab his hands and encourage him to dance too, he moved swiftly to Fran's side.

'May I have the pleasure?' Sid asked and held out his hands.

'The pleasure's all mine, sweetheart,' Fran said and rose to her feet.

After a few too many shots, everyone was glowing as the liquorice-sweet liquor took hold, and they surrendered to the infectious rhythm of the music. Spiros's mother came out of the kitchen with his sister, who beckoned Jimmy over, and they joined in too. Forming a wobbly line in the middle of the taverna, guests draped their arms over each other's shoulders and, with mixed steps and much laughter, attempted the sharp kicks of the dance. Don threw his leg too high and almost tipped over, while Fran fell against Colin as the music got faster. Sid, who couldn't escape from Neeta, looked away as her breasts, barely contained in her top, bounced in a rhythm of their own, the halter straps straining gallantly.

'SQUID!' they all called out as the music ended and they stumbled back to their seats.

'More oooozo!' Betty held up her glass. She'd abandoned her wheelchair and, staggering, held onto Carmen's shoulder.

Peter stared nervously at the party and clenched his hands. Everyone appeared to be red-faced and swaying and he was doubtful that he'd manage to manoeuvre his inebriated guests up the hill to the minibus.

'We're leaving for the return journey to the ship!' he suddenly announced.

Reaching for his clipboard, he was grateful that their driver had driven swiftly to the harbour following Peter's urgent call. Now, surveying the scene, he thought of the uncooperative goats they'd met on the road.

'I'm like a frazzled shepherd,' he muttered as he saw Debbie hug a lamp post as though it were a long-lost friend while Don, staggering slightly, attempted to ease her away.

Betty, meanwhile, was wobbling towards the bar.

'No! Betty, the bus is over here. No, over *here*!' Peter repeated, gesturing wildly.

He was relieved to see Sid and Fran take charge of the older woman and manipulate her into her chair with a fireman's lift.

As the giggling guests were finally ushered onboard the minibus, Peter closed the door, and the engine chugged to life. He wondered if his colleagues accompanying other cruise guests had as much trouble with their charges and with relief, settled deep into his seat and stared out of the window.

Spiros and his family stood with Jimmy, by their taverna,

and waved at the retreating guests. Raising his hand and forcing a smile, Peter considered if being a tour rep in Ibiza with a party of wild young millennials would be easier than caring for the vintage squad in the minibus. This lot made herding cats in the middle of a storm look easy.

As Peter waved goodbye to Spiros, he whispered, 'I should've taken that office job . . .'

Chapter Eleven

The following day, there was as an excited ripple amongst the passengers as one of the cruise's most anticipated highlights began. Today, the *Diamond Star* would navigate the Corinth Canal, a narrow waterway that connected the Ionian Sea to the Aegean. The ship would sail through the Isthmus of Corinth, a small stretch of land separating mainland Greece from the Peloponnese peninsula.

A little before midnight the previous evening, the *Diamond Star* had cruised smoothly away from Argostoli, her sleek hull cutting through the deep waters. Under the night sky, the island's green slopes faded into the horizon as the ship chartered her course eastward, and as many passengers retired, Captain Bellwood's voice issued a gentle reminder that they would sail through the night. For those eager to fully experience the wonder of the Corinth Canal, he urged them to make sure that they were on deck shortly after breakfast.

Fran and Sid stood in the sunshine at the bow and held hands as they eagerly watched the vessel approach the narrow entrance of the canal. Passengers clustered around, and it seemed as though everyone, including the crew, was ready to experience the breathtaking passage that was about to begin.

Fran waved energetically when she saw Carmen edging through the crowd. 'Come and join us, we've got a good view,' Fran added as Sid helped Carmen position Betty.

'I can't see why we had to get up so early,' Betty grumbled. 'I didn't finish my breakfast . . .' But her protest was quickly drowned out by the excited chatter around them.

'Room for one more?' called a familiar voice.

Don appeared, clad in running gear and Fran thought that Don's beige Lycra looked like sausage meat struggling to escape its casing. 'Yes, plenty of room,' Fran said as Don squeezed alongside. 'You must have been up early, have you been for a jog?'

'Got to keep in shape,' Don said, running a hand over his vacuum-sealed belly. 'Ten laps around the exercise deck before breakfast,' he added proudly.

'Does Debbie run with you?' Fran asked, silently thinking Debbie wouldn't be blamed for running in the opposite direction.

'No, she prefers a lie-in. I've left her searching our room.' Don frowned. 'She's misplaced a necklace.'

'I'm sorry to hear that,' Fran said, her curiosity piqued. 'Not that pretty chain with the diamond droplet she wore last night?'

'Aye, that one. Cost me a pretty penny, I can tell you.' Don shook his head. 'I've told her to stay below until she's found it.'

Fran was about to suggest that Debbie was missing a memorable part of the cruise, but to her relief, Debbie suddenly appeared. Fran offered a sympathetic smile but noted Debbie glare at Don, as she stood beside Carmen.

'Any luck with the necklace?' Fran asked, but Debbie shook her head. 'You need to report it to guest services and I'm sure it will turn up,' she added.

'Listen, the purser's speaking.' Sid's eyes were wide with anticipation, and he peered towards the tugboat that would guide their ship. Peter's voice crackled from the public address system, and a hush descended over the deck.

'Good morning, everyone,' Peter began, 'I hope you're all ready for this truly unforgettable moment because we will be entering the legendary Corinth Canal in a few minutes.'

'Look,' Sid pointed, 'the tugboat's ahead and is guiding us through!'

Bodies leaned in, cameras at the ready as the tugboat began its work.

'Captain Bellwood will take charge of this challenging and remarkable journey,' Peter continued, 'so find a comfortable spot with a view because this mysterious man-made marvel is going to be breathtaking.'

'The canal is too narrow for large vessels and cruise ships,' Sid explained to Fran as they gripped the railing, 'but as the *Diamond Star* is smaller, she will go through with only feet to spare.'

Everyone held their breath as they began to enter the canal. Carved out of the rocky land, it would reduce the journey by 185 nautical miles, and as they inched forward, Peter's voice resumed.

'This is one of the oldest man-made canals in the world. It took centuries to complete and requires immense skill by Captain Bellwood to manoeuvre such a large vessel. This famous canal was the brainchild of the Roman emperor Nero, who attempted the construction in AD67 by taking a pickaxe himself to dig up the first pieces of rock . . . Progress stalled after Nero's death and only restarted in 1881 and completed in 1893.'

'Why aren't we bumping into the walls?' Fran asked as she leaned back against Sid and the towering rock face loomed closer.

'Hold your breath, love,' Sid said, 'there's barely three feet on either side, but the captain is skilful.' He stared in awe at the tunnel-like surround, almost within arm's reach.

Don stepped away from the rail. 'The last time I saw something this dark, I was examining Debbie's bank balance,' he quipped. 'If it gets any narrower, we'll need butter to squeeze through.'

The canal seemed to stretch endlessly; the quiet hum of the ship's engines amplified beside the gentle whisper of water as they glided along. Long shadows closed in, casting darkness over the deck, and Debbie said that she hoped they didn't get stuck. When the cliffs appeared perilously close, the passengers gasped as they saw shafts of sunlight illuminating the golden tons of rock, a sharp contrast to the slither of blue sky above.

Fran felt Sid's arms wrap tightly around her body. 'It feels like time has stood still,' she whispered.

'Let's put it in our memory bank,' Sid said, 'for the days when we can't make memories like this anymore.'

'How much further?' Fran asked, snuggling close.

'Well, the canal is four miles long, and we've been going for nearly two hours, so we should be through soon.'

As Sid spoke, the cliffs gave way to open water and, moments later, they emerged into the Aegean Sea. The deck erupted with applause and cheers as Captain Bellwood safely delivered their unique experience.

'I'm so thrilled to have done this,' Fran said, 'do you think we should buy the captain a drink?'

Sid chuckled, taking her hand. 'I don't want Captain Bellwood to steer us off course. Next, you'll ask him to let you have a turn at the helm.'

From the navigation deck, Peter spoke up. 'On behalf of Captain Bellwood and the entire crew of the *Diamond Star*, we hope you enjoyed this historic journey. We'll be at sea for the rest of the day as we make our way to the beautiful island of Rhodes, and if you'd like to join us, we'll be serving complimentary Corinth Cocktails in the Mermaid Theatre.'

Don had a spring in his step. 'Free cocktails? It would be rude to say no.' He guided Debbie away.

'Did someone say cocktails?' Betty piped up from her chair.

Fran glanced at Carmen, noticing her worried expression. 'Sid told me that your author is talking today,' Fran said. 'It's scheduled in the *Diamond Star Daily News*.'

'Yes, Ruskin is giving a talk in the Neptune Theatre in half an hour.' Carmen glanced at her watch, 'But Mum seems set on trying a cocktail.'

'No problem.' Fran smiled. 'Sid and I will take charge. You get yourself off to the talk.'

Fran reached out to grab Betty's chair. 'Let's go, Sidney,' she called out. 'The Golden Oldies Gang are meeting in the Mermaid Theatre – and that's where the Corinth Cocktails are waiting!'

* * *

On the lido deck, Dicky stretched out on a steamer-style sunbed. It lay in a line curving around an oval shaped swimming pool, where at one end, a hot tub simmered. Dicky cradled a cocktail with a colourful umbrella and savoured the moment of solitude while everyone crowded on deck to experience the ship inching its way through the famed Corinth Canal. Dicky held a notebook and pen and wondered what jokes he could whip up to include in his act. He was due to host a quiz in the Mermaid Theatre for the Golden Oldies Gang, and later, would be on stage to compere the evening's entertainment.

'I've never seen land so close,' Dicky read from his notes, 'the captain must be demonstrating parallel parking.' He grimaced, then began again. 'Remember folks, sometimes the best part of a cruise is surviving the journey!' Deciding that the joke was inappropriate on a ship full of pensioners, he hastily erased the words.

He'd have to do better than that.

As the sun dimmed and the walls of the canal loomed high, Dicky flipped his Ray-Bans and glanced around the deck. Not a soul to be seen. Thankfully, not even the wealthy widow whom he'd entertained last night.

Earlier that day he'd been keen to leave the lady's suite.

Tip-toeing around, he'd hoped she wouldn't stir as he slipped into his clothes, and she slumbered heavily in the king-sized bed. The ornate chandelier and plush rugs were a long way from the dim lights and linoleum floor of his lower deck cubbyhole, and as Dicky edged into the palatial lounge of the suite, he grabbed a beer from the minibar before tripping over a silver sling-backed shoe.

'Bloody hell,' he cursed, thinking of the podgy foot the previous evening that had kicked off the shoe and most of her clothes as Dicky popped the cork from a bottle of expensive champagne. Seeing an open clutch bag, where a considerable stash of fifty-euro notes was tucked into a zipped section, Dicky pocketed four crisp notes. *She won't miss them*, he thought. As he left the suite, he'd checked the corridor to ensure there were no prying eyes to witness his escape.

Now, smoothing a layer of oily sunscreen over his conker-coloured chest, Dicky relished the fact that his encounters barely had any consequences. His targets, often too embarrassed to expose the comedian, usually dismissed the experience, if they remembered it at all, as nothing more than a fleeting holiday fling. A brief moment seized in the twilight of later life.

Let's face it, Dicky thought with a smile, *they got their money's worth!* Revved up and ready to go with the aid of a little blue pill, Dicky's stamina made a marathon runner look like they were off on a light jog. But when the effect of the enhancer wore off, Dicky was like a deflated balloon.

Now exhausted, he closed his eyes, hoping to catch a few hours' sleep away from the ship's engine that incessantly reverberated in his cabin. Daydreaming about his past mistakes, Dicky remembered Anne, who was closer in age to him. They'd enjoyed four glorious months on the Costa Brava but like the fool that he was, he'd messed it up. An unforgiving Anne hadn't accepted his dalliance with another woman nor his promise of reform. Before he could utter, 'It will never happen again!' Anne had left him with nothing but a suitcase of empty memories.

In the serene surroundings, Dicky was in his own little world and with the heat of the sun burning through a gap as the ship progressed through the canal, he felt drowsy and soon fell asleep.

An hour passed, and Dicky slept on. His dream took him to famous stages where he was greeted with standing ovations from the fantasy crowd that applauded his act. He had a foolish grin on his face as he shook the hand of the King, whose consort told the comedian he was brilliant.

'Thank you, your Highness . . .' Dicky mumbled aloud, his smile widening as he kissed the hand of the Royal and dreamed of his name in the new year's honours list.

'Wakey, wakey!' A voice pierced through his dream and jolted Dicky awake.

'*What the* . . .' he muttered. Shielding sunlight with his hand, Dicky realised a tall figure stood over him.

Melody Moon was a vision in a shiny red swimsuit. Dicky shook his head and slowly regained consciousness, noting her matching sarong, knotted at the waist. Melody looked as though she'd just strutted off a catwalk.

'Do you always talk in your sleep,' she asked, one hand on her hip, 'or are you losing your marbles?'

'Oh, it's you . . .' Dicky groaned and, reaching for his cocktail, drained the glass. 'Can't you find another spot to parade your . . . assets?'

'Been burning the midnight?' Melody smirked, unfazed. 'I could carry my shopping in the bags under your eyes.'

'Why don't you find a shaded corner to sit in?' Dicky retorted. 'You're blinding me with all that cosmetic work. Sunlight and surgery don't mix well.'

'Maybe you should try it,' Melody snapped, 'it might smooth out the train tracks on your face.'

Dicky lay back and, picking up his Ray-Bans, feigned sleep. The sniping dialogue with Melody could go on all morning, but he wasn't in the mood. It took too much brain power, and he needed his wits to concentrate on his act that evening. Peter had insisted that he work on something about the canal in a funny yet complimentary way.

He heard the flip flop of Melody's sandals and, opening one eye, squinted at the retreating figure. There was no doubt Melody was talented. She was a knock-out performer, and in beach apparel she looked like a super-model.

Dicky knew that his competition was fierce.

'Canals . . . Greeks . . . builders . . .' he muttered, trying to brainstorm.

'You'll have to do better than that,' came another voice behind him.

Startled, Dicky spun around. 'Bloody hell, it's like Piccadilly Circus out here today,' he said. 'Can't a man get a bit of peace?' Shielding his eyes, Dicky stared at the man before him.

Ruskin Reeve wore neat linen shorts, a short-sleeved shirt and a Panama hat.

'So, you're the comedian who's pushed my books to one side in the shop?' Ruskin drawled. 'Hardly funny, but then again, neither is your act.'

More criticism . . . Dicky eased to his feet. 'I don't believe I've had the pleasure?' he said, determined to keep things cordial.

Ruskin ignored Dicky's outstretched hand.

'Going swimming?' Dicky nodded towards the pool.

'I swam for an hour earlier.'

'You're the writer?' Dicky ploughed on.

'Ruskin Reeve, *bestselling* writer,' he emphasised.

'And I'm Dicky Delaney, comedy so sharp you'll need a safety net,' he grinned.

Ruskin's icy gaze swept over Dicky's perma-tan, gleaming teeth and Elvis-like hair. 'Move my books in the shop again,' Ruskin warned, 'and I'll destroy you faster than one of the victims in my novels.'

Before Dicky had time to quip a reply, Ruskin turned and marched across the deck. Slumping on his recliner, Dicky picked up his glass. It was empty. So much for the camaraderie between crew and entertainment members they mentioned in the *Diamond Star Daily News*, he thought. If anyone else disliked him, he'd have to plan a mutiny!

Dicky sighed and ran a hand through his carefully styled hair, his grin momentarily slipping. But maybe he didn't need their camaraderie? Perhaps he needed to shake things up! He signalled to a server for another drink. Mutiny wasn't the right word, he decided. Charm and punchlines sharp enough to cut were more his style.

Dicky's grin returned. Let Ruskin Reeve and everyone else underestimate him; he wasn't here just to make people laugh. He would use the cruise for his own devices and, cunningly, turn the trip into his own personal payday.

Chapter Twelve

Carmen sat on a velvet banquette in the Neptune Theatre, her fingers pulling nervously at the piping on the armrest. Three rows away from the front, she had a clear view of the stage, and glancing around, she heard a low murmur as passengers searched for seats.

'Anyone sitting here?' A man pointed to the empty space. Before Carmen could reply, he lowered his body and shuffled into place. 'Theo,' he said, 'pleased to make your acquaintance.'

Carmen winced as a beefy hand shook her own. 'Carmen,' she muttered and edged away. Theo was like a mountain, solid and unmoveable.

'On your own?' Theo asked.

'Er, well, yes, at the moment,' Carmen stuttered, unwilling to explain that her travelling companion, Betty, was probably three sheets to the wind in the Mermaid Theatre bar and upsetting anyone within earshot.

'Me too,' he said.

Unsure of whether Theo was attempting to make a pass

at her, Carmen clamped her legs tightly and gripped the notebook on her knee.

'Lost my partner a year ago, never felt so lonely.'

'I'm so sorry,' Carmen said and turned to Theo.

He looked familiar, but unable to place him she noted his ebony skin and short, tightly coiled hair, speckled with strands of grey that peppered his well-trimmed beard.

'It's a strange thing when you lose your partner. Grief is like trying to clear smoke with your hands.'

Carmen stared at Theo's hands, which looked large, strong, and accustomed to hard work.

'One minute, the smoke is thick with your loss, and you can't breathe,' he continued, 'then, the next, the smoke clears and he's there, like he never left.'

Carmen relaxed her grip. There seemed less danger of Theo hitting on her. 'Is that an Irish accent I detect?' she asked.

'I live in Donegal.' Theo's eyes, a deep brown, turned to Carmen. 'I still talk to Ruari, and often I feel as though he's right beside me.' He shook his head. 'It's madness.'

'Is that why you came on the cruise, to help you get over Ruari?'

Theo let out a breath. 'Yes, and I miss him something fierce.'

'I'm so sorry.' Carmen's tone softened. 'What happened?'

'A heart condition, we had no idea. It was very sudden. He died in his sleep.'

Carmen reached out and patted Theo's arm. 'Perhaps this talk will help you forget for a while.'

'Maybe . . .' Theo smiled. 'But I had a long flight and am very tired and that's when memories hit me.'

A spotlight beamed onto a podium and Carmen turned to the stage.

Strutting confidently, Peter appeared, and Carmen felt her heart flutter as the purser began the introduction. She was here! Moments away from experiencing Ruskin talk about his work – words that could inspire her own writing journey. This was what she'd been waiting for!

Carmen adjusted her glasses and opened her notebook. She wondered if she would ever stand on a stage like this – would her own stories create the buzz required to secure a huge following, eager to hang off her every word?

'So please, let's have a *Diamond Star* welcome, as it gives me great pleasure,' Peter called out, 'to bring to you the world-famous author, Ruskin Reeve!'

Carmen almost sprang to her feet, but fearing she'd shunt into Theo, she held her hands high and clapped. Gone was the memory of the unsociable man on the beach in Maxos. Here was the great author, Ruskin Reeve!

'Cruise Club members on the *Diamond Star*, friends, fans . . .'

To loud applause, Ruskin stood before the podium, tall and poised, his trendy linen suit as cool as his confidence. Pausing, he stared at the audience.

For a moment, Carmen felt sure that she'd caught his glance, and her breath quickened. She felt the air charged, full of anticipation as everyone waited for the great man to speak.

As his eyes swept the room, a smile played on Ruskin's lips as though telling the guests they were lucky to be in his presence. He raised a hand, and the room became silent.

'I imagine you all want to hear wise words on writing?' Ruskin gave a knowing chuckle and allowed a beat to pass. 'No doubt, many of you would like to understand the secret to my success. How did I dream up stories that have sold worldwide?' Ruskin shrugged and moved from the podium to slowly walk towards the audience.

Carmen sat forward and her hair fell softly onto her shoulders. As Ruskin came closer, she felt a magnetic pull as though being drawn into a world created by his imagination. Theo no longer sat beside her; instead, the Rainbow Sleuth had taken his place, and Carmen felt a fire of creativity burn in her pounding heart.

'But first,' Ruskin said as he scanned the crowd, 'let me tell you about the space between the words . . .'

Spellbound, Carmen's pen danced across the page as Ruskin talked about his life and what inspired him to write. He dropped nuggets of advice like gold coins, and Carmen collected them gratefully, each stroke of her pen capturing the wise and motivating words as his talk glued in her mind. Lost in the magic of his knowledge, nothing else mattered.

As the talk came to an end, she closed her notebook and took a deep breath. Ideas and plots filled her excited head. At last, she could start writing again! Ruskin Reeve had inspired her, and she'd begin what she set out to do on this cruise.

Maybe her writing block was over.

As Ruskin left the stage to thundering applause, Carmen turned in her seat. Beside her, the imaginary figure of the Rainbow Sleuth had gone, and instead, Theo, his head to one side, was slumbering quietly. Not wishing to disturb the man, Carmen placed her notebook in her bag and, with a smile that could light up the darkest night, slipped quietly out of the theatre.

* * *

The Mermaid Theatre was situated at the stern of the ship, and unlike the tiered seating in the Neptune Theatre, guests sat at circular tables grouped around the stage. The room was large, with two generous platformed areas and a well-stocked bar. Fran and Sid had chosen to sit by a window that offered stunning views during the day, and with Betty parked beside them, they ordered a round of drinks.

'If the Corinth Cocktail is free, I'll have two,' Betty said to a server, 'not too much ice!'

Her face was set in a permanent frown, and she sat upright in her chair, her bag like a shield, clamped to her knee. Betty's silver-grey curls were drawn back with a tortoiseshell band.

'I think I'll have the same,' Fran said, looking around. 'Isn't it lovely in here?' she added, admiring the theatre's theme, which blended with the ship's colour palette, where bright and bold blues reflected the sea and sky.

'It's very bright,' Betty complained. Dressed in a beige patterned blouse and slacks pressed to perfection, Betty's feet tapped impatiently. Pink toenails peeped out from her summer sandals.

'There's a good crowd gathered,' Sid said and picked up his beer. 'This is where the Golden Oldies Gang meet each day for quizzes and the like.'

'How exciting,' Fran said, 'I'm hopeless at quizzes, but it will be fun to join in.' She watched as the server slid coasters onto the table, reached for the cocktails on his tray, and placed them carefully beside a bowl of salted nuts.

'I'm not breaking my teeth on those,' Betty snapped, pushing the nuts away.

Fran thought that Betty's dentures could probably crush rocks, as she remembered the mounds of food she'd seen Betty consume in the last twenty-four hours. She watched the elderly lady reach for her glass and flip the garnish of mint before raising the drink to her thin lips and gulping it down.

'Steady on!' Sid smiled as he retrieved the mint. 'That's mostly vodka.'

'And lime and honey.' Fran took a sip. 'It's delicious,' she said and grabbed a handful of nuts.

The room had begun to fill, and as passengers gathered around tables and found their seats, Colin and Neeta arrived.

'Come and join us, we're having cocktails.' Fran inched her chair to make room. 'That's a lovely shirt.' She grinned at Colin and admired the pineapple pattern print, which matched Neeta's eye-catching minuscule vest.

Neeta pulled up a chair next to Sid. 'Hello, Sidney,' she whispered and fluttered her butterfly lashes.

'Ahem . . .' Sid nervously coughed. 'I think the quiz is about to start.'

All eyes turned to the stage, and seconds later, Dicky Delaney appeared.

'Hello Golden Oldies Gang!' Dicky called out. He stopped in his tracks, waiting for a response. 'Hello . . . Anyone out there?'

'Hello Dicky!' Fran enthused.

'You'll have to do better than that.' Dicky grinned. 'Are you all awake? Blink twice if you're conscious.'

Laughter began as everyone watched Dicky with amused anticipation.

'I hope you all had a second helping of lunch and are ready to stretch your brains because we are about to dive in at the deep end of trivia.'

'Get on with it!' a voice sliced through from the back of the room.

Dicky squinted and looked around the crowd until his eyes rested on Don. 'Ah, it's our Yorkshire friend,' he said. 'Did someone leave the farm gate open?' Dicky paused. 'I'm glad you're not giving me directions. Last time a Yorkshire man told me to "Tek a reet", I ended up in the sea.'

Dicky beamed. Everyone was enjoying his banter. 'All right, gang, let's get started,' he said. 'Has your team captain got a pen and paper, and have you chosen a name?'

On Fran's table, Betty whipped a notebook out of her bag. She tore out a page then reached for a pen. 'I'm in charge, and we are the Trivia Titans,' Betty declared as she wrote the name down. 'Everyone, up your game!'

Eyebrows lifted as guests around the table exchanged glances. The speed with which Betty took charge left the group speechless.

'Question number one,' Dicky shook out a sheet of

paper. 'You'll all know this one,' he smirked. 'What year did the Titanic sink?'

Sid held his hand over his mouth, 'I think it was 1914,' he whispered.

'No, nearer 1920.' Colin frowned.

'1912,' Betty snapped and wrote it down.

'What famous amusement park in California opened in 1955?' Dicky looked around the room where the competitive spirit was thick.

'Universal Studios!' Fran smiled.

'I'm sure it's Sea World,' Colin said.

'Mickey Mouse Land.' Neeta yawned.

'Disneyland,' Betty hissed and penned the answer.

'One for the astronauts amongst you.' Dicky nodded to the audience. 'What was the name of the first manned mission to land on the moon?'

'I know this . . .' Sid drummed his fingers on the table.

'It's Apollo 10, I'm certain,' Colin was adamant.

'I really don't care,' Neeta sighed.

'Wasn't it Gemini something?' Fran was puzzled.

'Apollo 11,' Betty spat out.

Tensions rose as Dicky switched the questions to a music round, and a man with a hearing aid banged his walking stick when he misheard a Frank Sinatra question. On Don's table, a scuffle almost broke out over Elvis's first hit, and when Don insisted that he knew the correct answer he was silenced by a dig of Debbie's elbow.

When the quiz ended, Dicky took a break as he collected papers. 'Time to refresh your drinks,' he called out.

Betty, on her third Corinth Cocktail, had a smug smile.

'I'm very impressed, Betty dear,' Fran said, 'you put us all to shame with your knowledge.'

'My late husband, Des, and I weren't known as the Quizards of Butterly for nothing.' Betty was confident in their victory. 'There's many a trophy on my dresser at home.'

When Dicky returned to the stage, any camaraderie in the room was forgotten as The Smartinis, shaken not stirred, pinged olives at the In It To Win Its. Drink coasters flew like frisbees from The Correctors, who aimed them at the Smarty Pints, while the Trivia Titans, awaiting news of the winner, held their breath.

'There have been some interesting answers,' Dicky chuckled and smiled at The Brainy Bunch. 'For example, in reply to "What was Elvis's first hit?" these good folk wrote, "Jailhouse Rock because Elvis accidentally locked himself in the bathroom . . ."'

'I don't think that's very funny,' Don said, 'didn't he die in there?'

'Exactly.' Dicky shook his head.

'What was the correct answer?' Fran asked.

Before Dicky could reply, Betty shouted, '"I'm All Shook Up!"'

'So, I've heard,' Dicky concurred.

'I knew that!' Don shouted and stared angrily at his team.

'But that doesn't take away from the fact that . . .' Dicky held up his hand for a drum roll. 'Betty Cunningham, you and your team, the Trivia Titans, are today's Golden Oldies Gang Quiz Winners!'

Fran and Sid leaped to their feet, and as Fran kissed Betty's powdered cheek, Sid patted Betty on her shoulder.

Dicky carried a bottle of champagne to the table and Colin and Neeta clapped their hands.

'I'll take charge of that,' Betty said and snatched the prize from Dicky. Standing triumphantly, all ailments forgotten, she held the bottle as though she'd won the lottery.

There was a murmur as numerous Golden Oldies, already plotting revenge, grudgingly clapped the winning team. Don and Debbie came over to congratulate the Trivia Titans, and Fran asked Debbie if her necklace had been found. But before Debbie had time to reply, Don shook his head. 'I told her not to bring the expensive stuff on holiday. It's a goner, I'm afraid, but if I catch the culprit, I'll skin them alive.'

Debbie rolled her eyes.

'Do you have any idea where you might have lost it?' Fran asked.

Debbie explained that she hadn't a clue. An officer from guest services had taken a description and checked Lost and Found. He'd frowned when Debbie mentioned that she hadn't used the safe in their room but assured her that a thorough search would be conducted and checked in the public areas.

'It's so upsetting for you,' Fran said, 'but someone will be sure to pick it up and hand it in.'

Debbie said that she hoped so and, taking hold of Don's arm, led him away.

Colin and Neeta said they were going for a rest and, holding hands, disappeared too.

'We must find Carmen,' Betty gave orders as she drained the last of her cocktail. 'She needs to press my outfit for tonight, and I want her to do my hair.'

Sid raised his eyebrow as Fran shrugged her shoulders. Releasing the brake, Sid took charge and wheeled Betty away.

'What a smashing afternoon,' Fran said as she linked Sid's arm, and they moved through the ship to Betty's cabin. 'I hope that Carmen had a lovely time too.'

Chapter Thirteen

Carmen was, indeed, having a lovely time. In the comfort of her quiet cabin, her glasses were perched on the edge of her nose and her fingers flew over the keys of her laptop. The Rainbow Sleuth had finally got back on his detecting horse to saddle up and set off on his mission to solve a mysterious crime. Lost in her make-believe world and inspired by Ruskin's talk, Carmen's brain whirled, and words raced across the page.

Unable to relax, Carmen suddenly felt that the story might evolve in a more intriguing way. Her sleuth was piecing together clues faster than she could get them down and as she envisaged the quaint village, cobbled streets, and cosy Cumbrian coffee shop where the story's pivotal scene occurred, Carmen focused.

'Thank you, Ruskin!' Carmen whispered as she scribbled notes and typed away.

Outside, the view from the open patio doors was like a painting, and as the ship glided through the smooth waters of the Aegean, muslin window drapes caught sunlight that filtered through the fabric. But Carmen didn't notice the slow-moving dance. She was in her own world, breathing life into her characters.

When a knock sounded on her cabin door, Carmen didn't hear. When it came again, banging furiously, she almost leaped out of her seat.

'CARMEN!' Betty yelled. 'Open up this instant!'

With a longing look at the screen, Carmen saved her work. Another few minutes and the chapter would have been reworked.

'Coming, Mum.' Carmen reluctantly pushed back her chair and brushed strands away from her face. Her fingers were clenched into fists as she marched across the cabin to fling the door open.

Standing on either side of Betty, Sid and Fran smiled apologetically. 'Hello, love,' Fran began, 'your mum wonders if you'd be kind enough to help her prepare for dinner.'

Betty waved her cane. 'You've been dilly-dallying all afternoon, Carmen. Anyone would think you didn't want to spend time with your poor old mother.'

'I've hardly been . . .' Carmen began to reply but knew that reasoning with Betty was useless. Instead, she followed the group to Betty's room where Betty flopped down on the sofa.

'Your mum won a bottle of champers,' Fran announced. 'Shall I pop it in the fridge so it will be chilled, and you can both have a drink before dinner?'

Betty, her knuckles almost white, gripped the bottle like it was her last loaf of bread.

'That's a great idea,' Carmen said and began a tugging match with her mother.

'Watch out, the cork will pop!' Betty cried as Carmen peeled Betty's fingers away and placed the bottle in the fridge.

'I hope you've had an interesting afternoon?' Fran asked Carmen.

'Yes, I did, and I must thank you both for caring for Mum.'

Betty, arms tightly folded, called out, 'I don't need carers. You haven't stuck me in a nursing home yet.'

'Any time,' Fran assured Carmen and patted her shoulder. 'Will you join us for dinner, or do you fancy a change?'

'Oh, no, I mean – yes,' Carmen stammered. She longed to sit with Fran and Sid again and not go through the agony of making new acquaintances.

'Lovely, if we get there before you, we'll save you both a place.'

'Thank you, Fran. You and Sid are very kind.'

'Don't mention it.' Fran smiled. As she reached the door, she turned and whispered, 'If you've time tomorrow, we could have a shopping trip in Rhodes?'

'Well, I don't know . . .'

'Smashing, that's settled. See you later.'

Carmen closed the door and moved back into the room to unbuckle Betty's sandals. 'It will be lovely to have dinner again with Fran and Sid, won't it?'

'I think they're terribly common.' Betty thrust out a foot, almost striking Carmen's face. 'That woman wears far too much makeup. If I wanted to mix with a clown, I'd join a circus.' Betty sniffed and wriggled her toes. 'And as for her husband, his cheap cologne almost gags me.'

Carmen leaned back on her heels and stared at Betty in disbelief. 'Mother,' Carmen said, 'how could you? Fran is just trying to be friendly.'

'Friendly? Oh, *please* . . .' Betty shuffled deep into the sofa and, with a nifty movement, raised her legs and placed a cushion behind her head. 'Pass me a blanket. I need a nap,' she said, 'and make sure you press my blue outfit. It's hanging in the closet.'

As Carmen searched for a blanket, she wished her mother was hanging in the closet from the strongest hanger on the highest hook. She flicked her gaze to her watch and sighed. Writing time was over, she'd never get the rhythm back today, and the Rainbow Sleuth would have to take a back seat, his sleuthing postponed until her inspiration returned. Betty dampened Carmen's writing like rain on a perfect picnic. But if her mother slept for an hour or so, with any luck, Carmen might steal away for a swim.

Carmen tucked the blanket around Betty, who'd fallen asleep, her false teeth clicking like castanets as her snores rose, filling the room with wheezes and snorts.

'Sweet dreams,' Carmen muttered and, with a shake of her head, tip-toed away.

* * *

Carmen arrived at the pool on the lido deck and, seeing that most of the loungers were occupied with bags, towels and hats, found a chair near the hot tub and sat down. As she slipped out of her sandals and eased the towelling robe from her shoulders, she became aware that the pool was full of pensioners, all standing around. Deciding that she'd never find room in the water to have a swim, Carmen was about to push her arms back into her robe when a hand reached out to stop her.

'Don't be shy,' a young man said, 'you'll feel much better when you've shaken off your excesses and got your body moving.' He tossed Carmen's robe to one side and pulled her to her feet. 'In you go!' He smiled.

Carmen felt herself propelled towards the water and guided down shallow steps until she was waist deep. To her delight, the water was warm and silky, and the late afternoon sun a caress on her skin as she joined Kyle's Senior Splashdown.

The warm-up began, and as Carmen placed her hands on her hips and turned from side to side, she was amused to see the varying get-ups surrounding her. Passengers of all shapes and sizes bobbed about, their brightly coloured swimming caps blended with floral swimsuits and Hawaiian patterned shorts in a blur of movement. She spotted Don in the shallow end, his red Speedos glowing like a lighthouse while Debbie, demure in a skirted tankini, wore rubber flowers on her headgear. Close by, Colin and Neeta stood out in minuscule swimwear. Neeta's bikini was tiny and as she moved, her enhanced breasts threatened to break free from her top.

Carmen felt like a slick of algae in the sludge-green one-piece that had been tucked in the back of her bedroom drawer. If Fran was still game for a shopping excursion, Carmen decided that a new swimsuit would be at the top of her list.

'Let's work those legs!' Kyle called out. Pacing around

the pool, his back straight and clapping his hands over his head, he lifted alternate legs in a goose step.

'Blimey, it's like being in the army,' Don could be heard to grumble. 'I feel as though I'm at a Victory Day Parade in Moscow.' He turned suddenly as Debbie, one kick too high, fell back and disappeared under the water. 'Come on, stop mucking about,' he said as a spluttering, red-faced Debbie choked her way to the surface.

'Feel the burn!' Kyle called out.

Carmen thought Kyle was taking the Senior Splashdown far too seriously as she struggled to keep up with his forward lunges and noted that others were also feeling the strain.

'Hang on to your noodle, Colin!' Kyle called out.

'He hangs on to a lot more than that,' Neeta laughed and ran her fingers over her long silver earrings, studded with emeralds that glinted in the sunshine. Ignoring Kyle's ongoing instructions, she slowly made her way out of the pool and into the jacuzzi. Her bikini clung to her shapely figure, and all eyes swivelled as Neeta gave a playful flick of her hair and dipped her toe in the bubbling water. 'Anyone coming to join me?' she asked.

There was a sudden scramble as many moved forward creating a surge of water, and partners' hands reached out to pull them back.

'Now, now, Neeta!' Kyle wriggled his finger in mock annoyance as he endeavoured to get his session back on track. 'Let's all do a jumping jack!' His megawatt smile encouraged the oldies but was soon replaced with a frown as everyone ducked to avoid flying limbs.

'The medics will be busy if he keeps this up,' Don said to

a red-faced Debbie, who gripped her noodle as she jumping-jacked up and down.

Kyle moved on to water-bound arm curls and exaggerated hip twists. With each knee-high, Carmen stared anxiously at other participants and wondered if joint replacement waiting lists were still achingly long. As the session cooled down, Kyle instructed his class to shimmy like chorus line stars. Bosoms and bottoms wobbled as everyone attempted to *shake it, shake it, shake it*, as Kyle sang along.

'Fabulooous!' Kyle called out, clapping his hands. 'Same time tomorrow everyone, don't be late!'

As the pool emptied of bathers and Carmen began to enjoy a swim, she watched Kyle towel down his neon Speedos and comb his immaculate hair. Kyle's body was that of an athlete, tanned, toned, and sprightly. *Oh, to feel and look so well*, Carmen thought, and wondered how many swimmers would be up to another Senior Splashdown. She knew that there was an excellent medical facility onboard and felt that after today's session, some might be making good use of it.

As Carmen leisurely made her way through the water, a voice called out. 'Well done, you survived!' Looking up, she saw Theo sitting beside the pool. Wearing casual shorts and a T-shirt, he held a cocktail in his hand. 'All a bit too energetic for me.' He smiled.

Carmen felt pleased to see Theo and paused in her swim. 'Hello, did you have a good nap?' she asked.

'Ah, I'm sorry about that, I struggle to sleep at night and sometimes find myself dozing during the day. I hope I didn't drown out the talk with my snores.'

'Not at all, I was engrossed,' she replied, tilting her head. 'You look happy, are you feeling brighter?'

Theo chuckled. 'I am,' he said, 'there's no smoke in my eyes now, and this drink is helping things along nicely. Why don't you hop out and join me?'

Carmen doubted that she could hop anywhere after her recent exertions. She wondered if Betty was awake and was about to turn down the invitation but as she looked at Theo's kind face, she decided that Betty could wait. Carmen couldn't remember the last time a man had wanted to share her company, and she wasn't about to let Betty spoil things. It would be churlish not to enjoy a drink with Theo.

'Give me a minute while I fetch my robe.' Carmen hoped Theo wouldn't see her aged costume as she moved through the water and climbed out of the pool.

'I took the liberty of ordering for you,' Theo said when Carmen joined him.

'Lovely,' she replied as she lifted a fruit-filled cocktail stick and took a bite. 'This looks interesting, what is it?' She lifted her glass and began to drink.

'A pina colada, made with rum and pineapple, it's my favourite. Now tell me, what's a delightful lady like yourself doing on a cruise full of old codgers?'

Carmen was about to insist that she was an old codger too, but realising that she was thirsty, she gulped the drink. The sudden effect of almost half a glass of rum made its way swiftly into her bloodstream and, for the first time since she'd boarded the *Diamond Star*, Carmen felt herself fully relax.

'I write cosy mysteries,' Carmen blurted, 'my leading man is called the Rainbow Sleuth.'

Theo clapped his hands together. 'I love it!'

'Well, I'm afraid the Rainbow Sleuth has done a disappearing act and I'm having a bit of a writer's block.'

'You mean you stare at the screen, and nothing happens?'

'Exactly,' Carmen nodded. 'I thought that this cruise would help clear my mind and having Ruskin Reeve onboard, to give a talk and workshops, might inspire me.'

'And has it?'

'Yes, after the talk I rushed to my laptop and found that words were filling the page.'

'Excellent. Mission accomplished.'

'Not really, my mother interrupted and now I'm back to the writing block.'

'Here, let me clean your glasses,' Theo said, reaching for a napkin, 'you're all steamed up.' He began to polish, turning the heavy rims between his fingers. 'Are these varifocals?' he asked.

'Yes, I'm as blind as a bat without them.'

'It sounds like your mum is a problem,' Theo said.

'I came on the cruise to get away from my mother.' Carmen finished the creamy cocktail, and Theo ordered another.

'And did you?'

'Not a chance. All my life she's been a constant shadow, trailing in my wake and bossing me about. Making friends or forming a relationship is almost impossible.'

'Well, that's a pity. Surely you have some time of your own to write?'

'Rarely. I live with Betty, unfortunately, and if I threaten to do my work, she suddenly becomes ill and incapable but conscious enough to warn me that if I don't pull my weight, she'll leave her estate to a cats' conservation charity.'

'Does she like cats?'

'Hates them.'

'Meow, that's tricky,' Theo mused.

They continued their conversation, even joking about the perils of having an elderly dependent parent, with Theo confiding that Ruari's father had been demanding. Carmen noticed that Theo's fingers stroked an expensive gold bracelet, in a slim simple design.

'Was that a gift?' she gently asked.

'How perceptive,' Theo said. 'It was a present from Ruari, I wear it all the time, especially during appearances.'

'Appearances?' Carmen looked puzzled.

'I'm a guest speaker on the ship, here to give a talk.'

'How exciting! What are your subjects?'

'Well, as a chef who has cooked here and there, I ramble on about my travels.'

'I'm so stupid!' Carmen burst out. 'What must you think of me? You're the famous Theo, from *McCarthy's Kitchen Adventures*, I'm so sorry I should have known. And to think that I have two of your wonderful cookery books too!'

'Please don't stress, there's no reason why you should know me and these days, I'm considerably more rotund than my last television series.' Theo smiled kindly and patted his belly.

Carmen was enjoying Theo's company and wanted to ask much more but realised that she'd been away from Betty for over two hours. 'I'm so sorry, but I must check on Mum,' she said. She was about to thank Theo for the drinks and say goodbye, when Ruskin appeared, wearing a monogrammed towelling gown that gaped to reveal swimming shorts. Carmen watched as he stopped and stared at Theo.

'Theo McCarthy,' Ruskin began, 'I'm not in the habit of sending my audience to sleep.'

'Ah, I'm sorry about that.' Theo grinned.

'Rest assured, I will find a front-row seat for your session and return the favour.'

'Ah, Ruskin, I was away with the fairies. I am beyond apologetic, but you have a fan right here. This lady thought you were outstanding.'

Horrified that Ruskin might see her old swimsuit, Carmen wrapped her robe tighter.

'I hope you enjoyed my talk?' Ruskin turned to Carmen.

'Y . . . yes,' she stammered. The sun was bright, and as Carmen held her hand to her brow, she was conscious that her damp, untamed hair frizzed wildly around her hot and now flustered face. 'It was fascinating,' she added.

Carmen wanted to tell Ruskin it was the most motivating and inspirational dialogue she'd heard in years. Within minutes of him uttering his closing statements, she'd rushed to her cabin to write. But Ruskin, showing no desire to spend time in her company, turned away before she could summon the courage and find the right words. Flinging his gown to one side, he dived neatly into the pool and began precise repetitious strokes as he pounded up and down.

Carmen picked up her bag and as she turned, she saw Peter pacing across the deck. He held up his hand and waved.

'There you are,' Peter said, almost breathless in his

haste, 'I'm sorry to disturb you, but your mother has guest services on speed dial and insists that she's unable to move. I need your help to assist her.' Peter shrugged and appeared apologetic.

Carmen sighed. 'Of course,' she replied. There was no doubt in her mind that Peter knew that Betty was a malingerer and made Carmen's life difficult.

'Sorry to dash,' Carmen said to Theo.

'The cat is in her cabin, and the mouse can't come out to play,' Theo said. 'Til we meet again.'

'Meow.' Carmen smiled.

At last, she had an ally.

Chapter Fourteen

The following morning the *Diamond Star*, having sailed through the night, docked in the ancient port of Rhodes. Passengers who'd risen early enjoyed stunning views as dawn rose over the island's coastline with its rocky cliffs and sparkling beaches. During breakfast, the guest services team made announcements reminding everyone of the disembarkation process and to have all necessary identification with them.

At a corner table, close to the buffet, Fran and Sid sat in the Deck Café. As Fran polished off her second slice of toast and Sid licked fried egg from his fork, they discussed the previous evening. Led by Melody Moon, the *Diamond Star* entertainment team had performed an enjoyable song and dance performance from the *Jersey Boys* show.

'I thought it was a bit left field for Melody,' Sid said as he cut into a slice of bacon, 'but her rendition of "Walk Like a Man" was brilliant.'

'It was,' Fran agreed and buttered more toast, adding peach jam with care. 'Dicky Delaney could have put more into "Can't Take My Eyes Off You", he hardly glanced at Melody during the number.'

'My favourite was "Big Girls Don't Cry",' Sid smiled, 'and Melody is a big girl.'

'I think she's marvellous, especially her outfits. Which reminds me,' Fran was thoughtful, 'I asked Carmen if she'd like a shopping trip today.'

'There'll be some fancy shops in Rhodes.'

'New clothes might lift her spirits,' Fran said, 'and you know how I love to browse.'

Sid smiled. He knew all too well that their savings pot of euros was about to take a hit, but he'd never begrudge Fran. His wife worked hard, and she deserved every luxury on this holiday. 'Can you handle Betty tagging along?' he asked, raising an eyebrow.

Fran reached out to stroke Sid's arm. 'The most important thing is to help Carmen come out of her shell, and I think that a few lovely outfits would give her the confidence she needs.'

Brushing sticky toast crumbs from his shirt, Sid said, 'I'll help with Betty.' He studied Fran's face. 'You've taken quite a shine to Carmen.'

'Betty dominates her daughter's life,' Fran said as she sipped her coffee. 'Carmen lives under her mother's thumb, and Betty has an invisible string that reels Carmen in every time she attempts to escape.'

'The old lady *can* be difficult,' Sid agreed.

'Controlling for sure, it seems to be in her nature, and it's drained any confidence Carmen might have had when her dad was alive.'

'Perhaps Betty is worried that Carmen will move away if she finds new friends, leaving her alone,' Sid reasoned.

Impressed, Fran stared at her husband. Sid had probably hit the nail on the head. Carmen was an unpaid carer.

'We all deserve a good life and to fulfil our dreams.' Fran nodded. 'Just look at us – we always dreamed of owning a fancy restaurant and *our* dreams have come true.'

Sid grinned. 'Aye, we've come a long way from selling candyfloss on the Golden Mile in Blackpool.'

'Folk flock from all over the north to dine with us, and our waiting list is long.'

'Who would ever have imagined it?' Sid chuckled.

'I know it's none of my business,' Fran lowered her voice, 'but Carmen needs time to fulfil her passion and write more novels, and I think she could use a friend or two.'

Sid pushed his empty plate away. His wife was kind and had a heart of gold. 'Perhaps this cruise will sort things out for her,' he said.

'I do hope so.'

'Isn't that Dicky Delaney?' Sid turned his head and pointed to a man standing by the coffee machine, programming a double espresso.

'Aye, he looks a bit rough this morning. He must have had a late night.' Fran watched Dicky as he drank his coffee. A tall man joined him, and they lowered their heads, deep in conversation.

'I think that's Theo McCarthy,' Fran said and leaned forward to get a better look.

'My goodness, I do believe it is!' Excited, Sid sat up.

Admiring Theo's dark skin and well-groomed salt and

pepper hair, Fran said, 'He's still a handsome man, despite the extra bit of weight that he carries these days.'

Sid knew that his idol, the Irish chef Theo McCarthy, was a guest speaker on the ship and one of the reasons Sid had looked forward to the cruise. For years, Sid had been enamoured with the lives of celebrity chefs who entertained the masses. It was the reason he'd sent Fran off to a cookery school in France to learn fancy skills. Under the watchful eye of a Michelin-starred chef, she'd enriched her cooking and transformed her endeavours, ultimately leading to their own culinary awards and accolades.

'He looks like he's been burning the candle at both ends, too,' Fran commented.

'The man's a legend.' Sid sighed.

'Didn't you tell me that Theo had recently lost his partner?' Fran's tone was one of concern.

'It was over a year ago, Fran, keep up,' Sid said. 'It was in all the papers, Ruari was an actor in one of the TV soaps. He was the love of Theo's life, and they say the chef hasn't recovered.'

'Lost his restaurant not long after, if I remember,' Fran said.

'Closed it down,' Sid corrected. 'But I'm relieved to see that he's taking gigs like this and hope his sadness is lifting.'

Fran's heart went out to Theo. Losing a partner must be one of life's cruellest blows, and she couldn't imagine being without Sid. They'd been together since they were teenagers, and despite never being blessed with the babies they longed for, she prayed there were many more years to romp happily down the road to the later years of their lives.

'I can't wait to hear his talk,' Sid said as he watched Theo and Dicky leave the café, engrossed in conversation. 'I've followed every episode of *McCarthy's Kitchen Adventures* over the years.'

The show was a nationwide hit and captivated audiences as the chef travelled globally. Fans followed his escapades and passion for great ingredients and fine wines. Theo McCarthy was known for his decadent 'slurps' both on and off-screen.

'Well, you won't have long to wait,' Fran said as she gathered her things, 'we've got a sea day in a couple of days when he's sure to be on stage.'

* * *

Dicky and Theo moved through the ship until they came to the library. The pair had met at the purser's welcome gathering when they'd joined the ship in Kefalonia, and now chose a quiet spot by the window. There wasn't a soul to be seen, and the ship was almost deserted as passengers, keen to go ashore, headed off to discover the delights of the island of Rhodes.

Taking a seat, Theo rubbed his fingers through his tightly curled hair and began to massage his scalp. 'Will you be off on a jaunt today?' he asked.

'I need some fresh air. It's like a cell in my cabin,' Dicky replied and wiped his brow. He thought of the relentless hum of engines that vibrated through the wall as he returned to his bed in the early hours that morning.

'I need to clear my head too,' Theo blinked.

'That was some party . . .'

'It wasn't what I expected, that's for sure.'

'What were you expecting?' Dicky turned to look at Theo.

'I have no idea. I'd had one too many cocktails during the day, and I stumbled across the cabin when an American chap opened the door and invited me in.'

'Ah, so you hadn't noticed the universal sign?'

'Not a clue, but I shall never look at a pineapple in quite the same way again.'

'On a cruise ship, if you see a pineapple sign hung upside down on a cabin door, you know you're in the right place.' Dicky grinned.

'Or, in my case, the wrong place.' Theo shook his head. 'I know that pineapples have a history of being a sign of wealth and hospitality, even good fortune, but I'd no idea they had a seductive association. It was my misfortune to stumble into the most unusual scene I've witnessed in years, and I've travelled the world,' Theo added, and remembered his discomfort . . .

Navigating the dimly lit atmosphere, Theo, clearly the worst for wear, had entered Colin and Neeta's suite. Instead of finding guests engaged in polite conversation and passing pleasantries, Theo's eyes popped when he realised that he was considerably overdressed in chinos and a shirt as everyone in the suite was almost naked.

A tall, well-built man with a paunch and a Yorkshire accent introduced a rotund, reticent woman whose acres of wobbling pink flesh reminded Theo of his grandmother's blancmange.

'Ey up,' the man had said, 'are you a vanilla?'

Theo hadn't a clue what was meant and wondered if he was about to be offered an ice cream. As he'd quickly turned away from the Yorkshire couple, Neeta's nubile body pressed against him.

'Welcome to the Upside-Down Pineapple Pensioner Club,' she trilled, taking Theo's hand and stroking his wrist. 'Or UDPPC as we like to call it. Colin and I are the founders of this exclusive club. Why don't you join in the fun?' Leading Theo towards another room, she reached out to unbutton his shirt.

As he tried to unscramble the scene before him, Theo wondered if he was hallucinating. Had his drink been spiked? Geriatrics in all their glory rolled around on a king-sized bed, and Theo recognised a quiff of black hair. Was that Dicky Delaney buried beneath a mound of bodies and bumps?

'We're oldies but naughties,' Neeta whispered, reaching for his belt.

Theo's eyes were wide as a woman made a beeline towards him. She wore nothing more than a diamond necklace and leaned heavily on a walking aid. Without pausing to witness any more elderly exposé, Theo, suddenly sober, had backed away.

Now, Theo watched Dicky, who yawned and stared out of the window.

'There was no mention of this sort of carry-on at the purser's welcome gathering for the entertainment team,' Theo said. 'Is it a regular thing?'

'Peter is hardly going to flag up the fact that his more able-bodied guests might be enjoying a later-life-lifestyle.' Dicky grinned. 'In fact, he panics when people like Colin and Neeta board his ship. It usually ends up with the medical facility being overloaded.'

'What do you mean?' Theo was puzzled.

'Use your imagination. Divorce, widowhood, and the need to spice up a relationship that's been stale for decades carries a risk.' Dicky smirked. 'But after a couple of Athenian Mules, inhibitions go out of port hole windows, creating more STDs than the UK's postal codes. Carpet burns, bingo-wing bruises, and the "knee-pain swagger" all form a lengthy queue for the nurse in the sober light of day.'

'Good heavens . . .' Theo shook his head.

'And, of course, there are the claims,' Dicky added.

'Claims?'

'Yesterday I heard that an elderly chap accosted Peter demanding compensation for slipping on the bathmat in Colin and Neeta's suite while engaged in . . . Well, think about it – he wasn't scrubbing his teeth.' Dicky paused. 'With a twisted hip, bruised nose and two black eyes, he's demanding that the Diamond Star Line compensate him.'

'Who'd have thought . . .' Theo looked wistful. 'Not what Christopher Columbus had in mind when he returned from the Lesser Antilles and introduced pineapples to Europe.'

Dicky smiled. 'And now, you too are officially a member of the UDPPC, whose motto is, "Engage first, regret later."'

'It's an organisation that I shall be swerving in future,' Theo replied, 'but I take it you're fully paid up?'

'Oh, I like to have an occasional dabble. It livens things

up a little,' Dicky said, 'and after several Athenian Mules, the partygoers appear twenty years younger.'

'They'd need to . . .' Theo mused.

'Of course, it might not be your scene.'

'No, certainly not. My relationship with a long-term partner was committed, and I never wanted to stray. Or swing both ways,' Theo added.

Dicky stretched out his arms and, yawning again, shook his head. His neatly arranged quiff quivered, and he combed it into place with his fingers. 'I need to crack on,' he said and stood up. 'There's a wealthy widow with my name on her day out, waiting for me to escort her.'

'Does Peter know?'

'He turns a blind eye.' Dicky shrugged. 'After all, guest relations are all about keeping the passengers happy.'

'So, you are providing a service?'

Dicky grinned lasciviously and rubbed his hands together. 'With a smile,' he said, 'you've got it in one.'

Chapter Fifteen

Stepping onto the firm ground, Fran and Sid were brimming with excitement as they disembarked from the ship. The morning sun was already casting its warm glow, and as Fran reached into her bag for her hat, Sid adjusted his cap to shield his eyes from the bright beams.

'Oh, look,' Fran called out and waved her hand, 'there's Carmen and her mum.'

Heading down the gangway, steering Betty's chair to avoid bumping into other passengers, Carmen, in crumpled shorts and a T-shirt, already appeared hot and bothered. Meanwhile, Betty was cool in a cream linen dress and straw bonnet, holding out her cane and threatening to poke anyone in her way.

'Cooee!' Fran jumped up and down, her yellow kaftan billowing like a balloon. 'Here we are, let Sid help,' she said as Sid stepped forward to relieve Carmen of the wheelchair.

'Be careful!' Betty snapped to Sid. 'My daughter has no sense of direction, and I'm lucky I'm not at the bottom of the sea.'

If only! Carmen thought and glanced at Fran, who winked with a playful smile.

'It's a short walk from the port into the old town of Rhodes. Shall we set off and see where we end up?' Fran asked. 'Sid has been reading a guidebook, so will point out things along the way.'

'That sounds lovely,' Carmen replied.

'Mind the cobblestones!' Betty yelled as they entered the narrow streets. 'My poor old back is playing up something awful.'

Fran linked her arm with Carmen's, and they began to stroll along, passing taxis and rental cars. 'Oh, just look at all those windmills!' Fran exclaimed and pointed to a long line of structures, their whitewashed walls standing majestically against a backdrop of brilliant blue. The large sail-like blades were still, and Sid, glancing at his book, explained that the windmills were reminiscent of the medieval period when they were used for grinding grain.

'It says here that some of the windmills have been converted into cafés,' Sid read aloud, 'and you can take in the view of the harbour while enjoying a drink.'

'I need a drink. My mouth is so parched I might faint.' Betty fanned her face.

'Sid, why don't you take Betty for refreshments while we pop into a couple of shops?' Fran smiled at her husband.

'All right, if that's what you'd like,' Sid said.

As Fran and Carmen set off, they heard Betty complaining about her aches and pains while Sid manoeuvred her away.

'Sid is a saint,' Carmen said, 'I don't know how to thank him.'

'He's one in a million,' Fran agreed, 'but don't worry, Sid loves wandering about old ruins and will ensure he has plenty of sightseeing.'

'Now he's in charge of an old ruin.' Carmen sighed. 'Mum never seems to let up.'

'Has it been a difficult morning?' Fran asked as they passed shops selling leather belts and bags.

'No worse than any other,' Carmen said. 'Betty is a law unto herself, and although I'm confident that she's perfectly capable of bathing and dressing, she has a way of manipulating me into doing everything for her.'

'Well, for the next few hours, you can relax and let someone else take over,' Fran reassured Carmen, sensing her need for a break. 'Time for a transformation.'

Carmen looked at Fran. She felt strangely comforted by the woman's warm arm, linked through her own, and the kind words that wrapped around her like a hug. Was this what having a friend felt like? The quiet thrill of knowing someone enjoyed her company. Carmen felt as though she was stepping onto unfamiliar ground. It was strange to be listened to by Fran and spoken to as an equal rather than a burden. Fran's kindness was a gentle tide, washing away years of isolation.

Carmen wondered why Fran was so generous with her time when she could have enjoyed Sid's company. But as she watched Fran head towards a quaint little shop, she decided to stop analysing everything, to do as Fran did, and live in the moment.

'Just look at these loofas!' Fran exclaimed as she stood beneath a rustic sign that invited passers-by to browse.

'Let's go in,' Carmen urged Fran forward.

They were greeted by the shop's earthy scent and the salty tang of the sea as they gazed at walls lined with shelves showcasing hundreds of natural sponges.

'What do you think they are made of?' Fran asked.

'They're an alternative to a synthetic sponge.' Carmen touched the coarse texture of a round object. 'I think they come from a gourd plant and soften when you get them wet. It's said that they promote circulation.'

'We all need some of that,' Fran said. She reached for an oval shape, beautifully packaged with a tag that explained the benefits. 'It's good for doing that escalating thingy . . .'

'I think you mean exfoliating.' Carmen grinned.

'In that case, we'll have one each.' Fran paid for her purchase and handed a package to Carmen. 'There's nothing like a good scrub to clear away the cobwebs.'

Accepting that Fran might be aware of Carmen's many complicated cobwebs, Carmen thanked Fran and tucked the gift in her rucksack.

Back in the bright sunshine, they walked past the ruin of a church until they came to a small parade of boutiques, where Carmen hesitated. 'I'm not sure if I feel like shopping for clothes today,' she said. With all her time taken up by Betty that morning, she'd not given a thought to her own outfit. Beneath her tired old shorts and T-shirt, Carmen wore an ancient bra and shabby knickers, and the humiliation of removing her clothes in front of others was causing her anxiety.

As though sensing this, Fran was firm. 'Now, let's have none of that talk,' she said. 'It's a little bit of "me-time" for you my dear, and I'll be looking after you all the way.' Without waiting for Carmen to argue, Fran guided her forcefully towards the shops.

* * *

Ruskin enjoyed wandering around the old town of Rhodes. There was much to see, and he felt like he'd stepped back in time as he inspected the ornate iron gates and inns where, during the Crusades, Knights had stopped off on their way to the Holy Land. Following the cobbled streets to the Palace of the Grand Master, he'd been impressed by the medieval castle, learning that it had been built in the fourteenth century by the Knights of St John. With tall towers and fortified walls, Ruskin was taken by the many beautiful mosaics, especially a central panel depicting a leopard.

Now, Ruskin sat in a café named Socrates Garden. He sipped a glass of chilled wine and dipped a slice of warm pitta into a bowl of tzatziki, his open notebook on the table beside him. How would Detective Inspector Blake enjoy these winding streets and hidden gardens where many a mystery might be uncovered? Ruskin's mind raced, and picking up his pen, he began to make notes.

Suddenly, a commotion at the next table caused Ruskin to look up.

Sitting in a wheelchair, a woman insisted that a place be found beside an ornamental waterfall. Waiting staff busied around, moving tables and chairs to accommodate the noisy old lady. The man at her side thanked them and took a seat.

Ruskin sighed. Probably cruise passengers, he thought. In

his opinion, some of the guests were pampered and spoiled, expecting everyone to bow to their demands.

Moments later, the couple were joined by a tall man and his partner, wearing matching polo shirts, Tilley hats and shorts. Ruskin heard the man say, 'Ey up!' as he sat down.

Ruskin sipped his wine, his thoughts returning to his detective.

'Let me buy you a drink,' a voice called out and Ruskin looked up to see Theo McCarthy towering over him. 'That is if you're tired of Alexander the Great, Hercules and the Persian Dynasty,' Theo added. 'Rhodes is full of history for your sleuthing mind.'

'I'll have a glass of this fine wine,' Ruskin said, holding out his glass, 'thank you.'

Theo sat down and ordered a carafe, then turning to Ruskin asked, 'Are you on your own on this cruise?'

'Yes, is there something wrong with that?'

'Not at all, I'm alone too.'

Ruskin sniffed. 'I'm very much single, having recently divorced and in no need of romantic liaisons, and in case you are wondering, I'm straight.'

'I wasn't, but don't worry, I'm not trying to pick you up.'

Nearby, two women appeared, laden with shopping. 'This is nice,' Ruskin heard one announce. 'Look who's here,' she continued, 'fancy meeting up with Don and Debbie, and if I'm not mistaken, that's the famous Mr Ruskin at the next table.'

Ruskin watched them deposit multiple bags.

'Why don't we all sit together,' the woman said and, with a wide grin, waved at a waiter who soon rearranged chairs, grouping them around the tables.

'Oh, Lord . . .' Ruskin heaved a sigh. The last thing he wanted to do was make conversation, and to his horror, the dowdy bespectacled woman, in crumpled clothes, who kept appearing like a bad penny, was being placed on a seat beside him. She appeared to know Theo and smiled at him as she sat down.

Ruskin drained his glass and closed his notebook. His peaceful day had ended. When his phone began to ring, he felt relieved and staring at the screen, saw that it was Venetia. Ruskin was reluctant to speak to his ex-wife but knew that their conversation would distract him from the café crashers surrounding his table.

Replenishing his glass, Ruskin took the call.

Fran eyed Theo McCarthy sitting with Ruskin Reeve, and having arranged seating next to him, was determined to seize her opportunity and speak to the celebrated chef.

'Mr McCarthy,' she began, 'we're thrilled you're on the cruise. My Sid here thinks you are amazing.' She grabbed Sid's hand and forced him to his feet. 'He's watched all your shows repeatedly and has collected all your cookery books.'

'Please, call me Theo. I'm honoured that you've enjoyed my work.' Theo reached out to shake Sid's hand. 'As it's my round, why don't you let me buy you all a drink?'

'Mine's a Santorini Sunset!' Betty piped up.

Theo took note of their drinks and advised the waiter.

'Cheers!' they all said, chinking glasses when their drinks arrived.

Fran smiled as she watched everyone begin to chat. Sid had removed his cap and twisted it nervously between his fingers. Speaking rapidly, he told Theo how he'd admired him for years and followed his career closely, while Don and Debbie described the delights of Mandraki Harbour to Carmen. Reading from a guidebook, Don explained that the Colossus of Rhodes, one of the Seven Wonders of the Ancient World, had stood at the entrance, then he droned on about their visit to the Fort of St Nicholas, explaining at length that it was built in the fifteenth century to protect the island from attacks by the Ottomans.

Fran sipped a mocktail and turned to see Carmen beside Ruskin. Sitting rigid with nerves, Carmen bit on her lip and twisted a ring on her finger, clearly uncomfortable in the author's company.

Ruskin, meanwhile, ignored Carmen and talked rapidly on his phone.

Whoever had made the call was in receipt of a telling-off. Ruskin's face turned red with obvious frustration as he struggled to keep his voice down, draining his glass and drumming his fingers. Fran thought that he looked as though he'd sooner be somewhere else. She wondered if Ruskin would be so rude if a well turned-out woman sat beside him? He hadn't noticed unfashionable Carmen nor passed a civil word.

Fran had enjoyed finding gorgeous outfits for Carmen, who, after her initial hesitation, soon got into the swing of things and swiped her credit card so hard that Fran thought it was probably on life support after the lavish spending spree. She'd purchased everything from gorgeous lingerie to daywear and glamorous evening dresses, but now, the carefree Carmen, with her lets-cripple-the-credit-card mindset, was back in her shell, obviously intimidated by the man beside her.

Fran nodded as she thought of the many outfits she'd persuaded Carmen to buy. At that moment, Carmen might look like a dusty old book, sitting silently on her shelf, but once revamped, Fran was confident that Carmen's story would emerge in glorious technicolour. She remembered the transformation as Carmen modelled the beautiful clothes. Beneath her drab and misshapen clothing, Carmen had a lovely figure and wore everything perfectly that Fran and a multitude of assistants had chosen.

Glancing at her watch, Fran realised that if they left soon, there was time for Carmen to have a couple of hours in the onboard beauty salon too.

She looked around at the group and wondered where the couple who liked pineapples were. Fran had chatted to them while shopping, when they'd met in a boutique. 'Has anyone seen Colin and Neeta?' she asked.

Theo was enjoying his conversation with Sid. It was cheering to be told you were someone's hero, and Sid seemed like a sincere bloke. Theo was fascinated to hear that Sid had a fine dining restaurant in Blackpool with his wife, and Theo nodded his approval. If the couple had conquered northwest England with their culinary skills, they must be good. They chatted about the crowded restaurant scene and Theo rubbed his wrist, his fingers searching for the comfort of Ruari's cuff bracelet, welcoming the smooth gold band that would warm to his touch.

But to his horror, the bracelet had gone!

For a split second, Theo was sure it was a trick of his imagination. Disbelief washed over him, and his heart missed a beat as he blindly ran his fingers up and down his arm. Scanning the floor, he hoped to see a flash of gold where the bracelet had fallen.

'Are you all right?' Sid asked. He noticed that perspiration had formed on Theo's brow, and he was fumbling about beneath the table. 'Have you lost something?'

'M . . . my bracelet,' Theo stammered.

'What does it look like?' Sid dropped to his knees.

'It's a cuff-like bracelet, gold and narrow.'

Theo stood as panic hit him like a punch. He wondered if he'd lost it as he wandered through Rhodes. Patting his pockets, he was relieved to find his wallet. If it was a thief, at least his cards and euros were safe.

'I hope it's not the cuff that Ruari gave you?' Carmen joined the search, her expression almost as anxious as Theo's.

'Yes, it's irreplaceable, so many memories, it's s . . . so . . . sentimental.' Theo looked as though he was about to burst into tears.

'I'll help you,' Carmen announced. 'Shall we retrace your steps?'

'That's a good idea,' Sid agreed, 'leave all your bags with Fran and me, and we'll follow on.'

'It'll be in the safe in your cabin,' Don joined in. Guzzling a cold beer, he added, 'You're as daft as Debbie. She's always misplacing her valuables.'

Unaware that Debbie had swung a size eight trainer into Don's shin, Theo was too upset to respond. His mind was a whirl. When did the cuff slip off? Or, worst-case scenario, had it fallen into the sea when he leaned on the rail of his balcony watching dawn rise over the island? Taking Carmen's arm, he set off as behind them, Sid piled a mound of bags onto Betty's wheelchair.

'Don't worry about me!' Betty's muffled voice could be heard.

'Rest assured, they won't,' Sid replied as Fran hooked more bags on the handles, and releasing the brake on Betty's chair, Sid set off.

Ruskin ended his call and, ordering more wine, shook his aching head. Venetia was like a shadow that refused to fade, lingering in the corners of his life. Her relentless obsession with him was so demanding, and she didn't seem to understand that their divorce was a reality, despite the papers being long signed and their lives severed.

And now . . . all this commotion over a bracelet!

Really! he thought. Panic over a piece of jewellery that probably had no value. But as he sipped his wine and watched Theo and the others leave the café, Ruskin breathed a sigh of relief. At least he didn't have to converse with the dowdy woman, who'd deliberately sat beside him.

Chapter Sixteen

Dicky was in his dressing room. He sat in front of a large mirror where soft lights lined the metallic frame, designed to eliminate shadows and allow the artist a clear view from all angles. Every wrinkle and flaw stood out no matter how he turned from side to side or tilted his head.

Dicky shrugged. After a sleepless night and a full day entertaining the wealthy widow, he'd need more than a layer of concealer to ready himself for the evening performance. He poked about on Melody's side of the table, picking up a Kryolan paint stick and a tube of MAC cosmetics.

'Dermacolor Camouflage System,' Dicky read from the side of the tube. 'That'll do nicely,' he muttered, squeezing a hefty measure onto his fingers.

Smoothing it into his skin, he was pleased to see his lines fade. He knew this expensive product withstood harsh stage lights, and adding a touch of Studio Fix Foundation beneath each eye, sat back to re-examine his skin. *Perfect!* He was camera-ready and looked at least ten years younger.

Dicky was about to replace the caps on the tubes when the

door burst open, and Melody strode in. She wore an emerald-green, shimmering silk cocktail dress with a glamorous auburn wig. Her complexion was as flawless as her figure.

Spreading his fingers, Dicky hastily covered the tubes.

'No wonder they call you Tricky Dicky,' Melody said as she stared at Dicky's reflection, 'you've got GUILT written all over your face.'

'I don't know what you mean,' Dicky shrugged.

'Your foundation can be seen from space,' she added, 'there's more life in Madame Tussauds. Surely, you're not going on stage like that?'

Dicky scowled and, taking a tissue, leaned into the mirror to dab at his face. Close-up, he had to agree. Perhaps he did look a little waxy.

Melody spied her tubes and, stepping out of her heels, held out her hand. 'Thief!' she growled, her voice growing deeper and fingers clenching into a fist.

'Oh, are these yours?' Dicky said, replacing the caps. 'They were on my side, and I thought I'd left them here earlier.'

'Yeah, likely story.' Melody pushed her chair to the end of the table and sat down. 'If I ever see you stealing my gear again, I'll make sure you're incapable of walking out on stage.'

As Melody removed her makeup, the sculpted chin and cheekbones slowly disappeared, revealing a layer of faint stubble. Her lips, no longer ruby red, lost their fullness and pulled tight like a washing line. She dabbed at her eyes with cleanser to remove the vibrant eyeshadow and reveal real eyes beneath. They stared at Dicky with menace.

Dicky thought Melody looked more like a prize fighter than a glamorous drag artist, and he didn't fancy a bout in her ring. He decided to drop the cutting quips, do what he was good at, and shower her with compliments.

Knowing Melody had been singing in the piano bar, he began, 'I hear there was standing room only for your performance. My spies tell me you were brilliant and had the audience eating out of your hand.'

Melody eyed Dicky suspiciously.

'In fact, one or two were overheard to say you are the best female vocal they've ever heard.'

Melody stood. She unzipped her dress and placed it on a hanger. 'Cut the crap, Dicky,' she said and, reaching for her robe, disappeared into the bathroom.

Shaking his head, Dicky gesticulated as the door closed. At a loss to understand why Melody disliked him, he decided there was no time to flatter her further. He would shortly be on stage. Swiping a stick of Melody's blusher, he dabbed at his cheeks again.

Nothing was going to quell his enthusiasm tonight.

He'd had a great day with the widow, and they'd stopped off at a jeweller in Rhodes Old Town, where she insisted on gifting Dicky an expensive chunky gold chain. He'd also privately sold many copies of his book in generous cash deals that he sealed with a smile, signing each one to the captivated guest, who would head home with tales of *personally knowing* the onboard entertainer.

He removed the towel protecting his brilliant white shirt and tossed it to one side. Standing, Dicky reached for his evening jacket, and straightening the lapels, smiled at his reflection and whispered, 'Showtime!'

* * *

Carmen was in her cabin. To her dismay, Betty insisted they have a lighter dinner in the Deck Café, where a buffet was served. Despite complaining of an upset stomach from an ice cream she'd eaten when visiting the windmills with Sid, Betty had polished off two plates of food and a cheesecake dessert. Back in her cabin after their meal, Betty feigned tiredness. But Carmen suspected that the moment she prepared Betty for bed and left her upright surrounded by cushions, the TV would be on, and a box of chocolates whipped out from beneath the covers. Betty would be channel hopping all night in a fluffy pink bedjacket and matching nightie, with her hair netted in place.

'She's like Barbara Cartland,' Carmen muttered as she paced around her cabin, 'lying in bed, scoffing chocolates while dictating her orders to the world.'

Carmen stared at her laptop and with a shrug, pushed it to one side. Writing was the last thing on her mind, and she wasn't sure what to do. Now, having missed dinner with Fran and Sid, she didn't feel like heading out to a show alone.

When they'd arrived back on the ship after their visit to Rhodes, Fran had whisked Carmen away to the onboard stylist, while Sid took Betty to the library where the Golden Oldies Gang had grouped for a game of pre-dinner Lingo-Livener. The oldies enjoyed a livener as the host used cruise-related phrases for the Lingo. Betty, grinning with delight, had romped through her card to win a giant box of chocolates.

Now Carmen sat before a mirror and stared, wide-eyed with disbelief at her reflection. In the onboard salon, at Fran's insistence, a beautician had given Carmen a makeover and the makeup she'd applied was subtle yet transforming. A hint of colour to her cheeks, soft eyeshadow and mascara made her eyes appear larger and peachy lipstick flattered Carmen's smile. The whole new look surprised her.

With Fran's encouragement Carmen had allowed a stylist to cut subtle layers into her hair that gave movement and body. Turning to study each side, she realised that this cleverly highlighted her cheekbones and brightened her complexion. A curling wand created soft waves, and a caramel-coloured rinse added depth. The stylist assured Carmen that she'd left enough length to sweep the hair into an up-style for formal occasions, and as light from an overhead lamp shone down, Carmen reached up to touch her face, reassuring herself that the image was real. She could hardly believe the revamped version of herself.

'Wow!' Carmen whispered as she took it all in. The dowdy look she was used to had melted away and she couldn't deny that an attractive face stared back.

Betty had told Carmen that she looked like an attention seeker. 'Your new hairdo makes you look desperate,' Betty sneered. 'You look like a buffoon with all that gunk on your face. I suggest you go to your cabin and wash it all off.'

Carmen pushed back her chair and stood up. She remembered Betty's words and felt determined to defy them. 'It's no use sitting here, twiddling my thumbs or staring at a blank page.'

Without time to change her mind, Carmen went to her wardrobe and stared at all the purchases she'd made that day. She hadn't a clue what to wear or where to go, knowing that she'd missed dinner in the Terrace Restaurant and the start of the show in the Neptune Theatre, but she felt confident that plenty was going on elsewhere in the ship.

'Goodness me,' Carmen whispered when she stood before a mirror, thirty minutes later.

As she'd dressed, Carmen had opened a half bottle of champagne, and now, twirling before the mirror in an off-the-shoulder, silky maxi dress, she was delighted with how she looked. Gone were her heavy-rimmed glasses, and without Betty nagging her to hurry along, Carmen had had time to insert her contact lenses. The delicate coral-coloured fabric of the dress was flattering and flowed elegantly to mid-calf. Fran had found a pair of gold hoop earrings and strappy sandals, and Carmen had to admit that the outfit was sensational.

She drained her glass and picked up a small gold clutch. As she dimmed the lights, the sound of a stick banging against the wall came from the room next door.

'Carmen!' Betty yelled. 'Are you awake? Come and make my cocoa.'

Pausing, Carmen felt a wave of guilt and was about to head to Betty's room when an invisible hand reached out to stop her. As though whispering from above and waving a heavenly wand, a ghostly voice said, 'Slip away, Cinderella!'

Within seconds, Carmen closed her door and set off.

Chapter Seventeen

Ruskin sat in a plush armchair in a softly lit corner of the bar. He was dressed in a well-tailored shirt, slightly undone at the collar, and paired with crisp navy trousers and soft suede shoes. He held a glass of his favourite malt and watched guests dressed for the evening, head to the casino or the late evening show.

Melody Moon had performed earlier, captivating the intimate crowd. Standing beside the baby grand, Melody wore an emerald green dress that shimmered in the low light as she moved to the music. Beyond large windows, the sea was a soothing backdrop, reflected in the moonlight as the *Diamond Star* sailed on. Ruskin enjoyed Melody's warm voice, full of emotion, and her setlist included a mix of sultry ballads and the occasional upbeat song. Now, drumming his fingers lightly on the arm of his chair, Ruskin decided that he was enjoying being at sea. Cruising life suited him.

Far away from his agent's daily calls and distant from Venetia, Ruskin was beginning to relax. His outline notes and research were taking shape, and he felt that he was on to something. Locating Detective Inspector Blake in a Mediterranean destination would bring a different dimension to the next book, and with a full day tomorrow, Ruskin planned to explore when they arrived in Crete, before prepping for his workshops.

At an adjacent table, a group of people were laughing as stories of their day unfolded. Ruskin recognised a couple he'd considered later-in-life honeymooners when they boarded the ship. The woman wore a smart, well-cut pineapple-patterned sleeveless dress with a plunging neckline that showed off more than her deep tan. He thought of Venetia, who loved the sun too, but Venetia always wore the strangest combination of bohemian clothes, unlike the woman at the next table.

Ruskin was content to soak up the sound of the piano and the energy of those around him and didn't at first notice a woman standing at the entrance to the bar. When a server moved swiftly forward to assist, Ruskin looked up to see her search the crowded room for a seat. Taking to his feet, he called out, 'There's a seat here.'

He noted that she was dressed in a sophisticated coral-coloured dress and her hair was perfectly styled, the caramel highlights caught the light as she moved. She appeared to be alone, and as he was keen for conversation, Ruskin hoped she'd accept his invitation.

Carmen was hesitant as she stepped into the piano bar. Despite the champagne she'd drunk earlier which softened the edges and gave her confidence, she felt her nerves flutter.

Leaving her room, Carmen had wandered through the

ship. She decided that the library was like a morgue at that time of night and the coffee area full of dozing passengers, weary after the day's exertions and a heavy dinner. The Neptune Theatre was packed, and Dicky Delaney was on stage, but Carmen didn't want to make a show of herself by trying to find somewhere to sit. Nor did she fancy the film in the cinema, which was already halfway through. In the Mermaid Theatre, the floor was crowded with dancers. She hadn't set foot on a dance floor in years, and as Carmen watched the energetic couples, she felt her feet firmly anchored as they effortlessly glided by.

Now, as a server approached her, Carmen decided that the piano bar looked inviting, and she searched for a seat. But every table was occupied, and the thought of drawing attention to herself made her stomach tighten.

'Can I help you?' the server asked.

'There's a seat here,' a man called out.

To her alarm, Carmen realised that it was Ruskin. She was unsure what to do but had little choice as the server guided her through the tables and past the pianist, who was playing 'Fly Me To The Moon'.

Carmen wished she *could* fly to the moon and as far away as possible. Ruskin obviously hadn't recognised her, and the moment he realised who she was, he would be off like a shot. Her cheeks flushed as she searched for excuses. But as the server pulled out a chair, Carmen knew it was too late to bolt. She'd have to sit it out and wait for Ruskin to leave.

Oh, God, he looks so handsome! Carmen miserably thought. Why was she attracted to a man who'd treated her so poorly? She could smell Ruskin's leathery cologne, and for a moment, was intoxicated and unable to shake off her nerves. For years she'd been numb to any hint of romance and the last time she'd felt this way, Carmen had been young and full of dreams, believing love was something certain, that everyone enjoyed.

Sitting down hesitantly, she remembered her betrayal.

The man she'd once pictured as the father of her children, her childhood sweetheart, had shattered her illusions. He hadn't just left Carmen; he left her for a woman who took the place Carmen had always believed was hers. Worse still, the woman was married. It had been a scandal, the kind that Butterly thrived on. Whispers in the hairdressers, pitying glances at the post office. Carmen could still remember the day Betty told her that she'd heard the news over the counter in their hardware shop, when a customer leaned in to mutter, *'Did you hear? Your Carmen's boyfriend has gone off with her!'*

That was when Carmen decided that love wasn't worth the risk. Not when the pain of losing it was so consuming. She accepted her life. The dream of a husband and family faded in the years that followed as Betty had dismissed any possible suitors, scaring them away, and ultimately Carmen had given up.

Now, as she looked around, bursts of laughter and lively conversation heightened her isolation and the butterflies in Carmen's stomach were relentless. She wished she'd stayed in her room. Cocoa and the remains of Betty's chocolates suddenly seemed appealing.

'Delighted to meet you,' Ruskin said. 'I'm Ruskin Reeve.'

'Carmen,' she replied, feeling tongue-tied.

'Let me get you a drink, please, what will you have?'

'Champagne,' Carmen blurted. The moment she spoke, she regretted it. *For heaven's sake!* she panicked. Who did she think she was, ordering such an expensive drink.

But Ruskin was unperturbed. 'What a good idea. I think I'll join you,' and he gave the server their order.

Moments later, a bottle sat in a cooler beside them, and Carmen held a chilled flute in her hand.

'Are you enjoying the cruise?' Ruskin began.

Carmen took a gulp of her drink. 'Yes, I'm having a lovely time,' she said.

'What's been the best part so far?'

She was about to confess to listening to his talk, then hurrying to her laptop to start writing, but for some reason, Carmen hesitated. 'I particularly enjoyed the day in Maxos,' she said, 'such a quaint village a charming place to visit.'

'I quite agree,' Ruskin smiled, 'there is so much history there. Did you know that Aristotle spent time in the region, which at that time was a centre of culture and philosophy?'

Carmen realised that Ruskin had no memory of sitting beside her on the bench where the old man sold his honey.

'I know that the Venetians took control in the fifteenth century,' she said, taking another drink, 'and I was interested to see remains of many of their buildings, but most of the structures were lost during the earthquake of 1953.'

'Yes, that's true, it was devastating,' Ruskin nodded, 'but thank goodness the village was rebuilt and is now a tourist destination, providing employment.'

'I'm sure the locals will be pleased when the season ends and the cruise ships sail away,' Carmen said with a tense smile. She held out her empty glass as Ruskin topped it up.

Could he really have no memory of their brief conversation on the bench? Did a new hairstyle and outfit create a creature Ruskin didn't recognise? Or had the impression she'd left been so fleeting he'd cast it aside? Clearly, Ruskin didn't remember Carmen from the pool either when he'd briefly stopped to speak to Theo.

'Did you visit the fort?' Ruskin asked.

'Unfortunately, no, but others from our party climbed the steep path and said how wonderful the view was.'

'It was built to protect the village from pirates and invaders.'

'It's not stopping invaders today – thousands of tourists must visit during summer.' Carmen felt Ruskin's eyes watching her closely.

Oh, Lord! Should she finish her drink and make her excuses? Carmen was sure he had no idea who he was talking to, but the moment he did, their conversation would end. Ruskin wouldn't want anything to do with the silly woman in the frumpy clothes, who wandered about pushing her nagging mother in a wheelchair.

'Would you like Maxos to be tourist-free?' Ruskin asked.

'Perhaps I would. I can't imagine a more perfect place to live and work.'

Carmen remembered the gorgeous three-storey villa she'd noticed near the horseshoe-shaped beach. Villa Galini. Galini meant tranquillity and the villa would be her dream home.

'Work?' Ruskin raised an eyebrow. 'What is it that you do?'

Carmen blinked. Rats! She hadn't meant to blurt that out. Now she'd have to explain herself, and her cover, rapidly melting like ice, would be blown.

'Oh, this and that.'

Carmen took a long sip of the champagne. She felt Ruskin's piercing blue eyes bore into her. As the butterflies in her stomach danced wildly, she looked around, praying for a diversion. What was happening to her, was it the champagne? Each tilt of Ruskin's head or even the way he held his drink seemed to pull her in deeper, igniting a spark she never knew she had. She'd come on the cruise to be inspired, not to fall for a man who had no interest in her.

To her relief, Carmen saw Theo come into the bar. He perched near the piano and ordered a cocktail. *Now's your chance!* Carmen thought and finishing her drink, she rose unsteadily.

'Thank you for the champagne,' Carmen said. She felt like Cinderella as the clock struck twelve. 'But there's someone I need to speak to. Please excuse me.'

With as much confidence as she could muster, Carmen gripped her clutch to her chest and trying not to wobble, quickly walked away. As she moved through the crowded tables, she realised guests were clapping along to the song the pianist was playing. Some were singing 'I want to break free!'

Carmen remembered the Queen number.

If only I could *break free* . . . she thought, and taking a deep breath, Carmen approached Theo.

He was staring at a half-empty glass of Santorini Sunrise when Carmen appeared alongside. 'Would you mind if I joined you?' she asked.

Hoping that Ruskin wasn't watching, Carmen was desperate to talk to someone, and Theo seemed the ideal confidante. She saw the surprise on Theo's face when he turned.

'Well, yes, but a beautiful woman shouldn't build her hopes up,' he said. 'I'm as gay as a rainbow at a pride parade.'

'Perfect,' Carmen said, 'you're exactly what I need.'

'I'm sorry?' Theo looked bemused.

Carmen touched his arm and leaned in close. 'Theo, it's me, Carmen,' she said.

Theo looked at his drink and then back at Carmen. 'Jaysus,' he said, 'what have you done?'

Carmen felt slighted but Theo shook his head before she had time to say anything.

'Hell, I'm sorry. I didn't mean that you don't look okay . . . I mean, well, I was just shocked.'

'What do you mean?'

'You look bloody amazing, and I didn't recognise you.'

'Oh, I see. Well, Fran insisted that I had a makeover.'

'Fran is to be congratulated. You're absolutely gorgeous, my darling.' He grinned. 'Not that you weren't before, well, just a little, er . . .'

'Dull.'

'If you say so.'

'Dowdy.'

'Perhaps . . .'

'I need your help.'

'Anything. Shoot.'

'Ruskin Reeve is in the corner, and he doesn't recognise me. He was being nice to me, and I've been drinking champagne, and . . .'

'You're feeling confused and tipsy and need to discuss the awkward situation,' Theo interrupted.

'Exactly.'

'Ah, then it's down to your friend Theo to whisk you away, and the casino is the perfect place for Caterpillar Carmen.'

'Caterpillar?'

'You've metamorphosised into a beautiful butterfly.'

'Oh . . .' Carmen allowed Theo to take her arm and, without daring to take a backward glance at Ruskin, was led away.

* * *

Ruskin watched Carmen leave the bar on the arm of Theo McCarthy. He was confident that she hadn't a clue that Ruskin had realised who she was when she joined him and they began to chat, and he wondered what Carmen was up to. As an author of crime and mystery, it wasn't difficult for him to suss her out.

A real-life Cinderella, he thought and grinned.

Ruskin remembered the occasions when they'd met and wondered if Carmen had deliberately tracked him down to the bench by the beach in Maxos. Had she purposely run into him during his morning jog, or sat next to him in the

Socrates Café in Rhodes? But, he considered, the meeting with Theo by the pool was probably accidental. She'd told him she was a writer, and he wondered if she wanted to feed off his knowledge. Whatever it was it didn't explain her transformation or her sudden departure from his company.

How curious, he thought and decided that he'd keep a close eye on Carmen and get to the heart of the matter, if only to use her character in his novel.

But there was a worrying development.

Ruskin had spent thirty years with a woman whose wild, bohemian way had been attractive. Now, those days were gone, and after his official separation from Venetia, he wanted nothing more than to be on his own, with no romantic involvement. But tonight, he'd felt something stir, and that was because of Carmen.

The woman who'd sat opposite him in the bar was enchanting.

Ruskin wished she'd stayed longer. He'd watched her hazel eyes sparkle, and as the minutes passed, something shifted, and Ruskin found himself listening intently, absorbing every word. It was clear that Carmen longed for a place of solitude to live and work. Until now, he hadn't given her more than a moment of his time and he wondered why she'd chosen to appear so plain and dull in the daytime, blending into the background in frumpy clothes that made her easy to overlook.

Ruskin felt a pang of guilt. Was he only seeing her now because she'd shed her inconspicuous look? She'd walked into the bar with an effortless confidence, her appearance completely transformed, and the attraction was instant.

But this was ridiculous! The last thing Ruskin wanted was any attachment, no matter how fleeting a fling. It would be easy to engage in an affair, he told himself, a brief onboard interlude, but he'd vowed to have a period of solitude after the agonies of his divorce. To be female-free and focus on his work.

Ruskin poured the last of the champagne and thought of Venetia. Wild, carefree and more concerned with saving the planet than cooking a family meal, his wife had embodied an unconventional lifestyle, from her weird and eclectic clothing to her numerous projects, and for years, Ruskin had supported her.

But Venetia's Dandelion Project, which promoted biodiversity and absorbed a chunk of the advance royalties for Ruskin's last book, was a step too far for the Kensington community where they lived. The gated communal gardens, transformed into Venetia's Gardens of Wildlife and Weeds, had upset the residents, who expressed heated objections and demanded their neat and orderly borders and carefully curated topiary be returned immediately. Likewise, Venetia's *Wheels for Wishes* – pop-up art installations of decaying old bicycles – hardly gave Banksy a run for his money. Ruskin remembered the rusting bodies when they appeared entwined in vines with broken flowerpots hanging from their handlebars. The decrepit metal frames and chaotic positions were hazardous to the residents of the borough, where every pram is pushed by a perfectly uniformed nanny, while yummy mummies sip oat milk lattes and discuss designer handbags and shoes.

'But it's art!' Venetia had exclaimed as the press got hold

of the story, and Ruskin suffered intense embarrassment when Venetia was ordered by the council to take it all down.

Ruskin glanced at his watch, and as the pianist played his final tune for the evening, he decided to go to his suite. He'd have a nightcap and rid his mind of women. His notes needed contemplation as he planned Detective Inspector Blake's escapades while visiting Crete the following day.

Romance, Ruskin vowed as he left the bar, must be the last thing on his mind.

Chapter Eighteen

As dawn broke over the town of Agios Nikolaos on the island of Crete, a soft mysterious mist slowly rose over the turquoise waters of Mirabello Bay and sun-bleached buildings, many with blue-domed roofs, emerged in the morning light. Awnings of tavernas lining the street were a vibrant splash of colour, fluttering in a breeze that carried the rich scent of wild thyme across the decks of the *Diamond Star*, now docked at the harbour. The town was slowly waking, and fishermen wrestling with nets set sail as their boats chugged gently to the Aegean Sea.

Leaning on the railing of their balcony, Fran and Sid savoured the moment, as they stared at the craggy mountain summits, softened by the light and standing protectively beyond the town.

'It feels like the place is welcoming us,' Fran said, her silk kimono flapping in the warm wind as she watched the palm trees sway along the quay. 'As though it's inviting us to enjoy this special place.'

'I could get used to this life,' Sid nodded, 'there's something dreamlike about waking up to a different destination every day.'

'Exactly,' Fran agreed, 'cruising is so relaxing with no rush or stress.'

Sid placed his arm around Fran's shoulder. 'Standing on this balcony, soaking it all up, feels like time is slowing down.'

'Aren't we lucky . . .' Fran turned to Sid, her eyes softening. 'Some folk our age never experience anything like this,' she said. 'Growing older can feel like watching your life shrink, when health and mobility go . . . But here we both are, and fortunately fighting fit.'

Sid gazed at the mountains. 'Aye, seeing the remaining years grow shorter is a reality check. Makes you realise what's important before it all fades away.'

'You are what matters to me, my precious.' Fran smiled at Sid.

'Ah, my Blackpool Belle, as the song says, "You to me are everything."'

'Oh, now don't get all soppy.' Fran held Sid's face and pulled him into a tender kiss.

As the sun warmed their skin, the couple closed their eyes, lost in the moment's happiness. Coming up for air and pulling away, Sid said, 'This cruise has made all the hard graft at the restaurant worthwhile. We should do this every year.'

'For as long as we can,' Fran agreed as she sat down. 'So, what's the plan for today?'

Sid picked up the *Diamond Star Daily News*, which earlier, had been tucked under their cabin door. Adjusting his spectacles, he scanned the list of activities. 'Well,' he began, 'there's several excursions, including a trip to a local market selling artisan goods, wines and olive oil. We could have a wander and see what catches our eye.'

'I think I did my fair share of shopping yesterday,' Fran replied, thinking of the hours spent with Carmen as they revamped her entire wardrobe.

Sid lowered the paper. 'How about a stroll around Lake Voulismeni? It's in the heart of the town. We could brush up on the area's history, then stop for a coffee at one of the lakeside cafés.'

'That sounds more like it,' Fran agreed. She fished a bottle of pearly pink varnish from a pocket and, resting her foot on Sid's knee, began to paint her toenails.

'Or there's a museum or a monastery?'

'No thanks.'

'All right, you don't fancy those, but there's a boat trip to Spinalonga Island that includes a walking tour. It used to be a leper colony.'

Fran winced. 'Oh, those poor people,' she said softly, 'what a terrible disease. Thank goodness there's a cure now.'

'If you don't want to do that, we could always go to the beach and have a go at water sports,' Sid grinned. 'Do you fancy a spin on a jet-ski?'

'Now, that sounds like fun!' Fran sat back to admire her nails, 'I could top up my tan too.'

'I'd like to try snorkelling.' Sid was warming to the idea. 'I suggest we have breakfast before we set off.' He folded the *Diamond Star Daily News*. 'Pack your towel and tanning cream, and let's get cracking.'

'Another free excursion – I'm so glad we're members of The Cruise Club,' he said and as Fran stood, he reached out, playfully patting her behind.

Fran giggled and slapped Sid's hand. 'Behave yourself, Sidney Cartwright,' she grinned before disappearing into their room, her kimono fluttering behind her.

'Ah,' Sid smiled, 'one more day of sun, sea and adventure.'

* * *

Carmen woke with the mother of all hangovers, and when Betty rapped on the cabin wall with her walking cane, Carmen thought that her head was going to explode. Every thud felt like a sledgehammer pounding her skull, and she cursed the Corinth Cocktails that she'd consumed with Theo in the casino the evening before.

Carmen hoped that the noise might stop or that the floor beneath Betty's bed would dissolve and send her mother to the ocean's depths, but the banging was as relentless as her headache, and with a groan, Carmen had no choice but to get up.

A little while later, when Carmen and Betty were dressed, Betty ate breakfast in her room and soon began to complain. 'It's far too hot to be wandering around the streets of the town,' she said as she shovelled a hefty mouthful of eggs Royale. 'I'll get sunburn if you leave me in another café while you go off galivanting.'

Carmen, unable to face food, sipped a black coffee and watched her mother. A slither of hollandaise sauce dribbled down Betty's chin, and viper-like, Betty's tongue darted out before it reached her blouse. The bitterness of Carmen's coffee mirrored her feelings.

Why couldn't Betty have stayed at home in Butterly? Carmen felt a heavy invisible chain wrap around her, one that yanked her back to her mother every time she thought she might escape. Whenever she'd found an opportunity to free herself of her mother's ties, Carmen realised that she was beginning to enjoy herself.

Last night with Theo had been a hoot.

Theo had been adamant that they should have a few drinks in the casino, and before Carmen knew it, he was teaching her how to play roulette. To Carmen's astonishment, she won a considerable amount, and they'd ended the night by celebrating with more champagne.

As the server poured, Theo raised his glass with a grin. 'To Caterpillar Carmen,' he said, eyes twinkling. 'Tell me all about your chat with Ruskin.'

Carmen grimaced, 'Ruskin terrifies me.'

'But you sat together?'

'He invited me to share the table and hadn't a clue who I was.'

Theo's gaze swept over her. 'He must be enchanted by you,' he said, studying Carmen from top to toe. 'You look beautiful tonight.'

'Hardly, and I don't feel beautiful, I still think I'm frumpy old Carmen.' She flushed as she sipped the cold champagne, the bubbles tickling her throat. 'It's all Fran's doing, this sudden change in my appearance. She seems to have an eye for a makeover, clothes, hair – the whole lot.'

'She did a great job.' Theo wasn't surprised that Ruskin

hadn't recognised Carmen. He hadn't recognised her either. 'But with no disrespect,' Theo continued, 'I trust you won't return to your old wardrobe tomorrow.'

'Don't worry, I've bagged up my crappy gear and asked Fernando to dispose of it all.'

'Fernando?' Theo asked, his eyes distracted as Colin and Neeta entered the casino.

'The lovely steward who services my cabin,' she explained.

Theo shuddered as he heard Carmen's words.

'Are you all right?' Carmen asked.

'Yes, fine, fine,' Theo replied quickly, turning his back on the couple. Mentioning services in a cabin brought back haunting memories of the previous night in Colin and Neeta's suite. A party he'd rather forget. He began to chuckle and decided to share his thoughts. 'Have you heard of the UDPPC?'

'No, what's that?' Carmen looked puzzled.

'The Upside-Down Pineapple Pensioner Club.'

Carmen's eyes widened, 'Is it something to do with the Golden Oldies Gang?'

'Not really.' Theo shook his head and remembered the golden oldies he'd seen in the suite. 'It's a swingers club for mature people.'

'You mean . . .'

'Yes, swingers, or *the lifestyle* as they call it. Sex for the over-sixties with no holds barred.'

'Good heavens,' Carmen said, 'I do hope Betty hasn't heard of it.'

Theo threw back his head and laughed. 'It might do your mother some good,' he said, 'and put a smile on her face.'

'I think it would kill her or anyone who came close.'

'Don't be so sure. Betty could be quite the dominatrix with that silver-topped cane. Discipline, dominance, asserting authority. It's right up her street.'

'But how do *you* know about it?'

'Let's just say I stumbled into a party last night by mistake,' Theo explained. 'I thought my drink had been spiked.'

As Theo explained his predicament, Carmen began to laugh. 'I wonder if the ship's management knows about the UDPPC?'

'I'm sure Peter does, and he probably turns a blind eye.'

'Fancy,' Carmen began to smile, 'seniors being a little more adventurous in later life?'

'Knitting by day, naughty by night.'

'Wheelchairs and wild times . . .'

'Bingo with a twist – dabbers at the ready!'

Theo and Carmen giggled like schoolchildren sharing a rude joke, but both looked up when Dicky appeared in the casino. Standing in the doorway, he paused. When his eyes alighted on a lady at a corner table, he moved swiftly across the room.

'Crickey, her diamonds are brighter than the chandelier,' Carmen said as she watched Dicky slide into a seat beside the woman, then snap his fingers to summon a server.

Theo closed his eyes to block the memory of the woman wearing only a diamond necklace as she leaned heavily on a walking aid. Returning to safer ground, he said, 'Tell me what you were talking to Ruskin about, and why does he terrify you?'

Carmen shifted in her chair. 'Oh, it was nothing really,' she deflected the question. 'But why don't you tell me about your life as a celebrity chef?' she asked. 'When I was shopping with Fran, she told me that Sid idolises you and you're going to be a guest speaker.'

'Come to my talk and you'll be bored in no time.'

'Don't be daft, you'll be brilliant, and I want to hear all about your illustrious career. I also meant to ask if you found your bracelet?'

'No, sadly I didn't, and let's save my career for another day.' Theo waved the subject away. 'I'm more interested in you right now.'

Carmen wasn't sure if she should confide in Theo, but as she took another sip of champagne, she decided to give it a shot. They seemed to get along, and she desperately wanted to discuss her feelings. 'I admire Ruskin for his writing,' Carmen began, 'and he inspires me.'

'But you've still got writer's block?'

'After Ruskin's talk, I felt inspired to write and my writer's block lifted for a short while.'

Theo's gaze softened. 'But it's more than admiration, isn't it?'

Carmen bit her lip. 'I'm not sure.'

'Does your stomach flutter and your heart race when he's near?'

'Oh hell,' Carmen slumped. Theo had figured it out.

'Are you tongue-tied and unsure of what to say? Does the smell of his cologne intoxicate you?'

'All right, all right,' Carmen held up her hand. 'You've clearly been there.'

'Got the T-shirt.' Theo nodded. 'I had all those feelings every time Ruari stepped into a room or walked beside me.'

'But what am I to do? Ruskin would never look at someone like me, and if I'm honest, I'm not sure I'd want him to.'

'Why on earth not?'

'Because I am a plain Jane at heart, stuck with my mother in a time-warp of a house. My life is nothing like his.' Carmen's voice was quiet. 'It was all mapped out for me long ago, and writing is my only escape.' Carmen explained the betrayal by her childhood sweetheart that had destroyed her trust and shaped her life.

Theo reached out his hand to encircle Carmen's. 'It's never too late to change your life,' he said. 'Look at the change you've made in your appearance, was that so hard?'

Carmen shrugged. 'Surprisingly, no, it's as though meeting Fran was meant to be and I simply let her help me.'

'No matter what obstacles there are in life . . .' Theo's voice was warm and sincere. 'Love can surprise you. Even when you think it's out of reach. You can be the heroine of your own story if you allow yourself to be.'

She stared at Theo.

'The world is your oyster, Carmen; it's up to you to go out and find your pearl.'

'I'm so glad I met you,' she said, grateful for his kindness.

'Me too, my darling girl, can we be friends?'

'Absolutely. Can I have another drink, please?'

* * *

'CARMEN!' Betty screeched. 'Are you going to sit daydreaming all morning?' She pushed her empty plate to one side and wiped at her chin with a napkin.

Suddenly back in the real world with Betty, Carmen winced and sat up. Reaching out, she popped two painkillers and swallowed them down.

'We'll miss our excursion if you don't wake up, and I need my hat and bag. And don't think I want to be seen with you in that fancy get-up,' Betty added. Her eyes were icy as she stared at her daughter who was wearing a floaty jumpsuit with shoe-string straps. 'Mutton dressed as lamb; you look ridiculous.'

Carmen sighed. Earlier she'd endeavoured to replicate the beautician's makeup and had found her beautifully cut hair easy to style. Now, as she stood, she felt her resolve harden.

'Sorry, Mum,' Carmen said brightly and moved to collect Betty's things. 'I haven't time to change, and besides, I rather like what I'm wearing.' Carmen ran her fingers over the peach-coloured jumpsuit and marvelled at Fran's choice of daywear. It felt luxurious and cool, and she couldn't wait to show it off.

Betty's eyes narrowed, but Carmen busied herself. Moments later, she opened the door and pushed Betty into the corridor.

'I hope the sea is calm today,' Betty chuntered and held her cane aloft. 'A boat trip is a silly idea, but I'll have to go along with it.'

'It will be lovely, Mum,' Carmen said cheerfully.

Her headache, thankfully, had begun to lift and a few

minutes later, they prepared to disembark. She hadn't mentioned to Betty that the boat trip was to the island of Spinalonga – a place Carmen couldn't wait to visit.

'Good morning, ladies,' Peter called out. He blinked in surprise when he saw Carmen. 'May I say how wonderful you look this morning?' Peter smiled. 'This cruise is working its magic.'

'Thank you,' Carmen said. Unused to compliments, she felt her cheeks redden.

'I hope there's a luncheon buffet on board,' Betty grumbled, 'and a shady place for me to sit.'

Carmen caught Peter's eye and shrugged. 'I'm sure I can find somewhere suitable,' she said as she pushed Betty onto the quayside.

As she caught a glimpse of the sun on the water, Carmen relaxed. She'd enjoyed the shopping trip with Fran and had a wonderful evening with Theo. A peculiar feeling swept over her, and she realised she was more assured and making new friends. Fran was like a rock and so kind, and Theo a confidante, someone who truly listened. Carmen hoped their connection wouldn't fade after the cruise when everyday life resumed. For the first time in as long as she could remember, Carmen felt almost ready for whatever might come next, and she mustn't let Betty's negativity creep into her writing or newfound friendships.

Returning home might not be as daunting as Carmen feared.

Chapter Nineteen

Fran had never ridden on a jet ski. The only moving thing she'd sat on at the seaside was a donkey named Dobbin on a Blackpool beach. But at Almyros Beach, where the tour bus took the cruise passengers, the turquoise sea was inviting, and Fran, encouraged by Sid, decided that she'd have a go.

Wearing her baby-pink tankini, Fran held onto Sid as he listened to instructions from the jet ski owner, who told Sid not to go too far out and to watch his speed.

'Aye, aye, Captain,' Sid said as he revved the engine and slowly set off. Fran let out a scream as Sid cruised away at a moderate pace. 'Give over, Fran,' Sid called out, 'it's hardly Formula One!'

Fran's hair splayed around her face, and sea spray kissed her skin. She pressed her body to Sid's, her eyes wide as she looked back at the beach, where stylish sunbeds lay beneath straw umbrellas on golden sands dotted with smooth pebbles. A bar with a Tiki-style roof was playing music and sunbathers gathered there for refreshing drinks.

The calm, shallow water was perfect for swimming, and many cruisers were in the sea.

'Oh look!' Fran called out. 'There's Dicky Delaney!' She thrust a finger in front of Sid's eyes and pointed at a man by the edge of the water. Dicky had both hands on his hips and wore colourful shorts, and, with his eyes closed, held his face towards the sun. 'Isn't that Peter too, playing bat and ball?' Fran held her hand to her brow as she scanned the beach. 'The fella he's playing with is wearing very brief trunks.'

'That's Kyle from Kyle's Senior Splashdown,' Sid acknowledged.

'I should get you a pair of Speedos like that.' Fran giggled as she eyed Kyle's brief neon beachwear and thought that he was glowing so brightly, he could probably be seen from space.

'Steady on!' Sid called out as he brushed Fran's finger away and swerved to avoid a swimmer who'd inadvertently drifted into the jet ski lane.

'It's that author,' Fran called out, 'you know, Ruskin Reeve.'

'Well, he needs to watch where he's swimming,' Sid mumbled, keeping his distance from Ruskin, who'd stopped to remove his goggles and held up an apologetic hand.

Fran gripped Sid tighter. 'Come on!' she urged. 'I haven't come out here for a Sunday stroll. Let me feel the wind whip into my wrinkles.'

Sid laughed, and as Fran clung on for dear life, he accelerated steadily.

'Blimey, I'll need a wrench to get off,' Fran said as

she gripped her thighs around Sid and felt her tightening muscles protest.

'Two paracetamols and a large ouzo will soon sort you out,' Sid shouted over his shoulder.

As they sped around the bay, Fran, enjoying the thrill of the ride, called out, 'This is the life, seize the day!'

* * *

On the island of Spinalonga, Betty seized her cane and pointed it angrily at anything that got in her way. 'I thought we were staying on the boat!' she grumbled to Carmen. 'I don't want to be on an island where I might catch an incurable disease.'

Carmen ignored her mother. Pushing Betty along the uneven surfaces was bad enough, but the constant commentary of complaints was even more wearing.

She tried to blank Betty out and thought of the enticing waters of Spinalonga that she'd seen from the deck of the boat as they gathered with other excited passengers. The island had risen dramatically from the sea as they approached, and Carmen was entranced by the rocky shores, vibrant greenery, and ancient stone buildings that lay beyond. She tried to imagine what it must have been like for a person afflicted with leprosy to arrive here, knowing that they would never leave.

The views were breathtaking as they made their way along the pathway and many visitors climbed to higher vantage points to photograph the panoramic vistas. Carmen stared at the olive trees and wildflowers and could almost feel the whirlwind of emotions that the lepers might have experienced when they arrived. Would it have been fear and despair? Or perhaps a sense of resignation as they faced a future separated from family and friends, not knowing if they would be treated with kindness or continue with the cruel stigma that had been inflicted on them. Carmen wondered what it might be like to be cast away from society and longed to discuss this, but as Betty moaned about the bumps in the path, Carmen kept her thoughts to herself.

Suddenly, a voice behind Carmen called out, 'It would be a very lonely journey all those years ago!'

Carmen turned and, to her delight, saw Theo. 'I didn't know you were on the boat?' She smiled as he reached her side.

'Last-minute decision. I was on a smaller vessel but have kept a low profile while the sea air got rid of my hangover.'

'I know the feeling,' Carmen laughed. She was happy to see Theo, who was dressed casually in shorts and T-shirt and looked relaxed as he walked alongside her.

'Hello, Betty,' Theo said and touched Betty's hand. 'I hope you're enjoying the trip.' But Betty snatched back her fingers and stared at Theo with an expression of horror before turning her head away.

'Probably thinks she'll catch something; given the island's history,' Carmen whispered, rolling her eyes.

'Here, let me take the load,' Theo said, 'these paths are impossible with a wheelchair. You relax and enjoy the island.'

'It's good to see you. What do you think so far?' Carmen

asked. Released from her duties, she shook the tension from her shoulders, enjoying her soft curls caressing her bare skin.

'I can't imagine the feeling of abandonment one must have felt, being deposited in this place,' Theo said as he looked around. 'Picture being dumped in a community of suffering, giving up all the dreams one might have had.'

'Heartbreaking,' Carmen agreed. She bit down on her lip and thought of her father's words. *You've got to have a dream to make a dream come true . . .* Dreams, for the residents of Spinalonga, would never have come true in this prison.

They were approaching the ruins of stone houses, and ahead of them, their tour guide waited for everyone to gather at Dante's Gate.

'It was the gateway to hell for the lepers,' Theo said as they walked through a tunnel that led into the village. Entering the main street, they studied the recently renovated houses where pots of geraniums stood beside a communal laundry, a bakery and a church.

The guide told the visitors that the lepers were thought to be cursed by God and the disease a punishment. But once on the island, he explained, they stopped being outcasts and formed a community that held elections, had families, and naturally, experienced every normal human emotion during their lives.

'Maybe life wasn't so bad,' Carmen reflected.

When they reached a bar and café, Theo suggested that Betty sit and have refreshments while he took Carmen to explore.

'At these prices?' Betty complained. She studied a menu

and gripped her purse. 'I could shop for a week for the cost of a coffee here.'

Theo purchased baklava and coffee with a large glass of Metaxa. 'Here you go, my love,' he said and made sure Betty was comfortable. 'Relax and refresh yourself. We'll be back very soon,' and before Betty had time to object, he grabbed Carmen's arm, and they set off.

'It's a good job you're wearing sensible shoes,' Theo said, staring at Carmen's glittery trainers, 'the paths will be difficult in places as we climb higher.'

For the next hour, they walked around the circumference of the island, stopping to view the ruins of a hospital and an eighteenth-century Venetian fort where they learned that the Turks took over the island in the nineteenth century. Theo studied a guidebook and told Carmen that the leper colony was established in 1903 for several hundred lepers and was known as the prison of no escape. Residents were called the 'living dead' because of their deformations and blindness.

'They were often brought in handcuffs, like criminals, under the escort of the Cretan police,' Theo said. 'Provisions to the island were exorbitant,' he added, 'suppliers insisted on high financial compensation for the risk to their health.'

In a museum, they saw games from the Ottoman period when paving slabs were used as boards with engraved dimples and lines. Alongside a cabinet of ancient glass bottles, Carmen studied a wall plaque and read, 'Guards were recruited from convicts and ex-criminals and often abused the sick.' She shook her head. 'This is truly a heartbreaking place.'

Theo lifted his sunglasses and continued to study his book. 'Fortunately, after the Second World War,' he said, 'a cure was discovered in America, and the colony closed in 1957.'

Now, they were standing in a little church.

Carmen stared at the simple artefacts and icons, almost sensing the history in what had been a place of worship for the lepers. Natural light shone through an open window, the beam falling on a vase of fresh wildflowers. *Thank goodness someone still cares!*

'I'm so glad I came here,' Carmen said to Theo as they came out of the church to stare at the surrounding view of the sea and mountains.

'It's very spiritual,' he replied softly, 'Ruari would have loved this.'

Carmen reached out to touch Theo's arm. 'Perhaps he is with you in spirit?'

'And perhaps your writing guide is with you.' Theo turned to Carmen and grinned. 'How do you feel?'

'Like I could suddenly write ten chapters!'

'I'd better get you back to your laptop, and we ought to rescue the staff at the café, too.'

'Hell, yes, I'd almost forgotten my mother.'

'As if you could . . .'

They reached the café and Theo and Carmen suddenly stopped when they saw Betty.

'Just look at her!' Carmen said and stared at her mother.

Betty was sitting on a wall, a glass of Metaxa in her hand, chatting to a tanned, grey-haired gentleman, who had a camera slung around his neck. Leaning in closely, she lightly touched his arm as she laughed at his joke. Flashing a radiant smile, Betty gazed at the elderly man with a girlish grin.

Carmen was open-mouthed as she heard Betty say. 'You know, if I wasn't on the cruise, looking after my daughter, I'd definitely steal you away!'

The man had an American flag on his baseball cap and wore a bright Hawaiian shirt. An expensive-looking gold watch gleamed on his wrist. 'Well, ma'am, I couldn't be that lucky.' He grinned and patted Betty's hand.

'Would you believe it . . .' Carmen whispered to Theo. Stepping forward, she said, 'Hello, my name is Carmen, and I'm Betty's daughter.'

'Holden Jackson the third, from Venice, Florida. At your service, ma'am,' the man said and rose to attention. 'I'm honoured to meet you. Your mom here has told me all about you.'

'I'm sure she has . . .'

'I guess you want her to take you back to the ship?' Holden Jackson the third raised a bushy eyebrow.

'Oh, I think I can manage,' Carmen replied, 'but Mum, shall we get you comfortable in your chair?' Carmen indicated that Betty sit down.

'She likes to think I'm infirm,' Betty giggled, knocking back the brandy. She nudged Holden, 'I go along with it to make her feel needed.'

'Sure thing,' Holden smiled. 'Good on you, Bet,' he added. 'I'll see you at the dance in the Mermaid Theatre later.'

With a wink and a tug on his cap, Holden turned and went to the bar.

'*Bet?*' Carmen voiced as Betty staggered to the chair, flopping down and wriggling to make herself comfortable. 'Did he just call you "Bet?"'

'Holden is being friendly.' Betty picked up her cane. 'Don't make a fuss and spoil my day like you usually do.'

With an incredulous stare, Carmen looked from Betty to Theo. 'And what's all this about the dance tonight?' she asked.

'Holden has asked me to join him,' Betty said, 'but only if my poor old bones can bear to be upright for a few minutes.' She raised her cane, 'Come on, hurry up, we don't want to miss the boat.'

Carmen was at a loss for words, and Theo, sensing her confusion, took the handles of Betty's chair. 'I've got this,' he said, tilting his head to indicate that they should be making their way.

'She's beyond belief . . .' Carmen muttered as the trio went along the bumpy path that led to the jetty.

'Holden Jackson seems like a gentleman,' Theo said as Betty's head slumped and she dozed. With the sun beaming down and the jetty in sight, Theo remembered the pineapple print he'd noticed on Holden's shirt and grinned as he thought about Betty and the American.

Was Colin and Neeta's UDPPC about to get a new member?

Chapter Twenty

When Theo, Carmen and Betty got back to the *Diamond Star*, they realised that there was a commotion taking place on the side of the quay. The coach that had taken passengers to the beach was emptying, and a crowd surrounded a woman lying prostrate on the ground.

'Move back!' Peter said, thrusting his clipboard to one side. The crowd, like a flock of startled birds, dispersed, giving the woman more space. 'Let her get some air,' he added, removing a towel from his bag to roll up and place under her head.

Betty, now wide awake, poked about with her cane. 'Let me through!' she called out, prodding the backside of a woman in tight Lycra shorts.

'Mother, behave yourself!' Carmen hissed and apologised to the furious-faced woman who was rubbing her rear.

'I want to see what's going on.' Betty's voice was as sharp as a knife. 'Someone's probably caught something terminal on that island, and we're all about to drop like flies.'

'Don't be ridiculous,' Carmen snapped. Thinking it

best to manoeuvre Betty away and head towards the ship, Carmen turned when Fran came hurrying towards them.

'Cooee!' Fran called out. 'Have you had a lovely day?'

'Yes, it's been wonderful, but what's happening here?' Carmen asked.

'Don't worry, dear,' Fran said softly, patting Carmen's arm. 'It's Debbie, she's had a drop too much.'

As Fran was speaking, Don appeared and marched towards them. 'Drop too much?' he angrily scoffed, 'She's three sheets to the wind and singing like a sailor.'

True to his words, a sound echoed across the quay.

'I DID IT MY WAAAY!' Debbie, now hauled into a sitting position, belted out the famous Frank Sinatra number and several cruisers who'd also been to the beach joined in.

'They're saying that she had neat ouzo in her water bottle,' Fran confided, her voice lowered. 'Don hadn't a clue and thought she was keeping herself hydrated.'

Theo began to laugh as the singing sunbathers chorused. 'And through it all . . . She took the fall . . . and did it . . . HER WAAAY!'

'She'll be doing it her own way when she sobers up,' Don huffed, 'all the way to the nearest flight home.'

'Oh, come on now,' Theo said, reaching out an arm and giving Don a playful punch. 'Your woman is on holiday, she's been having fun, and let's face it, we've all been where she is.'

Carmen wasn't so sure about that as she stared at Debbie, who now had a paper bag in her hand and was retching violently.

'Disgraceful,' Betty mumbled.

'Debbie's singing is the most I've heard her say all cruise,' Theo whispered to Carmen.

'That's true.' Carmen nodded. 'Don is always the mouthpiece for both of them.'

'Nothing to see here!' Peter called out. He flapped his hands to disperse the crowd and winced when Debbie projected two olives and a half-digested cherry onto his towel.

'Does Debbie need a hand?' Carmen asked.

'Probably not,' Theo said, 'it looks like the cavalry has arrived.' He pointed to two medics who were hauling Debbie to her feet. 'A rest and a black coffee and she'll soon be dancing again.' Theo grinned.

'Not likely,' Don complained, 'she's as wobbly as a three-legged stool.' He stared at the medics who were now red-faced as Debbie's weight fell against them. 'It's like lifting a sack of tatties . . .' Don added.

'At least you had a lovely afternoon.' Fran turned to Don. 'You were going for the jet ski speed record when we saw you whizzing around the bay.'

Fran remembered the look of terror on Debbie's face when she slid off the back of Don's jet ski at the end of their ride. Crawling through the water to the beach, her skirted swimsuit trailed heavily in the sand. No wonder the woman had downed a stiff drink. Don was deadly at the controls and had watched far too many action movies. He hadn't a clue what he was doing, Fran thought, unlike her safe and steady Sid.

Betty banged her cane. 'Can we please get moving!'

she griped. 'I can't sit here watching this nonsense, this is supposed to be a cruise, not a pub crawl.'

Carmen's fingers were firm as she began to steer Betty towards the ship.

'Shall we meet up later?' Theo asked, falling into step.

'That sounds like a plan,' Carmen replied with a smile. 'Betty has a date with Holden Jackson, and I'd hate to play gooseberry.'

'I've got to prep for my talk tomorrow,' Theo said, 'so I'll probably have dinner in my room. But how about we can catch the show in the Neptune Theatre?'

'Perfect,' Carmen said. 'Save me a seat.'

* * *

Dicky was in his dressing room. Pacing nervously around the cluttered area, he could feel beads of sweat form on his forehead as he rummaged in pockets and opened drawers. Dressed in his stage clothes, Dicky sifted through the tubes and bottles strewn over the table, pushing aside half-empty water bottles and notes with scribbled jokes.

'Where the hell is it?' he muttered, his fingers repeatedly going to his neck to search for the gold chain that had been gifted by the wealthy widow. She'd told him it would be his good luck charm and expected him to wear it when he was on stage. The chain had been missing for twenty-four hours, seemingly vanished into thin air, and despite his assurance that he'd forgotten to put it on, Dicky knew that he couldn't fool the lady further.

The door swung open, and Melody strode in.

'Stealing my stuff again?' she asked, her voice edged with sarcasm as she tugged off her wig and removed her heels before sliding onto her chair.

'I haven't touched anything of yours, but I could ask the same,' Dicky snapped. 'Have you seen a gold chain?'

'Hardly,' Melody said, 'do you mean the one that looks like it should be anchoring a ship?'

'Yes,' Dicky nodded, mentally agreeing that the chain *was* quite chunky.

'It's not my style,' Melody yawned.

Dicky checked his pockets for the third time, his gaze flitting around the room.

'I presume it was a gigolo gift from that portly diamond on legs that you've been servicing since you came on board?' Melody looked at Dicky's reflection in the mirror and raised her painted eyebrows.

Dicky was about to add that there were many more gifts in the pipeline if he played his cards right, but Melody's reference to a gigolo stopped him. Was that how others saw him?

'You're the human equivalent of an expensive sports car,' Melody said, 'always ready to hit the road but with a hefty price tag. Don't you ever tire of laughing at her unfunny jokes and bowing to her every command?'

'I don't know what you mean.' Dicky shrugged.

'Do you enjoy dishing out compliments that aren't true? You're a freeloader, Dicky, creating questionable services that are paid for by the hour.' Melody began to spread cleansing cream on her skin.

'You're imagining things.' Dicky tugged on his shirt sleeves to fasten the cuff buttons, then turned to the mirror and examined his stage-ready face. 'Most people would describe me as more of a life coach for passengers, a multi-tasker.'

'More like a Swiss Army knife for lonely old hearts, always ready with the right tool.'

Dicky scowled. 'Why do you dislike me, Melody?' he asked, genuinely perplexed as he stared at the singer. 'I've done nothing to offend you and have tried to be civil both on and off stage.'

Melody slowly wiped at the cream with a tissue. Tossing it in a bin, she pushed back her chair and turned to face Dicky. 'You don't have a clue, do you?'

'Eh?' Dicky was confused.

Melody crossed her arms and stared coldly. 'Benidorm. The Starlight Bar. Impersonation Night,' she said flatly. 'July 19th, 2014.'

Dicky scratched his cheek and frowned. He hadn't a clue what Melody was talking about. But as his brain unscrambled the years, trying to connect the dots, various gigs fell into place, and he was suddenly back on a dimly lit stage in the crowded room of the Starlight Bar in Benidorm . . .

'Tonight, for one night only!' Dicky announced. 'We invite you to our event, the Best Impersonation of Danni Del Rio!'

The lights in the auditorium of the Starlight Bar dimmed, and the crowd became hushed as Dicky started a routine that made fun of current events.

'I thought I was in a relationship, but it turns out I was

just a Netflix subscription. I was getting dumped every month!' Dicky joked. 'Have you heard the one about the ice bucket challenge that went wrong?' he asked. 'They used too much ice and are now auditioning for Titanic!'

Dicky raised his hand after several more gags, and the laughter died down.

'Now everyone, this is the moment you've been waiting for,' he said, 'I'd like to invite those audience members participating to come onto the stage with their impersonation of our resident drag queen and host, Danni Del Rio!'

To one side of the stage Danni Del Rio, a vision in sequins, stood in all her finery with a fake smile on her lips as she watched Dicky perform. It had been the club owner's idea to host this event, thinking it a novel way to fill the club with wannabe drag queens and their supporters, who flocked to Benidorm to find work in the many entertainment venues.

As the show began, Dicky encouraged the contestants to exaggerate and imitate Danni's over-the-top outfits and garish makeup, even emulating her every strut and pose. Caricaturing Danni's act, the wannabes lined up to await Dicky's final decision and pick a winner. The crowd roared with laughter, but for Danni, it felt increasingly uncomfortable, her routine ridiculed cruelly. Unable to take any more, she stepped forward and began a fierce retort, but the crowd continued to laugh, not with her but *at* her. Distraught and in a flash of rage, Danni stormed off the stage . . .

'You did nothing,' Melody said now as she stared at Dicky with icy eyes.

'What do you mean?' Dicky looked puzzled. 'I remember

the night, and it was all in good fun. It's not my fault if Danni couldn't take a joke and threw her toys out of the pram.'

'Danni was my best friend, and I was in the audience.'

Dicky shrugged. 'How was I to know you two were close? I didn't even know you then.'

'No. So neither would you know that Danni fell off our balcony in the early hours and was fatally injured.'

Dicky took a step back. His eyes wide as he stared at Melody. Shocked, he covered his mouth with his palm. Wracking his brains, he remembered leaving to join a cruise ship the day after the drag queen gig.

'The club owner sacked her when she left the stage.' Melody's voice was flat. 'He said she shouldn't have spoken out and viewed her action as disrupting a great night. You walked away, basking in applause and your own glory, leaving Danni horribly humiliated and without a job.'

'I had no idea . . .'

'And you have no idea of the emotional, transformative journey that we go through. The double-edged sword that cuts deep.'

'But . . . you can't blame me, surely?'

'But I do, Dicky. Danni was fragile, and it took great courage to hold down that job. She'd lost her family back home, through prejudice and backlash, just for wanting to be her true self. That job meant everything, and you took it away.'

Dicky didn't know where to look, and he glanced at his watch, realising that he was soon due on stage.

Melody stood. She picked up a robe and walked to the

bathroom. 'Go on,' she said, 'entertain them, but perhaps in light of what I've told you, you'll appreciate the true cost of a laugh.'

Dicky winced as Melody slammed the bathroom door.

'On stage in ten minutes, Mr Delaney!' a runner called out.

Dicky stared at his face in the mirror. The harsh lights reflected the turmoil that he felt. Self-doubt loomed as he swiped a finger across his heavily made-up cheekbone and thought of the thousands of times he'd stood in a theatre giving everything to each joke he told. Dicky turned pain and mishaps into material. It was his job.

'I'm a comedian, for God's sake!' Dicky yelled and swivelled his head to the bathroom door. 'It's what I do!'

Without waiting for Melody to reply, Dicky straightened his collar, squared his shoulders and thrust back his head. Ready to face his audience and with a resolute smile at his reflection, Dicky marched out of the door.

Chapter Twenty-One

Sea days on the *Diamond Star* began with the aroma of coffee, freshly baked bread and savoury treats drifting from the Terrace Restaurant and Deck Café. After breakfast, passengers strolled around the ship as it sailed to its next destination. Many sourced a sunbed by the pool while others joined instructor Kyle on the sun deck for his morning session of Yoga for the Young at Heart or Senior Splashdown. In the sports zone, strangers became friends over mini golf while the Golden Oldies Gang gathered in the library for a game of Trivia.

'It's like a floating paradise,' Sid said as he stretched out on a steamer chair by the pool and held a copy of the *Diamond Star Daily News*. 'There's so much to do.'

Fran sat beside him. She was studying a crossword. 'We could stay here and sunbathe,' she said, her pencil poised as she pursed her lips and looked thoughtful, 'and you can help me with this crossword.'

'Go on then, give us a clue,' Sid said.

'A drink that you might have on holiday. Eight letters. First four, C-O-C-K.'

'Tail,' Sid said, 'it's a cocktail.'

'Favourite form of activity after sixty. Three letters.'

'Nap.' Sid nodded.

'No, silly, and the first letter is S,' Fran added.

'Sex?' Sid looked hopeful.

Fran ignored Sid and licked her pencil. She wrote 'Sew' in the clue.

'Who's written these?'

'It's Brain Teasers for Seasoned Seniors,' Fran said. 'I picked the magazine up in the onboard shop.'

'More like brain teasers for two-year-olds,' Sid said. 'As you mentioned the shop, did you see Dicky Delaney's book on display?'

'Yes, I'm going to get a copy, and it was next to Ruskin Reeve's new thriller.'

'I fancy a thriller; it's just my sort of reading.'

'I'm sure Carmen said Ruskin is hosting a workshop today, you might get the book signed if you go along.'

'Does that mean I'll have to start writing a novel?'

'You might.' Fran looked up. 'You could call it *Sid's Guide to Getting Away*.'

'I'll never get away from you,' Sid grinned and ducked as Fran swiped his head with her magazine. 'Now, let's look at what else is on today.' Studying the front page, Sid suddenly sat up. 'Blimey Fran, I'd totally forgotten!'

'What on earth . . .' Fran looked startled.

'Theo McCarthy is giving a talk in the Neptune Theatre,' Sid announced, his voice filled with anticipation.

'Oh heck, you mustn't miss that. What time?'

'At eleven this morning, and I want a front-row seat.'

'Smashing, we can have another hour here and then get ready.'

'Oh, happy days.' Sid lay back again. 'This cruising life truly *is* paradise,' he exclaimed with a contented smile.

* * *

Carmen decided to try Kyle's Yoga for the Young at Heart, and with Betty playing Trivia in the library with the Golden Oldies Gang, she felt free to head off to the sun deck.

'Over here!' Kyle called out when he caught sight of Carmen. 'There's plenty of room, grab a mat.'

Carmen remembered taking a yoga course in her thirties, one freezing winter when the nights were dark, and she'd needed to get out of the house. Far away from Betty berating Des all evening, for the late hours her husband spent in the shop.

That was several years ago, and the suppleness she'd built up, despite being frozen to the bone in a cold church hall, had disappeared as fast as her motivation to join the local gym, where toned bodies paraded at all hours, making Carmen feel entirely out of place. Still, as she rolled out her mat and sat down, Carmen thought an hour's gentle exercise would be a great way to start the day before she headed off to listen to Theo's talk.

Keen to learn more about her new friend in his professional capacity, she also made sure Betty was booked in for the tea dance that afternoon, which would enable Carmen to take part in Ruskin's workshop.

Carmen made herself comfortable and as Kyle welcomed everyone, she watched the young man and remembered his performance in the Mermaid Theatre the evening before.

Carmen had escorted Betty to the theatre, where Betty's creaking joints and paralysing arthritis miraculously disappeared when she caught sight of Holden.

Unbeknownst to her mother, Carmen had delayed leaving, and after making sure that Betty was comfortably seated and Holden by her side, Carmen hovered at the back of the room to witness Holden order drinks. After the couple polished off glasses of wine, he escorted Betty to the dance floor. Holden looked dapper in snazzy red braces, a stars and stripes bow tie and a smart dinner shirt, while Betty wore a full-skirted ballroom gown that had seen many dancing days with Des. Holden gently led Betty into a waltz, and to Carmen's surprise, they made a very graceful pair.

You can't keep playing the frail old lady card, Carmen thought and shook her head in disbelief as she watched her mother moving with Holden as if they'd been dancing for decades.

Carmen was about to leave when one of the dance hosts made an announcement. He began by asking everyone to take a seat, then explained that they were to be entertained by two talented dancers. Many guests would remember the act from their performance on TV for *Britain's Star Search*.

'Ladies and gentlemen,' he said, 'please put your hands together for Kyle and Terry, the one and only Tango Tootsies!'

Intrigued, Carmen looked on.

The lights dimmed, and as the band began to play 'You Raise Me Up', a couple stepped into the spotlight. They were dressed in black, with shiny patent shoes and sequinned fringing on their shirts and trousers. The two men moved like graceful swans, their steps perfectly synchronised as they glided across the floor. At the pinnacle of the chorus, Terry raised a beaming Kyle high into the air, and the audience gasped.

Carmen glanced at the lady beside her and saw that she had tears in her eyes. 'It's the closest thing to heaven when you dance with someone you love,' she said, her voice filled with emotion. Carmen smiled at the lady and patted her shoulder, hoping Kyle and Terry's mesmerising routine wouldn't inspire Holden and Betty to attempt something similar. Then, realising that she might be late for the show, Carmen crept away from the entertaining performance.

'Good morning gang!' Kyle called out cheerfully, bringing Carmen back to the present.

Barefoot and wearing a bright headband that matched his stretchy shorts, Kyle wore a loose tank top and wristbands. 'Now, my young at-heart yogis,' he said, 'today we are going to align our chakras, but first, we're going to begin with a gentle stretch.'

Carmen wondered what a chakra was and looking around, was pleased to see Debbie close by, looking bright and eager. Wearing beige leggings and a flesh-toned top, Debbie appeared to have recovered from her episode of the day before.

As Kyle's yogis moved slowly and he encouraged them

into more adventurous positions, Carmen heard a sound like a whoopee cushion and turned to see Debbie, in the downward dog.

'Oops,' Debbie winked at Carmen, 'I shouldn't have had prunes for breakfast.'

Kyle held out his hands and balanced on one leg. 'Imagine you've a cocktail in each hand,' he said, 'and you don't want to spill them.'

Several yogis stumbled, and one man keeled over.

'Please, lie on your backs,' Kyle instructed to those still standing, 'time for our peaceful meditation.'

Around her, Carmen heard bones creak as they all lay down, but Kyles's words soothed as he explained a breathing technique, and Carmen gazed up at the sky, where wispy blue clouds floated lazily. One or two yogis had fallen asleep and to a background of gentle snores, she felt her thoughts drifting away to the show in the Neptune Theatre the evening before, where Dicky Delaney had hosted a Tamla Motown evening. He'd followed the acts with his own stand-up routine, and Carmen and Theo had agreed that Dicky was at the top of his game; it was a hilarious hour of comedy.

Next to her, Debbie had dozed off but suddenly woke when Don appeared by her side. Towering over her, he called out, 'Ey, up, Yogi Bear, it's time for our elevenses. By heck, you look like a crumpet in a nylon stocking in that get-up.'

Startled, Carmen opened her eyes as Debbie rose and glared at Don. Struggling to her feet, she elbowed him out of her way.

'Namaste,' Kyle said. The instructor was sitting cross-legged, holding his palms together in a pyramid.

'You've all done amazingly well, now don't forget to keep practising.'

* * *

Theo thought he might be nervous as he stood by the side of the stage, waiting for Peter to introduce his talk. But his nerves settled as he practised a breathing technique he'd learned while filming episodes of *McCarthy's Kitchen Adventures*. He thought of Ruari, imagining his partner in a front-row seat, together with Theo in spirit.

'You've got this,' Ruari's ghostly voice whispered, 'spread a little sparkle wherever you go!'

Theo remembered Ruari repeating those words every time Theo performed, whether on camera for his TV series or in media interviews, and the words had become a catchphrase that Theo used to end his shows. If only his partner was with him today! Ruari would have loved this cruise, the luxury, the ambience and visiting all the interesting places.

But Ruari was gone. Slipping quietly away, his heart took its final sigh as he slept beside Theo. Unable to wake Ruari the following morning, Theo was numb when the ambulance arrived, knowing that the man with whom he'd shared so much love and laughter, had taken an early curtain call. Their beautiful life together was no longer, and Theo had to go on alone.

Theo touched his wrist and wished that Ruari's bracelet was still there. Despite an endless search and reporting it missing, the gift had not been found.

'Are you ready?' Peter patted Theo's shoulder while a

technical assistant ensured Theo's mic was clipped to his jacket.

'Absolutely, let's go for it,' Theo replied.

He watched Peter head to a podium, where he introduced Theo. The familiar theme music of *McCarthy's Kitchen Adventures* played, and loud applause began as Theo walked out and took his place.

Sitting down on a chair beside a table, a spotlight shone on Theo as he reached for a bottle of wine, took a glass and slowly poured. 'Now, dear friends,' he began, 'I'm just going to have a little tipple.'

Laughter rang out throughout the Neptune Theatre. Every episode of *McCarthy's Kitchen Adventures* had begun this way, and Theo had become known for his tipples.

'You must think that I drink a lot?' Theo asked and studied the audience.

'Nay, lad, just enough to keep us entertained!' Don piped up from the back of the room.

Theo smiled. 'When I first auditioned for television, I was asked to cook, unscripted, for an episode which the production company would show to the commissioners, hoping they'd authorise a series.' Theo took another drink. 'But guess what? Like a rabbit in the headlights live on camera, I dried up halfway through . . . As the producer waved his arms wildly, urging me on, I saw the wine on the table and poured myself a glass. I thought the producer was going to have a fit, but as I drank, I said to the camera, "Now, dear friends, I'm just going to have a little tipple," and it gave me time to compose myself.' Theo held up his glass to toast the audience. 'And the rest, as they say, is history.'

Sid was in the front row. Fascinated by Theo's talk, he listened intently as the chef began to describe hilarious episodes from his travels as he cooked his way around the world. Recalling many of the chef's escapades, Sid thought that Theo had aged well, despite a girth that had expanded over the years; his hair, once tied back in long dreadlocks, was now closely cropped, and the grey tinge an attractive contrast to Theo's smooth dark skin. Always smartly dressed, Theo was known on TV for his colourful shirts, often worn with a contrasting waistcoat, which he wore today.

'Over the years, I modified so many recipes from the people I met in far flung destinations,' Theo said, 'most had never seen a TV show or read a recipe book nor weighed or measured an ingredient. Their timings came from the early call of a cockerel or the sun setting over a hillside.'

Fascinated, Sid wanted to make notes and was pleased to see that Fran, sitting beside him, had her pen and pad at the ready. Sid knew that their own cooking style wasn't a science but more an appreciation of nature and well-prepared local ingredients. Theo epitomised everything the couple admired and passed on to their guests.

'I loved my job,' Theo continued. 'Whether sitting on a mat in a mud hut eating with my fingers or dining in Michelin-starred splendour, food is love, and when, as Winston Churchill once said, you find a job you love, you'll never work again.'

Sitting comfortably at the table with his long legs crossed, sipping his wine, Theo held the audience in the palm of his hand. No one shuffled in their seat or fidgeted as they absorbed the culinary tales.

'You know, television has the effect of lessening our expectations,' Theo said, 'I've travelled to some amazing places and cooked in stunning locations. The glowworm caves of Waitomo, in New Zealand, the Grand Canyon, the Danakil Depression in Ethiopia. I've seen so many wonderful sights . . . and as marvellous as these sights are, when you see them on the screen, you think, "Oh yeah, that's so and so," and the grandeur is lost.' He shrugged. 'However, there is a place that I can honestly say blew my mind. But I also thought it might take my life . . .'

Sid was fascinated as Theo described Meteora, in central Greece, near the town of Kalambaka. Renowned for its breathtaking beauty, he'd visited the monasteries of Meteora, perched perilously on top of towering rock formations.

'I was terrified as I stood close to a sheer rock face, and it felt like I was cooking suspended on a cloud,' Theo said. 'My stew was simmering in a primitive pot, and as I stared at the breathtaking view of the valley, I wondered if I was going to fall from the face of the cliff and die. It was difficult to comprehend how on earth they'd built these incredible buildings using only pulleys and ropes.' He shook his head. 'Health and safety wasn't top of my producer's agenda at that time, and I needed more than my regular tipple that day.'

Sid grinned. He remembered that episode and the white bean and vegetable soup that Theo had also cooked, served with a garnish of stir-fried dandelions. Fran had replicated the dish in Blackpool, winning favourable reviews from their customers.

Sid relaxed as Theo continued to entertain, with tales

from as far away as Thailand and as close to home as his beloved Donegal.

'So that's it for now, folks,' Theo said, picking up his glass. 'If you see me around during the rest of the cruise, I hope that you, dear friends, will come and chat,' Theo raised his glass. 'Now don't forget to spread a little sparkle wherever you go!'

Chapter Twenty-Two

Betty had relished her morning at the library. She'd crushed the other Trivia participants, and when Carmen arrived, Betty was buried under a pile of prizes.

'What on earth am I supposed to do with this?' Betty said, holding up a T-shirt emblazoned with the *Diamond Star* logo.

'Why not wear it?' Carmen suggested as she wheeled Betty out.

'Don't be ridiculous,' Betty snapped, 'but I can find a home for these,' she added, stuffing a cruise-themed cap, mug, magnet and keychain into a tote bag.

'You've done well. Shall we go and get some lunch?'

* * *

They returned to Betty's cabin after a buffet in the Deck Café, and to Carmen's surprise, Betty casually told Carmen that Holden would be accompanying her to the afternoon tea dance. He was due to arrive at three.

'Dad would be pleased that you are enjoying some company,' Carmen said as she carefully styled her mother's hair.

'Your father? Don't be ridiculous, he wouldn't give me a second thought.'

Carmen was about to argue that Des had given Betty a very good lifestyle but knew that any mention of her father would only set Betty off. Her mother never had a good word for her deceased husband; she'd nagged him constantly, publicly and behind closed doors and Carmen hadn't been surprised that her dad spent so much time at the shop.

As Carmen fastened a string of delicate pink pearls around Betty's neck, she watched her apply a fresh coat of lipstick, her lips pursing in satisfaction.

'Be careful with my necklace,' Betty said as she thrust the lipstick into her bag and caressed the pearls at her throat, 'they are from the Queen Conch and are rare and very valuable.'

Carmen had heard the story of her mother's pearls a hundred times and knew that the vibrant pink tones of the necklace made it highly sought after. They had been gifted to Betty on her wedding day by Des, who, at that time, was in the merchant navy and had come across the pearls when visiting the Caribbean.

'Now, don't get in the way,' Betty said sharply, pinning a brooch to her lapel.

'I haven't seen that brooch before,' Carmen remarked, leaning in closely to study the enamelled pin. 'Is it new?'

'Holden gave it to me, so you can keep your hands off it.'

'It's very nice.' Carmen smiled. 'How thoughtful of him.'

Their conversation was interrupted by a knock on the door.

'That will be Holden,' Betty said, her voice brisk. 'I don't want him seeing you in that ridiculous outfit. You're past your prime so don't pretend otherwise. And he certainly won't want you to ramble on about chefs, and ageing authors who think they can write bestsellers.'

Carmen bit her tongue. There was no point in arguing about the guest speakers she'd enjoyed or justifying the lovely forest-green sundress that complimented her in all the right places. Fran's choice of outfit was gorgeous, together with jewelled sandals that matched perfectly. Carmen's hair was pinned up with tortoiseshell combs and she'd added a hint of makeup, pleased to see that she was developing a flattering tan. Thanks to Fran, she felt good about her appearance and refused to let Betty dampen her spirit.

'Don't dawdle,' Betty rebuked, 'answer the door. Holden's waiting!'

Carmen forced a smile. She wondered what Holden saw in Betty and whether his motives were genuine. Why would he voluntarily want to spend time with a woman who constantly moaned and complained? Indeed, there were far more attractive and better-placed passengers who might be eager to enjoy his company. After all, Holden was good-looking and probably wealthy. But Carmen reasoned that Holden hadn't seen the real Betty. His view was clouded, only knowing a pleasant, slightly infirm widow who enjoyed dancing but carried a burden in life. Holden probably thought Betty was a saint for putting up with a daughter who, Betty said, refused to be dutiful and had been nothing but trouble since birth. He had no idea of Betty's sharp tongue nor her manipulative nature.

'Hello,' Carmen greeted Holden, 'how kind of you to escort Mum to the dance.' She stepped aside as Holden strode into the room, carrying a bouquet of fresh roses. Acknowledging Carmen, he leaned down to kiss Betty on her cheek. 'Bet,' he said, 'don't you look swell.'

'Oh, Holden,' Betty giggled, fluttering her fingers, 'you flatter me, where on earth did you find these lovely flowers?'

'Guest services can be very accommodating for someone special,' Holden replied.

Betty took the roses and handing them to Carmen, told her to find a vase.

'You've done something new to your hair,' Holden said, gazing at her curls as Betty preened, her fingers brushing a silver strand into place.

As the compliments flowed, Carmen arranged the flowers then glanced at her watch. She'd miss Ruskin's workshop if they didn't get a move on.

'I hate to interrupt,' Carmen began, 'but you don't want to miss your dance.'

'Allow me.' Holden swiftly moved to Betty's wheelchair. 'Take it easy, Bet,' he said, 'save your strength for our waltz.'

Carmen stood aside as they left. Betty hadn't bothered to say goodbye, but Holden smiled as he wheeled Betty away.

Checking her bag for a notebook, Carmen shrugged. Anything that kept Betty occupied during the cruise was a blessing she hadn't anticipated. But as she made her way to Ruskin's workshop, Carmen gave a little smile. Betty's new brooch, approximately the size of a coin and perfectly crafted into a pineapple, was dimpled in appearance with a leafy crown.

Carmen thought of her prim and proper mother. If Theo was to be believed, 'Bet' was now wearing the universal sign for a secret club.

Perhaps Holden's gift wasn't as innocent as it seemed.

* * *

Ruskin's workshop took place in the games room, where chairs were neatly arranged around tables facing a large white screen. Carmen felt her nerves rise as she entered the crowded room. As she searched for a seat, she saw with relief that Sid, at a table in the middle, was waving.

'Over here!' Sid called and shuffled his chair to make room.

'Have I missed anything?' Carmen glanced at other participants, busy arranging notebooks and chatting as they fiddled with pens and pencils.

'Not yet, but look, the man himself is here.' Sid nodded towards the door as Ruskin strolled in.

'Greetings, everyone,' Ruskin said, moving confidently across the room to stand before the screen. 'I trust you're all ready to spark your creativity?'

The room hummed with anticipation, and Carmen stared at Ruskin. He looked handsome in a navy shirt and chinos, with a healthy glow on his face. She couldn't tear her eyes away. Was she really feet away from her idol, ready to worship at his writing shrine? Would the great man inspire her work and fuel her with ideas to get her redundant fingers dancing across her keyboard?

'Some of you may be here, hoping to polish a story,' Ruskin said, 'while others wish to test their writing skills. But whatever you want to achieve, we have two hours to make it happen.' With a winning smile, he stared at the expectant faces. 'So, let's dive into your imagination and see where the journey takes us.'

Carmen was hooked from the start.

'Why do you think I have anything worthwhile to teach you about writing?' Ruskin asked the class.

Carmen's hand flew up. 'Well, you've sold millions of books, so you must know something about writing.'

Ruskin smiled, and a few chuckles rippled through the room.

'That's one way of looking at it, but you're all here because you want to write. Am I right?' He paused for effect. 'I have only one rule, and that is, don't procrastinate – just write!'

Ruskin launched into his presentation, and Carmen's pen flew across the pages of her notebook as he explained his writing process. When he posed writing exercises, he presented them as a game with few rules and many possibilities. Ruskin explained that everything should be tried, from writing formulaically to writing wildly. Carmen was fascinated by his suggestion that writers can train their waking minds to sleep creatively and untangle plots in dreams.

Before she knew it, the two hours had flown by. Guests thanked the author for his inspiring workshop and filed out, and Carmen watched as Ruskin signed a copy of his latest book for Sid.

'We'll catch up later,' Sid called over his shoulder to Carmen. He clutched the book as he hurried off to find Fran.

Suddenly Carmen realised that she was alone with Ruskin.

'You're not wearing your glasses,' he commented as he packed away his lecture notes.

Carmen's fingers flew to her face. 'No . . . I'm wearing contacts,' she said.

'Shame, I rather liked those heavy frames, but it's good to see what lies behind them.' Ruskin reached for his satchel and fastened it securely. 'This cruise seems to be suiting you,' he added.

Carmen felt flustered. *Damn!* He did recognise her! Tongue-tied, she scrambled for her notebook, packing it hastily into her bag.

'You're an author, aren't you.' His voice was smooth. 'I was rude when we met in Maxos, I'm sorry that I didn't take the time to chat with you.'

Carmen narrowed her eyes. Was Ruskin for real?

She remembered their brief encounter in Maxos. She'd been wearing a frumpy outfit and had been invisible to Ruskin. Carmen remembered how discourteous he'd been. But in the piano bar, having revamped her appearance, the great man spoke to her, as he seemed to want to do now. Why should her appearance make any difference? Was he only interested in what he could see on the surface? Was she only worthy of Ruskin's attention when she fitted into his idea of attractiveness? Carmen's frustration bubbled and she wanted to ask if he even cared who she really was or if he was playing a game to create a scene in one of his novels.

She bit back her irritation. 'It doesn't matter,' Carmen said coolly, 'and I mustn't keep you, I'm sure you have a busy schedule.'

'No, please,' Ruskin's tone softened, 'stay and tell me about your work.'

Carmen was about to hurry from the room, but common sense suddenly got the better of her. Ruskin Reeve, the famous author, wanted to know about her writing and she would be crazy to walk away. She watched Ruskin pull out a chair as he suggested they both sit down then lowered herself into the opposite chair and placed her hands on the table. 'My debut, *The Rainbow Sleuth*, topped Amazon's cosy crime charts, and I secured a three-book deal.'

Ruskin nodded. 'Impressive. Have you started the next one?'

'Yes.'

'And your deadline?'

'Er, I've written the first draft but it's not good and I have a little over three months to submit.'

'So why are you here on a cruise?'

Carmen saw Ruskin reading her movements and sensing her discomfort as easily as reading one of his own manuscripts.

Carmen swallowed. 'I booked the cruise last minute because I needed to clear my mind.'

Ruskin tilted his head, waiting for more, but Carmen was tongue-tied.

'You have writer's block.' Ruskin's gaze was intent.

'I . . . I . . .' Carmen stammered and felt her cheeks flush.

'You are staring at the page, and it remains blank.'

'Well . . .'

'You saw this cruise, noted that a famous crime writer would be hosting a couple of workshops, and thought it might spark something, giving you the push you needed.'

Carmen was caught off guard. Her eyes widened in surprise, and she shifted in her seat. Fearing that her voice would falter if she attempted to respond, she scrambled to regain control, wondering how Ruskin had sussed her out.

'It's all right,' Ruskin smiled. 'Your reaction tells me everything, and I see it all the time.'

Carmen's shoulders slumped. He thought she was wasting his time. *Damn him!* He was going to kick her out of the workshops. She'd blown her opportunity to spend time with a mentor, and now she was back at square one. Her wretched book would never get written.

'You look very pretty when you blush,' Ruskin said.

Pretty? Seriously? How condescending. Now, he was patronising her.

Feeling trapped and unable to meet his stare, Carmen pushed back her chair, 'Thanks for the workshop.' She reached for her bag, longing to escape her humiliation.

'Carmen, wait,' Ruskin spoke firmly. 'Sit down.'

She blinked. 'But . . .'

'I know that you think I'm a smug bastard.' Ruskin's eyes scanned her face. 'My books sell like hotcakes, and I make a lot of money. It all seems to come to me so easily.'

Carmen sat. He was right. At that moment, she *did* think that.

She wondered how soon she could put an end to this torture. Ruskin must be inwardly laughing at this excuse of an author who acted like a groupie. She braced herself, glancing towards the door.

'All of that is true,' Ruskin continued, 'but I didn't start off that way.'

Carmen waited for the inevitable lecture on her lack of progress, laziness and stalling.

Ruskin placed his elbows on the table and made a pyramid with his fingers. 'I was like you once, full of ambition and writing dreams, hoping that one day my dreams might come true.'

Carmen's chest tightened. Ruskin's words echoed those of her father's talk of dreams.

'But no one helped me, and it was a lonely life. I hadn't a soul to turn to in the early days and only my own determination kept me going.'

Carmen bit her lip and nodded.

'I was married to a woman who was deeply committed to lost causes.' He paused. 'I found it inspiring initially, that Venetia could give her time to battles only she saw as winnable.'

'Did you have a family?'

'Yes, two boys, grown up now with families of their own.' Ruskin stared absently at a wall. 'It wasn't that she didn't love us, more that her heart always prioritised whatever do-gooding mission she was leading. Even though we craved her presence, Venetia's full attention was reserved for others.'

'Why are you telling me this?'

'I'm sorry.' Ruskin turned to Carmen. 'My point is that despite the circumstances, I felt determined, like her, to be passionate about a subject too, and writing not only gave me an escape from tolerating Venetia but became my *ultimate* passion, filling the gap in my marriage and eventually taking over.'

'I see,' Carmen said, 'and does Venetia support you now?'

Ruskin gave a slow smile. 'We're divorced. I'd had enough. Strangely, Venetia misses what she took for granted and is keen for us to reunite.' He shrugged. 'But tell me, how do *you* feel when you write?'

Carmen didn't hesitate. 'I feel alive.'

'How badly do you want this?'

Carmen thought of the career teacher at school, who'd smirked when she told Carmen that she didn't have the talent to write novels. 'More than anything,' she said, 'I write because there are stories within me that I want to be heard. Stories provide that escapism, for both the writer and the reader.'

Ruskin studied her, his furrowed brow smoothed, his eyes crinkling at the corners. 'Then I'll help you,' he said.

'What?' Carmen tried to process Ruskin's words.

'I said that I will help you.'

'B . . . but how?'

'We'll work together.' Ruskin stood. 'Early mornings, no distractions.' He pushed his hands into his pockets and began to pace the room. 'We'll meet in my suite at five tomorrow and begin to map out the framework of your novel. Beginning to end.' Ruskin stopped and faced her. 'You'll have your plot revitalised before this cruise ends, and when you get home, you'll rewrite the damn thing.'

'Oh . . ..'

Ruskin's words sank in, and Carmen's astonishment suddenly gave way to joy. Clasping her hands, she raised them to her flushed face.

Ruskin picked up his satchel and slung it over his shoulder. 'My suite is on the Bridge Deck, a steward will show you. Don't be late!'

Without a backward glance, he left the room.

Frozen, Carmen tried to process what had just happened. She wanted to call out and thank him, but the words didn't come. As she rose, her gaze fell on a poster of Ruskin promoting his latest book, and with a soft smile, she whispered, 'I won't let you down.'

Chapter Twenty-Three

When the first light of the new day touched the horizon, a silvery glow shone over the sea as the *Diamond Star* cruised towards Malta. Hints of pink in a rhubarb sky cast a dawn glow on the historic limestone bastions of Valletta and the Three Cities, perched on opposite peninsulas. Passengers who'd risen early to stand on deck took in the view and gazed at Maltese fishing boats, luzzus, bobbing on the water, their vibrant colours eye-catching as the ship berthed on the harbourside. In the distance, the soft chime of church bells echoed as the city awoke and Maltese folk began their day.

Beginning her own day, Carmen hurriedly dressed. The previous evening, an argument had ensued with Betty when Carmen told her mother that she wouldn't be available in the early mornings and had arranged for Betty to have breakfast in her room.

'So, you want to confine me to my cabin?' Betty raised her eyebrows and stared at Carmen with disgust. 'I can spend time alone at home. This isn't why I've come on a cruise,' she snapped.

'Mum, it's only for a short while,' Carmen pleaded. 'I have an opportunity, and I mustn't turn it down, and you are perfectly capable of dressing yourself.'

'For heaven's sake, why are you wasting your time with all that writing nonsense? This is supposed to be a holiday.'

Carmen was tempted to explain yet again why she'd come on the cruise, and that her reasons hadn't included her mother, but Betty stiffened with indignation and, turning away, became deaf to any persuasion.

Now, as Carmen packed her laptop into a bag, she assured herself that Betty would be fine. Fernando would arrive with Betty's breakfast at eight o'clock, and Carmen would return in time to help prepare for the day ahead. Glancing at her watch, Carmen realised she only had ten minutes to spare. With a last look at her reflection in a full-length mirror, she patted her hair into place and then hastened out of the room.

* * *

Ruskin stood on his balcony and watched the sun rise over the harbour, casting long shadows across the historic walls of Valletta. He noted the many luzzus, with their sturdy pointed bows designed to handle rough seas. Ruskin remembered the eye symbol carved into each boat, an ancient tradition rooted in Phoenician and Egyptian culture that was said to protect the boat and its crew from harm.

Arriving in Malta at dawn, he thought, felt like stepping back in time to discover a mysterious city that carries whispers of its past within its ancient walls. Ruskin had visited the island before but still looked forward to wandering around the vibrant capital that buzzed with life and blended the old with the new.

But first, he had work to do.

Ruskin turned and stepped into the living room. His breakfast order had recently arrived, and coffee, pastries, and fruit were laid out on a table in the middle of the room.

'A starved mind weaves no tales,' he said as he poured coffee. 'Feed the body and the muse will flow.' Ruskin tore into a croissant, and as he took a bite, he heard a tentative knock on the door. Glancing at his watch, he smiled. Perfect. She was on time.

Carmen's heart pounded as she stood outside Ruskin's suite. Clearing her throat with a nervous cough, she raised her hand and knocked.

'Come in,' Ruskin said as he opened the door. He held a pastry in his hand and brushed crumbs from his lips as Carmen meekly followed. 'Sit and eat,' he said, waving towards the table.

Carmen did as she was told. Placing her bag down, she reached for a coffee and then began to butter a warm, doughy roll. Ruskin peeled a banana, and Carmen watched as he moved around the room, taking bites. Barefoot, wearing shorts and a polo shirt, he didn't speak. She wondered if she should open the conversation by thanking him and assuring him that she was grateful for his time, but Ruskin was deep in thought and almost oblivious to her presence.

Carmen realised that she was hungry and felt grateful that

Ruskin had laid on food. As she ate, she couldn't help but marvel at the suite. It was on another level and far superior to accommodation in the decks below. The spacious living area was lavishly furnished, opening to an expansive sunny balcony and doors led to other rooms.

'Creativity flows better when the writer is well fed,' Ruskin announced a short while later. 'Now, let's begin.' He pointed to a desk and nodded when Carmen sat down and took her notebook from her bag. 'I read your book last night,' he said, 'it shows promise.'

Carmen jerked her head back. She was shocked that Ruskin had been online and downloaded *The Rainbow Sleuth*.

'Don't look so surprised,' he said, 'I have to assess your ability.'

'I'm impressed that you read so quickly,' Carmen said.

Ruskin took the opposite seat. 'Speed reading is a skill and retains the important details.' He folded his fingers together and stared at Carmen. 'As a debut, your novel is good, but your writing will be much better now. Think of the block you are experiencing as a locked door, and I will give you the tools to open it.'

As Carmen listened to Ruskin explain that she should get the words down, any words, and that the good stuff would come in revisions, she was mesmerised by his blue eyes and rugged handsomeness. Under the table, she squeezed her fingers into her palms, willing herself to focus.

'Let your ideas breathe then you can worry about shaping them later,' Ruskin said, 'you have a unique voice, so let it speak.' He leaned in, his eyes sharp. 'Now a challenge, I want you to write for fifteen minutes. Anything, it doesn't have to make sense.'

Ruskin stood and walked away.

Carmen was hesitant as she picked up her pen, but not wanting to annoy Ruskin, she began to write. To her surprise, after a faltering start, she thought about her reasons for writing, and words soon filled the page. When he held up his hand and told her to stop, she felt a sense of accomplishment.

'Was that so hard?' he asked.

'No, but it's mostly nonsense.'

'Unimportant,' Ruskin was dismissive, 'you've unlocked the flow, and this is how we will start each session. This is known as the morning pages, an exercise in journaling – a technique created by Julia Cameron in her book, *The Artist's Way*.'

Carmen scribbled down the name of the author. 'A book I should read?' she asked.

'Absolutely, it's a guide to living a more creative life.'

For the next three hours, Carmen was hooked as Ruskin explained how to structure her novel and build a framework from which to work. His calm yet commanding voice made the complexities of plotting feel surprisingly easy, explaining that time invested now would save countless hours of frustration later. Carmen's nerves were replaced with excitement as her story began to take on a new shape.

When Ruskin finally stood and showed her out of the suite, Carmen knew she was beginning to find the tools she needed. More than that, she was starting to believe in herself.

'Remember,' he said, his hand resting on the doorframe, 'an author's greatest asset is persistence. Keep going, and the magic will happen, even on difficult days.' As he closed the door, he called out, 'Same time tomorrow!'

Carmen moved through the ship, clutching her bag. As she made her way to her cabin, she realised that not only did she have a new plan for her novel, but the fear of the blank page returning was replaced now by determination. Ruskin was the inspiration she'd hoped for. Butterflies were dancing in her stomach, and she felt almost lightheaded.

But as she skipped down the stairs, Carmen thought of how she'd felt when Ruskin leaned over her shoulder to study her screen, his warm breath a whisper on her skin, as though an electric current had surged through her body, igniting every nerve. His cologne was intoxicating, the rich leathery scent sparking a craving she couldn't explain. When his hand stretched out to study her notes, she almost reached out to grab it, caught up in a longing so intense she'd had to look away.

'What on earth is happening to me?' Carmen murmured as she opened the door to her room.

She hesitated in the doorway, gripping the handle as a familiar ache stirred. It had been years since she had allowed herself to feel this way about a man.

And yet, here she was. Feeling something again.

The feelings for Ruskin that were bouncing around her body felt like a game of ping-pong, each jolt reminding her now, that even in her fifties, romance might not be dead.

A knock on the wall made Carmen flinch. It was followed by Betty's screeching voice.

'CARMEN! Are you there?'

Carmen closed her eyes, ignoring Betty's call. She must shake off her stupid crush. A man like Ruskin would never look her way. He was generous enough to be a mentor but anything more was too absurd to imagine. She shook her head to clear the foolish thoughts cluttering her mind.

There was only one priority to focus on. It was time to write.

* * *

Ruskin sat on his balcony and browsed the day's excursions in the *Diamond Star Daily News*. He toyed with a visit to St John's Cathedral with its opulent baroque interior and considered a taxi ride to Mdina, known as the silent city, which was surrounded by mysterious medieval walls housing dark and narrow streets. He also felt like a leisurely swim and considered visiting the clear waters of St George's Bay, but a tour of Valletta might be more promising. Unable to make up his mind, Ruskin found that his thoughts kept straying to Carmen.

It had been an easy decision to mentor the writer – after all, it was good to give something back. In the early days of his writing career, no one had helped Ruskin. With Venetia immersed in her make-believe world and uninterested in anything he did, support had been thin on the ground. While working full time in banking, he'd stolen hours whenever he could to write a story that had been building in his mind for many years. It was damn hard work, but with his gritty determination, he created Detective Inspector Blake. The fictional detective had been his passport to quitting the rat race of high finance where the hours were endless, the suits were sharp, and the smiles fake. No longer a cog in the relentless banking machine, as a successful author he had the freedom in his writing world to steer his own career.

Ruskin knew nothing about Carmen, but his intuition told him she was unhappy. With a demanding parent, her escape was through the page, and it was to her credit that her debut novel was a success. It was well written with many clever plot twists. He'd mentored writers in the past, and it gave him great satisfaction to see them benefit from his advice. A few hours each day on the remainder of this cruise came at no cost to himself, and the writing reward for Carmen could be fruitful.

But there was something else troubling Ruskin.

Details he'd overlooked were suddenly clear. Having previously dismissed Carmen as dowdy, her transformation had shaken him when she walked into the piano bar. After his messy divorce, Ruskin had vowed to give himself time and not get romantically involved. But there was something in the way Carmen tilted her head when she considered his questions and the warmth of the smile that lit up her face. Her heavy-rimmed glasses had a hint of allure, drawing his attention to her beautiful hazel eyes. Leaning in to study her screen, he'd caught the scent of her skin and the softness of her hair and longed to reach out and caress her.

Carmen was, in truth, quite captivating. The way she tilted her head, her laugh, and how she tucked a strand of hair behind her ear while she worked, unaware of her attractiveness, which made her even more appealing. Ruskin felt a stab of guilt for his shallowness and the superficial lens through which he'd viewed her before. His determination to be impartial to romance was crumbling, but more worrying was that he knew she would never feel the same about someone who'd failed to see her worth all along.

How could he have been so blind? Since his divorce, Ruskin had created an armour, a shield against the vulnerability of love. But now, something about Carmen was melting it and his defences had begun to unravel.

With a heavy sigh, Ruskin carefully folded the *Diamond Star Daily News*, and resolved that the only way to find something to occupy his restless spirit was to get dressed and leave the ship.

Stepping into his suite, he saw Fernando, a cabin steward, clearing away the breakfast debris.

'I knocked . . .' Fernando began.

'It's all right, I was outside on the balcony,' Ruskin said.

Fernando smiled as he carried a laden tray and moved towards the door. 'A day full of sunshine awaits, enjoy!'

Grateful for the warmth in Fernando's words, Ruskin smiled back. 'Indeed,' he agreed, 'it's time to write a new page.'

Chapter Twenty-Four

'Everyone! The walking tour of the city is this way!'

Peter clutched his clipboard and glanced down at a list of names. Thirty passengers were booked on the tour and, with any luck, he hoped to keep everyone together. Thankfully, a local guide accompanied them and Peter would only have to ensure that stragglers kept up, ideally ensuring that no one went missing.

'Listen, please,' he called out, 'we have six hours to discover the mysteries and delights of Valletta, but if you stray away from our party for any reason, make sure that you are back at the ship on time.' Pointing with his pen, Peter carried out a head count, and with everyone at the ready, they set off.

As the guide took control of the group, Peter thought of his conversation with Dicky Delaney the previous evening when the comedian told him that he'd mislaid a gold chain. Dicky hoped that it had been handed into guest services, but with no such luck, his concern caused him to inform Peter.

'It's a bit embarrassing to be honest,' Dicky explained, 'it was a gift.'

'Presumably not for your services to comedy?' Peter was cynical. He knew of Dicky's exploits with the ladies and, as long as they didn't get out of hand, chose to ignore them.

But what worried Peter that morning was that this was the third incident of missing jewellery. Debbie had mislaid a diamond drop necklace, Theo a gold cuff bracelet, and now Dicky was without a hefty gold chain. Passengers often mislaid items during a cruise, but to have three items of jewellery lost halfway through the holiday seemed less like a coincidence and more like a pattern forming. Misplaced items were generally found within a day or two, often in a cabin or left in the spa. Peter sensed mischief, and as he walked ahead of the group, he wondered if a thief was onboard. He decided to speak to the cabin stewards again, then initiate another sweep of all the public rooms with staff checking all areas including the spa and pool, and finally if theft *was* suspected, ask the passengers to file a formal report. It would be useful to have security review CCTV too.

If he wasn't careful, the passengers' whispers might turn into a full-blown scandal on the *Diamond Star*, which would never do!

* * *

'This is exciting, isn't it?' Fran said to Sid as she held his hand, and they began to stroll at the front of the walking party. 'What a lovely old town, I can't wait to have a look around.'

The charm of Valletta was evident, and it filled them both with a sense of anticipation.

'Aye, there's lots of things to see,' Sid agreed, 'and I'm sure we'll stop at some of the shops and pavement cafés.'

Sid wore his Opa T-shirt, with shorts and sandals, while Fran felt comfortable in a cotton playsuit and wide-brimmed hat. Her gold-coloured trainers glinted as she walked.

After passing the Grand Harbour waterfront, which was crowded with bars and restaurants, Peter halted the group when they arrived at the Barrakka Lift.

'We're going to take the lift to the upper gardens,' Peter said, 'it's an ascent of almost two hundred feet, which will save you the steep climb to the city's fortifications.'

The guide split the group into two, and Fran and Sid were first in the lift alongside Don, Debbie, Colin and Neeta. As the glass and steel structure began to rise, everyone gazed at the magnificent sight of the Grand Harbour.

Sid stood beside Don. 'I thought you might be jogging up to the top?' he said and gave Don a nudge.

'Bread don't rise without resting, and neither do I,' Don replied.

'These excursions are great, aren't they?' Sid remarked.

'They're great because they're free,' Don replied with a grin. 'That's why Debbie and I stick with the Diamond Star Line. You get your money's worth as members of The Cruise Club.'

Sid smiled. Don's Yorkshire thrift was alive and well, ensuring he squeezed every drop of value from his holiday.

The guide led the party to a prime spot and pointed out the panoramic view. 'You can see the Three Cities,' he explained. 'These are Birgu, Senglea, and Cospicua, and if we walk further, you will find statues of prominent figures.'

'Look, there's Winston Churchill,' Fran said as they wandered amongst shady tree-lined pathways, lush with plants and fountains.

Sculpted in bronze and dressed in his trademark suit and bow tie, Churchill struck a characteristic pose, and the guide explained that Churchill inspired King George VI to award the island of Malta the George Cross in 1942 in recognition of the Maltese people's bravery. 'The island played a vital role in the Allied efforts during the Second World War,' he said, 'and endured heavy bombing due to its strategic location in the Mediterranean.'

'Just think of all the money spent on that statue,' Don commented and gazed at Churchill's contemplative expression.

Sid folded his arms. 'I don't think the cost would have mattered,' he said to Don, 'considering the gratitude and respect the people had for Churchill's efforts during the war.'

In the gardens, the guide told them that the area and nearby building of Auberge de Castille were built as a private retreat in the sixteenth century for the Knights of St John and opened to the public in the nineteenth century. He added that the Auberge de Castille was now the prime minister's office.

'Those knights got everywhere,' Sid mused as they walked to the lower gardens.

'You have time to visit the museum here,' Peter informed the group, 'and those of you who wish to browse shops can head to Castille Place. We'll meet here again in one hour.'

Dressed in matching polo shirts, caps and khaki shorts, Don led Debbie to the museum.

'Shall we have a look at the shops?' Sid asked Fran. Taking her hand, they wandered along narrow cobbled streets and admired the beautiful baroque buildings.

'Look at these balconies,' Sid said as he stared at the overhanging box-shaped, carved wooden structures painted in bright colours.

Fran nodded and admired vibrant greens, reds and shades of blue. 'I'd love to sit up there on a hot day, enjoying shelter from the sun, while I take in the view of everyone bustling by below.'

'You'd spend all day chatting non-stop to the neighbours.' Sid grinned, noting the balconies' proximity in the row of stone-built houses.

'Look, there's a red post box, just like home,' Fran said as they entered a steep walkway where street stalls displayed fruit and vegetables piled high alongside herbs of every description.

'A legacy of British colonial rule,' Sid informed her.

As they rounded a corner, they saw Colin and Neeta sitting beneath a colourful umbrella at a café, enjoying a cooling drink. As they passed, they waved.

'That's a good idea,' Sid said and guided Fran to a shady spot at a café where tables lined the cobblestone street. The café played traditional Maltese folk music, and Fran swayed in time as they ordered a carafe of sangria spiked with fresh fruit.

'What's Carmen up to today?' Sid asked. He enjoyed people-watching as locals and tourists wandered by and servers, balancing laden trays, glided effortlessly between tables.

Fran bit into a slice of orange. 'She mentioned visiting the cathedral, I think she was going to take Betty to see it.'

'I heard our guide say that it was well worth a visit,' Sid said as he topped up their drinks.

Fran reached out and squeezed Sid's hand. 'Isn't this wonderful?' She smiled. 'Every port we visit feels like a new adventure.'

'Aye.' Sid returned the squeeze, a grin spreading across his face. 'We're a long way from Blackpool and the world is opening up to us, one port at a time.'

* * *

Carmen stood in a line that formed a queue slowly entering St John's Cathedral and studied two bell towers on either side of the doorway. She thought that they gave a fortress-like appearance to the entrance and was curious to see what the architecture was like inside. Her fingers tapped nervously on the handles of Betty's chair. She hoped they'd soon be through the large wooden doors as Betty's cane was poised and hovering dangerously close to the track-suited behind of a man ahead of them.

'Why can't we get a move on!' Betty moaned. 'I'll get heat-stroke if I sit here any longer.' Betty raised the cane and was about to poke the man to one side when the queue suddenly began to move forward.

To Carmen's relief, moments later, they stepped into

the interior. 'Wow,' she breathed, 'Mum, just look at this amazing place.'

'Too many people, and I can't see anything from this chair.'

'Perhaps you could try having a walk around?'

'What with my poor old bones?' Betty grimaced. 'You know I struggle; how can you be so heartless?'

Carmen remembered Betty waltzing around the dance floor with Holden and thought that her mother's poor old bones were leading them all in a dance of their own. But it was useless to argue and far simpler to give in to Betty's commands.

Pushing the chair along an aisle, Carmen stared at the marble tombstones underfoot, noting that each marked a burial site of knights and notable figures. She was fascinated by the coats of arms decorated with intricate designs. As she stared up at the vaulted ceiling, breathtaking frescoes came into view and every surface boasted complex detail.

The whole building seemed to be covered in gold and vibrant artwork.

'Isn't it incredible?' Carmen said. 'I've never seen such a lavish cathedral. It's quite breathtaking.'

She turned to study a balcony and, to her delight, saw that Theo was poised in the middle, waving his hand. He pointed to a small spiral staircase tucked away in a corner and signalled that she could come up, but Carmen indicated that she couldn't leave Betty. Moments later, Theo was by her side.

'Some place, isn't it?' he said, kissing Carmen on her cheek. 'And you're looking especially lovely today.'

Carmen was wearing a floaty dress with beaded straps. Her hair was scooped up in a clip, and trails of wayward curls framed her face. 'I love this outfit.' She smiled. 'Fran was so clever to pick it out.'

'You look like mutton dressed as lamb,' Betty snapped. 'Are we going to stay here all day?'

'Hello, Betty,' Theo said, taking over and moving the chair forward. 'It's good to see that you're enjoying yourself. Where's Holden today?' he asked.

'He's taking me to dinner tonight.'

Carmen and Theo exchanged a glance. 'That's the first I've heard of it,' Carmen whispered, giving Theo a thumbs up.

The previous evening, Theo had called Carmen to ask if she would join him at Kyle's Sunrise Senior Splashdown in the morning. Theo's waistline was expanding, and he felt that he should attempt to do some exercise. But Carmen had declined and explained that she'd be working on her novel with Ruskin.

'How was your morning's mentoring session?' Theo asked.

'Full on and very helpful,' Carmen replied. 'Ruskin is showing me how to create a framework.'

Theo looked puzzled. 'I can't wait to hear all about it,' he said, 'but first, we must find the oratory. Apparently, Caravaggio's masterpiece – *The Beheading of St John the Baptist* – is there and it's one of his most significant works.'

'Can't we find a café?' Betty complained. 'I don't want to see a lot of blood and gore. I've no idea why you've brought me here.'

Carmen was about to tell Betty that she'd hoped her mother would enjoy visiting one of the island's most famous buildings, but Theo interjected.

Patting Betty's shoulder he said, 'Now, my love, just as soon as we've seen this famous painting, I suggest that we head to an exit and find one of the many eating establishments that I noticed on my way here.'

'Not before time.' Betty pursed her lips in a tight line.

'I'm sure you'd like to try a delicious pastisi, filled with wild mushrooms and ricotta, and a refreshing glass of sangria, too.'

At the mention of sangria, Betty perked up. 'Well, as long as you don't linger by the painting,' she said, 'I *am* feeling quite thirsty, now you come to mention it.'

'Perfect.' Theo grinned.

* * *

Ruskin was making his way back to the ship. He carried two marionettes that he'd found in a gift shop and thought the puppets made perfect gifts for his granddaughters. Dressed in bright polka-dotted dresses with ruffled sleeves, and carrying tiny castanets, he looked forward to seeing the girls' faces when they received their Spanish souvenirs.

Now, he was eager to have a swim before the ship's pool filled with passengers returning from their day out.

He'd enjoyed travelling in a horse-drawn carriage around the sights of Valletta and it had been a most enjoyable form of transport and enabled the writer to view such sights as the Grand Master's Palace and the ruins of the Royal Opera House, destroyed during the Second World War. On previous visits to the island, Ruskin had visited many of the tourist hot spots, and today, he'd broken his sightseeing journey by stopping at a restaurant where he'd enjoyed a hearty lunch of slow-cooked traditional rabbit stew, a Maltese speciality, and two glasses of Gran Cavalier from Malta's Meridiana wine estate.

He was feeling mellow as he strolled along a walkway, enjoying the late afternoon sun that glinted on the still waters of the harbour. But the sudden sound of a horn made him jump to one side. Turning to see what was making all the noise, Ruskin saw a vehicle heading towards him. The wheels of the small land train slowed and soon came to a stop. As carriage doors opened, the walking party from the *Diamond Star* began to pile out.

'Damn,' Ruskin mumbled as he found himself surrounded by passengers, who, like himself, were heading back to the ship.

He was about to pick up his pace when he noticed that Carmen had stepped out of the train and stood to one side as Theo assisted her mother. Carmen was laughing as Theo attempted to jostle a folded wheelchair out of a narrow compartment. Ducking from the old lady's silver-topped cane, Theo stared at Carmen with mock frustration.

How lovely she looks . . . Ruskin thought as he watched the scene.

Carmen's hair, escaping from its clips, cascaded onto her shoulders as she bent forward to assist her mother. She was wearing a pretty dress, and the fabric caught the light, creating an almost translucent effect that hinted at the curves beneath.

Ruskin was mesmerised by Carmen's transformation. How had he not seen the woman beneath her anxious and dreary exterior? Whatever magic was happening to Carmen on this cruise seemed to be working. Even the way she moved suggested that she'd shed a heavy burden. Was it the sea air, the luxury of the ship, the daily outings to new destinations or something else entirely? Whatever it was, she was drawing him in like a tide he couldn't escape. Ruskin's determination to stay away from any romantic liaisons was weakening, and the more he fought it, the more he felt propelled to a place he wasn't prepared to go.

'I say, Ruskin!' A hand touched Ruskin's shoulder, and he spun around to see Peter standing before him. 'I wondered if I could have a word. Do you have a moment?' Peter glanced over his shoulder as he spoke. 'It's rather delicate, and I need your help,' he added.

'Er, yes, of course.' Ruskin tore his eyes away from Carmen and stepped aside to a shaded spot. 'What can I do?'

'A problem is emerging on the ship, and I don't want to create a fuss.' Peter paused, carefully considering his words. 'But you are a sleuth, someone who investigates crimes in your novels, and I wondered if you'd apply your skills and help me?'

Ruskin thought of Detective Inspector Blake and possible new plot lines. 'It sounds intriguing – tell me how I can help.'

Chapter Twenty-Five

It was a sea day on the *Diamond Star* and, with no shore excursions, many passengers rose a little later before having breakfast and heading off to the day's onboard activities. The Deck Café was busy, and those who sat at tables in the shade of overhead canopies stared out at an endless horizon where a golden sky melted like honey into the sea.

Sid stood by a railing, marvelling at the panorama, while Fran sat at a nearby table, sipping an orange juice. They'd enjoyed a cooked breakfast with softly poached eggs, buttery mushrooms and sizzling bacon, followed by slices of toast.

Returning to his seat beside Fran, Sid patted his chest. 'I think I'm overdoing it,' he said, reaching for a glass of iced water.

'Tummy too full?' Fran raised her sunglasses and reached out to stroke Sid's arm.

'Aye, with that big dinner last night and now this breakfast, my heartburn feels like a dragon is breathing flames in my chest.'

'Oh, love, have a drink of water.' Fran raised her eyebrows in concern.

'I think I need to go easy today.' Sid grimaced and rubbed his stomach.

'But food is one of the highlights of a cruise.' Fran smiled. 'After all, it says in the glossy brochure that one must enjoy the culinary voyage and savour every flavour.'

'It might be the sales pitch, but we're not used to so much gorging.' He thought of the porridge that generally started his day.

'Have an antacid,' Fran said, reaching into her bag to unwrap a foil-covered tablet. 'This will calm you down.'

'I've been chomping them all night,' Sid frowned, 'but I don't suppose another will do any harm.'

'Why don't I order a nice peppermint tea to soothe your tum.'

'That's a good idea. I want to feel okay when we sail past Stromboli. I'm looking forward to seeing an active volcano.'

'Talking of eruptions,' Fran whispered, 'here comes Don.'

'By heck, Debbie looks the worse for wear,' Sid observed.

'Morning all,' Don said as he strode purposefully to Fran and Sid's table, 'is there room for two more?' Don's electric blue Lycra sportswear hugged his stomach, emphasising his comfortable relationship with the culinary voyage.

'Help yourself,' Sid said and pulled out a chair. 'Are you all right, Debbie? You look a little bit peaky.'

Debbie wore fluffy slippers and a blanket wrapped around her shoulders, and her hair, generally styled with care, resembled a bird's nest. As she removed her sunglasses to squint at Sid, he wondered if she'd been in a boxing bout, the dark circles around her eyes giving her a haunted expression and the crumpled pantsuit she wore looking more like rumpled pyjamas.

'Have some coffee, love,' Sid said, reaching out to pour Debbie a cup.

'My wife had a drop too much last night and is paying the price this morning.' Don frowned at Debbie. 'I've told her that fresh air and a good fry-up will soon buck her up.'

Sid noted that Debbie's skin had turned the colour of custard. Instead of bucking up, she looked like she was going to throw up.

'Bit of a tummy upset?' Fran moved closer to squeeze Debbie's shoulder. 'My Sid hasn't been feeling too well. Perhaps you've both eaten something that hasn't agreed?'

'More to do with an excess of cocktails and too many tequila shots.' Don shook his head. 'I've told her that she should have joined me for Kyle's Sunrise Senior Splashdown. A session of exercise and fresh air would soon sort things out.'

Debbie groaned and, flinging an arm in Don's direction, swung her hand at his head. But Don, clearly used to ducking and diving, swerved away. Debbie closed her eyes and sipped her coffee, then sucked gratefully on the antacid tablet that Fran had produced.

'Did you have a late night?' Sid asked. He noted that Debbie never got a word in edgeways, Don being the undisputed champion of mouthpieces, with a black belt in talking over his wife.

'Yes, it was in the early hours before I managed to get Debbie safely back to our cabin,' Don said, picking up a menu. When a server appeared, he ordered breakfast.

'Fran and I turned in not long after the evening show in the Neptune Theatre,' Sid said. 'It was a great night with Melody Moon and the *Diamond Star* dancers entertaining us with an evening of Broadway hits.'

'Aye, we caught that too,' Don acknowledged. 'Did you stay for Dicky Delaney's late-night comedy and karaoke?'

'No, but I'm sure it was good.'

'It certainly was, with passengers joining in and the best singer turned out to be a welder by day and Neil Diamond by night.' Don grinned, 'It was a laugh a minute until Debbie took to the stage for her karaoke version of, "I Will Survive".'

'And did she?' Sid asked.

'Not for long; she shook her hips so hard we thought she'd dislodged a disc. It took me, Dicky and a stage assistant to lower her back into the audience.'

'No wonder she needed a drink, poor girl,' Fran interjected.

'Oh, that was at the party.' Don picked up a napkin and tucked it into the edge of his vest. 'Cocktails flowed like a waterfall.'

'Party?' Fran raised her eyebrows.

But before Don had time to answer, Debbie sat up and suddenly changed the subject. 'What time do we sail by the volcano?' she asked.

Sid looked at his watch. 'In a couple of hours, I think.'

The server returned with Don's order and placed a plate of fried eggs, bacon and sausages before Debbie. 'Would you like anything else?' he asked.

Debbie stared at the plump glistening sausages, their

surface split open and juicy fat oozing out. 'I'm going to be s . . .' Debbie exclaimed, thrusting a hand over her mouth and bolting from the café.

Fran pushed back her chair. 'The poor girl,' she said, and ran to help Debbie.

Don stared at Debbie's breakfast, then looked at Sid. 'Be a shame to waste this,' he said, picking up the plate. 'Fancy a sausage?' he asked.

'Gawd, no, not for me . . .' Sid frowned and rubbed his chest. 'My heartburn is already doing the cha-cha-cha.'

'Nowt beats a fry-up.' Don began to tuck in. 'That's what I tell the lads working on my sites, that and starting the day with a mug of builder's brew.'

'Well, bon appetit,' Sid said, sipping his peppermint tea. 'Here's to our first sight of the volcano.'

* * *

Carmen was returning from her session with Ruskin. As she wandered through the ship, she heard an announcement that informed everyone that they would be passing Stromboli in approximately two hours. Those wishing to enjoy the sight of the volcano should stand on the starboard side to watch the fascinating sight.

'I think Mum might enjoy that,' Carmen said to herself as she headed down the stairs to her cabin.

Depositing her bag and removing her laptop to place it on the desk in her room, Carmen sat down and felt tempted to continue with her novel while ideas spun in her head. That morning, she'd been immersed in the new ideas she was creating, and the outline of the current plot was starting to improve.

Ruskin insisted that she dig deep with character profiles, telling her that they had to come to life in her head. 'If you know them inside out, they will guide you through the story,' he'd said.

Eating a silent breakfast, Ruskin sat on his balcony, staring out to sea as he munched through a bowl of muesli, and Carmen began her morning pages.

The session was intense, and Ruskin was a tough teacher.

'What are the stakes?' he demanded. 'Is your protagonist achieving their goals? What do you think of your writing?'

'I thought it was pretty good.' Carmen bit her lip and immediately regretted her words.

'Pretty good doesn't get published, Carmen,' he snapped, 'it gets buried beneath a thousand submissions.'

Carmen's cheeks burned. Today, Ruskin had a way of stripping her confidence with his blunt instructions. Was he suddenly pushing her hard to get the best possible outcome in the limited time available? He paced like a caged lion as they worked, and his critiques were severe as he analysed the current chapter, tearing it apart before teaching her how to build it back up and make it better with every sentence. He illuminated cracks she'd never noticed and her head was spinning.

Determinedly immersed in her work, Carmen had no time to watch Ruskin, but he crept into her thoughts. She longed to breathe in his cologne and touch the warm flesh of his hand when it came too close, then feel the whisper of his breath on her neck. But he'd passed no pleasantries by the time the session ended.

Ruskin walked her to the door of the suite. 'You must make the very best of your talent and work harder, Carmen. Stop holding back.'

Carmen flinched as though struck by a blow as the door slammed in her face. Did Ruskin know how cruel he'd been? She wanted to brush it all away and not show her feelings, but the sting in his words lingered.

Carmen knew she ought to be grateful that he had no romantic interest in his student. This was a mentorship, nothing more. Reminding herself of that would make her ridiculous crush so much easier to bear.

'CARMEN!'

Betty's stick was banging on the adjoining wall. With all thoughts of writing dissolving with each bang, Carmen pushed back her chair. 'Coming, Mum!' she called out and, after taking a last lingering look at her laptop, hurried out of the room.

* * *

The *Diamond Star* sailed majestically through the shimmering waters of the Tyrrhenian Sea, with its course set to include a scenic route past the Aeolian island of Stromboli, a volcanic archipelago situated off the northeastern coast of Sicily. This allowed passengers to admire the volcanic island from the water. The weather was perfect, and with safety considerations relating to volcanic activity observed by Captain Bellwood, the ship travelled along the side of the island to get the best view of Sciara del Fuoco, a steep slope where lava often flowed into the sea.

Sid and Fran held hands as they stood on the ship's starboard side, gazing at the jagged land that rose dramatically before them. Fran wore a bright cotton dress, the floral skirt full, billowing around her legs. Clustered at the base of Stromboli, they could see a smattering of whitewashed buildings, and Fran pointed out the spire of a church.

'People must live on the island,' she said, reaching for her phone to take a photo.

'Aye, it says in the guidebook that it has a population of around four hundred folks,' Sid commented, 'and they are geared up for tourism. Stromboli is a popular travel destination.'

'I'm not sure I'd like to live so close to a volcano,' Fran shook her head.

'There are eruptions every ten to twenty minutes, but all low-level apparently.' Sid gazed ahead, hoping to see a burst of lava flow down the side of the mountain. 'It's known as the Lighthouse of the Mediterranean, and you can visit Stromboli by ferry. There are beaches of black sand, and guides will take you on a hike to witness the eruptions safely.'

'That might suit Don. He has an adventurous spirit.' Fran grinned as Don and Debbie joined them.

'Adventurous spirit?' Don questioned. 'Just as long as it doesn't cost more than a pint at my local.'

A group of maintenance engineers appeared and acknowledged the passengers gathered by the railings. They wore white boiler suits bearing the *Diamond Star* logo and held up their phones to capture the unforgettable sight of a volcano.

'I hope you lads have left someone in charge down below,' Don said, 'or else we'll be using paddles to get past Stromboli.'

Debbie rolled her eyes. Smiling at the engineers, she edged her way between them to join in with the sightseeing. A few moments later, Carmen appeared with Theo, who was taking charge of Betty.

'Room for a few more?' Theo called out and spun Betty's chair into position.

'How lovely to see you.' Fran beamed and hugged Carmen. 'And don't you look the business in your new outfit.' She stood back to admire Carmen's capri pants and matching lacey vest. 'Your gorgeous hair is getting lighter, and I must say again how much that cut suits you.'

Carmen smiled. 'You're a star, Fran, you've transformed me, and I love my new look.'

Seeing his hero, Sid held out his hand to Theo. 'Hello again, it's good to see you,' he said.

'I found these two loitering by guest services,' Theo explained, 'clearly lost. They wanted to know the best place to take in the view.'

'I wasn't lost,' Betty snapped. 'I don't know why everyone is crowded on deck to see a blackened hill.'

'It's a volcano, Mum,' Carmen explained, 'a very special sight and one of the highlights of the holiday.'

'Well, it's done nothing to highlight my holiday, and I hope that we arrive somewhere better than this very soon. I didn't shell out good money to stare at a blank horizon all day.' Betty gripped the railing and raised herself from her chair. Leaning out, she scanned from side to side, curious to study the onlookers. 'Has anyone seen Holden?' she asked. 'I'm having lunch with him today.' Turning back to the ship, she shoved forward. 'I'm doing my stretches,' Betty said and began to wave her arms. 'My doctor says I must try to move my poor old bones despite the excruciating pain.'

Staring at her mother, Carmen shook her head. Betty appeared to have forgotten her frailty. Now, using her cane, she crept along the deck with the agility of a cat burglar, any pain dispersing as fast as the smoke from the volcano. Her wheelchair had been abandoned in her quest to find Holden.

Theo noted Carmen's concern. 'Shall I go after her?' he asked.

'No, she'll be back as soon as she needs sympathy. But with any luck, she'll hook up with her lunch date and be gone for the afternoon.'

The ship had slowed, and everyone stared at Stromboli. In stark contrast to the clear blue sky, wisps of blueish-grey smoke began to billow from the summit as though the volcano had started to wheeze.

'It looks restless to me,' Don commented. His brow was furrowed as smoke swirled upwards, darkening the sky.

Fran turned to Sid. Tilting her head, she studied her husband. 'Are you all right, love?' she asked. 'You look a little pale.'

'Aye, my damn indigestion playing up again,' Sid replied with a sigh. 'Give my back a pat, will you?'

Fran began patting Sid's back then rubbed her hand in a circular motion. 'Any better?' she asked after a few minutes.

'Don't worry about me, my sweetheart, just enjoy the volcano.'

Reassured, Fran smiled at Sid, but as she turned, a sudden explosion made everyone jump back from the rails. Ash and lava flew high into the sky, and, grateful to be at a safe distance, onlookers watched in awe as the fiery red and gold torrent lightened the darkened sky above the summit of the volcano. Fran heard Sid cry out and smiled, pleased that he was enjoying this wonderful experience. But the sound of the thud that followed caused her to spin around.

Startled, everyone moved back, and Debbie gasped.

Sid lay on the deck, as still as a statue, his face pale and his hand clutching his chest.

'No!' Fran cried. '*No!* Not my Sid . . .'

Theo rushed forward and knelt beside Sid, taking hold of his wrist to check his pulse. 'It's okay, Sid, try not to panic; help is on the way.'

Theo looked up, his eyes searching for Carmen. Their unspoken words sent Carmen rushing off to find assistance.

Fran fell to the floor, her hand clutching Sid's. 'Someone help him, please,' she urged, her face streaked with tears.

'It's all right, sweetheart,' Sid mumbled, 'don't worry, I . . . I'll be right as rain in a moment.'

Perspiration broke out on his brow, and Fran dabbed at it with the soft fabric of her skirt. 'Oh, you daft old fool, you're scaring me,' she said, gently kissing his cheek and brushing the few strands of hair from his forehead.

'Make way!' a voice called out moments later, and Kyle appeared. He wore bright red spandex Speedos, his sliders slapping as he sprinted down the deck with a medical kit slung over his shoulder. Gripping his two-way radio, he yelled, 'Medics, to the viewing deck! Starboard side. Passenger down.'

Don leaped back, wide-eyed, and stared at Kyle. 'I feel like I'm on the set of *Baywatch* . . .' he said as Kyle reached Sid and flung a rainbow-coloured towel to the floor.

Theo knelt beside Sid and looked up at Carmen, who gave a shrug and whispered, 'He was the first crew member I could find . . .'

'Don't worry darling, I've got you,' Kyle soothed as he knelt beside Theo and leaned over Sid, padding the towel beneath his own knees. 'First things first, you need to breathe in and breathe out.'

Theo thought Kyle was stating the bleedin' obvious and resisted the urge to roll his eyes. Was that the best that he could come up with? He scanned the fitness instructor's face for a hint of medical expertise, knowing he'd heard more inspired advice on daytime TV.

'Is it his heart?' Fran whispered.

'Without a doubt,' Kyle replied. 'Prepare yourself . . .'

Fran almost collapsed, and Theo could scarcely believe what he'd heard. If there was any more loose talk from Kyle, Fran would need medical assistance, too. He reached out and gripped Fran's hand and smiled encouragingly, resisting the urge to fling Kyle to one side. 'It's fine, Fran,' Theo said, 'stay strong, your man is going to be okay.'

Passengers watching the unfolding scene stood back as two uniformed nurses appeared. Relinquishing his role, Theo breathed a sigh of relief as he let the professionals take over. He stood beside Carmen as Sid was examined with swift efficiency and wired up to a portable monitor. The nurses asked if the wheelchair by the railings might be used to transport Sid to the medical facility, and Theo moved forward to assist.

'Good job I was here,' Kyle said and neatly folded his towel.

Theo raised an eyebrow and stared at Kyle. 'I don't know what we'd have done without your towel-folding skills,' he said. 'You're the unsung hero of the day.' Placing his arm around Fran's shoulders as Sid was secured in the chair, he nodded as Carmen picked up Fran's bag, both knowing Fran would need their support.

Sid's eyes were closed. He held a hand to his chest and as the passengers parted, the nurses moved ahead with Sid, to a door halfway along the deck. Everyone else turned when a voice suddenly screeched out:

'CARMEN! Where are those people going with my chair?'

Chapter Twenty-Six

Ruskin was aware that there had been a commotion on the viewing deck. News of a passenger collapsing swept through the ship like wildfire, igniting speculation as guests gathered in groups, exchanging fragments of what they'd heard. As the whispers built, some said that Sid was struck by molten lava from the volcano and would need to be airlifted to hospital on the mainland, while others muttered that a giant seabird had crashed against his head, rendering him senseless.

Sitting on a steamer bed by the side of the pool, Ruskin wondered if a body would be removed from the ship at their next port of call in Ibiza. Deaths on cruise lines, he knew, were not something a company openly reported. However, given the average age of the passengers on the *Diamond Star*, Ruskin thought such an incident would inevitably occur, and it was a plot he might use in his novel.

With his pen poised and notebook open, Ruskin couldn't help but think about the ailing passenger. No one wanted their holiday to be marred by illness, especially on a cruise, which was a dream come true for many. But despite the commotion on the viewing deck, he felt that the atmosphere onboard that day was leisurely, and a sea day was the opportunity to relax beside the pool, sip a cocktail in an outdoor bar, and enjoy casual conversations.

Ruskin was hosting a workshop that afternoon but had decided to use his free time to think about Peter's dilemma. Missing jewellery was a delicate matter, and Ruskin thought that without any concrete evidence, the items may simply have been misplaced or accidentally overlooked. Peter had given him the names of the passengers who'd lost items, and now, to Peter's despair, one more missing item was added to the list. Neeta had reported that she couldn't find her silver and emerald earrings.

Taking his pen, Ruskin jotted down his preliminary thoughts.

When was their last sighting of the piece and had the jewellery been lost on a shore excursion?

He knew that Peter was having the public rooms checked again in case anything had been left behind, but so far there was no sign of the missing jewellery. The situation required diplomacy to avoid panic amongst the passengers and as his thoughts formed, he caught glimpses of the calming turquoise waters stretching out to the horizon. 'I shall enjoy this investigation,' he mused, as an occasional fishing boat sailed by and a cruise ship could be seen on the horizon. He decided to make a start by discreetly speaking to those who'd suffered a loss.

A steward approached, and Ruskin ordered a beer.

As the ice-cold nectar refreshed his thirst, his thoughts

returned to the earlier session with Carmen. Ruskin was aware that he'd been too tough with her. Foolishly pacing in his suite like a caged lion as they worked, he was aware that he was overly critical and that tearing apart each chapter of her book was unnecessary. But whatever he threw at her, Carmen seemed to soak it up. She was like a sponge, keen to improve, never buckling under the weight of his harsh comments. He couldn't help but admire her resilience when every cutting suggestion was met with a quiet nod of acceptance.

But in his heart, Ruskin knew there was more to it all.

When Carmen entered his suite, he felt like a light had been turned on. Senses that had been dormant for years suddenly woke up, and he saw past the eager student to the woman stealing his heart. As she hesitantly took her place at his desk, he'd noted her features softened by the frame of perfectly styled hair. A faint blush coloured her cheeks as she tilted her head to avoid his gaze. Carmen had a quiet allure that drew him in, and when she looked up to listen to his harsh critique, her eyes held a hundred unspoken thoughts. What was she thinking?

He wondered if she hated him for how he'd treated her that morning. No one had to put up with rudeness but perhaps by overlooking it she was using him to achieve her goal?

Ruskin was battling with his feelings. Venetia had deadened his longing and lust, but Carmen's vulnerability stirred it, despite his decision to lead a solitary life free from the demands of romance.

'Sort yourself out, man,' Ruskin told himself. He mustn't let a longing for Carmen take control or complicate his life.

Draining his glass, he lay back and, enjoying the tranquillity, closed his eyes to nap. A little while later, voices from the side of the pool suggested that Kyle was about to start a Senior Splashdown session and as Ruskin slowly roused himself, he realised that someone was hovering by his bed.

'What on earth are you doing?' Ruskin asked as he opened his eyes and stared at the crouched figure of Dicky Delaney, who was flailing his hand beneath Ruskin's bed.

'Er . . . sorry mate, I thought you were asleep and didn't mean to disturb you, but I often sit in this section, and I'm looking for an item I've misplaced.'

Ruskin was about to tell Dicky that he wasn't his mate but realised that this was an opportunity to speak to the comedian.

'Don't worry, you haven't disturbed me. Do you fancy a beer?'

Dicky shuffled back, and Ruskin noted his look of surprise. The pair didn't get on, but Ruskin knew he needed to mend the situation if he were to question Dicky about his missing chain.

Dicky, ever eager for free booze, nodded his head.

Ruskin caught a steward's attention and ordered two beers. 'Have a seat,' he said to Dicky.

Comfortable with a cold drink, they watched the group of passengers by the side of the pool. Kyle was handing out noodle flotation aides and encouraging everyone to enter the water.

'Did you say you'd lost something?' Ruskin casually asked. He focused on a man with a Yorkshire accent almost pulling his partner into the pool.

'Yes, a chunky gold chain.'

'A chain that you wear around your neck?'

'Yes, mad, really. It weighs a ton, and I feel like a heavyweight champion when I wear it, so I can't understand how I might have misplaced it.'

'You've searched your room?'

'My broom cupboard, you mean.' Dicky sighed. 'Yes, many times and it's not there.'

'Is it likely to have fallen off when you've gone ashore?'

'Nah, I don't think so, I'm sure I would have noticed.'

Ruskin thought that a heavy, weighty chain *would* be a noticeable loss unless the comedian was preoccupied.

'Was the clasp inadequate?'

'I wouldn't have thought so.'

'At least you'll have it insured; that must be some comfort.' Ruskin turned to Dicky, but noticing the look of horror on the comedian's face, realised that the chain wasn't insured.

'Well, not exactly . . .' Dicky was hesitant. 'It was a gift, and the person who gave it to me will be apoplectic when she finds out.'

'Ah, I see.'

Ruskin did indeed see. Whoever had gifted the chain would want to show off their trophy companion, bedecked with their expensive gift.

The two men were distracted by a commotion in the pool, where Kyle had grabbed a flotation aid and jumped in, dragging a woman to the surface.

'Never let go of your noodle!' Kyle shouted.

Red-faced and spluttering, the woman was assisted to

the steps by Kyle and the Yorkshire man, who spoke loudly, berating Kyle. 'A couple of Yorkshire puddings would be more buoyant than your noodles,' he growled. 'I told you my missus can hardly swim.'

'That's Debbie and her husband Don,' Dicky mused as he saw Debbie's arms flapping like a freshly caught fish as she shrugged off Kyle and Don and, steadying herself on the steps, waddled away like a penguin.

Ruskin remembered Peter's list of passengers who'd misplaced jewellery and realised that Debbie was included. 'Do you know her?' he asked.

'Er, sort of.' Dicky was evasive. 'Well no, not really,' he added and looked away.

A couple, hand in hand, wandered past, and when they saw Dicky, they both smiled and waved.

'Morning Colin, Neeta,' Dicky called out.

'You must get to know everyone,' Ruskin said. He stared as the couple moved away, remembering that Peter had told him that Neeta had lost her valuable earrings.

'It's a small ship, and I must entertain,' Dicky continued. 'As a crew member, it's part of my job to be friendly.'

'Of course.'

'Well, thanks for the drink, but I need to get on. Rehearsals are calling.' Dicky stood.

'I hope you find your chain,' Ruskin said, rubbing his chin thoughtfully as Dicky walked away.

'Any room for two tiddlers?' the Yorkshire man called out and approached the vacant chairs beside Ruskin.

'Help yourself,' Ruskin said. He winced as the man shook his hair and droplets of water sprayed everywhere.

'You're that writer,' the man said. 'We're Don and Debbie,' he continued and sat down.

'Have a towel.' Ruskin reached out, handing Debbie a large fluffy towel. 'You appeared to have got into a bit of trouble in the pool.'

'Nowt to worry about,' Don said, 'Debbie likes to think she's a mermaid but keeps forgetting she hasn't got fins.'

From beneath the towel, Ruskin heard Debbie groan. Emerging with wet hair plastered over her face, she shot Don a withering look.

'Can I get you both a drink?' Ruskin asked.

'Aye, a couple of beers would refresh our parts.' Don settled back, his face turned to the sun.

Their drinks arrived, and Debbie dug into a dish of peanuts as she sipped her beer.

'Dicky was telling me that he's lost a gold chain,' Ruskin began, 'he's quite upset about it.'

Don sat up, and Debbie began to fidget in her chair. 'Not as upset as I am,' Don looked angry. 'Debbie misplaced a diamond droplet necklace that cost me a fortune, and Peter, that useless purser, is doing nothing about it.'

'Oh dear, I am sorry, Debbie. Do you know where you lost it?'

Don rolled his eyes and interjected, 'If she knew where she lost it, we'd have found it by now.'

Don's face was red, and as Debbie stretched out her foot and kicked his ankles, Ruskin decided that if Debbie wasn't going to speak for herself, it was time for him to move away.

'Well, it's been pleasant meeting you, but I have a workshop to prepare.' Grabbing his bag and placing his notebook deep in the folds, Ruskin slipped into his sandals and stood up. 'I hope you find the misplaced jewellery.' He gave a courteous nod.

As Ruskin walked away, he heard Don angrily say to Debbie, 'The only thing misplaced around here, is your necklace and my patience!'

Chapter Twenty-Seven

Carmen stood by the railings on the promenade deck of the *Diamond Star* and stared out to sea. Then, closing her eyes, she whispered a grateful prayer to whatever higher deity protected cruise ship passengers during their voyage.

They'd thought that Sid was at death's door, suffering from a heart attack, but tests in the medical centre confirmed nothing more serious than acid indigestion, causing Sid's severe pain, probably brought on by an overload of rich and fatty food. There was a possibility that Sid may have a hiatus hernia, and he was to make an appointment with his own doctor as soon as he got home. Now armed with medication, Sid was advised to avoid trigger foods, watch his diet and drink soothing peppermint tea.

Opening her eyes, Carmen studied the deep blue of the Tyrrhenian Sea, stretching endlessly, the horizon occasionally dotted with passing ships and cruise liners. She thought about Fran as they'd anxiously waited for Sid to undergo tests. Fran had battled to stay calm for her husband's sake, but Carmen knew her new friend was suppressing her distress.

'He's the centre of my world,' Fran said as she gripped Carmen's hand and dabbed at her eyes. 'I can't imagine life without him. We've known each other since we were teens.'

'Tell me about your life together,' Carmen asked, keen to divert Fran from the activity in the adjacent room.

In the small waiting room, Fran leaned back in her chair and explained that Sid had always dreamed of putting their hometown of Blackpool on the culinary map. During the dark days of the pandemic, when their takeaway business had soared, their bank balance reached a level they'd never imagined.

'Now that we can afford it, let's give a fancy restaurant a go, lass,' Sid pleaded. 'If it doesn't work out, we can always return to selling fish and chips.'

'Why don't we buy a place in Spain?' Fran asked, still reluctant to commit and conscious that her cookery skills wouldn't quite cut it. After all, they had money to buy a nice villa and retire early.

'I want to serve the best food in Blackpool.' Sid was emphatic.

Fran told Carmen that as innocent teenagers, they'd sat on the Blackpool prom in deckchairs overlooking the crowded beach. 'Look at all these folk,' Sid had said and spread out an arm to point at holidaymakers enjoying donkey rides and Mr Whippy ice creams. Straightening his button-down Ben Sherman shirt, Sid fiddled with braces supporting two-toned trousers while Fran dunked a straw in a bottle of Babycham.

'The best grub is fish and chips,' Fran replied, 'that's what Blackpool is known for.'

Sid lit a Woodbine. 'All right,' he'd agreed, 'I know you're right, but no one can take a dream away, and it's my dream that one day Sid and Fran Cartwright will have foodies flocking to our door.'

'We worked two jobs each,' Fran continued, 'and eventually saved enough for a lease on a shack on the Golden Mile.'

Selling candyfloss and burgers, in time, they rented a fish and chip café by the central pier, which they eventually purchased. But Sid never lost sight of his dream, and as the years rolled on, Fran anxiously kept a silent counsel, knowing that it would take great courage to change course from the life they knew.

'Sid sent me to France to learn about haute cuisine.' Fran smiled and patted Carmen's arm. 'I didn't want to go and nearly had a panic attack when I met the Michelin-starred chef running the school, but the cookery course was brilliant, and I learned so much that I was buzzing when I got back.'

'Is that how you started your fine dining restaurant?' Carmen asked.

'Yes,' Fran nodded, 'and it's been a success.'

'No wonder you love each other so much. You've shared quite a journey together.'

'Oh, lass, you've no idea. Don't get me started on the babies that we lost and health scares, too. I was impossible to live with at times and I have no idea how Sid stayed with me when he was grieving so badly himself.'

'I'm sorry, Fran. I had no idea. Please don't feel you have to explain anything to me.'

'It's all right, dear, we overcame our difficulties, but I've always known that if the day came when I'd lost Sid, it would be the one difficulty I'd never overcome.'

'Thankfully, that day hasn't arrived.' Carmen hugged Fran. 'Look, here's Theo,' she said and turned to see Theo carrying two mugs of tea.

'Any news?' he asked, handing Carmen and Fran the tea.

But before they could respond, a nurse appeared, and she wore a beaming smile. 'Mrs Cartwright? You can see your husband now . . .'

Carmen looked at her watch. She must stop daydreaming, or she would miss Ruskin's concluding workshop. She began to wander through the ship, past the library and the lounge where afternoon tea was being served, and as she made her way, Carmen thought of the adoration between Fran and Sid. Standing with Theo as they heard the good news about Sid's diagnosis, she'd witnessed the profound outpouring of love and relief between the couple. Fran held onto Sid as if to shield him from anything further while Sid stroked Fran's hair and kissed her forehead, gripping her tightly.

Carmen wondered how it must feel to be loved like that. To be wholly adored, cherished, and the centre of someone's universe. As she left the room with Theo, she'd heard Sid say to Fran, 'I love you, my darling, and I'm going to be okay.'

Exchanging glances with Theo, she saw that he had tears in his eyes. Carmen knew that he was feeling his own loss of Ruari, as he witnessed the unshakable bond between Sid and Fran. She felt a lump rise in her throat, her emotions threatening to overwhelm her, knowing she'd never find a love so deep.

As though embarrassed by his tears, Theo wiped at his eyes quickly, but Carmen didn't look away. Instead, she wrapped her arm around him and pulled him into a hug. They began to walk in silence, and Sid's words lingered in her mind. *I'm going to be okay!* Carmen wasn't sure if she believed it yet – for Sid, for Theo and even for herself. But hearing the words made her want to try.

And that, she realised, was a start.

Reaching the door of Ruskin's workshop, Carmen's hand hovered over the handle, her fingers curling uncertainly. She could see the class through the glass panel – a sea of eager faces turning towards Ruskin as he prepared to begin. There was energy in the room, but for Carmen, it only made her feel like an outsider.

If she went in now, she knew she'd slip into a chair at the back, feeling small and insignificant. She'd spend the next two hours watching Ruskin, with his easy charm, dominating the room with a smile that promised brilliance. The same man who, hours earlier, had torn into her work and left her reeling.

Carmen was rooted to the spot. Ruskin was her hero. Wasn't he? The author whose opinion mattered most. But at that moment, Carmen wasn't so sure.

Her eyes studied his gestures, his confident smile, the flick of his wrist as he brushed a lock of hair from his forehead, and the way his mouth moved as he spoke. That was the Ruskin everyone else saw. The one who made Carmen want to write better, to be better. But he was also the man who'd ignited a fire in her heart that no one else ever had. She wanted to melt into his arms, to lose herself in the tenderness of his kiss and longed for Ruskin to be the man in her dreams.

But she knew there was another side, the one she'd been on the receiving end of earlier. Yes, his feedback had great value, and every critical comment carried a lesson as he forced her to try harder. But he made Carmen feel like a child desperate for approval that never came.

How could she long for a man like that and crave his affection?

Carmen realised that her fantasies were pure fiction, and she'd spent too long believing he was her salvation, her muse and now . . . her love?

The stark reality was that the man could lift her up and tear her down in the same breath and she was only hurting herself. After his treatment of her that morning, she knew that she must let Ruskin go. Her thoughts churned as she watched him. Did she really want to put herself through this workshop when there was every chance his behaviour towards her would be unforgiving?

Laughter erupted from the room, and Carmen saw that everyone was already hooked on Ruskin's every word. *What am I doing?* The urge to escape became overwhelming.

Without pausing to think, Carmen turned on her heel.

Oh, how it hurt, the pain was like an old coat, heavy and all-encompassing and her heart ached as she moved away. Blinking back tears, she knew she had to stop dreaming about a man who'd never be hers. It was time to write her own ending, and it didn't include Ruskin's approval. Carmen had written a bestseller before and was determined to do it again.

Whatever wisdom awaited inside that room would have to go on without her.

Chapter Twenty-Eight

Betty Cunningham and Holden Jackson were celebrating when Carmen got back to her cabin and heard music. 'Are you all right?' Carmen asked as she knocked on her mother's door.

The door swung open, and Betty stood with a glass in her hand. She wore a *Diamond Star* T-shirt and cruise-themed cap. 'Here she is,' Betty said, moving back as Carmen entered the room. 'My daughter has come to put a downer on our day.'

'Of course I haven't,' Carmen said as she looked around the room, where Holden was sprawled on the bed wearing a T-shirt and cap that matched Betty's. He spun a keychain between his fingers and sipped champagne from a logoed mug. 'What have you both been up to?' Carmen asked.

'You might be surprised to hear that we won first prize at the Golden Oldies Dance Like No One Is Watching afternoon event.' Betty grinned. 'Holden and I showed off a few moves that impressed the judges and added a little humour to win us a few extra points.'

Carmen thought that the judges must be blind, and the audience certainly wasn't watching. Her mother's humour could clear a room faster than a fire alarm, and her wit was probably best enjoyed with earplugs and a stiff drink.

'How wonderful, I'm very happy for you both.' Carmen smiled. 'Was the prize champagne?'

'A bottle each and a bag full of *Diamond Star* goodies.' Betty wandered over to the bed and sat down beside Holden.

'How are your poor old bones after all that dancing?' Carmen asked.

Betty sighed dramatically and reached out for Holden's hand. 'I'm in constant pain,' she said, 'but I wouldn't want to hold my Holden back with my suffering. I just quietly grin and bear it.'

Carmen saw 'My Holden' smile sympathetically at his Bet and she knew it was time to leave the couple alone. Whatever magic he was weaving over Betty in the form of spiritual pain relief, Carmen hoped it would continue, at least until the end of the cruise.

'Don't wait for me this evening,' Betty said. 'Holden is treating me to dinner in the Atrium restaurant.' She smiled lovingly and stroked Holden's fingers. 'He's reserved a table for Jaden Bird's tasting menu.'

'That sounds like an amazing treat,' Carmen said.

As Carmen closed the door, she thought about the cost of a meal in the Atrium and knew the tasting menu would cover a month's shopping at home. Holden must be loaded. Entering her own cabin, she wondered if the dinner was to celebrate something special. Perhaps Holden was celebrating his birthday? Carmen flopped down on her bed, and as she kicked off her shoes, she fantasised wildly about Betty jetting off to the States to live in Holden's Florida home, which was probably luxurious. Had Holden come on this cruise specifically to meet someone? After all, Betty was single and had assets that amounted to a tidy sum. Despite needing updating, Desbett House, set in an acre of grounds, was worth a great deal, and Carmen's dad had left his family more than adequately provided for with investments that had paid substantial dividends over the years.

Carmen stared at the ceiling and considered that many older couples met on cruises. Sometimes, they even tied the knot on the ship. Carmen couldn't imagine that Betty's serendipitous meeting with Holden would lead to anything more than enjoyable company for both during their holiday. No one in their right mind would put up with Betty for long.

Carmen sighed and daydreamed about life without Betty. It would free her to pursue her own dream, filling her days with writing in a place of her own, somewhere that Carmen could truly call home.

She remembered Villa Galini in Maxos – the charming retreat overlooking the sea with steps patterned in pretty mosaic tiles and terracotta pots on either side of a blue front door. The villa, three stories high, boasted overhanging balconies and a terrace, and she could almost imagine the pleasure of sitting there, watching the world drift by.

Carmen stretched, turning to hug her pillow, allowing herself a fantasy of the lonely writer blossoming in her new home. Every morning, she'd wake to the soft rustling branches of the fir tree outside before throwing open the shutters to reveal the horseshoe-shaped beach below. Carmen would eat breakfast on a balcony, enjoying local yoghurt laced with delicious honey supplied by the elderly man who slept on the bench. Isolation would feel like a companion, and her words would flow in this peaceful place.

The phone rang, waking Carmen from her dreams. Wondering if Betty needed assistance with dressing for the evening, she answered it.

'Hello, Mum, what can I help you with?'

'Hello, my darling, isn't it a fine evening to be alive?' Theo's voice held a hint of humour.

'Hello you,' Carmen began to smile, 'I thought it was an emergency call from my mother, insisting that I zip her into a dress that she insists makes her look twenty years younger.'

'It sounds like Betty has a special evening ahead?'

'The Atrium, no less, for Jaden Bird's tasting menu.'

'A financial commitment, for sure,' Theo laughed. 'Do you think Holden is going to propose?'

Carmen nearly dropped the phone. 'What! Propose to my mother?'

'Why not? Stranger things have happened at sea. At their age, the only thing left to lose is time.'

'B . . . but Betty, married again? She's been set in her ways for decades,' Carmen spluttered.

'Well, she seems to have embraced the whirlwind that is Holden, and you might be in for a surprise.'

Carmen was momentarily speechless. 'Let's not get ahead of ourselves. He could be after her money.'

'Let him have it. It'd be worth every penny and you can always come and live with me. Just think,' Theo said, 'freedom beckons for you.'

Theo's voice was warm and sincere, and Carmen hugged the phone to her ear. She might not be lucky in love, but she'd struck pure gold in friendship.

'But in the meantime,' Theo continued, 'Fran has asked us to their suite for drinks to thank us for today.'

'She doesn't have to do that,' Carmen said. 'I'd do anything for Fran and Sid.'

'Me too, but I say we accept their kind invitation, and I'll pick you up in an hour. Would you consider having dinner with me, too?'

'My lovely Theo, there is absolutely nothing in the world at this moment that I'd like more. Thank you, I'll see you soon.'

Carmen replaced the phone and sat up.

She felt bittersweet at the thought of parting ways with Theo, Fran and Sid. Their friendship added a new brightness to her days. She spent so much time alone, wrapped up in her writing and the demands of Betty's daily life, that she didn't know how good companionship could feel. Saying goodbye and returning to her predictable world was strangely disheartening.

This fleeting escape, the cruise of her dreams, would end soon, and she would head back to the grey routine of her life in Butterly. The pleasure of interesting excursions and spontaneous conversations would fade, replaced by the familiar quiet of Desbett House and solitary hours spent coaxing words onto a screen.

Carmen suddenly decided that with only two more sun-drenched days ahead, she should make the most of them and stop worrying about her novel. Now that she had the framework of her book in place, it was time to put it to one side. Feeling anxious that she was rejecting the main reason for being here, Carmen knew that she was grateful for Ruskin's time and tuition, but as she swung her legs over the side of the bed, she made her mind up that she couldn't take any more of his critical comments and wouldn't be attending the early morning mentoring sessions.

'I'll send him a note,' Carmen decided, aware of the need to be polite, and taking a pen and a sheet of *Diamond Star* stationery, she began to write.

> Ruskin,
> I want to express my gratitude for the time and effort you've invested in me, but I won't be continuing with your mentoring sessions. They have been invaluable, and I appreciate the expertise you've shared in our discussions. That said, I have decided that I need to enjoy every moment before the cruise ends and I return home to finish my current novel.
> Thank you for all you've done to support me.
> With my best wishes,
> Carmen

Trusting that she'd hit the right tone, Carmen slipped the note into an envelope. She'd ask Fernando to deliver it to Ruskin's suite and hope that Ruskin wouldn't be offended. But she reasoned he was so thick skinned, she had no doubt that he wouldn't notice her absence.

Now, the most important thing she had to decide was which of her new fabulous outfits she would wear that evening.

* * *

In the comfort of Fran and Sid's suite, the setting sun cast a breathtaking backdrop as Theo and Carmen stood on the balcony alongside the reunited pair, who were happily back in each other's arms, and watched the horizon transform into a canvas of pinks and purples merging with the deep blue of the sea.

Dressed for the occasion, Fran wore a flowing dress of rainbow colours with silver bangles jingling on her arm. Sid, in smart trousers and a bright yellow shirt, wore a smile as vibrant as Fran's outfit.

'I could live on a ship,' Sid said, 'everything feels so peaceful at times like this, as though the moment is suspended while we pause to take in the beauty of the amazing world out there.'

'Blimey, you're getting all lyrical.' Fran laughed. 'Sid Cartwright, the writer, who'd have thought it?'

'Fran has a point, Sid,' Theo added. 'Have you ever thought about writing?'

'No,' Sid sipped from a glass of ice-cold sparkling water, 'not until now, but my little upset this morning has made me think.'

'What about, my sweetheart?' Fran asked.

'How hard we work when we should be thinking about slowing down and enjoying our golden years.'

'Well, that's the first time I've ever heard you say anything like that.' Fran touched Sid's arm. 'I thought you liked our working life.'

'I do, but the dreams we built have all come true, and I want to spend my days enjoying life with you.'

'Ha!' Theo said. 'You see, Sid, you're a poet, and you don't know it.'

They all laughed, and Theo topped up their glasses, smiling when Sid declined any champagne.

'Are you watching your diet, my friend?' Theo asked.

'With this one's eagle eye permanently trained on me, I'll have no choice.' Sid took hold of Fran's hand. 'We had a bit of a scare today, and I never thought that acid reflux could be so painful. It's taught me a lesson.'

'But all that matters is that you're well,' Fran said, 'and if we must watch our intake more closely, then so be it. I could do with losing a few pounds.'

'You're gorgeous, Fran,' Sid said, 'and I'll always love you just as you are.'

'I promise not to turn into the food police, but I want you to be in fine fettle.' Fran winked at Sid. 'Besides we ought to include some healthy options on our restaurant menu.'

Theo raised his glass. 'I propose a toast to health. May it be the only thing we need to worry about.'

Everyone chinked glasses, then Fran held a plate of nibbles and encouraged Carmen to try a bite of smoked salmon topped with caviar on a slither of blini. 'Go on, fill your boots,' Fran urged. 'You've no fear of gaining a pound or two, and I must say that you look absolutely fabulous in that dress.'

'Hear, hear,' said Theo, 'I shall be the envy of everyone tonight.'

Carmen dipped her head. She wasn't used to compliments, and they could see that she felt uneasy.

Fran took hold of Carmen's hand, lifting it and twisting her into a twirl. 'Just look at you!' She laughed. 'Where did that shy woman go who boarded the ship and wouldn't say boo to a goose?'

'You mean the dull, dowdy, downtrodden person who's blossomed since she met the three of you,' Carmen replied.

Sid grinned, and Theo nodded as Fran gave Carmen a hug. They wordlessly acknowledged that Carmen looked stunning in her evening gown. The satin fabric caught the light, the mix of blues the colours of the ocean, flattering her figure as it hugged her curves before cascading to the floor. Delicate beading on thin straps added glamour, and Carmen had pinned her hair in a soft, flattering updo that framed her delicately made-up face.

'Now,' Fran announced, her voice warm with gratitude, 'don't let me and Sid stop you both from enjoying your evening.' She gently set her glass down on a table. 'We're planning a quiet night in, but before you go, we both want to express our heartfelt thanks for your kindness and support today. I was hopeless in a crisis, and the fact that you were both there, rooting for us, means the world, and we won't forget it.'

'Nonsense,' Theo said, 'of course we would be there, and I know I speak on behalf of Carmen too when I say that meeting you and enjoying your lovely northern company has enhanced this cruise for me. Can I come and dine at your restaurant soon?'

'Any time!' Sid and Fran chorused. 'Both of you, come and stay at Dunromin, our home at North Shore.'

Carmen placed her glass beside Fran's. 'I'd love to and hope that when we leave the ship, we'll continue to be friends.'

Sid nodded. 'I've told Fran that this cruise is the first of many for us. We love everything about it, and no matter where life takes us all, let's keep in touch and have many more adventures. When this holiday ends, our friendship doesn't have to.'

'Now off you go and enjoy yourselves!' Fran shooed Theo and Carmen out of the suite.

On their own, Sid held Fran's hand and led her back to the balcony. Standing side by side with the gentle sound of the sea beneath them, they felt the warm air on their skin and breathed the faint scent of seawater.

'Who would have thought that plain old Sid from Blackpool would make friends with the celebrity Theo McCarthy?' Sid said.

'We're all the same Sid, just flesh and blood, breathing the same air, so why shouldn't you two be friends?'

'Aye, I guess so, but a cruise *is* magical, isn't it,' Sid whispered. 'It's like time slows down.'

'I can't believe how perfect it is.' Fran squeezed Sid's hand. She rested her head on his shoulder and snuggled into his arm.

In the comfortable silence that followed, as they stared out at the pitch-dark night, Sid whispered, 'It's a blessing to be alive.'

Chapter Twenty-Nine

In Dicky's brightly lit dressing room, the comedian sat in front of a mirror and adjusted the collar of his shirt. A clipboard with a handwritten setlist rested on the counter alongside a few last-minute punchlines scribbled hastily onto sticky notes. Dicky felt nervous as he ran a hand through his hair, carefully arranging the quiff. Staring at his reflection, he reached for a half-empty water bottle and took a long drink.

Dicky's afternoon had been spent with his lady friend. After an exhausting session in her bedroom, she'd presented him with a bracelet that matched his missing chain. His eyes bulged when he saw the gift, knowing it had come from the onboard jewellers and would have cost a bomb. His usual practice was to gather his gifts, promise undying love at the end of the cruise, and then disappear to the nearest pawn shop when he hit dry land. But this lady was proving difficult and appeared to have taken ownership of Dicky. Curious about the absence of the gold necklace, she warned Dicky that she expected him to be wearing both items during his show. How could he tell her that he'd lost the damn thing? He could kiss farewell to her generous goodbye gifts in the remaining days of the cruise. It wasn't as though there was time for Dicky to line up a replacement, and if she insisted on creating a fuss about the loss, Peter would string him up. Dicky had been warned about his onboard exploits, and if Peter reported back to Clive, Dicky Delaney's days at sea would be over. He wasn't at the top of his agent's Christmas card list, and his only hope now was to avoid Peter's wrath and somehow make it to the final stop in Malaga without his future career sinking into the sea.

'Ten minutes, Mr Delaney!'

Dicky slipped into his jacket. He knew he had to find the necklace because he didn't want to stop working on cruise ships.

'Let's face it,' Dicky said to his reflection, 'I need the money.'

Taking a deep breath, he straightened his lapels, took one last look in the mirror and exited his room.

It was showtime!

In the Neptune Theatre, Melody Moon stood under a cascade of golden lights, her sequinned gown shimmering with every step she took. With the audience clapping to the beat of her song, Melody's voice soared above the backing singers who moved in synchrony behind her. Dancers in feathered costumes and rhinestone-studded headwear executed perfect choreography as Melody strutted across the stage, blasting out the lyrics to Lady Gaga's 'Born This Way'.

Dicky stood at the side of the stage. He had to hand

it to Melody, she had the audience in her hand, and as he hummed along to the song, he thought, like the song lyrics, that it really didn't matter who you were, whatever your orientation. If you believed in yourself, like Melody, you were 'On the right track, baby'.

Melody's performance was captivating, but when a spotlight shone on a grand piano and she gracefully took a seat, the charged atmosphere softened. Her fingers caressed the keyboard, and she began to sing Adele's ballad, 'Hello', the emotion in her voice raw. Resonating with the poignant words which brought tears to the eyes of many, Dicky was in awe as he listened to a voice that could evoke such profound emotion.

For her finale, Melody invited the audience to their feet and began a medley, concluding with Queen's 'Don't Stop Me Now'. The crowd clapped and swayed, then cheered as Melody hit the final show-stopping note, her arms outstretched as she bathed in the rapturous applause.

'Bloody hell,' Dicky said as he ran his perspiring hands along his suit jacket, 'she's stolen the show. How do I follow that?'

An audio technician adjusted the mic on Dicky's lapel, and as a nervous Dicky mentally ran through his opening lines, his knees felt unsteady, as though the floor was shifting beneath him.

'You've got this,' he mumbled, trying to convince himself.

The stage manager gave Dicky a nod, and knowing that the spotlight was waiting, Dicky stepped into its glare.

As Melody moved towards him to leave the stage, Dicky grabbed her hand. 'Let's hear it again, everyone, a big

Diamond Star cheer for the one and only Melody Moon!' He moved Melody forward. 'Isn't she amazing?' Dicky called out and began to clap his hands.

Many in the audience took to their feet and Melody basked in the standing ovation. After several more minutes of whistles and cheers, she strutted off the stage, but as she passed Dicky, he was surprised to see the artist smile and mouth the words, 'Thank you.'

Dicky turned to the audience who'd settled into their seats. 'And now, you get *me*,' he shrugged. 'It must be like enjoying a five-star meal, then being offered a bag of chips.' To the sound of laughter, he added, 'If I sing "Hello", you'll all say, "Hello, Dicky, there's the exit . . ."'

Dicky was settling into his rhythm, and after a few more jokes, he nodded to the band and the audience soon joined in with Dicky's version of Barry Manilow's 'Copacabana'. As he strutted and danced across the stage, his eyes fell on a band of diamonds glinting brightly around the neck of his lady friend. Sitting in the front row, she ran her fingers over her jewellery and raised a heavily painted eyebrow.

Dicky moved away from the microphone, deciding that mid-act was not the time to address the mystery of his missing gold chain. With the song wrapping up, he thanked the band and began a repertoire of one-liners.

'Do you like takeaways?' he asked the audience with a sly grin. 'The last time I phoned our local, I said, "Do you deliver?"' Pausing just enough to build anticipation, he continued, '"No," they told me, "we do lamb, chicken, and fish . . ."'

The room erupted in laughter, and Dicky let it settle before continuing. 'I introduced my third wife to my mate,' he said, raising his eyebrows for effect. 'Do you know what he said? "She wouldn't have been my first choice either."'

Not missing a beat, he placed a hand on his hip. 'I wanted to put the magic back in our marriage, and it worked. *She disappeared.*' The laughter rippled again. 'We shared a house, my wife and me. She got the inside, and I got the outside.'

Dicky was in his stride, and the audience, who were age-appropriate for his jokes, lapped it up. Posturing with every punchline, his body language was amusing as he paused to pull the audience in with a knowing look.

'We had a power cut in our road the other night,' Dicky said, 'but I knew it was all right when a bus went by with its lights on.'

His timing was impeccable, and with the audience hanging on his every word, as his act ended Dicky's heart was racing with post-show adrenaline from his performance.

'That's it from me, folks!' he called out, 'Don't forget that it's Ibiza tomorrow. The party island! So, enjoy the sun and have a great day out, but remember that at our time of life, you're only a party animal if the party includes a nap . . .'

* * *

Carmen was having a wonderful evening with Theo. They'd dined in the Terrace Restaurant and enjoyed a meal of tantalising Mediterranean flavours which blended through three delicious courses. Theo chatted about his life as a chef, his love of Ruari, and his TV shows.

Carmen was fascinated.

Theo enthralled her with tales of his travels while filming *McCarthy's Kitchen Adventures*, including his time in America, where amongst many eclectic characters, he'd met a chef in Texas who was so obese that he used an electric hoist to lift him into his truck and his business partner, another chef, who was so thin he could barely lift a spoon.

'It was a strange contrast,' Theo explained, 'they had an incredibly successful restaurant, but one couldn't move without assistance, and the other appeared too fragile to chop vegetables. Both were brilliant chefs, and I learned much about their undeniable passion for food, which I hope came across in the programmes.'

'You must have enjoyed travelling around the world?' Carmen said, as she finished her dessert and sipped a delicious, honey-flavoured wine.

'Not really. I was living out of a suitcase much of the time and had no friends or family with me on the long stints away.' Theo was thoughtful. 'I was drinking too much, and I didn't know where the exit was when I reached the bottom of the bottle. It's hard to leave booze alone when you can't find the door.'

'What happened?' Carmen's voice was soft, and she gently touched Theo's hand.

'My life suddenly changed. I met Ruari in London. He was an actor in one of the soaps, and everything took on a new meaning.'

'New meaning?'

'I fell in love, Carmen. Deeply. Love isn't something you search for. It hits you blindside when you least expect it, and it would be a fool who pushes it away.'

'So, what happened next?'

'I went to Donegal and, together with Ruari, whose roots were there too, bought a gorgeous old property. I opened a restaurant, and we settled down.'

'Was he still working in the soap?'

'Yes, until they killed his character off.' Theo smiled. 'We were delighted because it meant more time together, little knowing that my beloved would be killed, too.'

'A heart attack.'

'Yes.'

Theo poured the last of the wine into their glasses. 'Enough of me,' he announced, 'what of you, Carmen Cunningham, the author. What about the rest of your life?'

'There's nothing to tell. It's as boring as it can be. Working in a hardware shop with a dad I adored was nothing spectacular, but I enjoyed it in my own way. It took a downturn when he died, and Mum sold up. Suddenly I was out of a job, but my writing has given me a new interest and determination in my middle life, to do something for me. This cruise and meeting people like you have helped enormously.'

'People like me?' Theo asked. 'Don't you mean someone like Ruskin?'

Carmen felt herself blush. 'Well . . . he has been invaluable,' she stuttered.

'Come on, Carmen, you can't fool me.' Theo smiled. 'Fairies and birds are tweeting around your head whenever you mention him, and you get a faraway look in your eyes.'

Carmen bit her lip. She'd always been a terrible liar. 'It's not like that,' she said.

Theo raised an eyebrow, clearly unconvinced. 'Really?' he asked. 'Then what *is* it like?'

'I didn't go to his final workshop today,' she began. 'Ruskin was tough with me this morning. I know he wants to get the best out of my writing and is doing all he can to help, but I spend every day on the receiving end of Betty's cutting blows and don't need more from anyone else, and now . . .' Carmen paused. She traced the silk fabric of her dress, then touched the soft curls of her hair. 'Since Fran insisted on my makeover, I've discovered that Carmen Cunningham quite likes herself.'

'And you won't put up with any nonsense?'

'Well, something like that.'

'From where I'm sitting, I think you are head over heels in love with him,' Theo said, out of the blue.

'WHAT?' Carmen was stunned. 'No, you're w . . . wrong. Ruskin has helped me a lot, and I'm grateful, but that's all.'

Theo began to laugh. 'If you say so, my darling girl, but you deserve someone who worships you, and Ruskin might just be the man.'

'A man who is horrible to me?'

'Perhaps that's the only way he can overcome his feelings for you; he may be scared of being rejected or, like you, of falling in love?'

'Oh, Theo, really, you should write romance novels. I'm sure love doesn't work like that.'

'Love works in many ways, and Cupid has a habit of throwing a few curved arrows before he hits the target.'

Carmen placed her hands on the arm of her chair and stared at Theo. 'You're a good friend,' she said quietly.

'And this good friend is now going to take you to the bar for another drink and then we'll go dancing.' Theo held out his hand to Carmen. 'What a shame I'm gay. As a chef, I'm savoury, spicy and impossible to resist, and with your author's imagination, think what we'd cook up together.'

'Thank goodness you *are* gay.' Carmen giggled as she took his hand. 'You'd lead me into far too much mischief.'

They left the restaurant and stepped into the foyer, where they saw Holden and Betty descending the stairs from the Atrium. Betty smiled smugly and gripped Holden's arm, nestling into his arm.

'Did you have a pleasant dinner?' Carmen asked.

'It was wonderful,' Betty said, her eyes sparkling. 'I haven't had a meal like that in years.'

Holden patted her arm. 'It wasn't just the food, Bet. It was your delightful company,' he said and smiled adoringly.

Betty closed her eyes as though the taste of the dishes were still lingering. 'The dessert,' she exclaimed, 'the mousse was so smooth and velvety.'

'We're about to go for a drink,' Theo said, 'would you like to join us?'

'No, no.' Betty shook her silvery perm. 'Holden has a surprise for me.'

'How interesting,' Theo said. 'I hope you have a perfect evening.'

'I can't wait to hear all about it,' Carmen added as they moved away.

'Do you think he's going to take her to his suite to propose?' Theo asked as they waited for the lift.

'A surprise in his suite? With heart-shaped rose petals on

the bed and champagne cooling beside a gift-wrapped gift for Betty?'

'It's a foregone conclusion.' Theo laughed. 'The deal is sealed, and you will wake up tomorrow knowing you are about to lose your mother and gain a stepfather.'

Carmen shot Theo a worried glance. She barely knew anything about Holden, and if Theo's suspicions were correct, her mother's new companion might soon be a permanent part of their lives. The thought unsettled her.

'Hell, can we head to the piano bar?' Carmen shook her head, 'I need a strong drink.'

A short while later Theo and Carmen chinked glasses. 'We must celebrate,' Theo laughed, 'Carmen Cunningham is about to become footloose and fancy-free!'

Carmen laughed with her friend, but as her eyes swept the room, she suddenly realised that Ruskin was sitting in one corner. For a moment, their eyes met, and Carmen felt a stab in her heart so sharp that she winced and quickly turned away.

Had one of Cupid's curved arrows just landed?

But she knew that Ruskin was unaware of the woman who was aching for him with a desire he didn't know, and all she could do was carry the ache in the quiet hope that one day, it would fade forever, with her fantasies of Ruskin and her dreams of romance.

Chapter Thirty

When the *Diamond Star* arrived in Ibiza, its smaller size had a distinct advantage, and guests disembarking that day were pleased to find the ship docked within walking distance of the old town. In contrast, much larger vessels loomed further out in the harbour, their giant silhouettes resembling floating hotels where passengers on those ships relied on shuttle buses to cover the three-mile trek to the city centre.

As the ship's crew prepared for a day in port, the turquoise waters of the Mediterranean glinted under the sun, and the rugged coastline shimmered in the heat. The backdrop revealed a mix of whitewashed buildings and rolling hills.

Ruskin stared at these whitewashed buildings. Having disembarked early he decided against breakfast on the ship, and chose instead to walk to the iconic Dalt Vila, a UNESCO World Heritage Site. As he stepped out at a brisk pace, he thought of Carmen and the note that had been delivered to his cabin the evening before.

'With my best wishes?' Ruskin muttered furiously, remembering the closing lines of her letter. What the hell was

Carmen playing at? He'd given her a golden opportunity to improve her novel, and not only had she chosen to miss his workshop the previous afternoon, but now, she'd decided to stop the morning mentoring sessions.

'How many aspiring authors would be that foolish?' he asked himself as he walked past sleek yachts and colourful fishing boats bobbing about in the water. Voices talking in different languages could be heard, as yachties and crews from the more luxurious boats called out to each other and wandered into harbourside cafés lining the promenade to enjoy a café con leche and crisp tostado glistening with olive oil.

Ruskin ignored the boutique shops offering artisan goods as he continued to walk, climbing higher, and went through the Portal de Ses Taules's grand stone gateway, the Dalt Vila's main entrance. He barely glanced at the Roman statues on either side.

But as he entered a plaza bustling with life, he suddenly stopped, realising that he was filled with disappointment, and nothing, not even the incredible architecture and beautiful landscape, could soothe his thoughts.

Deciding to sit down, he chose a café table under a broad canopy and ordered water and a coffee. Nearby, he recognised the Yorkshire couple, Don and Debbie, from the *Diamond Star*. The woman was tucking into an ensaimada pastry. Filled with cream and chocolate, the local delicacy was dusted with powdered sugar, which left a white moustache on her lip as she bit into it.

'Debbie, if you keep eating them, we'll need a bigger ship,' the man cuttingly said.

Ruskin noted the pained look on the woman's face as she lowered her head, placed the half-eaten pastry down and then pushed the plate to one side. Oblivious to his wife's feelings, the man read a paper and sipped a cold beer.

Ruskin wondered at the ability of one human to inflict pain on another, where words hit harder than blows. Without even noticing the hurt in her eyes, the husband had cut deep with his comment, and Ruskin was struck again by the thought that his own comments might have been too harsh for Carmen to bear.

Sipping his coffee, he tried to remember Carmen's body language as he barked out instructions and critiqued her work. She'd kept her head lowered, and her eyes focused on the words on her screen. Remembering her note, it suddenly occurred to Ruskin that perhaps she'd had enough of his aggressive teaching method.

But how else could he hide his feelings?

He sighed and stared at the busy plaza, recalling the previous evening when he'd sat alone in the corner of the piano bar. When Theo had entered the room with Carmen on his arm, Ruskin looked up. Against a hum of conversation and the gentle chink of glasses, the couple unknowingly commanded attention. Theo's handsome face, impeccable suit and colourful waistcoat were a much-loved sight for those familiar with *McCarthy's Kitchen Adventures*. Carmen turned heads in her elegant silky gown, the deep blues catching the dim lighting, the fabric skimming her figure and swirling gently like the sea, with her hair pinned in a sophisticated style adding to her allure.

From his corner, he'd watched her. His gaze traced every

detail, from how her head tilted as she listened to Theo, to the fluid movement of her hands as she held a flute and carefully sipped champagne. When her eyes swept the room, he thought that for a moment, they met his, but she'd turned back to Theo, unaware of the man in the corner, who was aching for her with a desire she didn't know.

The man at the adjacent table scraped back his chair, rousing Ruskin from his thoughts.

'If you've finished filling your face, we'd best get a move on,' Don said to his wife, studying the bill and carefully counting out euros. 'This place must think it's feeding royalty,' he grumbled. Turning to leave, he grinned when he recognised Ruskin. 'It's you, that writer bloke, we meet once more,' Don said. 'I expect you can afford these prices.'

Ruskin ignored the comment, knowing that if the couple could afford the cost of the cruise, they could afford refreshments in this café. Taking the opportunity, he asked Debbie, 'Did you find your necklace?'

'No, and we're never likely to,' Don cut in before Debbie could reply. 'Debbie is so damn careless I've told her she's not to wear her jewellery when we're out.'

Debbie's lips pressed into a thin line, and her hands clasped around her cup as though it was the only thing anchoring her. She stared at Don, and Ruskin caught the flicker of pent-up anger as Don continued, 'She's a liability wherever we go.'

Fearing that Debbie was about to hurl the cup at the back of Don's head, Ruskin stood and placed his payment on the table. 'Well, I hope you both enjoy your time on the island,' he said, smiling at Debbie.

Deciding that he must salvage the day and not be carried away with his unrequited longing for Carmen or the sting of being stood up for their early lessons, he told himself that for a few hours he wouldn't agonise over what he could have done differently. As he walked away and climbed higher through the old town's narrow lanes, he vowed to enjoy the day and remind himself why he loved travelling.

* * *

Carmen and Theo strolled through the charming streets of Ibiza together, having decided to do some sightseeing while leaving Betty to enjoy a quiet day aboard the ship.

'Is your mum all right?' Theo asked as they walked along a tree-lined avenue where the gentle gradient led to the Dalt Vila.

'Yes, I think she's tired though,' Carmen said. 'I heard her come back to her cabin at silly o'clock when she began to bang on the wall with her cane.'

'Announcing good news?' Theo's brows were raised with an expectant expression as he turned to study Carmen.

'No, there was no talk of a proposal. She said the surprise had been to go to the Mermaid Theatre where he'd arranged a spotlight dance for just the two of them.' Carmen paused. 'But as I was helping her to bed, she told me that Holden was taking her to a party tonight.'

'The plot thickens! But I am sure you'll have news of an engagement before the cruise ends.'

Carmen nodded. 'Wouldn't that be nice.'

Reflecting on Betty's chatter the previous evening,

Carmen recalled a marked change in her mother. She'd completed the usual elaborate routine of removing Betty's makeup, unpinning the pineapple brooch from Betty's dress and placing her pearls in their leather box, carefully hanging her clothes, then arranging her hair in a nighttime net, and Betty seemed almost gentle instead of her usual bossy self.

Carmen could just about remember a kinder Betty reading her bedtime stories as a child, wrapped in the warmth of her fleecy dressing gown as they snuggled together in bed. Back then, cocooned with her mother, Betty's arms had felt warm and safe. She remembered the rich, spicy scent of Youth-Dew by Estée Lauder, Betty's favourite perfume then, as she brushed Carmen's hair in long, patient strokes, humming a nursery rhyme. Tonight, Carmen felt that a trace of the gentler Betty of Carmen's childhood had returned.

Taking a pot of face cream, Betty spoke with an uncharacteristically soft tone as she smoothed the lines on her face. When she reached out to thank Carmen and kiss her goodnight, the gesture left Carmen struggling to conceal her surprise.

'Are you enjoying the cruise?' Carmen asked.

'Do you know something?' Betty settled back on her pillows. 'I think I am.'

Carmen was astonished to see Betty smiling, and the shock made her sit down. Instead of the painful endurance etched permanently into Betty's expression, Betty's normally guarded eyes almost twinkled as she reached out to take her daughter's hand.

'Does Holden make you happy, Mum?' Carmen softly asked.

'Yes, I feel like a young girl again. Holden is kind, and it's lovely to have a man flatter and cherish me.' Betty appeared wistful. 'I haven't felt like this in years, not since your dad and I courted.'

'Goodness . . .' Carmen was momentarily lost for words as she studied Betty's face. 'But Dad was kind too,' she whispered, 'and he loved you.'

'Ah, your dad and love . . .' Betty squeezed Carmen's hand. 'That's another story,' she said and shook her head. 'But love has a funny way of finding you when you've stopped searching for it, like a flower that blooms in the most unexpected place.'

Now on her way to the Cathedral of Santo Domingo, Carmen couldn't help but think about Betty's words as Theo led her through an alley. Had love blossomed for her mother on the *Diamond Star*? Betty surely hadn't been searching for it, but love seemed to have appeared in the most unlikely of places for a woman of Betty's sharp demeanour, which could deter even the most devoted admirer – though that wasn't the side of her nature that she showed to Holden.

'Mum has undergone a transformation,' Carmen said to Theo as they stopped beside an arched entrance where a jar of fresh flowers sat on a small table, beside two metal chairs.

'Then that's two of you, and the magic of this Mediterranean cruise is helping both mother and daughter.' He smiled. 'But look, I want to show you something.'

He took Carmen's hand and guided her into a contemporary art studio and large open space.

'What is this?' Carmen asked as she stared at a variety of eclectic paintings and souvenirs.

Theo looked around with a contemplative smile, 'I came to Ibiza in the 1970s when the island was a magnet for artists, writers and musicians, since the 1960s. The relaxed pace made it a perfect refuge for carefree young wanderers.'

'Were you a carefree young wanderer?' Carmen asked.

'I'd taken time out, after finishing college, and together with a friend we bought an old VW caravanette and drove through Europe. Finding Ibiza was like finding the holy grail.' Theo picked up a silver pendant. 'It was a haven for countercultural youth during the 1960s and 70s and I'd read a book called *The Drifters* by James Michener, and it had become a bit of a bible for me,' he explained. 'In the story, a group of young people from all over the world came together here. It was one of the key settings that Michener wrote about and greatly influenced me. I wanted to see what Ibiza was like.'

'Did it meet your expectations?'

'God, yes, it was anything and everything. We lived in a commune that summer and led a very bohemian life.'

'How lucky you were to experience something so different,' Carmen said, thinking of her repetitive days behind the counter in the family hardware shop.

'I eventually came home, to my parents' relief, and remember my father tearing the Afghan jacket off my back and ripping up my cheesecloth shirts then removing the cowbell from my neck,' Theo laughed. 'He handed me a chef's jacket and told me he'd found me an apprenticeship in a restaurant, and that was the end of my hippie era.'

Carmen stared at a framed, black-and-white image of a couple, signed *Traspas y Tozejano* and dated Ibiza 1976.

'That was the couple who owned this gallery,' Theo said as he watched Carmen study the photo of the handsome bearded young man beside an attractive girl.

'Did you know them?' she asked and stared at the suntanned girl in minuscule white shorts with a bandeau top and legs that seemed to go on forever.

'Yes, I met them, and they were generous, charismatic figures.' Theo looked around. 'I understand they still live here and run this gallery, which shows their commitment to the island's cultural scene.'

Still holding the silver pendant in his hand, Theo sought out an assistant and paid for it. As he stepped out of the gallery and into the sunshine in the alley, he handed the gift to Carmen.

'What's this?' she asked with surprise as she stared at the smooth polished disc. At its centre, she traced a symbol with her fingers.

'The design of a rising sun represents new beginnings and the promise of brighter days,' Theo said, 'while the open hand signifies support. It's most appropriate.'

'B . . . but it's lovely, I couldn't possibly accept . . .'

'Shush,' Theo tutted and, taking the pendant, fastened it around Carmen's neck. 'There, it suits you.' He grinned. 'And it will remind you of this holiday,' he added.

'And of our friendship,' Carmen said. 'Thank you, Theo.'

A little while later, they stepped out of the cathedral, which was a peaceful and cool escape from the fierce sun. They'd admired the beautiful artwork, and Carmen was fascinated by the focal point of the high altar, which showcased intricate woodwork and religious symbols of saints and mythological creatures.

'Shall we find somewhere to have a drink and a bite to eat?' Theo asked.

They stood by a honey-coloured stone wall and stared out at the view. 'Look, there's our ship.' Carmen pointed towards the harbour, where the *Diamond Star* was berthed.

For a moment, Carmen thought of Ruskin. Was he still on the ship, and had he read her note and missed her at the workshop and morning mentoring session? Carmen thought that Ruskin was probably relieved that he didn't have to devote any more time to helping with her novel, and now that his workshops were over, he was, no doubt, thoroughly enjoying the cruise. She remembered that he loved swimming and imagined him on nearby Talamanca beach, which she could see close by. The waters were ideal for a dip where the calm, clear sea stretched out to the island of Formentera in the distance.

'Penny for your thoughts?' Theo asked.

'Oh, nothing . . .'

'You're thinking of Ruskin, I can tell.'

'How on earth . . .'

'It's the Irish gypsy in me.' Theo laughed. 'I have psychic powers.'

'If I'm being truthful, I *was* wondering what he might be doing?'

'Oh, Carmen, when will you ease up on yourself and let go a little?' Theo shook his head. 'The man told me that he is divorced and not in a relationship, so what have you got to lose?' Theo omitted to add that Ruskin had also told him that he had no intention of being *in* a relationship.

'But he isn't very nice to me.' Carmen's excuse sounded lame, even to herself.

'He was all over you when you had a drink with him in the piano bar, until you stood up and left. It's only in a classroom environment that he pushes you – can't you see that he wants the best for your writing?'

'Well, I sent him a note saying I didn't want any more tuition and would enjoy the time I had left enjoying the cruise.'

Theo took Carmen's arm and began to march her through the cobbled, zigzagging alleyways until they found a bar overlooking the central plaza. They'd almost finished a carafe of sangria and several plates of tapas when Theo looked up and saw Ruskin sitting at a café on the opposite side of the square.

'It's a sign, now's your chance!' Theo said excitedly. 'Go over and offer to buy him a drink in return for help with your novel.'

Carmen hesitated as she listened to Theo, her mind swirling with unspoken thoughts. Would Ruskin notice her if she walked by his table, and more importantly, would he make his excuses and leave if she offered to buy him a drink? As Carmen studied Ruskin, she could see that he was lost in thought, seemingly miles away from the buzzing atmosphere all around. The afternoon sun caught his face, highlighting the charm that Carmen found so appealing and as Carmen heard Theo ask her what she had to lose, she suddenly felt a sense of excitement, and with her nerves softened by the sangria, she grabbed the sides of her chair and stood.

'Atta girl!' Theo grinned. 'Go for it!'

'Do I look all right?' Carmen asked, reaching out to tidy her hair.

'You look beautiful. Sun-kissed and sexy in your gorgeous outfit.'

'Okay, here goes.'

Carmen's heart pounded as she stepped into the open plaza, each footfall heavier than the last. She rubbed her clammy palms against the fabric of her sundress and whispered a prayer that Ruskin wouldn't turn her away. Rehearsing her words, she felt a knot of fear in her stomach. *What if he says no and laughs at the suggestion of sharing a drink with me?* But Theo's encouraging words drummed in her ears and urged her forward.

Carmen was behind Ruskin and close enough to catch the leathery scent of his cologne. Her voice felt trapped, and she forced herself to swallow her fear. But just as Carmen was about to step forward into Ruskin's vision and ask her question, a woman hurried through the crowd to his table.

'Darling, darling!' the woman called out. 'I've missed you so much!'

Carmen froze. Her breath caught in her throat as she watched the woman embrace Ruskin with unguarded joy, her laughter ringing out. Her sun-kissed hair fell in loose waves, streaked with silver, and she'd tucked a red hibiscus behind one ear. A flowing off-the-shoulder dress, patterned with embroidery, displayed deeply tanned skin, and huge, heavy amber beads were draped around her neck. The woman epitomised the island's soul, and as Carmen stared at the timeless beauty, she suddenly felt frumpy and old.

Carmen quickly looked away. Tears dampened the corner of her eyes as she began the agonising walk back to Theo.

No wonder Ruskin never noticed her furtive glances! Or her quiet attempts to be near him. He had a partner! A bitter inner voice told her that she'd been foolish and suddenly she felt stupid and hurt for letting her heart chase something so clearly out of reach.

As she reached the café, Theo was waiting. 'Come here, sweetheart,' he called out.

Theo's face bore the pain she felt as he stood with his arms outstretched, and as he embraced and stroked her softly, Carmen buried her head into his shoulder and whispered, 'At least I know now that there's no hope . . .'

Chapter Thirty-One

Fran and Sid stopped in the old town to enjoy refreshments, and found a spot, shaded from the sun under a brightly coloured parasol at a café in the plaza's centre. The sunlit haven was encircled by bustling shops, colourful stalls in a fresh produce market, and buildings where balconies spilt over with vibrant pots of sweet-smelling herbs.

'It's grand to be here, despite the climb to get to this spot,' Sid said as he drank a glass of sparkling water and then topped it up from a bottle on the table. 'I feel like we've stepped back in time, sitting and watching the world go by.'

A nearby fountain trickled softly, its gentle sound mixing with the hum of conversation from tourists and locals. As the smell of freshly baked bread and rich espresso drifted over from a table nearby, Sid gazed longingly at the fluffy white dough.

Fran noticed Sid's expression and reached into her bag. 'Have a banana,' she said, 'keep your heartburn at bay.'

'This is a lovely place,' Sid said as he watched children

chase each other around the fountain. 'Can you imagine all the history over the years?'

They stared at the sturdy stone walls of the Dalt Vila, where from this vantage point, the shimmering Mediterranean could be glimpsed in the distance.

Sid, intrigued by the town's rich history, reached for his guidebook. Flipping through the pages, he began to read aloud, 'The old part of Ibiza spans more than two and a half thousand years and is one of Europe's oldest towns.'

'I expect lots of cultures have left their mark,' Fran commented as she drained a glass of orange juice.

'They certainly have, from the Romans, Byzantines, Arabs and Catalans. The book says that the architecture reflects all those different cultures.'

'I think we should make the most of our time,' Fran announced. 'Did you say there was an art gallery and a cathedral?'

'Aye, and a museum if we can manage it.'

'Best get going, then.' Fran smiled and reached for her bag. 'That's if you feel well enough?'

'Of course. A silly bit of heartburn won't stop me from enjoying as much as we can on this cruise.'

Sid and Fran set off, and hand in hand, they wandered through the vibrant gathering place. 'I think I'm going to like Ibiza,' Fran said, 'it's such a beautiful island.'

'Me too. The cruise is like a journey through time where every port is a postcard of pictures and memories,' Sid said as they made their way through the labyrinth of narrow, cobbled streets and charming squares.

An old bicycle painted white and supporting a wooden

crate filled with fresh herbs leaned against the wall of a shop where a sign above read *Curiosidades de Ibiza*. Peering through the window, Fran gazed at the diverse mix of items.

'Let's go in,' Sid said, 'you might find some souvenirs.'

As they stepped into the shop, a bell jingled, announcing their arrival. Fran's eyes sparkled as she took in the charming interior. The air was filled with the scent of incense and the shelves were lined with an array of hand-painted ceramics, trinket boxes and neatly folded cotton sarongs. Fran smiled as she studied a display of puppets. The Spanish marionettes were dressed in bright polka-dotted dresses with ruffled sleeves and carried tiny castanets. Nearby, a rack was stacked with brightly patterned scarves, and a glass-fronted case showcased delicate silver jewellery.

'I like these pendants,' Sid said and pointed to silver discs of different shapes mounted on thin chains. Each carried a design of a rising sun on an open hand.

'Oh look,' Fran said, 'there's shelves full of gin. She picked up a bottle and studied the lilac-coloured label. 'LAW – the Gin of Ibiza,' she read. 'I fancy a local tipple, let's take one home.'

They moved deeper into the shop but stopped when they noticed Colin and Neeta by a table in the centre of the room. As the pair picked up an object and turned it from side to side, Fran saw a handwritten card. *Pineapple Ice Bucket – Perfect for Parties & Summer Soirées, €45*. The gold exterior gleamed in the soft glow of a hanging bulb, and Neeta's face lit up as she stroked the texture that mimicked the fruit's spiky skin.

'Looks like you've found a bargain,' Fran called out.

Colin and Neeta looked up, and when they recognised Fran and Sid, they smiled.

'I rather like this cocktail shaker,' Fran added, picking up the item shaped like a palm tree. 'There are some quirky gifts in here. I think we'll have this,' she said, adding the shaker to her basket.

'This ice bucket is perfect,' Neeta enthused and moved towards Sid. 'We can use it tonight for our party.'

'Party?' Fran's ears picked up.

'Yes, why don't you come?' Neeta leaned close to Sid. Her eyes were soft with mischief as her body brushed against his arm, and she flicked a strand of her long hair, skimming it along Sid's cheek.

Like a cat caught off guard, Sid stiffened, and his shoulders rose.

'How fortuitous that we should meet you both here,' Colin added. 'Do say you'll come to our little soirée. Your friends Don and Debbie will be there.'

Sid began to inch away, but Neeta followed, undeterred.

'Excuse me, I need to see something,' Sid muttered nervously, 'from over there.' His hand waved vaguely and as he bolted, he almost knocked into Fran.

'Don't mind my Sid.' Fran smiled. 'He had a bit of a turn yesterday and isn't quite himself, so despite your kind invitation, we'll probably give the party a miss.'

The bell jingled, announcing the arrival of new customers. As Fran went to pay for her items, she called out, 'Enjoy your party!'

Taking hold of Sid's arm, Fran guided him through the shop. Depositing her wrapped items into her bag, she glanced back at Colin and Neeta and with a knowing smile, whispered, *'Don't forget to place the pineapple upside down . . .'*

* * *

Ruskin was back on the ship and pounded through the corridors. Letting himself into his suite, he headed for the bar, grabbed a bottle of malt whisky, and then poured a considerable measure. His jaw was clenched, and his face wore an expression of barely contained frustration as he snatched up the whisky, swirling it hard. His grip tightened, and Ruskin emptied the glass before pouring another.

Stepping out to his balcony, he stared blankly ahead, unaware of the afternoon sun casting a glow over the sea, as he placed a steadying hand on the metal railing. The rugged cliffs appeared amber in the light, and the sky was streaked with pinks and fiery orange, promising a spectacular sunset. But Ruskin took no notice of nature and the timeless appeal of the island, nor the sound of the music from the ship and the lively world aboard. A storm was brewing in his mind, as was the whirlwind that had created it.

Venetia. Would the day ever come when she stopped stalking him?

Ruskin had been enjoying his sojourn in a café at the centre of the plaza in the old town. The sun was a tonic, and as he sipped a glass of chilled wine, he found the tranquil rhythm of the island infectious. As nearby tourists chatted happily, he felt himself relax.

He'd pondered his problems while climbing the

meandering alleys to the cathedral. The plot of his forthcoming novel was forming, and he was enjoying thinking about the missing jewellery, which was still a mystery he'd yet to solve. Ruskin determined to get to the bottom of things and, who knew, maybe even use it in his next book.

Carmen, however, was a source of frustration and it occurred to him that if he really wanted to get to know Carmen, he should man up and ask her to have a drink with him. Never mind working on her novel or any conversation over the requirements needed to pen a good story, he should heed her words that she wanted to enjoy the final days of the cruise and finish her novel once she arrived home. What harm could it do to share a cocktail or two?

There was only one way to find out.

Despite his intentions to stay celibate and alone, Carmen filled his thoughts, and until she turned him away in person, he wouldn't be free of her hold on his mind. And if she said yes, he might find himself ripping up his romantic rule book and risking everything to see where it led.

With his mind made up to track Carmen down as soon as he returned to the ship, he felt comfortable in the café and sipped his wine, savouring the soporific effect. Ruskin's eyes felt heavy, and with his sunglasses shielding him from the sun's rays, his lids began to close.

'Darling, darling!' a woman suddenly called out. 'I've missed you so much!'

Ruskin felt his body freeze. With a suppressed dread, he slowly looked up to see Venetia standing before him.

'Imagine finding *you* here!' she said, leaning in. She cupped Ruskin's face and began to kiss him.

'Venetia, what the hell are you doing?' Ruskin said through gritted teeth.

'That's no way to greet me,' Venetia replied, pulling out a chair she pouted as she made herself comfortable. 'You could at least smile.'

Venetia ordered wine and began to speak, the words tumbling out like a faucet Ruskin couldn't turn off. She spoke as though they were still married, oblivious to Ruskin's new single life. He stared at her hair, which fell in loose waves, and noted that it was streaked heavily with grey, and despite the playful hibiscus tucked behind her ear, his ex-wife was showing her age. The short, embroidered off-the-shoulder dress wasn't flattering and appeared far too young for a woman in her sixties. The depth of her tan was ageing her skin beyond her years.

Venetia's incessant rambling about their shared memories droned on, and Ruskin knew that he had to end the situation he didn't want to be a part of.

'Venetia. Stop!' he suddenly announced. 'Why are you stalking me?'

'Well, I knew the *Diamond Star* would be in Ibiza today and thought it would be nice for us to meet up.'

'Are you deliberately going out of your way to antagonise me?' Ruskin was aghast. 'Are you telling me that you've flown out here just to sit and chat?'

'Er, sort of, well no, I mean . . . I have my jewellery in several shops and am going to check on sales.'

Ruskin recalled the silversmith course that he'd funded for Venetia after they'd parted. He'd hoped that it would inspire her to settle down and channel her energy into something meaningful rather than pursuing her harebrained schemes that had occupied their lives up until the divorce. He had to admit that her silver pendants were marketable, and he knew that she still had connections to several outlets in Ibiza, remnants of her hippy days before they met. But checking on sales was something she could do with a phone call from home.

'Venetia . . .' Ruskin removed his sunglasses and, leaning forward, spoke quietly. 'We are divorced, we are not together, nor will we ever be a couple again.' He looked into her misting eyes. 'You are a talented woman with much to offer, but not to me.'

'How can you be so cold?' Venetia crossed her arms, then childishly scrunched her nose. Reaching for her wine, she took a long drink.

'I'm not cold, I've been as kind as possible, but you must stop this ridiculous stalking.'

'I don't know how to live my life without you,' she muttered, twisting the stem of the glass in her fingers.

Ruskin thought that Venetia had lived her life exactly as she wanted when she was with him and wouldn't find it too difficult to continue doing so.

'Why don't you stay out here for a while? You love Ibiza,' he said.

'Oh, it's all so commercialised now with superstar DJs, electronic music and luxury hotels, I'm far too old for all of that.'

'Nonsense, there are wellness retreats, yoga centres and cultural experiences that you love.'

'I want to be with you, Ruskin. *Please*, won't you give me another chance?'

Ruskin took a deep breath. He chose his words carefully, his voice low and gentle. 'I need you to hear me, Venetia,' he began. 'We had good moments, moments I'll always remember, and we have two wonderful sons. We are blessed with grandchildren, our precious little girls. But our life together is a chapter that is closed.'

Venetia opened her mouth as if to protest, but Ruskin raised his hand. 'You are talented, creative, and much stronger than you think.' His voice was tinged with genuine admiration. 'You have so much to offer, but not with me.'

Her eyes glistened, and Ruskin felt a pang in his chest but knew he had to press on. 'I want you to find someone who makes you truly happy and will let you shine in the way that I know you can. But to do that, you must let me go.'

Leaning back, Ruskin gave her a moment to absorb his words. Then, standing, he reached into his pocket and drew out enough euros to cover the wine.

'Take care, Venetia,' he said softly, and, turning, began to walk away. As Ruskin crossed the plaza, he kept his gaze fixed forward and he didn't look back.

But the words he'd spoken to Venetia echoed loudly in his mind.

I want you to find someone who makes you truly happy . . .

Ruskin thought of Carmen and wondered if he'd ever truly find happiness for himself.

The sun was still hot as Ruskin stood on his balcony and finished the last sip of his whisky. A tiny bird fluttered down, perching lightly on the railing beside him, its beady eyes sharp with curiosity. As if studying Ruskin, the bird tilted its head and chirped.

'You're not done yet,' the bird seemed to say, 'there's still work to do.'

As the bird flew away, Ruskin turned his attention to Peter's request for help. There was no clear explanation, but could there be a pattern? Was there a thread connecting these seemingly unrelated incidents?

Mentally listing the victims, Ruskin considered their backgrounds, the location of their cabins and possible movements around the ship. Had they dined at the same table or attended the same events? Or was there a more subtle link that Peter and his team had missed? His years crafting mysteries told Ruskin that there had to be a common denominator, something everyone was unaware of. Surely, if the passengers had been careless, the lost items would have turned up by now?

Yet they hadn't.

Ruskin stepped back into his suite, the warmth of the whisky lingering on his tongue. The steady hum of the ship beneath his feet reminded him that they were all trapped in this floating world together, and the missing jewellery wasn't just a coincidence. Something, or someone, was at the heart of the matter.

And Ruskin intended to find out who.

Chapter Thirty-Two

Carmen was preparing for the evening ahead with Theo and stood in her bathroom under the soft glow of the light above the mirror. The face that stared back seemed unfamiliar, and she felt she was seeing herself in a different light. Her skin was slightly tanned and glowing, and her eyes sparkled confidently. Even her hair appeared softer, lightened by the sun. In such a short time, the plain and drab woman who'd boarded the ship seemed to have vanished, replaced by someone she hardly recognised but liked. A lot.

It was wonderful to be on this cruise, feeling its magic take hold and bring her to life. A pendant nestled at her throat, and as it caught the light, Carmen reached out to touch the engraved pattern, silently thanking Theo for his kindness. Stepping back, she smoothed her evening dress, marvelling at how it hugged her figure. Fran's impeccable taste was still a revelation, and with the help of the boutique's assistants, every outfit her new friend had chosen mirrored the changes Carmen was feeling.

Even her mother had undergone a transformation, and

spending time with Holden had softened Betty beyond recognition. Carmen could hardly believe the change, for her mother had been brusque and impatient for as long as she could remember.

Earlier, as Carmen helped Betty dress, there had been an unfamiliar ease in her mother's demeanour. Reaching for the long-handled comb to smooth Betty's hair into place and spray it with lacquer, Carmen braced herself for the usual sharp remark about being too rough.

Instead, to Carmen's astonishment, Betty murmured, 'Thank you, dear.'

Carmen nearly dropped the comb. Had she heard correctly? Her mother had thanked her! She'd watched Betty's reflection in the mirror, searching for some trace of annoyance, but Betty's face was soft and as Carmen fastened a pearl necklace, her mother smiled warmly then reached out and patted her daughter's hand, with a gentle, reassuring touch.

A lump formed in Carmen's throat. Who was this woman, and what had Holden done to her? Whatever it was, Carmen wasn't sure if she should be wary or relieved.

'Where are you dining tonight?' Carmen asked.

'We'll eat in the Terrace Restaurant. Holden has reserved a window table,' Betty replied, pinning her brooch and slipping rings onto her fingers.

'You seem to have grown very fond of him,' Carmen said softly. 'Do you think he might propose?'

'Oh, Carmen . . .' Betty giggled like a girl. 'Don't be so silly.' But as she reached for her cane, she paused and looked at her daughter. 'But then again . . . I have very strong feelings for him, and stranger things have happened. It might be fun to have a change at my time of life.'

As Carmen slipped into her jewelled sandals and picked up her clutch, she hoped that Betty would find happiness with Holden. Carmen wouldn't allow herself to think of her own feelings for Ruskin, but as she flicked off the lights and opened the cabin door, she couldn't help but think that between Betty and herself, at least one of them had found love.

* * *

Perched on a chair in front of a mirror, Dicky sat in his dressing room rehearsing his punch lines. His face broke into a well-practised smile, and he chuckled at his reflection as though hearing the audience's rapturous applause. Beside him, his outfit for the evening, prepared by the wardrobe department, was neatly laid out.

The bathroom door opened, and Melody appeared. Gripping her silky gown, she moved across the room to sit beside Dicky. Her fingers searched through the array of cosmetics until she selected her Kryolan paint stick and held it out. 'Here, try this. It will get rid of those dark shadows,' Melody said.

'Cheers,' Dicky replied. He dabbed it lightly under his eyes.

After Dicky had generously paused the start of his act to ensure that Melody received more applause and a standing ovation from the audience in the Neptune Theatre, an amicable rapport had struck up between the two performers. Now they treated each other with respect, sharing conversation and discussing improvements to their acts.

Melody talked about her friend, Danni Del Rio. The memory still haunted her, but she admitted now that Danni's fall from the balcony in Benidorm had been a tragic accident. On reflection, Dicky wasn't to blame. Danni had alcohol issues, and although Melody had tried to get her to slow down, Danni lived a chaotic life, and it was inevitable that, ultimately, her ending would be messy.

'I'm sorry,' Dicky said, 'it must have been very painful for you to watch her decline.'

'It was and still is when I think of her. Danni burned brightly. Too brightly.' Melody fastened a sparkling bracelet to her wrist. 'How's your wealthy widow?' she asked.

'Remarkably amenable since I took your advice and got the courage to break the news that I'd lost the gold chain. I thought she'd have a meltdown, but instead, it turns out she's more concerned that I might misplace myself.'

Melody chuckled, her fingers teasing her hair under a nylon cap before reaching for a towering blonde wig. 'Perhaps the chain was a fake?'

'Hardly, I was with her when she purchased it.'

'She must think a lot of you?' Melody arched an eyebrow as she tweaked her hair into place. 'Maybe you mean more to her than a piece of jewellery.'

Dicky leaned back, a grin playing on his lips. 'She's fallen for me all right, they always do.' He shook his head. 'Ironic when you think about it as I've made a career of telling jokes about middle-aged dating disasters and ridiculing old age.'

'So, what's your next move?'

'My usual move. What happens on the cruise stays on

the cruise.' Dicky shrugged. 'When this journey ends, so does the relationship.' He swivelled in his chair, suddenly thoughtful. 'The thing is, though, she makes me feel good, even when my jokes bomb.' He lowered his head and stared at his hands, 'I know she's a bit older than me, but I think I'm starting to fall for her.'

'Bloody hell, Dicky!' Melody's mouth dropped open, 'That's not in the script. Love 'em and leave 'em is the motto on any ship.'

'Yeah, I know, and I also know I'm just a temporary fling for her. There are a thousand Dicky Delaneys out there, sailing the seas, available for anyone wealthy enough to buy a few hours of their time. She'll move on to someone else as soon as she boards the next cruise.'

Melody was quiet as she began to apply eyeliner. Then, as she dusted her cheeks with shimmering highlighter, she said, 'I don't know what to say.'

'Don't stress, I'll get over it, and in the meantime, we have a show to put on.' He stood and, reaching out, unhooked Melody's outfit from a rail. It was a dazzling concoction of fringe, sequins and rhinestones. 'Tonight, Melody Moon, you are Dolly Parton!'

'And you need to get changed.' Melody smiled, nodding towards Dicky's outfit.

'Fifteen minutes, Kenny and Dolly!' a voice called out.

Dicky and Melody exchanged a look of solidarity, and with a firm nod to the other, finished their preparations for the show.

* * *

There was a gentle murmur of conversation and the clink of glasses as Carmen and Theo sat in the Terrace Restaurant and enjoyed their evening, dining with several new faces, at a large circular table. Guests delighted to be in Theo's company urged him to tell tales of his time on television and in escapades during *McCarthy's Kitchen Adventures*. As Theo told an amusing story of making ostrich egg omelettes on an open plain in the Serengeti, in Tanzania, while several ostriches got perilously close to his cooking pots, Carmen looked around and noticed Betty and Holden, sitting at a corner table by a window.

The glow of candlelight enhanced Betty's face, and her usually sharp features softened as she leaned slightly forward, her hand nestling in Holden's.

Carmen watched with quiet astonishment.

Betty had been the dominant one all of Carmen's life, setting the rules for her daughter and delivering the last word in a tone that could cut through steel. But now, her mother was unrecognisable, clearly doting and hanging off Holden's words, it was almost bittersweet that Betty had found love on the cruise despite her years.

Carmen raised her glass. She knew that she should be pleased for Betty, but at that moment, she could only feel relief. If there was the slightest chance that Betty had the opportunity to sail off into the sunset with Holden, Carmen would encourage it. The prison gates were opening, and Carmen saw the possibility of life without Betty.

'If he proposes,' she whispered, 'I hope you accept.'

* * *

After dinner, Theo and Carmen went to the Neptune Theatre and found a seat near the stage. When the lights dimmed, the show started, and the *Diamond Star* Dance Troupe began to entertain the audience. Starting with a sultry tango, the dancers moved across the stage with precise steps, executing daring lifts and dramatic spins. The females wore revealing, flowing red gowns, while the men performed in sleek tuxedos.

Carmen joined in with the audience, clapping along to the high-energy rhythm of the music. Her eyes widened as a spotlight followed a solo tap dancer, whose rapid-fire footwork created a whirlwind with each flawless move. For the grand finale, the dancers transformed the stage into a carnival spectacle in feathered headdresses and vibrant costumes, they spun and twirled like flames leaping and dancing in a fire, closing their show with a high octave performance.

'That was wonderful,' Carmen said to Theo as they applauded.

Peter came onto the stage and thanked the dancers. Raising his hand, he smiled and said, 'Tonight, everyone, for one night only, we have a very special act, and I'd like you all to join me and give a big hand as we present a *Diamond Star* tribute to . . . Kenny Rogers and Dolly Parton!'

Multi-coloured lights danced across velvet curtains that slowly drew back, and the band began an introduction medley of country music.

Hand in hand, Dicky and Melody walked forward.

Dicky was convincing as Kenny Rogers. With a perfectly trimmed snow-white beard and wig, and wearing a suit with a western-style tie, he carried the aura of the country music legend. Beside him, Melody, as Dolly Parton, was spectacular. Her blonde wig towered and fell gently on her shoulders and her sequined dress emphasised a shapely figure. Gliding across the stage, when she spoke, her voice perfected Dolly's southern drawl.

'Good evenin' y'all,' she said, flicking her curls. 'I'm not offended by any dumb blonde jokes because I know I'm not dumb . . . and I know I'm not blonde.'

'Well, Dolly,' Kenny replied, 'I'm still tryin' to figure out if I'm dumb and using the wrong shampoo.' He smiled and stroked his pure white hair.

Dolly adjusted her exaggerated bosom and began to sing, and Kenny stood back as the sound of 'Jolene' filled the auditorium. Their act continued with 'Jackson', a duet by Johnny Cash and June Carter. The pair continued to move seamlessly through several more numbers, and each song found the crowd clapping along.

The performance ended with a track familiar to all.

'Islands in the stream . . .' Dolly and Kenny sang the final chorus, encouraging the audience to join in, and as the music faded, they took a bow. To everyone's delight, confetti cannons erupted, showering the crowd with a cascade of paper petals and colourful streamers.

'That was brilliant!' Carmen shouted to Theo above the applause as Dolly and Kenny left the stage.

'A great evening, shall we find somewhere for a nightcap?' Theo asked. 'Perhaps the piano bar,' he suggested and taking Carmen's arm, led her out of the Neptune Theatre.

Chapter Thirty-Three

In the dimly lit piano bar, the pianist played familiar jazz tunes, his fingers gliding over the smooth keys of the baby grand, where several passengers sat at tables, their conversations blending gently into the music. Carmen's heels clicked softly against the polished floor as she entered with Theo, and they looked around for a seat. Settling onto a banquette by a window overlooking the moonlit sea, they chose a cocktail.

'I've never tried an Aperol spritz,' Carmen said as she studied the menu.

Theo was thoughtful. 'I'm going to have a limoncello; it's good for digestion,' he said and sat back. 'We're in Cartagena tomorrow and it's our last day for sightseeing. Do you know anything about the place?'

'I know there is a Roman theatre, and guest services have a tour there that includes a tapas trail.'

'That sounds interesting, although, after the meal tonight, I'm not sure that I can eat another thing for at least twenty-four hours.'

Carmen smiled. 'Nonsense, the whole point of a cruise is to try foods from different countries, although I realise you've been doing that for years.'

'I'm sure I'll recover for the farewell dinner tomorrow,' Theo said.

'This time tomorrow we'll be preparing to leave the ship,' Carmen shifted in her chair, 'I feel sad that the cruise is ending. Are you flying home when we berth in Malaga?' she asked.

'I think I might go back to Greece for a little while,' Theo mused. 'I've nothing to rush to Ireland for and I rather fancy island hopping for a few weeks.'

'That's a great idea and you might find solace in the islands.'

'I was hoping it might ease the pain of returning again, to the house I shared with Ruari.' Theo was thoughtful. 'I've been thinking about writing my memoir.'

Carmen beamed. 'Your fans will welcome an account of your fascinating life.'

'Perhaps, when you have time, in between setting the Rainbow Sleuth off on any more mysteries, you can help me?'

'Theo, I'd love to.'

As Carmen spoke, she looked around the bar. Suddenly, she realised with a shock, that Ruskin was sitting in the far corner. For a moment, their eyes met, but she quickly looked away and, reaching for her drink, took a large swallow, her hand wobbling as she placed it down.

'Are you okay?' Theo asked. 'You seem flustered.'

'Ruskin alert at twelve o'clock,' Carmen whispered.

'Ah, I see.' Theo grinned. 'But he's no longer at twelve o'clock. In fact, I think he's about to join us.'

'Oh hell,' Carmen breathed. 'Don't leave me alone with him,' she pleaded.

'Deep breaths . . .' Theo replied. 'You've got this.'

Ruskin had spent the earlier part of the evening in his suite, dining on a light chicken salad and a couple of glasses of Ibizkus white, a wine he'd picked up in Ibiza. He'd enjoyed a happy half-hour FaceTiming his granddaughters, and his face lit up as they chattered about their day, both girls giggling with excitement as he promised to bring them each a gift from his cruise. Though miles apart, seeing the little ones eased the ache of missing them. They were growing up too fast.

Deciding to head to the Neptune Theatre and watch the show, Ruskin was entertained by the dancers and enjoyed the Kenny and Dolly gig. Dicky Delaney, he realised, was a versatile artiste, and Ruskin wasn't surprised that the all-round entertainer was a popular cruise ship act.

Knowing there was only one more day on the cruise before it sailed for Malaga and everyone departed for their flights home, he thought he'd end his evening with a nightcap and decide on his plans for tomorrow when the ship berthed in Cartagena.

Taking a seat in the piano bar, in the corner he favoured, Ruskin ordered a malt and made himself comfortable. He was contemplating a walk the next day, around the modernist buildings in the city, or maybe a boat tour of the bay, when Theo and Carmen appeared. Ruskin traced his fingers around the rim of his glass and watched as they took a seat and ordered drinks.

Carmen looked elegant and happy as she sat down and studied a cocktail menu, and Ruskin couldn't tear his eyes away. For the hundredth time, he asked himself why she'd stopped the mentoring sessions. 'There's only one way to find out,' he muttered, knowing that he must go over and join them and somehow instigate the conversation.

He scolded himself for staring and turned back to his drink. But when he looked up again, he caught her glance as she studied the room, and their eyes met before she quickly turned away. Draining the last of his whisky, he set the glass down. To his surprise, Ruskin was hesitant and, for a moment, wondered if she would stand up and leave the bar. The thought of never knowing if things could be different between them gnawed at him and, staring at his empty glass, Ruskin straightened his shirt cuffs, raised his fingers to straighten his hair and stood.

'Hello, Ruskin,' Theo said and stretched out a welcoming hand. 'We're having a nightcap. Why don't you join us?' Theo felt Carmen's eyes bore into him, but he ignored her silent protest and indicated that Ruskin pull up a chair.

'I don't want to interrupt,' Ruskin said, his eyes drawn to Carmen. She was wearing one of Venetia's pendants. It was a sign!

'Not at all,' Theo said, 'but as I'm suffering from acute indigestion and don't want to end up in the infirmary like our friend Sid, I think I'll call it a day and leave you two authors to chat, as I am sure you have a lot in common.'

Theo reached for his limoncello and, with a courteous smile, walked away.

Carmen was flummoxed. She'd kill Theo when she next saw him! How could he leave her in the company of Ruskin, aware of her feelings and knowing damn well that Ruskin wasn't footloose nor fancy-free? Her cheeks felt warm, and she couldn't look at Ruskin as he ordered a drink and offered her another.

'No, thank you,' she snapped and reached for her glass. 'I'll finish this and then head off to my room, too. My mother will need me to assist her to bed and I need to think about things I want to do tomorrow . . .'

Carmen knew she was babbling, and Betty's chances of needing Carmen's help while she dined and danced the night away with Holden, were as likely as a snowstorm in Cartagena the next day. She could feel the awkwardness between them, and felt her stomach churn, like a washing machine on full spin.

'Of course,' Ruskin said softly, 'but if you are going to be stuck with me for the few minutes it will take you to finish your drink, shall we make the best of it?'

Carmen looked up. Ruskin's blue eyes were like magnets drawing her in, and for a moment, the memory of his harsh critique of her writing and of the blonde woman's kiss as Ruskin sat in the plaza were forgotten. His rugged handsomeness was a drug, and as Theo had advised, she took a deep breath, trying to steady herself.

'What's wrong?' he asked.

'N . . . nothing,' Carmen mumbled. But as she tore her eyes away, she suddenly felt a stab of indignation.

Why shouldn't she stand up for herself and tell this man how she felt?

The Carmen Cunningham who had silently shut up and put up for most of her life, had faded on this cruise, and a new Carmen had emerged. She had an impulsive burst of clarity that suddenly overcame her usual doubt and fear, and unsure of whether the alcohol she'd consumed during the evening was making her braver, without thinking about the consequences, Carmen began to speak.

'Very well,' Carmen said, 'I'm confused.'

'Confused?' Ruskin frowned. 'Why would you . . .'

'Please,' Carmen held up her hand, 'let me say what I need to before I lose my courage and retreat into that frumpy woman you met in the early days of this cruise.'

Her words hung thickly between them, and when a server placed Ruskin's drink on the table, he reached out and took a sip. 'Of course, I'm sorry, do go on.'

'I admire you massively; you are the reason I booked this holiday,' Carmen said, her voice quieter than she'd intended. 'I thought that by listening to your talks and attending a workshop, I would be inspired to finish my novel, my so-called work in progress.' Her words felt clumsy, but she willed herself to go on. 'When you offered to mentor me, it was as though a dream had come true, and I lapped up every second of the time you generously gave.' Carmen paused. 'But you berated my writing and pushed me so hard, I felt that I couldn't continue with our sessions.'

'I'm so sorry, that was the last thing I intended,' Ruskin said, his voice soft with apology.

Carmen bit on her lip. How on earth could she tell Ruskin

how she really felt about him? She knew she was making a hash of the whole thing and was about to reveal too much. Clenching her fingers, Carmen decided that it would be best to make an excuse and leave.

Ruskin sensed that Carmen was about to bolt. 'Would it help if I spoke for a moment?' he asked.

'Well, if you think . . .'

'I can't tell you how sorry I was that I was so rude to you. You must feel as though you were insignificant in my eyes when we first met, and for that, I apologise.' Ruskin drew breath. 'Knowing this, I also knew that you would consider me crass for only noticing you when you revamped your appearance.'

'Yes . . . I did think that of you.' Carmen looked confused.

'The truth is that I think you are an incredibly talented author, and you don't really need my help, but there is more.' Ruskin paused and took another sip of his whisky. Looking at Carmen directly, he said, 'I am divorced, and the whole process has been difficult. When I received the decree absolute, I told myself I wouldn't get romantically involved and focus only on my work.'

Carmen was even more confused. She didn't understand what Ruskin was saying. He'd just admitted something quite raw and personal, and all she could do was stare. Was he trying to compliment her or push her away?

'It's not just the way that you write that enchants me,' Ruskin continued, his voice steady but filled with sincerity. 'It's your mind, the way you think, the kindness you show everyone around you. There's something about your presence that draws me in.' He paused, swallowing his emotion before adding, 'You see, I realised several days ago that I think I'm very attracted to you.'

Carmen's breath caught in her throat. The world seemed to spin, the music in the bar fading into a distant hum. She tried to process Ruskin's words but could only see the memory of the woman kissing him.

'But . . . you are involved with someone else,' Carmen stuttered. 'I s . . . saw you kissing in the plaza, in Ibiza.'

Ruskin smiled and began to shake his head. 'Oh, my dear girl, please don't read anything into that. The woman was my ex-wife, Venetia, who has a habit of stalking me, but it won't happen again.' He sat back. 'In fact, you are wearing one of her pendants, she sells them at several outlets in Ibiza.'

Carmen's fingers flew to her throat, and as she felt the soft silver disc, she remembered the design.

'It shows a rising sun which represents new beginnings and the promise of brighter days,' Ruskin explained. 'I think it's most appropriate.'

Carmen's voice came out in a whisper. 'I don't know what to say.' The idea of Ruskin feeling this way about her was everything she'd secretly hoped for but was almost too much to take in.

'It's a beautiful evening,' Ruskin said, 'would you like to take a stroll with me on the promenade deck?'

Carmen hesitated as she watched Ruskin hold out his hand. Then, trance-like, she stood up and felt his strong fingers wrapping around her own.

'Yes,' she smiled, 'I'd like that.'

Chapter Thirty-Four

As the *Diamond Star* sailed smoothly through the open sea, making its way to Cartagena, Ruskin strolled alongside Carmen on the promenade deck, her hand nestled gently in his. He'd walked on countless decks, travelled across many seas and experienced the triumphs and heartbreaks that inspired his novels, but at that moment, a sense of long-forgotten happiness washed joyously over him.

He glanced at Carmen beside him. In the dim glow of the ship's lights, her smile seemed to light up the deck ahead. Relaxed and happy, the sight of her face ignited something in Ruskin that had lain dormant for too long. They chatted about books and authors they liked, the things that motivated them and their favourite time of day to write. Carmen asked if he based his characters on people he knew and if travelling inspired his work. She spoke of her aspirations, and Ruskin told her of the time that had passed since the ink had dried on his divorce papers. In the last couple of years, he'd shut himself off to many things. He hadn't felt the rush of infatuation for decades, yet walking with Carmen, he felt like a young man again and was happy to tell her about his family and his two granddaughters, who he couldn't wait to see again.

When his arm accidentally brushed hers, and he felt the warmth of her skin, she turned to meet his gaze. With the sea stretching out beside them, shimmering in the moonlight, he tilted her chin and kissed her longingly on her lips.

'I never thought . . .' he began, then stopped, shaking his head and running his fingers through his hair. 'I'd ever feel like this again.'

'I never thought I *could* feel like this,' Carmen whispered.

'Like what?'

'Like I'm a young girl, and everything is possible.'

'I don't know what is happening here,' Ruskin said, 'it must be the magic of this cruise, but can I suggest that for the little time we have left on the ship, we both just sail along and enjoy it?'

When Carmen nodded, he wrapped his arms around her and kissed her again.

* * *

Carmen felt as though she were dreaming. The promenade deck's warm breeze still lingered on her skin, and as she raced back to her cabin, she touched her lips, remembering the passion she'd felt when Ruskin kissed her. Her chest felt tight with exhilaration and disbelief.

Had the last few hours really happened, and had Ruskin told her he was attracted to her?

Things like this never happened to Carmen Cunningham;

she only heard about it happening to other people or read about love in a novel.

But facts were facts, and on this Mediterranean cruise, she'd strolled along a deck in the moonlight, hand in hand with her idol, her heart thudding in her chest as her fantasies came to life and the man of her dreams kissed her. And it didn't end there! She was meeting him the next morning, and they planned to spend the last day together discovering the Roman Theatre in Cartagena and taking the tapas trail tour.

Carmen felt lightheaded as she flung open her cabin door and wandered into her room. She saw her reflection in a mirror, a wide-eyed woman beaming from ear to ear. Her hair had fallen from its clips, and she shook it wildly as a giddy laugh began to bubble up. *Thank you!* She thought of Ruskin and how his eyes had softened in the moments before they kissed.

Ruskin told her that Peter had asked him to help solve the mystery of the missing jewellery items on the ship. 'I've been making my own enquiries,' he said, 'and liaising with Peter and the ship's security team and I'm convinced we're missing something.'

'It sounds intriguing – and good research for a future story perhaps.'

He'd considerately asked her about her family, and she'd explained her past, adding that she thought Betty was about to become engaged and married to an American.

'So, you will have time to yourself?' Ruskin asked.

When Carmen nodded, he said he hoped she'd share as much as possible with him.

She remembered the granddaughters he'd spoken about, and smiled. Little ones that brought joy to his life!

This is all happening so quickly. Carmen kicked off her sandals and flopped onto the bed, staring starry-eyed at the ceiling. But why overanalyse it? This wasn't a novel where every plot had a hole, and every twist begged scrutiny. Ends didn't have to be tied, and she'd let her time with Ruskin unfold and see where it took her. Ruskin admired her writing, and she admired his. This mutual respect was a foundation, and when their schedules aligned, she'd make the most of every moment she had with him.

Carmen closed her eyes and soon felt herself drifting into a dream where butterflies hovered, and birds tweeted as Cupid skilfully aimed his arrow. When she heard someone sobbing, she thought that the dream had taken an unexpected turn, but as the sobbing got louder, Carmen opened her eyes and realised that the sound was coming from the other side of the wall.

Betty! Was her mum sobbing her heart out?

Carmen stood and grabbed the spare key card and barefoot, hurried into Betty's room where she found her mother sitting on the bed with her head in her hands, sobbing uncontrollably.

'Mum, shush, what's happened?' Carmen spoke softly, placing her arm around Betty's shoulders. 'Please stop crying and tell me what has upset you.'

Betty's sobs wracked her body. Her silver hair was dishevelled with wisps clinging to her tear-streaked cheeks as her fingers clutched a crumpled handkerchief. 'It's

Holden . . . but I can't talk about it,' Betty stuttered, 'I don't want to remember.'

Carmen slid to the floor and knelt beside Betty. 'It's all right,' she said as she stroked Betty's arms in soothing circles. 'Please tell me.'

'Oh, you won't understand.' Betty shook her head. 'Just for once, I thought that a man really liked me,' she said.

'What do you mean?' Carmen asked. 'It's obvious that something has happened with Holden, but Dad adored you.' Carmen was puzzled. Surely, Betty hadn't forgotten her marriage to Des already.

'Oh, Carmen,' Betty focused on her daughter with misty eyes. 'You think that your father adored me?' she asked in surprise. 'You haven't a clue, have you? Well maybe it's time I told you the truth.'

'I don't understand, what truth?'

Betty let out a heavy sigh, folding her hands in her lap. 'Your precious dad had an affair with Marion for most of our marriage. Why do you think he kept such long hours at the shop?'

Carmen froze, stunned into silence. '*Marion?*' she asked.

Betty gave a bitter laugh. 'Took you long enough. Have you only just put two and two together? I thought you'd worked it out years ago.'

Carmen blinked rapidly, staring at her mother. A part of her wanted to cover her ears, to block out Betty's voice, but the quiet that followed forced her to sift through her memories of home and the hardware shop. Slowly, she processed what her mother had said and piece by piece, the reality sank in, followed by the realisation that Betty might be right.

Marion, a woman who worked at Cunningham's Hardware, assisted in the shop, then helped Des with the books while her husband, a projectionist at the local cinema, worked evening shifts. Now, as Carmen slowly nodded her head, she understood that Marion had been helping herself to more than a few hours of bookkeeping. She remembered how Marion's hand lingered on Des's arm and the knowing glances they shared.

She thought of the late nights when Des came home, seeming preoccupied, and how Marion had started driving a newer car even though she always claimed that money was tight.

'Marion?' Carmen repeated, remembering the woman she'd always been fond of and who had been kind to her. She'd trusted Marion and felt a warmth in her presence, but now, as the pieces began to fall away, Carmen wondered how the woman could have betrayed Betty and herself so cruelly.

'I stayed for you,' Betty said. 'Having a daughter together meant that I could never leave your father, but he wanted more babies, and I couldn't let that happen. I didn't want to be the laughing stock of the neighbourhood. His lies tore me apart.'

'But Mum, you could have left. I would have understood.'

'Hardly, you were the apple of your dad's eye. With him filling your head with silly ideas of making dreams come true.' Betty sighed and spoke slowly. 'His affair with Marion started soon after you were born and went on for years. They were different times, and I couldn't blow up our lives, so I played the dutiful wife.'

'Did Marion's husband know?'

Betty snorted. 'Yes, he found out all right. There was a huge row, and that's why she left the shop abruptly, but for your father, old habits die hard.'

Carmen's mind reeled. She'd always wondered why Marion departed so suddenly. What else was this strange evening going to reveal?

Betty began to cry again, and then, suddenly, threw back her head and yelled, '*WHY, why does it always happen to me?*' She reached for the brooch on her dress and tore it from the fabric.

Carmen's eyes followed the flying pineapple, and suddenly realised what might have happened. Taking Betty's hand, she gently asked, 'It's all right, Mum, thank you for explaining about Dad. You've had a shock, but I need to ask, did Holden take you to a party in Colin and Neeta's suite?'

'He most certainly did, and I've never seen anything like it,' Betty bristled then recovered her composure, suddenly seeming more like her old self. She dabbed at her nose. 'If only I could erase the memory,' she sniffed.

'Oh, I think I understand,' Carmen said, resisting the urge to smile as she remembered Theo telling her about his unintentional visit to the Upside-Down Pineapple Pensioner Club.

Holden had given Betty a pineapple brooch. He was obviously a member of the *UDPPC*, as were others on the ship.

'I thought we were going to a nice party,' Betty explained. 'It all seemed perfectly innocent, canapés, champagne and the works, until Holden disappeared into another room, and someone asked me if I was a new member.' Betty grimaced. 'The next thing I knew, he was showing me *his* member, and I told him I'd seen more meat on a toothpick . . .'

'Where was Holden?' Carmen bit her lip, suppressing a giggle.

'He suddenly appeared in a pair of budgie smugglers with that Neeta woman hanging half-naked off his arm. She came over put her hand on my shoulder then offered me a glass of champagne, but I told her, "No. Thank. You!"'

'What did Holden have to say for himself?'

Betty crossed her arms. 'He said it was all in good fun and not to be so serious. *Fun?* I told him that the only fun thing was seeing him squeezed into those budgie smugglers and that he looked like a hot dog ready to explode. Then I left as quickly as I'd arrived.'

Carmen finally laughed as the image of Holden in his too-tight leisure wear burned into her memory. 'Oh, Mum, I'm so sorry,' she said, 'it must be an awful blow for you to realise that Holden isn't all he seemed to be.'

'You might think it's funny, but Holden has some very odd ideas,' Betty grumbled, 'and if I'm completely truthful, he's like a dinosaur on the dance floor. My poor old feet are trampled.'

Carmen marvelled at her mother's ability to change her mood so swiftly. Holden was no longer the blue-eyed all-American man, and now, Betty was ripping him to pieces.

'Why don't I make you more comfortable and get you settled in bed?' Carmen suggested. 'I'll order some cocoa too, and things will look brighter in the morning.'

'Never mind cocoa, pour me a large measure of brandy,' Betty snapped as she leaned forward for Carmen to unzip her dress. 'My poor old nerves are in pieces.'

Carmen sighed. Already her mother's bad temper had returned. But as Carmen reached for the hook at Betty's collar, she noticed something was missing. 'Mum,' she slowly asked, 'where are your pearls?'

Chapter Thirty-Five

Carmen was wide awake. Having settled Betty with two herbal sleep aids and the brandy she'd insisted on, her mother was away with the fairies in no time at all. As Carmen crept out to the sound of loud snores, she let herself into her own room and sat down at her desk. Her mind was buzzing with lost memories as the chaos of Betty's confession refused to let go.

Her dad. The man she'd always considered steady and kind, had been living a profoundly different life from the one she remembered. Had his marriage to Betty meant anything at all?

Carmen might have had siblings. A brother or sister to befriend and share the burden of Betty with as she aged. She thought about her parents as young lovers and the vows they must have made, then the life they built together as they welcomed a baby to their family. Had it all been a façade for Des?

And then there was Marion. The other woman.

As a child, Carmen had called her, 'Aunty Marion'. A

wave of anger rose in Carmen's chest, but it was quickly followed by a deep sadness that Betty had lived all those years, pretending that all was well. No wonder she was so bitter.

Tears dampened Carmen's eyes, but she held them back even with the realisation that the image she had of her father was crumbling fast. For all his talk of making dreams come true, he'd been unable to fulfil his own.

'Oh, Dad,' Carmen sighed, 'why didn't you have the courage to change things? You might have given everyone a chance to be happy.'

Carmen stood and stepped onto her balcony. Her bare feet were cold against the metal floor. Gentle waves glinted under the pale moonlight, and the night felt vast and endless. Betty's confession had shaken Carmen, but here, in the stillness, she thought of Ruskin. Their kiss felt like a hundred years ago, but as she touched her lips, the warm feeling returned and wrapped around her like a hug. She thought of his laugh and the way her hand fitted in his, his steady voice and how his eyes softened when he looked at her. Whatever lay ahead, whether fleeting or enduring, she would grab what happiness she could. Life was messy and unpredictable, but here, on this balcony, her heart felt full of hope despite the storm that raged around her mother.

And for now, that was enough.

Carmen headed to the bathroom to take off her makeup, and while brushing her hair, she recalled her mother's missing pearls. Don, Debbie and Dicky Delaney had all lost jewellery, Theo too and more recently, Neeta. Remembering that Ruskin had told her Peter had asked for his help, she realised she needed to inform Ruskin that Betty had joined the list of passengers with missing items.

Carmen distantly remembered Theo telling her that he struggled to sleep at night and she glanced at her watch. Perhaps he was awake? She longed to tell him of the latest developments and reached for the phone. After a few rings, he answered.

'Theo, it's me,' Carmen spoke softly.

'Hello, Cinderella. You don't need to whisper. I'm wide awake and intrigued to hear your news.'

Carmen remembered that she'd cursed Theo when he left her alone with Ruskin, but suddenly, she wished that he was beside her.

'Shall I come to your room, and we can snuggle like roomies while you reveal all about Ruskin?' Theo asked.

'Would you?'

'I'm on my way.'

* * *

'What a surprise,' Theo said as he sat beside Carmen on her bed.

'Oh goodness, Theo, I feel terribly sorry for my mother. She thought Holden was someone she could enjoy herself with.'

'But not at an upside-down pineapple pensioner party. Do you think Betty will be heartbroken that Holden wasn't the man she thought he was?'

'I don't know,' Carmen shrugged, 'she seemed to regain her bad temper quite quickly, especially when she described the party and Holden's revealing outfit.'

Theo began to laugh and, unable to help herself, Carmen joined in.

'I've led such a sheltered life,' she said, dabbing at her eyes. 'Who would have thought there was such a thing as the Upside-Down Pineapple Pensioner Club?'

'Apparently, upside-down pineapple parties are a global phenomenon, and we shouldn't be surprised that they happen on cruise ships,' Theo said. 'Where better for people to relax and enjoy these . . . er . . . activities?'

'Beware the upside-down pineapple,' Carmen giggled, 'I doubt my mother will ever buy one again.'

'I heard a story that in Spain, a supermarket chain encourages shoppers who, on certain nights, place a pineapple upside down in their trolley as a sign that they're *available*.'

Carmen's eyes widened. 'When you say "*available*," do you mean . . .?'

'Absolutely,' Theo said with a mischievous smile. 'Supermarket seduction or whatever else takes your fancy.'

'My goodness.' Carmen shook her head. 'I need to get out more.'

'But more importantly, dear girl, tell me about Ruskin.'

Carmen sank back in the pillows, her expression softening as she thought of her time with Ruskin on the promenade deck. 'It was . . . nice,' she admitted.

'*Nice?*' Theo raised an eyebrow. 'Carmen, please spill the beans.'

'Well, we talked, walked and held hands and . . .'

'Oh, pleeease . . .' Theo rolled his eyes. 'Get to the point. Did he take you back to his suite and ravish you?'

'No, of course not.' Carmen blushed. 'But we did kiss.' Carmen remembered their kisses and quietly wished it had led to something more.

'Well, it's a start, and I couldn't be happier for you.' Theo sat up. 'Now, what's on your agenda for today?'

'Ruskin invited me to visit the Roman Theatre with him. There's a tour that includes tapas tasting too.'

'Perfect, your last day of the cruise spent together.'

'But I can't, can I?' Suddenly anxious, Carmen swung her legs over the side of the bed, 'I need to make sure Mum's all right, and I can't leave her alone after everything that's happened, especially on the last day.'

Theo rose and took Carmen's hands in his own.

'Here's what I suggest. I will take Betty to guest services to report her missing pearls. You must also tell Ruskin about Betty's necklace, while you spend the day with him.'

'But I can't leave Betty.' Carmen sighed.

'Of course, you can.' Theo tugged her to her feet. 'You've spent most of your life taking care of Betty. Today, it's my turn to sort her out and keep her amused. Go and enjoy yourself. You deserve it.'

Carmen stared at Theo. 'Are you sure?' she asked.

'Positive, no arguments,' he said with a reassuring smile. 'After all, what are friends for?'

* * *

As they wandered around the Roman Theatre, Ruskin and Carmen were struck by the size of the amphitheatre as their guide explained that this was one of the most significant and well-preserved examples of Roman architecture on the Iberian Peninsula. Together with a group of passengers from the *Diamond Star*, they learned that the seating area in the theatre would have accommodated around six thousand spectators. Carmen was fascinated as she gazed up at the three seating tiers, which were divided by aisles and staircases, then, turning to look at Ruskin, she saw that he was engrossed in the wide semi-circle where an orchestra would have played.

'There would have been marble flooring there.' Ruskin pointed and read from a tourist pamphlet. 'The stage's backdrop has decorated columns, with sculptures created from locally sourced stone.'

'It's magnificent. Do you think it's still used?'

'Yes, cultural events are held here, and modern entertainment too, I imagine.'

Their guide informed the group that they had an hour to spend in the theatre and to wander at leisure before reconvening. Ruskin took Carmen's hand, and they climbed to the top. There, they paused to catch their breath and take in the stunning view of the modern city of Cartagena amidst ancient ruins.

'Look, we can see the sea in the distance,' Carmen said, reaching for her phone to capture the moment.

'Let's take a selfie.' Ruskin hugged her.

Carmen wore her floaty dress with beaded straps. As she nestled into Ruskin's arm, she felt a thrill as his bare skin brushed her own. A breeze caught her hair, and as he reached out to tuck a stray strand behind her ear, their eyes met, and he kissed her.

'I so enjoy doing that.' Ruskin smiled.

Sitting on the sun-warmed stone, Carmen was thoughtful as she looked at the view. 'I almost feel sorry for Holden, and for Mum too,' she said. Earlier, she'd explained the events of the previous evening.

'Theo will have taken Betty to speak to Peter about her necklace. And try not worry about her relationship with Holden, it wasn't meant to be.'

'I know Holden's idea of fun doesn't match up with Mum's, but in the brief time they had together, he made her happy.'

'When he wasn't stepping on her toes . . .' Ruskin laughed.

Carmen smiled and checked her watch. 'We'd better go down. The guide will be gathering everyone for the tapas trail.'

A little while later, in the lively streets of Cartagena, the guide led the group to a hidden gem of a bar. There, in a sunny courtyard, they were greeted with a glass of sangria and invited to try fried potato cubes in a rich tomato and garlic sauce.

'It's called patatas bravas,' Ruskin said, 'and these meatballs are albóndigas.'

'Delicious.' Carmen smiled as Ruskin held out a small dish. 'And what have we here?'

'Pulpo a la gallega. It's octopus, tuck in.'

At each stop, everyone passed dishes back and forth, sharing small plates that included salty anchovies, tiny green peppers with a spicy kick, melt-in-the-mouth Iberian ham and hot clams in a delicious seafood sauce.

'Try this tortilla,' Ruskin urged and forked a wedge of thick creamy omelette.

'I'll have no room for the gala dinner tonight,' Carmen said, rubbing her stomach, but despite her words, and encouraged by several glasses of wine, she eagerly took a bite.

By the time they came to the final stop, the nervousness Carmen had felt when setting off with Ruskin had lifted, and now she felt a comfortable intimacy as they sat together, tasting tiny slices of creamy flan and sipping from glasses of sweet sherry.

'I've loved being with you today,' Ruskin said. 'We have a lot in common, from a love of history and architecture to guzzling a great deal of food.'

The air was filled with chatter in the bustling bar as glasses chinked around her, but Carmen barely noticed any of it. Ruskin was smiling and leaning in to listen to her every word, and Carmen couldn't help but replay the moment in the piano bar when he'd told her he was attracted to her. It all felt surreal, like a dream she didn't want to wake from. Ruskin's quiet intensity intrigued her, and she looked forward to any time they spent together in the future.

But as their guide called out that everyone was to return to the ship, reality pressed in. Freed from Holden, Betty would reclaim her time and attention and the weight of it felt heavy. When the cruise ended tomorrow, Carmen would no longer be a woman with fleeting freedom on a luxurious ship.

As she strolled hand in hand with Ruskin through Cartagena's cobblestone streets, they paused by a square where a musician played a guitar. To her surprise, Ruskin let go of her hand and pulled her into a slow, impromptu dance. Carmen rested her head on his shoulder and thought how much she'd enjoyed the Roman Theatre and the centuries of history. As the warmth of his body touched her own, she realised that she hadn't just fallen in love with the cruise and everything it offered, she'd fallen in love with the man whose arms enveloped her so effortlessly.

Ruskin wasn't just part of this journey. He'd become her journey.

Chapter Thirty-Six

As the sun dipped towards the horizon, a gentle radiance fell over the harbour in Cartagena, casting shadows over the elegant ochre façades of buildings along the waterfront where intricate ironwork balconies and arched windows were framed with carved stone friezes. Carmen and Ruskin walked arm in arm along the Paseo del Muelle, the wide promenade beside the water, lined with swaying palm trees and bustling with activity. Tourists and locals sipped drinks at outdoor tables, and Carmen browsed handmade crafts in stalls and looked at the many glamorous shop fronts.

'I adore the old-world charm of this city,' she said as they approached the ship where the decks of the *Diamond Star* buzzed with passengers returning from their day out.

As they made their way aboard, Peter came forward to speak to them. 'Holden Jackson has reported that he's misplaced a valuable watch.'

'Holden has lost an item too?' Carmen was flabbergasted.

'Between you and I,' Peter confided, glancing over his shoulder, 'Holden's lost watch is a fake, a copy of a gold Rolex.'

'He wears a fake?' Ruskin chipped in.

'Very sensible too.' Peter nodded. 'Holden took me to his room to show me the real Rolex, which was in his safe, in a box with papers authenticating its provenance. I was impressed.'

'Why does he travel with such an expensive item?'

'Oh, passengers like to show off their wealth, especially on the last night of the cruise, but it would be foolish to go ashore wearing the real thing. The old boy is worth a fortune. I've met him on previous cruises.'

Ruskin nodded, listening thoughtfully.

'If you have any views on the matter now that another passenger is missing an item, you need to let me know.' Peter sighed. 'If we can't find out where the items are I will have to file a report with the authorities ashore tomorrow.'

As they walked away, Carmen turned to Ruskin. 'Some cosy crime author I am,' she said. 'I hope my Rainbow Sleuth would do a better job of unravelling this whodunit because I haven't a clue.'

'The situation is serious,' Ruskin said. 'I must find the answer to this mystery.'

Carmen nodded. 'I'm going to find Theo and buy him a large drink for putting up with my mother all day.'

'Do you know where they are?' Ruskin asked.

'Theo sent me a text to say that they were by the pool on the lido deck.'

'Probably relaxing in the last of the day's sunshine.' Ruskin reached out to take her hand. 'Let's go and find out.'

* * *

'Come on, Betty, one more duck, and you share the lead!'

Carmen and Ruskin arrived on the lido deck and could hardly believe their eyes when they saw the commotion in the pool as Kyle, standing by the edge, wearing a rainbow sunhat and neon Speedos, shouted out instructions.

'Colin! That's a foul!' Kyle yelled and blew a whistle. 'Three ducks scooped at once constitutes a final warning; if it happens again, you will leave the pool.'

The pool was full of pensioners and brightly coloured rubber ducks bobbed about on the surface. With elbows out and water flying, each person carried a small net on a pole as they splashed and dived to net a duck.

In the middle of the pool, Fran sat on an inflatable blush-coloured flamingo, wearing her baby pink tankini, while Sid paddled around her on a fierce-looking crocodile. Don was riding a dolphin, while Debbie had a doughnut around her waist.

'Good heavens,' Carmen said, her eyes wide as she saw Betty at one end of the pool wearing a safety strap and sitting in a waterproof chair next to a wheelchair ramp, thrusting out a noodle to shove Neeta out of her way. Betty wore Carmen's sludge-green swimsuit and a flowered rubber cap, and as she extended her net, she scooped up a duck and flung it on the side of the pool.

'Another duck for Betty!' Kyle called out. 'She shares the lead with Sid. Two minutes to go, everyone. Put some effort into it!'

As a pensioner tumbled into the water from the steps and another dived chest-deep, Carmen and Ruskin smiled when they saw Theo, comfortable in an inflatable chair, wearing heart-shaped synthetic sunglasses, paddling towards them.

'Hola!' Theo called out. 'Did you have a good day?'

'Yes, but possibly not quite as much fun as you appear to be having here,' Ruskin laughed.

'How on earth did you get my mother into a swimsuit?' Carmen gawped. 'She can't even swim.'

Theo slid off his chair. 'That was down to Fran, I'm afraid she raided your closet.'

'I thought I'd thrown that dreadful bathing suit away,' Carmen said.

'Betty looks as though she's having a great time,' Ruskin said as Betty hurled another duck out of the pool, narrowly missing his head.

'It's been full on.' Theo eased out of the water. 'Fran decided that Betty needed cheering up, so we took her for a wander around Cartagena and had a most enjoyable lunch, then back to the ship for poolside trivia, and now, as you can see, the floating duck hunt.' Removing the novelty glasses, he reached for a towel and began to dry himself.

'I have a feeling that you're going to tell me Mum won the trivia.' Carmen thought of her mother's quizzing skills.

'She certainly did, and it looks like she's about to secure first place here too.'

Everyone stopped and turned towards Kyle as he blew his final whistle. Breathless with anticipation and fuelled by rivalry, they waited for the result.

'Drumroll, we have a winner!' Kyle called out. Checking the scores on a clipboard covered with glitter stickers, he let the tension mount. 'In third place for the dolphin that appeared far too interested in the flamingo, we have Don with fourteen ducks!'

A cheer went up for Don, who looked miffed not to have scored higher. 'Kyle, you have the game rigged tighter than a ferret in a rabbit hole!' Don yelled.

Kyle ignored the comment. 'In second place, give it up for Debbie, who dived extra deep and achieved a fantastic fifteen ducks!'

'Fix!' Don shouted, ducking as Debbie walloped him with a noodle.

'But in first place . . .' Kyle paused, to build the tension. 'With not only sixteen ducks but she also netted two golden chuckies, our queen of the hunt and winner of our Danny the *Diamond Star* Dolphin is . . . Betty!'

Everyone clapped as Kyle presented Betty with a tiara-wearing Danny the Dolphin. Sid tossed his cap into the air as Kyle posed beside Betty, and the ship's photographer snapped away.

'And that was our final senior splashdown,' Kyle said sadly, 'but remember darlings, this isn't goodbye. It's just a see-you-later, as I know many of you will be meeting me again on another cruise.' He stood poolside in a pirouette pose. 'You've all been the sunshine in my day during my time on the *Diamond Star* Mysteries of the Mediterranean cruise. I want you to promise me that you will keep splashing, keep laughing and never let your trivia cards get wet. Go out there and show the world that you seniors know how to make waves!'

To the sound of applause, Kyle blew a kiss to the crowd, then spun on his sliders and strutted towards the bar.

'We'd better rescue Betty.' Carmen saw her mother grappling with her safety strap.

'Don't worry, I've got it,' Theo said, 'it was me who fastened her in.'

Theo sped off to assist Betty as Fran and Sid appeared.

Fran's hair was wet and clung to her face as she grabbed a towel. 'Gosh, that was fun,' she said, rubbing Sid's back. 'We don't get games like that at the Sandcastle Waterpark at home in Blackpool, but I might suggest that they do.'

'I hear that you've been looking after Betty,' Carmen said. 'Thank you so much, I'm so grateful for all your help.'

'Oh, get away with you, it was our pleasure, we've all had a wonderful day.' Fran beamed and gave Carmen a wink, nodding towards Ruskin. 'But more importantly, I must ask, are you ready for the gala evening and what are you going to wear?'

'Goodness, I hadn't really thought about it,' Carmen said.

'Well, I need to head off and get ready. I've a lot to do.' Fran ran her fingers through her damp hair and laughed. Are we all going to sit together for our last night?' She looked at Ruskin, her eyebrows raised.

'I'd love to join you, if I am invited,' Ruskin replied and squeezed Carmen's hand.

'That's settled then, Sid will reserve the table.'

As everyone turned to leave the pool, Theo appeared with Betty, now sitting in her chair. She gripped an armrest as the flowers on her cap bobbed as though trying to avoid the storm brewing beneath.

'Carmen!' Betty cried out, waving her cane. 'You've abandoned me all day, and the least you can do is help me to my room and get me out of this horrible swimsuit. I look like a slimy slug.'

Carmen took the chair from Theo and gave him a grateful wink. 'See you all later,' she said, then turned to Betty and added, 'Normal service resumed . . .'

* * *

Dicky had enjoyed his day in Cartagena. Still glowing from the success of the Kenny and Dolly show the previous evening, he was happy to escort his lady friend, who'd insisted that they find a jeweller's shop where she treated Dicky to an emerald signature ring with matching cufflinks. Now as he sat back in his chair in his dressing room with Melody alongside, Dicky showed off his latest acquisitions.

'Who's a lucky boy?' Melody said as she held the ring and watched it sparkle in the lights from her makeup mirror. 'Emeralds are gorgeous, the birthstone of Taurus.'

'Correct,' Dicky said, 'and as I am born under that sign, I am known to be ruled by Venus, the planet of beauty and love.'

'Taurus is also known to be stubborn and resistant to change, making me think that you won't pursue this relationship when the cruise ends tomorrow. Was this a goodbye gift?'

'I am sure it is,' Dicky said, taking the ring from Melody and placing it on his little finger. But his smile faded and, looking for a distraction, he reached for the call sheet for the evening's performance.

Melody saw the shift in his mood. 'What's wrong, Dicky?' she asked. 'You don't sound so sure about things.'

Dicky glanced up, his eyes meeting Melody's, and for a

moment, there was a flicker of something unspoken between them.

'It's okay. I'm Taurean remember, and I'm stubborn,' he said.

'Well, stubborn or not, sometimes you need to talk, and you might find that what you want is worth fighting for, even if you must break a few of your own rules along the way.' She reached for a tube and began to apply her makeup.

'What are your plans when we leave the ship?' he asked.

'I'm looking forward to heading home to Benidorm for a few months, where I can get plenty of work in the clubs. Then, I'm booked to join this ship again for a Christmas cruise in the Canaries.

'That sounds good,' Dicky said and forced a smile.

'And what about you?'

'Oh, I've no doubt my agent has me work lined up for months. Clive considers my talent to be the best on his books.'

Dicky thought of Clive. His agent hadn't contacted him, and Dicky knew that there wasn't any work coming his way. Clive had moved onto pastures new with younger, edgier comedians who fitted the bill for the larger cruise ships with more youthful audiences. Their appeal meant bigger fees and a healthier cut for Clive.

Dicky shrugged and diverted his attention to the call sheet. 'But right now, we've a show to deliver, so let's focus on giving the guests a grand spectacle and a last night they'll never forget.'

Chapter Thirty-Seven

As darkness descended, passengers gathered on the decks of the *Diamond Star* as the ship's horn signalled its departure. Spanish music played for the sail-away, and many held glasses of champagne as the ship left the harbourside, where the shimmering waters of the Mediterranean caught the city's lights and bathed Cartagena's historic skyline in the twilight. Under a canopy of twinkling stars, they passed a lighthouse, and as the port lights faded in the distance the *Diamond Star* set course for Malaga.

'I'm going to miss this,' Fran whispered to Sid. She felt wistful that their cruise was nearing the end of its voyage.

'It's not an ending, lass. Don't be sad,' Sid replied, his arm around her shoulder. 'This is the start of something special for us, and we'll have many cruising days ahead.' He kissed her cheek, then stood back to admire his wife. 'I have to say I have the most beautiful woman on my arm tonight.'

The kaleidoscope of colour that Fran wore was perfect with her glitzy jewellery, and the long flowing lines flattered her full figure. Fran had swept her hair into a towering topknot and fastened it with a sparkling clip that was as bold and bright as her makeup.

'Get away with you,' Fran laughed and punched Sid's arm playfully. But as Fran smoothed the fabric of her colourful kaftan, she felt good. This cruise had been the perfect tonic to refresh her tired bones.

A few feet away from Fran, Don and Debbie stood with Colin and Neeta. The men were smart in their dinner suits, and Debbie wore a long, sapphire blue tunic with beadwork at the neck. Neeta, meanwhile, carried a pineapple-shaped clutch and turned heads in a skimpy dress adorned with a lively tropical pattern.

To Debbie's dismay, Don watched Neeta's hemline sway in the breeze, and he grinned salaciously when her tanned thighs were revealed. With her back ramrod straight, Debbie shook her head and began to stride away.

'Eh, up! Come on love, I'm only admirin' the craftsmanship on Neeta's crutch, I mean clutch . . .' He turned to Colin and winked.

On the promenade deck, Theo, handsome in a midnight-blue jacket, formal trousers and a loud checkered waistcoat, pushed Betty along in her chair. 'What a wonderful evening,' he said, gazing at the stars.

'I'm cold,' Betty grumbled, 'why on earth are we out here when we could be inside in the warm restaurant?'

A little further behind, Ruskin and Carmen fell into step. 'Don't worry, Mum. We're on our way,' Carmen said, frustration etched across her face. She hoped that Betty wouldn't spoil the evening and, holding onto Ruskin's arm, took a slow, deep breath.

'You look amazing,' Ruskin whispered and squeezed Carmen's arm. 'That colour is fabulous on you.'

Carmen's tension eased. 'Thank you,' she said, glancing at Ruskin and wondering how she was strolling along with this man on her arm. Tall and poised, Ruskin's dinner suit was perfectly tailored, the satin lapels catching the light. His chiselled features softened when his blue eyes caught her own, and his cologne's scent was almost overwhelming.

The rich colour of Carmen's scarlet dress enhanced her sun-kissed skin, and she knew she'd never look better. How clever Fran had been to find this gorgeous garment. Carmen's hair was swept to one side in a soft updo, and a few strands fell lightly onto her shoulders. Carmen had treated herself to sparkling earrings from the onboard jeweller, and as she caught her reflection in a window, they caught the evening light.

Carmen watched as Theo gripped the handles of Betty's chair and carefully manoeuvred her through a doorway. Carmen crossed her fingers, hoping that her mother's grumblings wouldn't continue.

The past days aboard the cruise had stirred something deep within Carmen, nurturing plans that felt like new fresh shoots. After a magical day with Ruskin, Carmen was sure there was more for her in life. No matter what happened with him, she *had* to gently escape her mother's shadow and find a new path. But as she stared up at the sky, she smiled. Tonight was the final chapter of this unforgettable cruise, and she was determined that she would enjoy every moment.

Ruskin followed the group through the ship and into

the Terrace Restaurant, where the dining room had been transformed. The baby grand now sat at the entrance, and the pianist played familiar melodies as everyone found their seats. White linen covered the tables, and candles flickered above elegant floral arrangements where subdued lighting added a romantic air to the night.

Ruskin stood beside Carmen as everyone took their place. Her scarlet dress caught the glow, and for a moment, everything faded as he watched her. The dining room was impressive, but it paled compared to the transformation of the woman he'd encountered at the beginning of the cruise. Ruskin's feelings for Carmen were complex, and he couldn't explain why he was drawn to her. All he knew was that he wanted to be with her and thought about her all the time. Seeing Carmen come into her own was exhilarating, and her transformation mirrored his unexpected feelings, making his heart sing and his whole being feel lighter. He knew that he'd emerged from the aftermath of his divorce and felt optimistic and excited that he might find happiness in whatever time they carved out for each other.

As he sat with this varied group of people, Ruskin wasn't sure where things might lead with Carmen, but one thing was sure. He didn't want it to end with this cruise.

Dinner was a delight, and guests enjoyed a starter of gazpacho followed by seared scallops with a saffron sauce. Betty couldn't understand why anyone would want to eat a cold soup and pushed her plate away. However, her eyes soon lit up as a wine waiter topped up her glass and when a filet mignon with truffle jus was placed before her, she heartily tucked in. A chocolate fondant with pistachio cream followed and the meal ended with a magnificent selection of cheese.

Don commented as each course arrived and as a server offered more jus with his steak, he said that he'd prefer a jug full of gravy. In between a course he asked, 'What's this intermezzo nonsense? If I wanted to cleanse my palate I'd use a tube of toothpaste.'

Debbie's expression hardened as she glared at her husband and shaking her head, looked away.

At the end of the meal, as everyone departed to make their way to the Neptune Theatre, Colin and Neeta invited them all to a party in their suite when the evening's entertainment had concluded. Betty, now walking beside Theo, looked up in surprise and called out. 'One of your upside-down pineapple parties? Not for me. Pineapples belong in a fruit salad, not in whatever plans you lot have.'

Ruskin studied Neeta as she grinned at Betty and shrugged her shoulders. Her tan had deepened and offset the silver jewellery that sparkled on her skin. Noticing his stare, Neeta appeared surprisingly self-conscious, and her hands flew to her head to loosen her hair, ruffling her blonde locks around her ears.

Ruskin reached for Carmen's hand as they took their seats beside Theo and Betty with Fran, Sid, Don and Debbie in the row behind. Their murmur of excited conversation filled the air. When colourful lights sparkled across the stage and the band began to play, the room was hushed and after the opening medley, Peter appeared.

'Good evening, everyone,' he began, 'welcome to our

grand finale for the last night of your unforgettable cruise. I can hardly believe that this is our final night together, but before I introduce you to tonight's show, on behalf of Captain Bellwood and the entire crew of the *Diamond Star* we want to say a heartfelt thanks to everyone for choosing to sail with us.'

There was a round of applause then Don held up his glass and called out, 'Aye with prices like this I could have bought a new car but at least a few drinks were included.' He winced when Debbie dug an elbow in his ribs and one or two guests booed.

Peter ignored Don. 'So, tonight, we're pulling out all the stops – we have a fabulous line-up and to kick off the night we have the one and only . . . Dicky Delaney!'

There was a drum roll as Dicky danced onto the stage and the audience began to clap along as the band played the opening chords of 'I Gotta Feeling'.

'Tonight's the night!' Dicky called out before launching into the chorus encouraging everyone to join in.

'How are *you* feeling?' Dicky asked when the song ended, and he searched the crowd. 'I see a few familiar faces.' He pointed to Debbie and waved. 'This beautiful lady sang "My Way" so many times this week, Sinatra's turning in his grave. But all credit to you – you certainly sang it . . . your way!'

Debbie took to her feet and blew Dicky kisses while slapping Don's hand away as he attempted to pull her back down.

'Is that your husband?' Dicky asked and laughed when Debbie replied that, unfortunately, it was.

'Ah, Don, our Yorkshire friend, who is so careful with his money,' Dicky said and remembered the countless times Don had heckled him during the cruise. 'Why did Don sit on a coin?' Dicky questioned the audience. 'Because he wanted to make sure it didn't roll away.'

Don turned a shade of red as Debbie cupped her hands to her mouth and called out to Dicky for more.

'Hey, Don, don't worry, mate, just keep doing whatever Debbie does, and you'll get somewhere in the end.'

Striding across the stage, Dicky asked the audience if they'd enjoyed the food on the cruise. 'That twenty-four-hour buffet is a dangerous place, isn't it?' He raised an eyebrow. 'You tell yourself you'll just have a salad, and five minutes later, you have a plate stacked higher than the ship, balancing a pudding on top!'

Laughter spread, and many guests nodded in agreement.

'Have you been on the excursions?' Dicky looked out at the audience. 'You know, like the one where you're made to walk for hours to see a pile of rocks? My favourite is a trip to a local market where it's all about the culture, but do we really need an embroidered tea towel and a glow-in-the-dark statue of Adonis?'

'*We* do!' Sid called out, then turned to Fran, and the pair began to giggle.

Dicky continued with more senior-friendly humour, and by the time his act ended, everyone was in stitches. 'Anyway folks,' he said, catching his breath, 'you've been a fabulous crowd all cruise, and since tonight's the big send-off, don't forget there's still plenty to do. You can dance the night away in the Mermaid Theatre, and if you don't fall asleep, an open-air movie will be shown under the stars, but don't forget your blankets. My favourite is the midnight fireworks on the promenade deck, and I hope to see many of you there.'

Dicky paused, and the room became quiet. 'Always remember that you're all part of one big family to us. And now, as members of the *Diamond Star* Cruise Club, let's have some fun and enjoy the rest of the show!'

As Dicky made his exit, the curtain rose to reveal the *Diamond Star* Dance Troupe, who delivered a jaw-dropping performance to high-energy tunes. With choreography paying homage to the many places they'd visited on the cruise, the dancers brought to life a blend of samba, flamencos and Zorba, blending all in a whirlwind of colour.

When the dancers took their final bow, Melody took to the stage, and her presence lit up the room. Wearing impossibly high heels beneath her floor-length silver sequinned gown, she shimmered with each confident step, the voluminous skirt cascading like a waterfall of diamonds. Melody's towering blonde beehive, studded with sparkling gems, held a tiara perched on top. As she strutted with confidence, the audience was mesmerised by her powerful voice and belting out lyrics to classic diva tracks and popular songs, she invited everyone to sing along. Every twist and turn were met with cheers, and as the final song approached, Melody turned towards the side of the stage, where Dicky stood watching her with a proud smile. With a graceful movement, she reached for his hand, pulling him towards her as they made their way to the centre of the stage.

Together with the *Diamond Star* Dance Troupe, the

entire cast united for the final song. 'We'll meet again, don't know where, don't know when . . .'

The audience was on its feet, clapping and shouting their appreciation, when suddenly, bursts of golden light erupted from the front of the stage, as stage fireworks brought the act to its showstopping conclusion.

'Goodness me,' Fran said as she collapsed back into her seat, her eyes wide with wonder. 'Wasn't that magnificent?'

'Does anyone fancy a dance before the midnight fireworks?' Theo called out.

His suggestion hung in the air momentarily, then Betty piped up as if on cue. 'Well, I'm up for it, and unless you lot are ready for bed, I suggest we all make our way to the Mermaid Theatre.'

In an instant, everyone rose, eager to continue the evening.

Chapter Thirty-Eight

The Mermaid Theatre, filled with guests dressed to impress, hummed with music, clinking glasses, and the sound of conversation. Tonight, the band, in fine form, played an upbeat mix of classical and modern music that coaxed even the shyest onto the dance floor. Captain Bellwood was in attendance and circled the room, chatting with guests and exchanging friendly words, curious to know how everyone had enjoyed the cruise. Gold epaulettes enhanced his crisp uniform, and his presence added an elite air to the evening.

Betty had already danced with the captain and now her poor old bones seemed to find another new lease of life as she danced with Theo, her head held high, guiding him in a waltz.

At the centre of the ballroom, Debbie was having the time of her life and laughed aloud as she cavorted with Kyle, the pair playfully swirling across the floor. At the same time, Don, unimpressed with his wife, looked miserable as he stood by the bar and ordered a pint and a whisky chaser.

Colin and Neeta were doing their own thing and

had leaped on the stage. Colin's tie was loose, and he'd unbuttoned his jacket. Lunging forward, he offered Neeta his arm and in one smooth movement, she was in his grasp, and he spun her mid-air. Several guests applauded, but Betty, not to be outdone, upped the ante as she glided past the stage and dipped dramatically backwards, her gown sweeping the floor. Theo, caught off guard, managed a heroic, backbreaking save.

The number ended, and many guests returned to their seats, including Theo, who collapsed and looked as though he needed a stiff drink and several painkillers, but he raised a hand when he saw Carmen and, with a wink, gave her a thumbs up as the music began again.

Ruskin asked Carmen if she'd like to dance.

'I'd love to,' Carmen said, and in moments they were moving around the floor.

Ruskin held her close, his hand on her waist and, initially nervous, she was grateful for his expert moves. With her hand resting on his shoulder, their eyes met, and every smile they exchanged seemed to Carmen to carry the discovery of something new and wonderful.

'Whoops!' Fran called out as Sid barged into Ruskin. 'Sorry, Sid's got his dancing shoes on the wrong feet and has forgotten how to use them.'

'All part of the fun.' Ruskin smiled.

Around them, the ballroom was full of life, with couples twirling gracefully and others laughing at their missteps. As the music swelled, Ruskin leaned closer to Carmen, his voice low. 'I think I know where the missing jewellery is,' Ruskin whispered, 'and I'm going to let Peter know.'

Carmen leaned back to meet his gaze. 'So, your sleuthing mind has cracked the case?'

Ruskin pulled her closer. 'Yes, and it's fairly obvious if you think about it.'

'Go on,' Carmen urged, 'do tell me.'

Ruskin whispered his theory. 'Am I right?' he asked when he'd explained.

Carmen's eyes widened. 'Yes, you could be.'

The dance ended, but guests stayed on the floor, and when Dicky and Melody came into the room, they were loudly applauded. Melody smiled and, noticing Don alone, asked him to dance. Glancing at Debbie, Don put down his pint and followed Melody to the floor. Dicky meanwhile caught the eye of his lady friend, whose diamonds glowed in the soft lighting. He extended his hand, and placing her walking aide to one side, she stepped forward to join him.

After several more dances, Ruskin asked Carmen if she'd like a drink, and they returned to their seats. Sipping champagne and enjoying every moment of the evening, Carmen suddenly sat up as she saw Betty taking the arm of an elderly man. Her mother's poor old bones were off again as the band struck up once more.

Offering his arm to Betty with a gentlemanly flourish, Holden exuded charm. His immaculately tailored tuxedo and crisp white shirt were complemented by a stars and stripes bow tie. His tanned skin glowed with sunbathing days, and his silver hair shone.

'They make a striking couple,' Ruskin remarked.

Carmen slowly smiled, shaking her head. 'And his gold watch is almost as blinding as Betty's smug grin,' she added.

Just then, Peter stepped onto the stage, announcing that guests wishing to view the midnight fireworks should make their way to the upper decks. As dancers moved forward and guests rose from their seats, Betty – still holding Holden's arm – glanced towards Carmen and gave a mischievous wink. This time, Carmen's smile was genuine. Her mother looked truly happy, and that was all that mattered.

Ruskin extended his arm. 'Shall we?' he said to Carmen.

On an upper deck, couples stood together, and guests gathered in groups, still caught up in the energy of the evening as they perched by the railings, staring up at the night sky. A cool breeze swept across the deck, creating a refreshing contrast to the warmth of the ballroom inside. Ruskin and Carmen found a spot, and as they waited, they heard the subtle sound of waves below.

Suddenly, a burst of light erupted, and a cascade of colour filled the sky. A collective gasp could be heard from the cruisers, their faces illuminated by the beginning of the fireworks display. Fiery reds mixed with brilliant blues and purples, and Fran was heard to call out that it was like stars being born.

Each explosion sent waves of colour rippling across the sky, every new burst more dazzling than before. Guests stood in awe, their eyes wide at the sound of a rapid-fire explosion. They cheered and applauded as a final burst of sparkling white light hung, almost suspended, before cascading diamond-like droplets that slowly melted into the water. The silence that followed felt almost mystical, as though the magic of the Mediterranean Sea had paused to say goodbye to this cruise and wish passengers a safe onward journey.

'This has been the best thing I've ever done,' Carmen said as she stared at the starry sky. 'It's the perfect end to the cruise.'

Ruskin's gaze lingered on Carmen before he gently turned her toward him. With a soft smile, as their eyes met and the world around them faded, he whispered, 'And maybe . . . it's the perfect beginning of something new.'

Chapter Thirty-Nine

Twelve months later

Carmen Cunningham no longer fought the urge to murder her mother. These days, as she sat at her desk, she even looked forward to her long-distance calls with Betty, who'd mastered a 'newfangled laptop' and delighted in skyping her daughter several times a week. Betty's poor old bones were rejuvenated in the therapeutic heat of the Florida home that she now shared with Holden, and Carmen hardly ever heard her mother complain. Nestled on a private estate in a tranquil coastal neighbourhood in the town of Venice, Betty adored the house, which boasted panoramic windows framing the sparkling waters of the Gulf of Mexico.

Carmen had visited the couple when they married in a discreet ceremony at Holden's church. Her beaming stepfather was proud of his new wife, and enchanted by his English rose.

During her stay, Carmen had become fond of Holden as he escorted her around Venice to explore. Holden had a keen interest in the former Cunningham's Hardware store, and Carmen found that they could converse easily. His successful chain of stores, Jackson's Power Tools, which he sold when he retired, shared many similarities. A prolific reader, Holden had shelves lined with books. He favoured popular crime writers, including Ruskin Reeve, and was delighted by Carmen's cosy crimes. They'd sat in quaint coffee shops, while Betty went to the beautician for her hair and nails, and they soon go to know each other.

When Carmen wandered along the white sandy stretches of beach that fronted Holden's house, she marvelled at the abundance of fossilised sharks' teeth to be found along the shoreline, glistening in the sun.

'Who'd have thought I'd ever leave cold, damp Butterly?' Mrs Holden Jackson the third said, as they sat beside the pool. 'You should come over for the annual shark tooth festival, in April, Holden tells me it's a hoot.'

Carmen was amazed at the change in Betty, who once again wore her delicate pink pearls, a brightly patterned bathing suit and enormous designer sunglasses, and had recently learned to swim.

'Holden and I shall carry on cruising, of course,' Betty continued, 'especially while my visa sorts itself out,' she said and sipped a key lime Martini that Holden had expertly prepared. He moved attentively between them, refilling glasses, and Carmen couldn't help but smile when she noticed the pineapple emblem on Holden's cap.

Noting her daughter's expression, Betty leaned closer. 'I don't bother with all that sort of stuff,' she confided, 'but I can't deny Holden his occasional bit of *fun*.'

* * *

From her desk by the open window of her balcony, Carmen gazed thoughtfully at the branches of a fir tree, swaying in the breeze, as she remembered her time in Venice. She hoped her mother would find lasting happiness with Holden in their golden years, sharing morning coffee on their sunlit terrace or watching sunsets over the Gulf.

After all, everyone deserved a chance at happiness. Even Betty.

* * *

When Carmen and Betty had returned from their *Diamond Star* cruise, the house in Butterly sold quickly. Holden had proposed to Betty on the last night of the cruise and Betty, without hesitation, accepted.

'You'll have a tidy sum from the proceeds of the sale, and I'll be glad to see the back of it,' Betty generously said. 'I don't need much, Holden has more than enough to support me. You can begin a new life.'

Though Desbett House was outdated, the land appealed to a local developer eager to build six modern homes on the site. With Betty now settled in Florida, Carmen took on the task of packing up the house before the sale was finalised. Betty had no interest in bringing memories to America, and Carmen found it surprisingly easy to part with their possessions.

'It's all just stuff,' she reminded herself, sorting through the 1970s kitchen as she placed a macramé plant hanger and a set of Pyrex dishes into the growing charity shop pile.

On a cold, rainy day, Carmen boarded a plane with nothing more than her suitcases of new clothes and her laptop. She felt a wave of liberation as she left Butterly behind to begin the next chapter of her life.

When her flight touched down in Kefalonia, Carmen rented a car and drove to the village of Maxos. She headed straight to the Villa Galini, the adorable property overlooking the beach and the place she'd dreamed of since her visit to the island on the *Diamond Star* cruise. To Carmen's absolute joy, it was still for sale and the owners were agreeable to Carmen's offer on the charming three-storey Villa Galini. They agreed to rent it to Carmen while the sale was finalised.

To Carmen's further delight, she discovered that Theo was in Maxos, and the moment he heard she was there too, he rushed to see her.

'Where are you staying?' Carmen asked when they reunited.

'I have a cramped space above the bar at Jimmy's, it's not ideal but it's impossible to find anywhere during the summer months, in this tiny village, that isn't already booked.'

'Why don't you take the top floor of Villa Galini,' Carmen offered. 'There's plenty of room and it will give you peace and space to finish your memoirs.'

Theo agreed that Villa Galini was roomier and far quieter than the bar and moved in the next day. Carmen was thrilled to have her friend nearby and enjoyed his company during their breaks from writing.

Maxos turned out to be everything that Carmen had dreamed of.

As the weeks passed, she grew to love the quaint village even more. After her daily swim at the horseshoe-shaped beach, Carmen would head into the village square, where she was greeted by the woman who owned the gift shop, and spent hours sweeping needle-shaped leaves from the cobbles outside her business. At the bakery, Carmen chose her favourite koulouri, a sesame-covered bread, before selecting provisions from the tiny mini market, where the open-air counter displayed sun-kissed produce and towering crates spilt over with deep red tomatoes, bright yellow lemons, bundles of fragrant herbs, figs and earthy potatoes.

She cherished the simple pleasures, flinging wide the bright blue shutters of the house, watering the terracotta pots on her balconies, brimming with vibrant oleander, and waving to the sleepy honey seller who napped daily on the bench below her window. When awake, he stared down the passing tourists until they handed over fifteen euros for a jar of his golden treasure.

'That's inflation for you,' Theo quipped, one sunny afternoon, as he and Carmen sat on the patio of her home, sipping wine and watching the old man. Theo caressed the gold cuff on his wrist and leaned back in his chair. 'You can't stop the world from turning.'

Suddenly, a voice called out, startling them both.

'Kalimári!' the voice called out again, louder this time.

'It can't be . . .' Carmen whispered, gripping the wrought iron railing as she peered down the lane.

'Kalimári! Oi! Anyone there? Squid! Squid!'

'Kaliméra Fran!' Carmen and Theo shouted together, rushing to meet their unexpected visitors.

Carmen laughed with delight as she embraced Fran and

Sid. 'What on earth are you doing here?' she exclaimed, pulling back to stare at them both.

'We're off on another cruise and flew into Kefalonia last night,' Fran said with a chuckle. 'As members of The Cruise Club, we thought we'd take advantage of the wonderful offers.' She unbuttoned the waistband of her shorts and collapsed onto a chair. 'Blimey, it's a scorcher today!' she added.

'Aye, we thought we'd surprise you,' Sid added, grinning as he shook Theo's hand. 'Got a taxi here with Debbie.'

'Debbie?' Carmen asked, eyebrows raised. 'But where's Don?'

'Oh, you really must keep up, dear,' Fran said, fanning herself dramatically. 'She kicked Don into touch ages ago and moved out of their marital home. We left her at the Psaro Taverna, down by the harbour, where she's pestering Spiros for a job.'

Carmen laughed, remembering Debbie's manner. Spiros would do well to refuse.

As Theo brought out wine and a platter of olives, the group settled in and began catching up.

'Have you given any more thought to retirement?' Carmen asked.

'We have,' Fran mused, 'but we still enjoy what we do and like to keep a hand in. We've a good team now to run things at the restaurant, and given the scare we had with Sid's health, it's prompted us into taking plenty of holidays.'

'I'm not surprised that the restaurant is busy,' Theo said, 'the food you serve is incredible, and I loved my visit to Blackpool.'

'And we loved having you all to stay with us,' Fran said, smiling at the memory. 'Having a famous chef at our table didn't half do our street cred some good.' She thought fondly of the centre page spread in the *Blackpool Gazette* that had featured Theo in Sid and Fran's kitchen, standing proudly with his arms around them both as they prepared for the evening service.

'And you came back to Kefalonia,' Sid said, addressing Theo.

'He can't stay away,' Carmen teased, winking at Theo.

Before Theo could reply, a voice broke into song from the lane:

'Toreador! Love, love awaits you!'

Fran sat up and suddenly remembered the singing bar owner from their visit to Maxos during the cruise. Was this the same man, she wondered, as she saw Theo swiftly turn.

Theo's eyes fell on Jimmy's handsome face, and his smile widened. Leaning over the railing, Theo embraced Jimmy and kissed him on the lips.

'Ah, the puzzle is solved,' Fran said with a knowing nod as she watched the two men gaze lovingly at each other.

'Now, *you're* the one who needs to keep up,' Carmen laughed.

As Theo made room for Jimmy at the table and expertly uncorked the wine, he turned to Fran. 'By the way, whatever happened to Dicky Delaney?'

Fran held up her glass to be filled. 'Peter is on our cruise again and told us that Dicky's moved to Malaga. He's settled down with his lady friend in her humongous villa, and she happens to be his new manager. Apparently, he's doing well, gigging in shows all over southern Spain and having a high old time.'

'To Dicky!' they all cheered, clinking glasses.

Fran reached into her oversized bag and pulled out a recent copy of the *Daily Mail*. 'I brought this for you,' she said, smoothing the paper on the table and pointing to a page.

Carmen and Theo leaned in to read the bold headline.

Ring of Trouble! Jewellery Thief Couple Caught Red-Handed After Stepping Off Ship!

Theo began to read out loud: 'A couple arrested after disembarking from a cruise ship have been sentenced to lengthy prison terms following a recent court appearance.' He paused to nod at Carmen before continuing. 'Colin and Neeta Scott believed they'd got away with their thefts when the *Diamond Star* berthed in Málaga at the end of a twelve-day cruise. However, a guest speaker on board, an acclaimed author of detective novels, tipped off the ship security.

'"*I saw Neeta Scott wearing earrings, on the last night of the cruise, that she reported to have been stolen,*" the author told the purser. "*I was certain that the couple had directed suspicion away from themselves by claiming to have lost jewellery too, and the ship's security team was informed.*"

'Local authorities followed the pair when they disembarked, and they were arrested while attempting to pawn the stolen jewellery in the town.'

Theo and Carmen studied the image of Colin and Neeta following their arrest.

'It took a while for it to come to court,' Sid interjected.

'And they don't *exactly* explain how the sleuth figured it out,' Fran added, her eyes narrowing as she turned to Carmen.

Carmen smiled. 'It had me baffled at first, but it all came down to Neeta foolishly wearing the earrings she'd reported stolen, then, when spotted, trying to cover them by ruffling her hair over her ears.'

'Silly girl,' Fran tutted.

Sid shook his head. 'Thieves think they're clever, but it's the small mistakes that catch them out. She might have got away with it if she hadn't been so careless. Neeta practically convicted herself.'

Carmen took the paper from Theo and began to fold it. 'But of course,' she said, 'it had a lot to do with passengers attending the Upside-down Pineapple Pensioner Club.'

Jimmy looked puzzled. 'Pineapples and pensioners? What is this?'

Carmen grabbed a towel and moved to the villa steps. 'Perhaps you should ask the sleuth himself,' she said and gestured towards the beach. 'I'm sure he'll be happy to explain.'

A man emerged from the sea, shaking droplets of water from his hair as he walked along the beach then climbed the steps beneath the fir tree.

'Ruskin!' Carmen called out. 'We've got visitors!'

Acknowledgements

When asked to write another book about a cruise, I began by digging through my memory bank to find cherished moments from Mediterranean holidays. This was a delightful part of the research, and some of the destinations in *The Cruise Club* are inspired by places that hold a special place in my heart. Many moments shaped this story, from laughter-filled annual Greek holidays with girlfriends to the unforgettable experience of cruising as a guest speaker with Fred Olsen Cruises.

One destination stands out above all others: a small Greek village, on a peninsula in a stunning bay at the end of a steep and winding road. Years ago, while exploring the island of Kefalonia, we stumbled upon this gem. What was meant to be a one-night stay turned into a longer adventure, and we found ourselves returning time and time again. In this story, I've given the village the fictitious name Maxos, but many of you may recognise the place as Assos.

This village became even more magical because of the two brothers who owned a beach bar and a taverna by the harbour. Their kindness made every visit unforgettable. They called us the Ouzo Ladies, and I'll never forget how they'd head down the beach to the edge of the water, bringing trays of ouzo to us as we lounged in the sea. Among those ladies was my beautiful sister, Cathy, whose memory I treasure. I think she's enjoying an ouzo now in her heavenly place, and I thank her for the many happy holidays we shared.

Cruising the Mediterranean also brought special memories. Ibiza was particularly magical. I mention *The Drifters* by James Michener, a book that profoundly affected me as a young girl, much to my parent's horror, causing me to leave home like the young people in his story. Years later, after walking miles in the Ibizan sunshine with my lovely hubby, we found ourselves at a pavement bar, savouring tapas and sangria. I don't know why it felt so special, but surrounded by the vibrant energy of Ibiza, that delicious lunch stayed with me and found its way into the story.

Through the characters in *The Cruise Club*, I want to highlight the beauty of friendship and the importance of kindness. Fran, in particular, who appeared in *The French Cookery School*, has emerged again. It was pure joy to send her and her husband, Sid, on this cruise adventure.

I am indebted to my agent, Lorella Belli, and her talented team. With Lorella in your corner, you know you are in safe hands. Helen Huthwaite, my editor, what would I have done without your wise advice and kindness? Kindness – there it is, that word again. Thank you, Helen. You are a superstar.

One of the kindest people I have had the honour of

knowing is my hubby. Like many of my character's love stories, ours is a later-in-life romance – a marriage I never expected. How lucky I am. Thank you, Eric. ILYTTMAB.

To all my readers, thank you for joining me on this journey. So many of you contact me through social media with your precious holiday memories or tell me that you are on a cruise, or that my stories have inspired you to book a cruise, and I treasure every comment. Please keep your words and photos coming.

May *The Cruise Club* bring you as much pleasure as the memories that inspired it, and I wish you all wonderful holidays and many happy reading hours.

With love,
Caroline
www.carolinejamesauthor.co.uk

Disclaimer

The *Diamond Star*, its crew, passengers, and all other characters depicted in this story are fictional creations of the author's imagination.

Any likeness to actual individuals, or ships, is purely coincidental. The story incorporates locations visited by the author when cruising. However, the ship's itinerary uses artistic license and does not reflect actual cruise ship journeys, places or events.

Loved *The Cruise Club?* Keep reading . . .

**Three women.
One widowed.
One unmarried.
One almost divorced.
All aged 63, but not ready to give up on life!**

Will the three friends find the comfort and joy they seek aboard the *Diamond Star*?

What happens at the spa stays at the spa . . .

A weekend at the spa will leave four
old friends with a whole lot more
than they'd bargained for . . .

The recipe for a perfect summer . . .

Step 1: Mix together a group of mature students
Step 2: Add in a handsome host
Step 3: Season with a celebrity chef
Step 4: Bring to the boil at a luxurious cookery school in France!